GO CLOSE

AGAINST THE

ENEMY

Also by Takis and Judy Iakovou:

So Dear to Wicked Men

Takis and Judy Iakovou

GO CLOSE

AGAINST THE

ENEMY

St. Martin's Press ❧ New York

Library of Congress Cataloging-in-Publication Data

Iakovou, Takis.
    Go close against the enemy / Takis and Judy Iakovou.—1st ed.
      p.   cm.
    ISBN 0-312-18587-1
    1. Restaurant management—Georgia—Fiction.
    2. Georgia—Fiction.   I. Iakovou, Judy.   II. Title.
    PS3559.A45G6   1998
    813'.54—dc21   98-13532
                                                   CIP

First Edition: June 1998

10 9 8 7 6 5 4 3 2 1

To our parents
Greg and Eulalia Kerley
and
Angelo and Maria Iakovou,
with love

Acknowledgments

The authors would like to thank the following individuals for their assistance: Dr. Thomas J. Conahan of Havertown, Pennsylvania, and Dr. Boling S. Dubose of Athens, Georgia, for their advice regarding medical questions; Alan Schwartz and our agent, Joan Brandt, for their counsel and guidance; and our editor, Kelley Ragland, for her considerable expertise and help. We would also like to gratefully acknowledge the criticism and support of our many writer friends, specifically Diane Trap, Beverly Connor, Charles Connor, Jim Howell, Nicky Ashcraft, Harriette Austin, and the members of her writer's workshop. And finally, our deepest gratitude to the two people who have sacrificed the most in the pursuit of our dreams—both owning restaurants and writing about them—our daughters, Angie and Mari. We love you.

For no man ever proves himself a good man in war
unless he can endure to face the blood and the slaughter,
go close against the enemy and fight with his hands.

from Courage: heros mortuus: heros vivus
Tyrtaeus of Sparta
seventh century b.c.

Chapter One

poly-phy-let-ic-\päl-i-(,)fi-'let-ik *adj*. [ISV, fr. Gk *poly-phylos* of many tribes, fr. *poly-* + *phylē* tribe—more at PHYL] (1875): of or relating to more than one stock; *specif*: derived from more than one ancestral line.
—*Merriam Webster's Ninth New Collegiate Dictionary*

Once upon a time, many thousands of years ago, a mortal named Sisyphus offended the ancient gods on Mt. Olympos. Although the exact nature of his offense is somewhat obscure, his punishment has been well documented. Sisyphus was doomed to spend eternity rolling a huge boulder up a steep hill, only to reach the top and watch it career back down again. A never-ending, thankless task was Sisyphus's. Then the Greeks discovered the restaurant, and the rock was rendered obsolete.

So it was that my husband, Nick, a descendent of the wretched Sisyphus himself, was once again toiling at his rock—that is, the Oracle, our cafe in Delphi—when the door opened and trouble sauntered in. The badge glittered in the morning sun, and the man who held it next to his shoulder smiled humorlessly.

"Let me call my husband," I said, backing away from him. I scurried through the wait station and into the kitchen. Nick was on the floor with a plumber's snake, twisting it into the floor drain. The expletives were flowing thick and fast. Although I didn't know their exact translation, I caught on to the spirit quickly enough.

"Nick, we may have a problem."

"We do have a problem." He pulled the snake back, coiling it as he pulled. "Otis. I've told him and told him to sweep the floor before he hoses it down. I don't know how he does it, but he can force more garbage through this grate—" He struck his bare arm down into the pipe and pulled out a bottle cap, holding it up for me to see.

"Look at that! He must be taking the grate off before he hoses it down. If I catch him . . ."

"Nick, there's another problem. He's waiting for you in the dining room. You have to come now. Now, Nick!"

"Who is it?"

"It's—"

"Mr. Lambros?"

The man himself stood behind me in the kitchen door. Nick scrambled up, grabbed the snake, and tossed it onto the skirt of the dish machine. "I'm Nick Lambros."

The man held up his badge again. "Richard Fortunata. Internal Revenue Service."

His voice had a godfather rasp to it, and he pronounced his name in thick Bronx—Faw-chu-nah-tuh. Nick extended his hand, but Fortunata backed away, flipping the badge case closed and returning it to the breast pocket of his jacket. He stared pointedly at Nick's hand.

"Just a minute," Nick said, stepping over to the hand sink. He lathered his hands and arms thoroughly. Fortunata, meanwhile, stayed in the doorway, but his glance roved over the kitchen as though he were taking inventory: one double convection oven, one Hobart dish machine, three stainless steel work tables . . . I imagined numbers ringing up in his eyes, like a human adding machine. Nick dried his arms and hands on a clean bar mop and beckoned Fortunata back out into the dining room.

"Can I get you some coffee?" I said, following them.

Fortunata shook his head somberly. He laid his briefcase on the family table and popped it open, withdrawing a thick manila file and dropping it on the table. Inside the briefcase, a picture ID was clipped to an inside pocket. The face that stared out of the picture was dark, swarthy, stern to threatening. A face without humor—an agent who would take no prisoners.

Although they were not visible in the photograph, his most outstanding features were the long, black hair he wore in a heavy ponytail at the nape of his neck, and the single gold earring—a thick, filigreed hoop—that dangled from his right earlobe. I thought his resemblance to Blackbeard was not entirely incompatible with his job.

"Nick, I need to find Spiros and discuss, um, the . . . um . . . Lions Club meeting with him."

"But it's all worked—" he called to my retreating back. When I glanced over my shoulder he was glaring at me. DESERTER was scrawled across his handsome features.

I don't like badges. My hands shake whenever I pass a sheriff's car on the road. My legs dissolve to grits when the deputies come in for lunch. Brown cars, brown uniforms, blue lights—they all evoke that same knee-knocking terror. One day in jail was all it took, conditioning me to fear authority figures from that time forward. B.F. Skinner would have had a field day with me.

I hurried back to the private dining room, dropped into a chair next to Spiros, closed my eyes, and tried to swallow my heart back down where it belonged. Our big cook didn't even seem to notice. He was poring over the morning copy of *The Delphi Sun*, just as he does every day.

I don't know why he does this, since he speaks very little English, never mind reading it. But as soon as the Buffaloes and the rest of the breakfast crowd clear out, Spiros grabs a mug of coffee, tucks the paper under his arm, and heads for the back dining room. There he carefully studies the printed word, grunts meaningfully as he turns it page by page, scrutinizes the world weather map, and ends with the daily horoscope. The latter, he scrutinizes at considerable length, often copying it word for word into a small notebook he carries in his breast pocket.

After the lunch rush, he returns to the table with his Greek-English dictionary and carefully translates the predictions for Aries—the sign he shares with Nick. It strikes me as a laborious task—especially when Nick would willingly translate it for him—but Spiros is highly superstitious and seems to feel that, when it comes to his horoscope, confidentiality is of the utmost importance. I have not pointed out to him that millions of people are reading the same words, probably at the very same time of the morning, right along with him.

He snapped his notebook shut, returned it to his pocket, and methodically refolded the newspaper before rising. *"Poli zesti stin Athena,"* he said, fanning himself with his hand. I was not especially interested in the heat in Greece.

"But." He held up an index finger. "Today, Zulia," he solemnly announced, "world still ex-kwee-zeet." With that, he took his cup and returned to the kitchen.

Spiros Papavasilakis is from the island of Crete, which, Nick tells me, distinguishes him from other Greeks in countless ways. He approaches every new task with the determination of Theseus facing the Minotaur. As a merchant seaman for many years, he learned to speak several languages fluently. English, unfortunately, was not one of them. But on the evening of December 31, as the clock tolled twelve times, Spiros announced his intention to spend the next year learning to speak English as well as the Queen Mum herself. Toward that end, Miss Alma had given Spiros a word-a-day calendar, thinking that it would broaden his grasp of the language. It had, instead, created some very perplexing situations in the kitchen.

If I was guessing correctly, I could go into the kitchen, check his calendar on the wall, and find that *exquisite* was Spiros's word for the day. He would have tried to find its equivalent in his extremely inadequate Greek-English dictionary, and failing that, would have translated the definition word for word as best he could. One of the definitions of *exquisite* would be *fine*, thus "today the world is still fine."

I had to give him credit—he was certainly trying to learn. In fact, not only did he practice his word for the day, but he kept a lexicon of his new words at the ready in his notebook. He did not try to conjugate these words, nor was he always clear on their part of speech, but I had found, early in the game, that trying to explain the finer points of English linguistics usually added to the general confusion. I was leaving that task to Miss Alma. Revenge is sweet.

Well, maybe the world was exquisite, but I wasn't doing too well. What did the IRS want with us? We filed our quarterly reports on time. We never cheated on our expenses. We withheld regularly from our employees' paychecks and always got their W-2s out before the end of January. But Richard Fortunata had not just stopped by for a cup of coffee and a little chat. Whatever he was here for, it was serious business.

And I was not going to think about it. I may be a Yankee, but Scarlett O'Hara and I share certain idiosyncrasies that I consider valuable for self-preservation. *Get busy. Do something else, get your mind off it. Read the paper.*

I snagged the *Sun* and spread it out on the table in front of me, wishing I had a cup of coffee but loath to return to the wait station to get it. The board of education was still fighting over redistricting. *What could he possibly want?* A professor at Parnassus University was being accused of sexual misconduct by a female student. Any other time, that might have made interesting reading. But not today. *Maybe it has to do with tipping. Tammy probably isn't reporting all her tips. It would be just like her.*

I flipped over to the horoscope for Virgo. "Day revolves around work. Get your priorities straight. Stay in touch with friends." Nothing new there. And how about that Aries message? "Obtain clue from Virgo, Sagittarius messages. Do not be sidetracked by trivial problems. Concentrate on the task at hand." Not a word about employees, taxes, badges. I returned to the front page, but couldn't work up any real interest in school redistricting.

Life in Delphi being a somewhat insular and self-important existence, world news was encapsulated in a single column on the second page. Trouble in Bosnia again. A minor earthquake in China. The First Lady's newest hairstyle was, once again, big news. *Who cares, when the IRS comes knocking?*

Billy's byline caught my eye. The headline read "Trouble Over Funeral Splits Mount Sinai Tabernacle Church." Above the article, two faces stared solemnly at me from a stark photograph taken in front of the little church. I knew one of those faces, the white one. Billy has been working on his writing style. The article was brief and to the point.

Trouble broke out at the meeting of the congregation of the Mount Sinai Tabernacle Church last night, when the pastor of the church, Reverend Allen McNabb, took the part of his daughter, April Folsom, over the burial of her stillborn child. Mrs. Folsom and her husband, Davon, appeared before the congregation to plead their infant son's right to be buried in the church cemetery.

The opposition, led by Walter Fry, a deacon in the 650-member church, claimed that it was not an issue of race, although Mr. Folsom is an African-American, but a matter of tradition.

"It's just always been that way," Fry declared. "You go to a black congregation and ask them to be buried in their cemetery, why, they'd laugh so hard they'd wake the rest of the dead! They got a perfectly good cemetery out there in Markettown. No reason the Folsom baby can't be buried there. There's a lot of us would even go to the funeral."

Asked to comment on the situation, Louis Thatcher Humphries, attorney for the Folsom family, stated that the church's refusal to allow the Folsom child to be buried in the Mount Sinai Tabernacle Cemetery is in violation of federal statutes.

"If the congregation persists in this position, I will have no recourse but to file charges of discrimination against the church. I don't want to do it, but they may leave me no alternative."

Fry responded to Humphries's allegations, stating that he would consult with the church's attorney before the congregation voted. Reverend McNabb was unavailable for comment. Reaction among other area churches was unanimous in its shock and condemnation of the position of Mount Sinai Tabernacle Church *(see sidebar).*

I skimmed the sidebar before my gaze returned to the photograph—to the narrow, girlish face of April McNabb, her fair complexion turned sallow, her pale eyes underscored by black bruises of grief. Next to her, with his arm over her shoulder, stood her husband, Davon. So they had married after all. And had a child. And the child was born dead. How much more tragic could life get?

I met April only once, during my brief stay in jail. She was there purely to be harassed for having a black boyfriend, a ploy instigated, she said, by her own father, in the hope that it would scare her into giving up Davon. April didn't really know how she felt about Davon then, only how she felt about her father. It was, at the time, a matter of principle with her. A matter of doing the right thing—fighting bigotry. I wondered again, as I had then, where Davon—the living, breathing man with feelings, needs, and dreams—fit into the whole scheme. In the picture, he stood with his feet apart, his left fist clenched, his jaw set. But his eyes were large, liquid, and sad. My heart went out to them both.

April couldn't know how she had affected me that day, giving me the courage to stand up and fight for myself and Nick. I owed her something. I wanted her to know that I shared her grief. I turned over to the Obituary section of the newspaper and scanned the column for the name Folsom. It was there. Only a few lines, as there were no accomplishments to list—no schools, jobs, marriages, children. No life. The baby, the article had said, was stillborn. The family would be receiving visitors at Statler's Funeral

Home tonight between seven and eight o'clock. I grabbed the paper and hurried toward the front dining room, Fortunata all but forgotten. I found Nick sitting at the family table, glassy-eyed as he stared at a white paper in his hand.

Out in the parking lot, Agent Fortunata opened the door of a nondescript white sedan, tossed his briefcase on the seat, and shrugged out of his jacket. He hung it on a hook in the backseat, turned and stared at the Oracle for a moment before climbing into the car. Probably doing a casual property assessment. He gunned the ignition and tore out of the parking lot, on his way, I supposed, to deliver more bad news to some unsuspecting tax-payer. I turned back to Nick, who sat in the same position, with the same glazed expression. I pulled out the chair next to him.

"Okay," I said. "Tell me what he wanted."

Nick handed me a paper and my glance went straight to the bottom line. "Six thousand seven hundred and twenty-three dollars!"

"And forty-six cents," he added.

"We owe them that?"

"So he says."

I let the paper drop from my fingers, staring as it fluttered slowly to the floor. "How is that possible?"

"Penalties. Penalties and interest, accumulating for three years."

"What? Accumulating on what? We've always filed on time, paid quarterly. How can this be?"

Nick shrugged and jerked his chin toward the empty parking lot. "He says we've owed it for—" he counted backward on his fingers. "—eleven quarters. Claims they've sent us letters and we've ignored them. He's going to file a lien. On the house."

"On our house?"

"No, Julia. On Spiros's house. Of course, our house."

"Wait a minute. We haven't gotten any letters from them. Did he say he sent them himself?"

Nick shook his head. "Some other field agent. Fortunata just took over our . . . case."

I stared at the figures in front of me. It couldn't be right. They had us mixed up with someone else. But it was our name on the notice. And it was our address. Nick's normally olive complexion had turned a dismal ocher. I took his hand and squeezed it.

"It's just a mistake, Nick. We'll get it straightened out. Don't worry."

Nick could not accompany me to the funeral home that night. He was busy resurrecting three years worth of tax records from the attic. I left him surrounded by files in our little makeshift home office and swung through Markettown to pick up Miss Alma.

Alma Rayburn is a retired teacher and a dear friend. We met her through Spiros, who lives next door and has assumed the care and tending of this very senior citizen. I didn't want to go to the funeral home alone, and Miss Alma was gracious enough to agree to go with me.

"I saw it in the paper this morning," she said as she climbed into the car. "But I didn't realize you knew the family."

"I don't. That is, I met April only once, but I feel so . . . sad for her. I guess I just want her to know that I care." Miss Alma accepted this without question. Although she knew about my jail time, and was instrumental in solving the crime that had put me there, it was something we never discussed. The experience was too humiliating, too painful, for me to want to relive it.

I pulled into the parking lot of Statler's Funeral Home a few minutes after seven. A battered pickup truck, a black BMW sedan, a shiny green Jaguar, and four or five less distinctive cars were lined up in the lot. Not an overwhelming crowd. Potholes and weeds pockmarked the asphalt, confirming what I already knew—that Statler's was not the nicest funeral home in town. Their hallmark was low-budget bereavement.

Just as we reached the peeling double doors of the building, one of them flew open, slamming back against the clapboard wall of the building. "Oh my!" Miss Alma cried, as a man brushed past her, knocking her precariously back against the doorframe.

"Hey!" I grabbed her elbow to steady her, and spun around on my heel prepared to give him a piece of my mind. But I only caught a glimpse of his back before he climbed into the Jaguar and slammed the door. We watched openmouthed as he spun the wheel and tore out of the lot, leaving the weeds trembling in his wake.

"Walter," Miss Alma sighed, and shook her head. "He always was so impulsive."

"You know that man?"

"Indeed I do. I taught him, oh . . ." Miss Alma closed her eyes for a moment. "I guess it's been well over thirty years ago now."

"Who is he?"

"That, my dear, is Walter Fry. Deacon of the Mount Sinai Tabernacle Church."

Chapter Two

es-trange\is-`trānj\\vt **es-tranged; estranging** [ME *estrangen,* MF *estranger,* fr. ML *extraneare,* fr. L *extraneus* strange—more at STRANGE] . . . **2:** to arouse esp. mutual enmity or indifference in where there had formerly been love, affection, or friendliness: ALIENATE.
—*MerriamWebster's Ninth New Collegiate Dictionary*

"Please come in." The funeral director held the door open for us, cutting off any further conversation about Walter Fry. "You're here to see the Folsom family, I take it?"

What is it about funeral directors that makes them so amorphous? It's as though they work at it, which, I suppose, in a way they do. It's their business to be unemotional, yet somehow properly grave and sympathetic—to be inconspicuous while imparting the comforting feeling that they're there if you need them.

"Helluva job," I muttered to Miss Alma. She nodded. Despite her eighty some-odd years, she's always right with me.

"Right this way," he said. We followed his erect back, carefully clad in charcoal gray worsted, through the entryway and down a softly lighted hallway. To our left and right, cherry veneer tables and thinly padded Duncan Phyfe chairs invited us to sit down and relax in this most subdued of atmospheres. No, thanks. I'd just as soon get on with it and get out.

The ambience of funeral homes strikes me as a sort of suspended reality—as though life were not crashing and careening just outside those double doors. It's hazardous out there— painful, often miserable, but occasionally wonderful. Given the choice, I'd take my chances out there. But duty called in here. "Lead on," I said, under my breath.

When we reached the door of "The Savannah Room," the man stood back, allowing me to precede Miss Alma. I took a long breath and walked in.

To my right, a tiny, white wicker casket stood on a platform draped in forest green velvet. I turned away immediately, but not before glimpsing a tiny body in a white christening gown laid out on white satin. A knot formed at the back of my throat as I wondered why I had thought coming here was a good idea.

Beyond the casket, a black couple hovered together, talking quietly with a tall, well-dressed black man. Behind them, seated in a slightly battered armchair, was a young black woman. She picked at her fingernails, glanced at us, and cocked an eyebrow. The love seat next to her was occupied by another black man who might have been a few years older than the girl. He was a tall man with large hands that dangled ineffectually between his knees.

On the left side of the room, a tall, gaunt white man stood, hands behind his back, rocking on the balls of his feet. He looked neither right nor left. Beside him a woman who looked to be in her mid-forties sat in another armchair. She was twisted slightly away from him, looking down at hands that opened and closed around a wrinkled lavender handkerchief. And beyond them both, April and Davon sat in a pair of folding chairs. They faced each other and whispered quietly. I headed directly for them.

"April?" Her head came around in apparent surprise. Her complexion looked bleached against the austere black blouse she wore under a loose-fitting black and white houndstooth jumper. Her hair had a lifeless, slightly dusty look to it, with none of the healthy glow that had shimmered under the fluorescent lights of the jail. No recognition sparked in her pale eyes.

"I don't suppose you remember me. We met, um . . ." I glanced over at the gaunt man who had to be her father—the man who disapproved of Davon and who'd had his daughter arrested not once, but many times. I leaned close to her, hopefully out of earshot.

"In jail. We met in the holding cell. My name is Julia." She stared at me for a moment, recognition dawning slowly.

"Yeah, I remember. You were there for . . . ?"

"I was charged with . . . murder. But my husband, Nick, he bailed me out and then . . ."

April leapt up and took hold of my hand. "Yeah, I remember now. I read about you in the paper. Something to do with foreigners. You solved the crime yourself!"

"Well, I had a lot of help," I said. But this was not a subject I wanted to dwell on anyway. "I just wanted to see you. You helped me a lot that day, and I wanted you to know that I . . . well, I'm just so sorry about your baby. I saw it in the papers."

Davon had risen and waited patiently to be introduced. I turned to him. "You must be Davon." I held out my hand and felt it sink into a warm, firm handshake. "April told me about you." He glanced over at the girl beside him, but she was staring at the rigid posture of her father.

"I'm Julia Lambros," I said. "And this is my friend . . ." But Miss Alma was not behind me. I glanced around the room and found her conversing with the distinguished black man I'd noticed earlier. They moved toward the casket. Miss Alma looked into the little bassinet, shook her head, and turned back to the man. He said something and she nodded.

"It was nice of you to come, Julia." April's voice was tremulous. "Did you see Damien?"

"Damien?"

Her chin tilted toward the casket. I shook my head, realizing that there was nothing to say. I couldn't talk about my own loss— a miscarriage in the fifth month. Miscarriage that late in my pregnancy was difficult at best. But to carry a child to term, and then to have it cruelly taken away, born dead, never having had even a chance at life—no, there was nothing to say.

Damien. I hadn't thought of him as having a name. But there, in that little bassinet, was a child. A human being. And he deserved a good, strong name. April took my hand and led me across the room. I didn't want to go. What would I say? All sorts of platitudes sprang to mind, but I quickly discarded them. He didn't look like he was sleeping, he hadn't lived a long life or accomplished his goals. And everything did not, always, work out for the best.

His skin was a soft caramel color, and black curls peeked out from under the white christening cap on his head. His tiny fist was curled around a silver barbell rattle. Stiff white lace tucked up under his chin, looked like it would scratch his tender skin.

April stood stoic before the casket, but Davon reached out to pull the lace away from Damien's face. A heavy tear dropped onto the eyelet gown so carefully arranged over the baby's body. I squeezed April's hand.

"I'm so sorry, April."

"What a sweet baby." Miss Alma to the rescue. She turned away from her companion and introduced herself to the young couple beside me. "I believe," she said, "he has his father's chin."

"Oh yes." April's voice rose a bit. "But that's definitely a McNabb nose. And his feet are just like mine. But his hands—the fingers are long and narrow, like Davon's." She grabbed Davon's hand and held it up for us to see. We all nodded vigorously, willing the awkward moment to pass.

"Julia, I'd like you to meet a former student of mine." Miss Alma turned to the man who had stood silent at her side. "This is Louis Humphries."

He reminded me of Sidney Poitier—tall, handsome, confident. The gray at his temples added to the overall impression of dignity, and his perfectly fitted navy pin-striped suit was positively elegant. He smiled ruefully.

"I don't like to think about how many years ago that was, Mrs. Rayburn."

Miss Alma studied him thoughtfully. "Let's see, you were class of 1967?"

"Six," he corrected her.

"Of course! National Merit Scholar of 'sixty-six. Oh my, that was a long time ago. Life in Delphi has certainly changed since then, hasn't it, Louis?"

He smiled and nodded. "A lot." He glanced over at Reverend McNabb, and his smile grew hard. "But not enough." Miss Alma noticed the change, too.

"Louis," she added hastily, "was one of my best students. He went on to Duke University on scholarship, then came back to Parnassus for law school. He's one of the most successful attorneys in this part of the state."

He looked at her with some surprise. "I'm amazed you remember all that, Mrs. Rayburn." She took him by the arm, and me by the hand, leading us away from the casket.

"Some students just stick in your mind, I suppose. The good ones . . . and unfortunately, sometimes the bad ones." She patted Humphries's arm and turned to the black couple who seemed to be waiting for us in the corner. "And this must be the grandparents."

Louis Humphries made the introductions to Davon's parents—Chester and Candice Folsom—before Davon stepped in to introduce us to his sister. D'Anita offered me a limp hand before returning to the inspection of her fingernails. I turned expectantly to the young man next to her. He was staring at D'Anita, reached over and gave her a sharp nudge with his elbow.

"Oh," she said. I could practically hear her yawn. "This is my friend Rodney."

Rodney rose, towering over me—at least six and a half feet tall, and every foot of him as heavily muscled as George Foreman. He took my hand and shook it, gently for a man of his size, nodding gravely. He didn't speak, and I knew why as soon as I got a close look at his face.

His upper lip bore two lines of thick scar tissue which extended into the lower edge of his nostrils. The repairs were not the most skillful I had ever seen—uneven, pulling the lip slightly up and to the left. Rodney had been born with a complete bilateral cleft palate. Even with early intervention and years of therapy, his speech might be interspersed with harsh bursts of air from his nose. I accepted his silent handshake and turned to Davon's mother.

Candice Folsom was a strikingly handsome woman. Her hair was neatly pulled back in a bun at the nape of a long, regal neck. The severity of her hairstyle accentuated the taut skin stretched across high cheekbones, and the slightly uptilted shape of her eyes. She had an exotic beauty that reminded me of Egyptian queens on ancient friezes. Her simple black sheath was accented by a single gold chain. A gold watch and plain gold band were her only other accessories. Her voice was throaty, her demeanor gracious. "It was kind of you to come," she said, and glanced over at her husband. My gaze followed hers.

Chester Folsom stared at the shiny, black toes of his shoes. His gray suit had none of the cut of Humphries's, but was neatly pressed and fit his slightly slouching posture as well as could be expected. He was a man of moderate height and breadth, with a wide face and broad nose. When he offered me his hand, I couldn't help noticing that the skin was scarred and the palms callused. Several hangnails protruded around his fingernails, a whitened contrast to the ebony skin that stretched over enlarged knuckles. He nodded at me, but said nothing.

"I'm so sorry about your loss." The words didn't come easily, and felt bitterly inadequate. Both grandparents nodded. And that was it. Nothing more to say. I turned to April.

"I'd like to pay my respects to your parents, too."

April heaved a deep sigh and nodded. Wordlessly she turned and led Miss Alma and me to the other side of the room. Davon remained with his parents.

"Mama?" The woman in the chair looked up but did not stand. "Mama, this is Julia . . ."

"Lambros," I added, offering her my hand. "And my friend Mrs. Rayburn. I'm happy to meet you, Mrs. McNabb."

Mrs. McNabb fiddled with the lace collar on her pastel flowered dress. She smoothed it on her shoulders and ran her hand down over her breast. "Joy," she said. "Everybody calls me Joy. You're a friend of April?"

"Well, yes. We met when—"

"Daddy—I want you to meet someone. This is Julia and her

friend." The man was so patently hostile, I didn't even bother to introduce him to Miss Alma. He nodded curtly, not extending his hand. I turned back to Joy.

"We really must be going," I said. "But I just wanted to stop by to express my condolences."

"Nice of you to come by." Joy McNabb looked back down at her hands, took the lavender handkerchief and began methodically folding it, running a broken nail over the edges to crease it.

"April," I said, taking her hand. "If there's anything I can do . . ."

"Funeral's tomorrow afternoon. Two o'clock. At the church cemetery—Mount Sinai Tabernacle," she said. Her glance searched my face. A protest grew in my throat, but I couldn't bring it out.

"Of course," Miss Alma added quietly. "Julia and I will be there." April nodded happily.

We said good-bye to Davon and Humphries, stopping at the door to sign the guest book. There were only three other names in the book: Dr. Martin Glazer, L.T. Humphries, and Vivian Spaulding. Miss Alma pointed to the blank page.

"That's why she wants us to come," she said.

We couldn't have been there more than fifteen minutes, but it felt like hours. The June evening sun was still high when I dropped Miss Alma at her house, promising to pick her up at one-thirty the next day, and turned the Honda for home.

I couldn't get them out of my mind. Billy's article said that Allen McNabb had supported his daughter on the issue of burying Damien in the church cemetery, but he certainly had not seemed supportive to me. The animosity in that close, almost fetid atmosphere was palpable. I should have realized that it augured badly for the funeral.

Nick was deep in paperwork when I got home. Bank statements and deposit slips covered the office floor, and three feet of tape curled out of the adding machine on the desk. Jack looked up as I came in, his tail thumping heavily on a stack of IRS forms.

"Get off that, Jock!" Nick gave our little Scottie a playful swat on his rump. Jack reacted with his usual manic behavior, scurrying for his ball and scattering bank statements and canceled checks everywhere. Nick groaned. "I just got them all organized. Put him out in the yard, will you?"

"Come on, Jack. Let's go out," I said, leading him downstairs and opening the back door. He hit the backyard with a volley of barking. The neighbors love Jack.

"So what have you found?" I asked, as I returned to the office.

"Just three years worth of tax returns, checks, statements," Nick muttered. He punched a few numbers into the adding machine. "I figure it must have something to do with that refund they sent us a couple of years ago. The one I sent back, remember?"

I certainly did. He had returned the check with a letter suggesting that the IRS check their records, since our records did not indicate that we were due a refund. The IRS had complied by sending us a second check for twice the amount—approximately three thousand dollars and some vague cents. The second check had also been returned with a lengthier and slightly more strident letter requesting that they review their records. We had not heard from them—other than to make our usual quarterly deposits and filings—since.

"But, Nick, those checks didn't total anywhere near six thousand dollars."

Nick raked his fingers through his black hair. "I know. But it's the only thing I can figure out." He bundled up his papers, stacked the statements and checks neatly inside a box, and tore the ribbon of paper off the adding machine.

"Fortunata's coming back day after tomorrow. I'm going to ask him about it then."

"Good, then you can go to the funeral with me tomorrow."

"Oh no, now, Julia—" he said as I tickled his earlobe with my fingertip.

Chapter Three

pre-sage \ˈpre-sij, pri-ˈsāj̇ *vb* **pre-saged; pre-saging** *vt* (1562) [ME, fr. L *praesagium,* fr. *praesagire* to forebode, fr. *prae-* + *sagire* to perceive keenly—more at SEEK] **1:** to give an omen or warning of: FORESHADOW, PORTEND.

—*Merriam Webster's Ninth New Collegiate Dictionary*

The little church was several miles outside of town on the Industry Road on the edge of the county line. We had to watch carefully for the sign, as neither the church nor the cemetery was visible from the main road. Miss Alma had been there once before for a student's wedding. She spotted the sign just in time for Nick to hit the brakes and careen down the driveway.

The church sat nestled back in the woods, a squat building with a short steeple that barely tickled the limbs of the pine trees around it. The white clapboard evoked fond memories of New England, but the sultry weather reminded me that we were in the deep South. I was surprised, and pleased for April, when we found the parking lot filled with cars. Pleased, that is, until I realized why they were all there.

There was to be a graveside service only, conducted by Allen McNabb, the baby's own grandfather. The hearse was drawn up to the side of the church, and behind it, the black BMW, followed by several other cars. We pulled in behind the last one. A white van, lettered WPAR-TV, the university television station, tilted precariously on the edge of the grass near a ditch. Nick took Miss Alma's elbow as we carefully stepped over gray cable lines spewing from the van's open doors to follow a brick walkway around to the back of the church. The gates of the little cemetery stood to the left. To the right, a deep thicket of kudzu vines and wild muscadines reminded me of Eden after the Fall. Beautiful—but treacherous and filled with serpents.

The afternoon was still and hot, with an oppressive humidity hanging over the cemetery and the bright green canopy that sheltered the grave. A line of six folding chairs, swathed in green felt, waited empty at the graveside. April, Davon, and their families stood next to the chairs and stared across the cemetery to the pathway where we stood.

D'Anita wore a sleeveless column dress of stark white, contrasting with her skin like piano keys. Louis Humphries stood next to her in a black sport jacket and neatly creased camel slacks. The rest of them looked like they had walked directly from Statler's to the cemetery, without so much as combing their hair. April looked particularly haggard in a skimpy dress that appeared to have been hastily dyed an uneven black.

The tick-ticking of a video camera and the murmuring of the newscaster's voice drifted over the otherwise silent graves. The crowd didn't chant, just quietly paced in a narrow oval in front of the cemetery gates, carrying their placards and homemade posters. Miss Alma drew a sharp breath.

"How can they do this? How can they be so cruel?"

"Religion," I offered, "sometimes has a nasty twist to it."

They were mostly women. I suppose their righteous husbands were out working, leaving it to the womenfolk to set the virtuous standards for the family. Here and there a toddler clung to his mama's skirt and paced with the rest of them. One or two men, flushed of face by the sweltering heat and the knots in their neckties, meekly followed the women. And to the side, Walter Fry smiled upon his work, for clearly he had orchestrated the event.

He was a tall, lean man, with a round-shouldered stature that caused his torso to cup and created a slightly rounded belly unsuited to a man of his weight. His dark brown hair was beginning to gray. It emanated from a widow's peak and was worn slicked back with a thick layer of gel and long enough to curl up at his collar. His features could only be described as coarse—a heavy brow ridge overhanging small eyes, the nose long and blunt, lips thick, and ears large and heavy—as though the sculptor who chiseled them had not bothered to refine them. Had more care been taken to perfect them, he might have been considered handsome. There was a rugged energy about him, as if his veins were filled not with blood, but with black crude oil. His sleeves were rolled up, his forearms darkly matted with curling hair. He carried a book in one hand and divided his attention between the demonstration and the large, ruddy man who was speaking to him in agitated bursts. At length the man threw up his hands and backed away, glaring at Fry from the sidelines.

The signs were vicious—phrases extracted from the Bible and twisted to their own purpose, God's mandate for purity of race. One particularly venomous sign reminded us all that the sins of the father would be visited upon the children. Davon's child was dead.

"Come along, Julia." Miss Alma linked her free arm in mine. "Hold your head up. We're marching right through this picket line."

I followed as directed, and the three of us crossed between a barrel-shaped woman in a pink polyester pantsuit and a man whose eyes would not meet mine. We were no more than a foot or two across the line when I felt something hit my ankle. I glanced down and back up at the woman who had spat at my feet. She smiled insolently as I turned away, shaken to the core. Miss Alma loosened her grip on me to clutch Nick's arm with both hands. She whispered something in his ear and pushed him through the cemetery gate.

"That baby don't belong here." I glanced around to find the woman in pink glowering at me, and as I met her eyes she raised her fist. "Let 'em bury their own dead." I opened my mouth, ready with a rejoinder, but Miss Alma shook her head.

She left Nick and me standing at the gate and turned back, making straight for Walter Fry. "I am ashamed, Walter," she said, in a voice loud enough for all of us to hear. She turned on the crowd of picketers. "I taught so many of you—you, Nelda Conrad, and you, Dub Cantrell. And," she said sadly, turning back to the deacon, "you, Walter. But I can see now that I taught you nothing."

Without waiting for a response, she turned on her heel and rejoined us. The crowd began jeering, screaming hateful, ugly epithets. A handful of muscadines buffeted our backs and splattered in our hair as we dropped behind Miss Alma and followed her into the cemetery.

Louis Humphries stood next to the Folsom family wiping his forehead and neck with his handkerchief as the June heat boiled up under the canopy. He took Miss Alma's arm and guided her to a seat with the family before taking his place behind her. I stood between Humphries and Nick, behind D'Anita Folsom, who twisted to glare over her shoulder at the picket line. Candice touched her arm, urging her to turn back around. Allen McNabb, holding an open Bible, was standing behind the wicker basket at the head of the grave.

" 'The Lord is my shepherd,' " he began.

The service was mercifully brief. I was aware, from the corner of my eye, of the cameraman and newscaster moving around just outside the canopy. I wanted to snatch their equipment and hurl it into that open grave. Billy English quietly stepped up behind me. Although he had a microcassette recorder in his hand, he lowered it to his side, discreetly directing the microphone toward Allen McNabb, and bowed his head.

As the service drew to a close, April stood and went to the lone flower arrangement positioned next to the casket. She extracted a white rose and laid it on top of the wicker bassinet. D'Anita's shoulders collapsed in a tremor and Humphries leaned around to pass her his handkerchief. Candice Folsom pressed her hand to her mouth while her husband, Chester, stared despondently at his feet. A hard knot formed in my throat, and I reached for Nick's hand. Davon followed April's lead, and one by one the family members stripped the arrangement and offered their flowers to the baby. Candice Folsom lingered a moment at the casket. "Godspeed, Damien," she said.

Miss Alma, Nick, and I withdrew to the back of the canopy to say a final good-bye to the family. The picketing crowd had stopped their pacing to watch the funeral. They had then gathered around their leader. Walter Fry was speaking to them, his Bible slung open on his hand, his index finger wildly waving in the air. His drawl was deep—drawing out the vowels—and seemed affected to appeal to the crowd. ". . . the holy race has intermingled with the peoples of the lands . . ."

Fry was an astute showman, the very picture of righteous indignation. He shook his head slowly, almost compassionately, as though pitying the wayward sinners who had brought him here. And his congregation was taking it all in, nodding their heads and greeting his remarks with resounding amens.

Davon stood beside me, his fists curled and jaw rigid with anger. Joy McNabb twisted the lavender handkerchief in her hand and dabbed at her upper lip. To her left, Candice and Chester Folsom stood on either side of D'Anita, their arms entwined through their daughter's. D'Anita stood utterly still, eyes sharply focused upon the crowd, muscles tense under her smooth skin—like a black panther poised to attack. Louis Humphries spoke quietly near her ear, but she didn't seem to be listening to him. Allen McNabb stood alone next to the casket, his gaze fixed upon Walter Fry. McNabb's expression was no more readable than it had been the night before at the funeral home.

And April stood alone, at the edge of the canopy. Freckles mottled her otherwise white, waxy skin. Her jaw was dropped, slackened, as she stared across the cemetery at Fry and his followers. Davon walked over to her, but she brushed him away, turning to fumble in her purse.

" '. . . therefore give not your daughters unto their sons, neither take their daughters unto your sons . . .' " Fry's voice rose above the hush of the cemetery. He held up his Bible in both hands, turning in a semicircle so that everyone might see.

"It's right here in the Word," he cried. "Ezra nine: twelve."

"No!" The cry sounded as though it had been wrenched from a heart. April was halfway across the cemetery before any of us realized she was gone. She absently stepped over and around markers, her eyes fixed on Fry all the while.

"Follow her," Miss Alma whispered, and shoved Nick and me out from under the canopy. I moved as quickly as I could, the heels of my shoes sinking into the soft earth and hanging on foot markers. Nick and Davon shot past me, with Humphries and Candice close behind.

By the time I caught up with them, April was facing Walter Fry. The crowd had backed away, but the cameraman had angled in to get a better shot. Sunlight flashed on the shiny barrel of a small gun. April's hand trembled violently. Fry's face was pasty, but he had not stopped reading. She took several slow steps toward him as he droned on through the passage.

"I have heard that all my life," she said. Her voice rose scarcely above a whisper, guttural, filled with rage. Humphries and the family stumbled behind her, muttering confused warnings. She swung the gun around at the crowd and screamed.

"Get away—all of you. Damn you to hell! Get out of this cemetery before I shoot every one of you. I will! I'll kill you all! You leave my baby alone!"

Miss Alma had reached my side. Her hand squeezed my arm in a vise grip. "Oh God in Heaven," she whispered. Nick pulled us back toward the cemetery and out of harm's way.

"And you . . ." April jerked the gun back at Fry. "You'll be the first. Do you hear me?" Fry stepped back, his glance darting left and right. He waved his open palm at her as the Bible drooped in his other hand. His lips curved in a placating smile.

"April," he said. "April, honey, I've known you since you were—"

"Shut up! Shutup shutup shutup! I hate you. I always have . . ." Her hand grew steady as she brought the gun up level with Fry's chest.

"April!" Allen McNabb stood behind his daughter. His voice

was so loud, so deep and masterful, that the headstones in the cemetery seemed to tremble. She froze.

"Give me the gun, April," he commanded. He strode confidently past her, swinging around in front of Fry to face her off. He held out his hand. "Give me the gun," he demanded again.

"Do it, baby." Davon walked steadily toward her. "Give him the gun."

She confronted her father, her face white with fear and rage, and his granite-hard as he stared at her through small, glittering eyes. She shook her head slowly.

"No. I don't have to listen to you. Not anymore—not ever again. You—you're worse than all the rest of them." Her teeth were clenched, and she ground out her next words. "I hate you the most."

Allen McNabb was more than equal to her. "You will do as I say! Honor your father, girl."

"Stop it! Don't say it!" She staggered, her hands coming up to cover her ears, and the pistol went off in midair. Its crack reverberated in the bell tower of the church, even as the bullet splintered the clapboard siding. Children shrieked. Mothers screamed. McNabb lunged for his daughter, grabbed the gun by the barrel, spun, and with the strength of Samson, hurled it out into the thicket behind the church.

And then, as we stared and the videotape rolled on, Allen McNabb stepped up to his daughter and backhanded her a slap that sent her reeling into her husband's arms.

I dropped into a chair at the family table and fumbled with the silverware in front of me.

"What's the matter, Julia? You look sick. You want me to get you an aspirin or something?"

I nodded. "Thanks, Rhonda. I don't feel very well."

Rhonda returned quickly with the aspirin and a glass of water. "Here," she said. "Take this. You look like you're going to faint."

I wasn't going to faint, and I knew that aspirin wasn't going to make this particular illness go away, but I took it anyway. Rhonda pulled out the chair across from me.

"You want to tell me what's the matter?"

No. I didn't want to tell her, but I told her anyway. Rhonda listened patiently and without interruption until I was finished. "What happened after he slapped her?"

"Davon attacked him and would have beaten him to a bloody pulp, I suppose, if his father hadn't pulled him off. Candice took care of April, got her into their car, and Chester managed to wrestle Davon in behind her. Davon was threatening McNabb, and . . . oh, it was a mess. D'Anita was screaming at Fry, but Humphries got her under control, I guess, and hurried her away. Reverend McNabb and Fry were going at it in the parking lot. The rest of them—the demonstrators—couldn't get out of there fast enough. Neither could we."

Nick returned from the kitchen just then, a solemn Spiros behind him. He shook his head. "I am hob-gob-lins, Zulia."

Hobgoblins. Bad spirits. "Yes," I agreed. "Me too."

Rhonda and Spiros readily agreed to close for us and we left them to it. I stared out the car window as we drove home, unable to get April out of my mind—her grim, pale face, eyes sparkling with hatred. And her father, unyielding in the face of his daughter's raw pain. Maybe *hobgoblins* had not been such a bad choice of words, although *demons* would have been better, for surely evil had been present in abundance in the churchyard that afternoon.

Chapter Four

as-sess \ə- ˋses, a-\ *vt* [ME *assessen*, prob. fr. ML *assessus*, p. of *assidēre*, fr. L, to sit beside, assist in the office of a judge—more at ASSIZE] . . . **3:** to make an official valuation of (property) for the purposes of taxation **4:** to determine the importance, size, or value of *syn* see ESTIMATE.

—*Merriam Webster's Ninth New Collegiate Dictionary*

Jack was delighted to see us, scampering for his toy box and returning with his leash tightly clamped in his square little jaws. "I guess you'd better," I said to Nick, pointing to the leash. "You know how he is. If you don't take him, he's liable to take it out on the furniture."

We changed our clothes, and I saw them off at a trot, down the driveway and heading for parts unknown. At five o'clock the air was still and heavy, without the slightest whisper of a breeze to cut through the June heat. They'd both return panting, and quickly. I surveyed the contents of the refrigerator—in our house, always an interesting foray into the unknown. Very little presented itself for our dining pleasure. Instead, I pulled out a couple of wineglasses, filled them, and took mine to the den. I flopped down on the couch and closed my eyes, where, uninvited, the events of the afternoon replayed themselves.

Jeering picketers. Prayers droning over the relentless ticking of a videocam. A flower laid on the wicker casket. Weeping. Joy had wept. Candice had wept. Even D'Anita had wept. But not April. April had not shed a tear. She had listened to the prayers of her father without interest, ignored her husband's gentle efforts at condolence, and finally she had pulled a gun from her purse and turned it on the man who represented everything she hated. I could still hear the crack of the shot and the answer from the bell tower, the soft plop as the gun landed in the kudzu thicket.

The gun! I bolted off the couch, nearly spilling my wine. Where was the gun? It was vacation Bible school time. What if some children were to find it? One dead child was enough. I grabbed the phone book and pawed through it, trying April first, and when I didn't find her at home, the Folsoms. But there was no answer at either place. I met Nick coming in the door and quickly explained the situation.

"The family probably didn't even think about it, Nick. Everyone was so upset . . . and the picket line cleared right out."

"We'd better go back out there," he said. "Someone has probably already picked it up, but just in case . . ." He grabbed my hand. "Come on, let's go."

Jack was on our heels and hopped into the backseat of the Honda as though we'd invited him along. I glanced at my watch. "It's been three hours. Surely someone will have thought about it by now."

"Maybe we should have just called Sam. He would have sent a deputy."

I shook my head firmly. "Why? No crime was actually committed. Besides, they've got enough trouble already. There would be questions and April might be charged with . . . I don't know. Something."

Sam Lawless is the sheriff of Calloway County, and the newly wedded husband of our waitress, Rhonda. Sam is a kind man and a good friend. But he takes his job very seriously, as well I know, and he would not look upon the incident at the church with favor.

"We'll have to call him if we can't find it," Nick said.

"Please, let's spare April and Davon if we can."

The parking lot was deserted when we arrived. Although it was still light, a smoky mist was oozing in for the night, hovering over the church steeple and clinging to the tops of the low mountains around us. We sprinted around the back of the church and ground to a stop. The blanket of kudzu spread much farther out behind the church than I had thought.

"Maybe this wasn't such a good idea after all," I said, considering the many creatures that call kudzu home. Spiders. Snakes. Rodents. "I'll just get Jack," I said. "He probably needs to be walked anyway."

Nick plowed into the vines in the vicinity where we thought the gun had landed, stooping to pull them apart as he went, while I returned to the car for my protector. Jack was, of course, delighted to be included in the party.

Territorial marking is a high priority with Jack. And mark it, he did—on a flattened, weather-stained Sunday bulletin in the parking lot, and on an abandoned Kodak film box, and on one of the picketers' signs, hastily discarded as she retreated from April's gun. He even stopped at a crumpled handkerchief on the ground, snuffled, and raised his leg before sighting Nick deep in the thicket. The leash snapped taut and we were off at a brisk pace, Jack's square little nose parallel with the ground and moving straight for the vines. I gulped hard and plunged in after him.

"Found anything?"

"Plenty. Four beer cans and an empty bottle of Southern Comfort. And these." He held up his foot, around which was looped a limp pair of pink bikini panties. I shivered. The kudzu looked soft and inviting—a perfect place for a little splendor in the grass if you didn't mind the company of vermin. But really—behind a church?

"No gun?"

"No gun."

I told myself that Jack would scare them away—the bugs, the snakes. The rats. And I dogged his tracks, lightly lifting the vines, peeking under them carefully, only to find more abandoned trash. Mosquitoes and no-see-ums swarmed up in our faces and stung our necks. Something swished in the underbrush and Jack's head came up, ears pointed tall and alert, before he returned to his snuffling along the ground.

"Okay, that's it," I said, scrambling out of the vines. "I'm not setting another foot in there. I've had it with creeping, crawling, slithering things I can't see. We need a scythe, only . . . I don't really want to see what's under there anyway. Come on, Nick. Let's go. We're not going to find it."

"It fell right here," he called back. "I'm sure this is where—"

"Nick, please!"

He stood up, arched his back, and swatted a mosquito on his cheek. "All right. I guess you're right."

Scotties are small-game hunters, never more in their element than with their noses in the underbrush on a promising scent. It took a few minutes to convince Jack that the party was over. We made all the same stops on the way back to the car, reaffirming our territory.

"I'm worried," Nick said, as we pulled back out onto the Industry Road. "It should have been there. I'd better call Sam when we get back to the house."

"Is that really necessary? April's got so much on her shoulders right now without having the law breathing down her neck."

"Julia, possession of a gun without a license is illegal. Anyone could get hold of it, don't you understand that? If that gun is out there, it has to be found. I hope Sam has better luck than I did."

I had to admit he made sense. "Well, he'll probably take mowers in there." I shuddered. "I'd hate to live around that area when he ousts those . . . creatures from their natural habitat."

But I didn't have much time to think about that after we got home. I tried April and the Folsoms again, still without success, reluctantly agreeing to let Nick call the sheriff. Sam called us back the next day. He had finally reached April and Davon, only to learn that neither they nor the Folsoms had returned for the weapon. Under the supervision of a deputy, a crew from public works had cleared the area. The news was not good.

"The gun is gone."

The gun was found three days later. It was lying on the floor right next to the body of Walter Fry. I didn't hear about it until the morning after the body was discovered, when Rhonda arrived for work. She gave me a quick rundown shortly before Roger Mumford arrived for his daily dose of ice water.

Roger is one of the Buffaloes—that is, the Sunrise Businessmen's Club, a group of local, self-styled entrepreneurs who meet at the Oracle every morning. Most of the time they just clutter up the place, make a lot of noise, and leave without paying for their coffee. I'm not crazy about them, but my optimistic husband thinks they're eventually going to start buying breakfast. Hope springs eternal.

Roger always arrives first, eager, I suppose, to escape the aging mother with whom he lives, and whose foot is firmly planted on his neck. Eleanor still controls the family jewelry business, as well as her sixty-something-year-old son. Roger is a misogynist.

Sonny Weaver, our insurance agent, was right on his heels. He grabbed his "Insure and Feel Secure" mug from the wait station and vaulted onto A deck.

"Hey, Roger, seen *The Sun* yet this morning?" He slapped a paper down in front of Roger and pointed to the headline: "Local Businessman Found Shot to Death in His Home." I followed Sonny onto the deck with a full pot of coffee. His face fell when he saw me.

"Where's Rhonda this morning?"

"Good morning, Sonny. Nice to see you, too."

"Aw, I didn't mean anything, Julia. You know that. I just wanted to see Rhonda, that's all."

"She's not going to tell you anything, Sonny." In fact, we had agreed that she'd work B deck for this very reason. Sonny is an incurable gossip. He couldn't wait to start questioning her about Walter Fry.

"Now, hold on a minute, Julia. I got a right to know. I'm the one who wrote his life insurance. He's my client." His expression lit up. Rhonda was coming down off the deck, across the cafe to the wait station.

"Hey, Rhonda?"

She ignored him and kept on walking. In a minute she was back, carrying a syrup pitcher and a bowl of creamers.

"Rhonda . . ."

"You're going to have to talk to Sam, Sonny," she called over her shoulder.

"Aw hell, he won't tell my anything till they're finished investigating." He dumped cream in his coffee and sulkily studied the article in the *Sun*. In a moment his expression brightened. "You know, I think Charley knows, er . . . knew Fry pretty well. Goes to the same church." He twisted around on the deck and gazed out the window. "Where the hell is he, anyway?"

The Buffaloes were arriving pretty steadily by then. Warren promptly spilled the steaming mug I'd set at his place. By the time I returned with a fresh cup and a bar mop to sop up the spill, Mitch Yoakum had arrived. He'd brought a box of Dinah's Donuts, which he swiped off the table when he saw me coming. Some things just never change.

As soon as the breakfast rush slowed, I met Rhonda in the wait station. "So you were saying . . ." I prompted her.

"Just that they found him last night on the kitchen floor."

"Who found him?"

"His wife, I guess. She came home from a Ladies' Circle meeting at the church and there he was, shot in the head."

"How awful for her. Any suspects yet?"

Rhonda pursed her lips. "Judging by what you told me about the funeral, I'd say there'd be about a dozen suspects, wouldn't you? But Sam never got home last night, so all I really know is what he told me on the phone. They have the weapon, and they'll be taking prints. They're dusting the house now—at least that's what they were doing last night. And taking pictures. You know the drill."

Unfortunately, I knew it all too well. I inadvertently glanced around the cafe, remembering the crime-scene team—the photographers, fingerprint men, the evidence bags. The memories were as fresh and crisp as Spiros's Greek salad. "Yeah," I said. "I know the drill."

Rhonda squeezed my shoulder. "You have to let some things go, you know?"

I nodded. I did know. But still, it was hard. I had felt so violated, so used. As much a victim as Glenn Bohannon, whose murder had almost cost me my marriage and my freedom.

I glanced back up at the Buffaloes, their morning "meeting" in full and rowdy swing. Harry Gaines, used-car salesman and relative newcomer to the group, was holding forth with an off-color story from his college days when Richard Fortunata, laden with briefcase, folder, and adding machine, trudged through the front door. Why was I worrying about the problems of the past? Now that the IRS was nipping at our heels, murder seemed the happier alternative.

"Good morning, Mr. Fortunata," I said. He nodded curtly. "Would you like a cup of coffee before you get started?"

"No."

"Well, my husband is waiting for you in the back dining room. Let me just show you—"

"Find it myself," he muttered.

"No, really. It's no trouble. Right this way." I wasn't about to let him wander the place unescorted. Nick had told me that Fortunata had demanded a list of our equipment. I would put it together for him sometime during the day, but I wasn't going to make it any easier for him. He followed me down the hall past the rest rooms to our small private dining room. The voluminous files, register tapes, and tickets had swelled to three years worth of records, making it impossible to work in our little office. Thus the back dining room had been relegated to preparing for battle with the most powerful agency in the federal government.

Nick had pushed four tables together and was carefully stacking canceled checks, bank statements, deposit slips, copies of forms 940 and 941, FICA and FUTA deposits, profit and loss statements, and payroll records, all organized by year, in their respective places. Fortunata shoved them aside and slapped his briefcase on the table. He held up the plug to his adding machine. "Where can I put this?" he said. I bit my tongue.

By the time I returned to the front, the Buffaloes had departed, leaving their customary droppings behind them. Rhonda heaved a bus tub onto her hip and started for A deck.

"I had to hide out in the cooler until they left," she said. "Sonny just wouldn't let up. As if I'd tell him anything, even if I knew."

I would have helped her, but she insisted on doing it alone. "You go ahead and help Nick out back there. I can get this."

I had no intention of helping Nick. In fact, he didn't want my help. "You're too nervous," he said. "He'll think we're guilty of hiding something from them. I'll handle him." I was only too happy to turn the whole mess over to him. Nick keeps his head in a crisis far better than I do. But I did have that list to compile, and a hospital consult to schedule. I headed for the kitchen.

Spiros stood at the steel table folding a chicken and mushroom mixture into triangles of phyllo pastry for the day's lunch special—*kotopita*, one of my favorites. Too bad my appetite ebbed every time Fortunata showed up. Beside Spiros, a battered tape player vibrated with the twang of a bouzouki: *"Da, la, la, da, dir-la-dada."* Spiros grinned at me under his wide mustache and sang along in a rattling base. It was a happy song. But I was in no mood for happy. I waved at him and went on to the office to make my phone call.

I don't take many patients anymore—only the really unique cases. Speech pathology had seemed like a good career choice until I realized that I couldn't leave my patients at work. It takes a special type of personality to overcome the temptation to take every case to heart. My last regular patient had lost a hand in a grenade explosion on D day. He was eighteen at the time. He had returned home, disabled, to a failed wartime marriage, and slipped into an alcoholic haze where he had remained, off and on, for over thirty years. Until he met Lois, his second wife, at an AA meeting. He became an active speaker in AA, married Lois, and six months later had a devastating stroke. He gave me tapes of his speeches so that I could hear how he had sounded before the blood vessel burst in his brain. I listened to them, and I wept off and on for a week. Then I cut my practice in half and started working part-time with Nick.

But occasionally a patient comes along that interests me. This case was a referral from a local ENT, a voice problem he thought I should hear. Due to an insurance snafu, it was necessary to hospitalize the patient for some pretty routine tests. I would have to go over to Delphi General for the consult. The patient was scheduled, I was told, for an MRI that morning. He was expected back in his room in time for lunch, but had other tests scheduled for the afternoon. I would have to be at the hospital by one o'clock or I would miss him. I glanced at my watch and the day's schedule. Otis, our dishwasher, was due in at ten, and Tammy would be in at eleven. Spiros could handle lunch without Nick, if he could press Otis into service. And Otis, who was thoroughly intimidated by him, would reluctantly comply. I decided I would have time to compile the list by then, and told the nurse on the floor that I would be there no later than twelve-thirty.

One large fryer, one small fryer, one flattop grill, two steam tables (four wells each) . . . The list was far longer than I had anticipated. I looked it over carefully and wondered just why Richard Fortunata wanted it. He didn't enlighten me when I handed it to him. In fact, he didn't say anything at all, just tucked it inside a folder and slid it into his briefcase before returning to his adding machine. Nick didn't even look up, but continued tapping keys. *Chink, chink, whir.* The tune of dueling adding machines followed me out the door and most of the way to the hospital.

The patient had myasthenia gravis, the debilitating disease that took the life of Aristotle Onassis. There wasn't much doubt about the diagnosis—the voice began heartily, but quickly fatigued and faded away. I soon realized that I had been called in only to confirm what the doctor already knew. But he needed my report, describing vocal symptoms, to complete his chart. I thanked the patient for his time, said that I would report to the doctor and he would make the final diagnosis. An unfortunate choice of words. I left, castigating myself as I felt, again, the helplessness that so often accompanies the job.

As I passed the nurses' station, I stopped to ask for Candice Folsom. I wanted to find out how April was doing. The nurse on duty called up to Candice's office, soon hung up the phone, and turned back to me. "Apparently she left about eleven, gone home for the day. She must not have been feeling well or something. She's had some family matters to take care of lately."

"Yes, I know," I said. "I was at the funeral."

"You were?" The nurse licked her lips and leaned over the counter confidentially. "Then you saw April?" I nodded. "And you know about him, the man they found dead last night . . . He was the one that April——"

"Yes, I know. How did Candice take the news?"

The nurse—by now I had seen her name tag and knew she was Coral Hanson, L.P.N.—glanced around the station and lowered her voice. "I didn't see her this morning myself. But I hear that . . . well, that she laughed when she saw the paper. I mean, somebody in her office, I don't want to name names, was there. And she said that Folsom laughed!"

Coral Hanson fidgeted with her nursing pin, straightened a chart in the rack, and looked away from me. "Imagine that," she said, as if to herself. "Folsom laughed."

The parking lot was all but empty when I got back to the Oracle. Spiro's monstrous Pontiac and Fortunata's generic government car were neatly lined up near the door. Poor Nick. He was still in the back dining room with Richard Fortunata. When I arrived, they were nose to nose, Nick impatiently waving a photocopy in Fortunata's face.

Nick rarely loses his temper, but when he does it gives one pause. Richard Fortunata seemed to be impervious to the possibilities, most of which were not pleasant, some of which could get Nick twenty to life.

"Look," Nick growled. "We've been over it and over it. You've seen the damn forms, the deposits, everything. The total was three thousand one hundred and sixty-seven dollars." He brandished copies of the checks and letters in front of Fortunata's eyes. "Here they are. I never cashed them. I returned them both."

Fortunata shrugged impassively. "Not credited in the computah."

Greek expletives. Long ones. Some of them I'd never even heard before. "I don't give a damn for your computer!"

Fortunata smiled thinly. "We didn't owe you that money, Mr. Lambros. Didn't you read the disclaimer enclosed with the check? If you cashed it, and we determined that we did not owe it to you, you are subject to penalties and interest."

"But I didn't cash it—them—either of them. I sent them back!"

Fortunata shook his head morosely, although I suspected he was secretly enjoying it. "Not in the computah—not paid."

"What are you," Nick shouted, "a rowboat?" Fortunata's gaze was puzzled.

"He means a robot. Are you a ro—"

Nick swung around to me. "Not now, Julia," he snapped. But the interruption did defuse the tension, if only for a moment. Nick dropped the papers onto the table and ran his hands through his thick, black hair. He sighed heavily.

"How do we get it in the computah?" I said.

Fortunata turned to me with a little sneer. "One way's to pay it," he replied.

A slow burn started creeping up my neck. A hot rejoinder was hovering on the tip of my tongue when, out of the corner of my eye, I glimpsed Spiros beckoning to me from the kitchen door.

"Zulia, *o andras,*" he whispered, pointing at the IRS agent's back. "*Eine . . .* plen-uh . . ." His brow furrowed. He took my arm, pulled me into the kitchen, and rustled through a box of loose calendar leaves until he came up with the one he wanted.

plen-i-po-ten-tia-ry *n:* a diplomatic agent with full discretionary power to transact business.

"No. Well, yes and no." Diplomacy was not Fortunata's forte, but I knew enough about the IRS to realize that "full discretionary powers" was too apt a description.

Spiros nodded gravely. "I feex," he said, grabbing a salt shaker and bounding toward the back dining room. When I caught up with him, he was tiptoeing through the back of the room, liberally sprinkling salt in the carpet behind the IRS agent. He tilted his head sideways and put a finger to his lips.

"*Efere ee kyra to fege panayia mou na fege,*" he whispered. Evoking the gods? Chanting away the evil spirits? Satisfied, he nodded abruptly and lumbered out of the dining room. Richard Fortunata started packing up his briefcase.

"And if I don't pay it—*again?*" Nick said.

Fortunata had mastered the art of the impassive shrug. "Seized assets," he replied.

"What do you mean? You've already put a lien on our house!"

"Just in case."

"In case of what?"

"Case you got no assets to seize."

"But if you take my money, and my equipment, how do you expect me to pay off what you *say* I owe you?"

"That'll be up to you." Fortunata snapped his briefcase shut and picked up his adding machine. "You might try paying your taxes, Mr. Lambros."

"It doesn't make any sense, Julia," Nick said, as we walked back to the main dining room. "Why can't I just send them copies of the letters? Then they can put it in the computer and everything will be okay."

"It can't hurt," I agreed. "Just send it to the local office, with another letter explaining that they've made a mistake. I'll type it for you tonight."

Nick's jaws were clamped tight as a clamshell, the muscles flexing. "I'm not paying them," he said. "I'm not going to do it. It's not right. They can seize whatever they want. I'm not paying them." He sat down at the family table and crossed his arms. Feet rooting into cement.

"Well, now, wait a minute . . . I'm not sure that's a good idea, Nick. Nobody takes on the IRS and wins, least of all us!" But his mind was made up. He sprang out of his chair and grabbed the phone book at the register. In a minute he was jabbing the numbers on the telephone dial. When he returned to the table, he was considerably calmed.

"What was that all about?"

"I've got an appointment with a tax attorney tomorrow. I'm not giving that son of a—" he checked himself in midcuss "—that pirate the satisfaction of collecting money I don't owe them."

I agreed that a tax attorney sounded like a very good idea. "By the way, what was Spiros doing with that salt?"

Nick grinned. "When you want someone to go away, you sprinkle salt behind him."

I rolled my eyes. "You know that's just a superstition," I said, not entirely convinced that he did know it.

"Well, it worked. He left."

"Yeah, but he was getting ready to go anyway. I think."

"Excuse me." Davon Folsom stood in the door. "Is it okay for me to come in? Are you still open?"

"Sure, Davon. Come on in. It's almost closing time, but—"

"I'm not here to eat anyway, Miz Julia. I need to talk to you."

Nick excused himself and left to pack up our tax records for the attorney. Davon took a seat, jiggled the change in his pocket, and shifted uneasily.

"I just came to tell you," he said. "They've arrested April."

Chapter Five

ma-lev-o-lent \-lənt*adj* [L *malevolent-, malevolens,* fr.
male badly + *volent, volens,* prp. of *velle* to wish—more at
MAL-, WILL] (1509) **1:** having, showing, or arising from
intense, often vicious ill will, spite, or hatred . . .
> —*MerriamWebster's Ninth New Collegiate Dictionary*

I'd been expecting it. "When?"

"They took her in for questioning about ten-thirty this morning. I went along behind them. Didn't get to see her, though, until
two o'clock. She sent me to you."

"To me? Why to me?" Her family was the logical place to turn
for help. But I thought about Allen McNabb and understood. "I
mean," I continued, "is your family helping out? Do you have an
attorney?"

Davon nodded. "L.T.'s been with her while they questioned
her. But she wanted me to come see you."

I really was perplexed. Davon's family seemed supportive and
loving—at least to him. I didn't really know how they felt about
April, but at least someone had contacted Louis Humphries.
Where did I fit into the picture?

"She said you'd know what to do," he continued. "You gotta
help her, Miz Julia."

"Davon, I'm willing to do what I can, but Nick and I don't have
any money." As if to underscore the point, Nick came out of the
wait station and punched the register. The drawer popped open
and he flipped back the money clips.

"We don't want your money!" Davon's dark eyes looked hurt.

He pushed his chair away from the table and stood up. "I've given you enough trouble. I'll be going on now."

"Davon, wait. I'm sorry. I just don't know what other kind of help I can give you. Please, sit back down and tell me what I can do."

He stood there for a moment before dropping back into his seat. But he sat with his weight perched on the balls of his feet, as if he might lunge out the door at any moment.

"Wait here," I said, patting his hand. I went into the wait station, returned with a cup of steaming coffee, and set it in front of him. "Now, let's start over again. Has she been formally charged?"

"Not yet. They're still questioning her. But L.T.—he's pretty sure they will."

"All right," I ventured carefully. "If I can't help with bail money or attorney fees, what can I do?"

He didn't answer right away. Instead, he tore open a packet of Equal and stirred it into his coffee, stared at the dripping spoon, and searched for a place to lay it down.

He was very young, I realized. Not more than twenty, and probably not that old. And he was very tired. His eyes were sunken into deep hollows. He knuckled them hard, massaged his temples, and took a long sip of his coffee.

"April. She said you'd know what to do. She said you know about catching murderers. She didn't do it, Miz Julia. I know it looks bad, with that gun and all, but she didn't kill Fry. The man . . . uh, the sheriff, I mean. He saw the video the TV crew took, and that made up his mind for him. But she didn't do it. She wasn't there. She was at home by herself last night."

"By herself? Were you working or something?"

He hesitated, taking another sip of his coffee and a measuring glance at me over the rim of his cup. "The garage isn't open at night. But I wasn't home."

"You were gone all night?"

"Yes, ma'am. But I wasn't at Fry's place either, if that's what you're thinking. It was just something I had to take care of." There was a perplexing obstinacy in the way he was fending off my

41

question—wanting me to know that he was not at the scene of the crime, but unwilling to disclose his whereabouts. He held his head up with a hint of pride in the challenging tilt of his chin.

"And you won't tell me where you were."

"No, ma'am. You wouldn't understand. It's not important anyway. April—she's what's important. We gotta get her out of there, Miz Julia. She's the only thing we gotta think about now."

I glanced over at Nick, sorting tickets at the register, and remembered what it felt like to be deprived of the person you love. Davon was hurting. He really loved his wife. I wished I were as sure of April's feelings for him. I remembered our conversation in the cell. I had come away feeling that April had used Davon to get back at her father. I had been surprised to learn that she'd married him.

"Tell me about you and April," I said. "And please, call me Julia," I added.

Davon's gaze went to the door as it opened and his eyes widened. He glanced around nervously as though he were looking for an escape. Two men had come in and were moving toward A deck, leaving behind the scent of something not quite right.

"Tammy," Nick called, and gestured toward the customers.

They were both tall, easily topping six feet. One was beefy— a thick belly rolling over his belt and spilling onto his blue-jeaned lap. He wore a baseball cap in a camouflage print over a ragtag mop of rusty hair. He kept his big hands curled into fists, even when he wiped his nose, which he did often, like a cliché of someone spoiling for a fight.

His companion was slender in a wiry, muscular way as though, if he stripped his shirt off, a surprising set of biceps and a tight solar plexus might be waiting underneath. The pearl buttons on his western shirt sparkled in the afternoon sun. A leather tooled belt encircled a narrow waist that tapered into snug hips. His jeans were tight, clean, even creased, and fit smoothly down over a pair of highly polished western boots. The whole effect was of a man who cared about his appearance.

In another time and place I might have thought he was good-looking. Very tan, with a square set of gleaming teeth, dark hair, and eyebrows that framed crystal blue eyes. Not bad at all. But there was an essence that emanated from him—a cocksure grace, almost charismatic, but also faintly evil. A Tantalus—a man with insatiable hungers. Vain and reckless. He lazed back in the chair, one long leg extended, and knuckled his lips. And watched Davon.

Tammy snapped her gum, raked her hands through her hair, and took her place in front of them. "What can I get y'all?" Doing her best Dolly Parton, I noted with some annoyance.

Davon glanced at his watch and drained his cup. "I gotta get back down there and find out what's happening, Miz Julia." His eyes darted back up to A deck, then back to do a second check behind him, with the wary nervousness of a cornered animal.

He was about to make his escape, leaving me to wonder what I was expected to do for April and where he had been the night of the murder. But he had come to me looking for help, and the thought of that free-spirited girl confined to a cold, terrifying holding cell was too much to bear.

"Wait," I said. "Look, if I'm going to help her, then you're going to have to talk to me. If you leave, you're tying my hands. Let me get you a refill." I got up and went into the wait station, leaving him to think about it. Tammy came in behind me.

"What did they order, Tammy?"

She parked her pencil behind her ear, tore the ticket off her pad, and poked it through the window to Spiros.

"*Birra,*" he cried. "You get, Tammy. Is your job. Spiros is beezy."

Tammy rolled her eyes. "Just a couple of beers. Why can't he get it, Julia? He's already in the kitchen. Did you see that thin one—the one with the black hair? Hot, huh?"

This last comment, I ignored. It's best not to encourage Tammy to fraternize with the customers. Not that she needs any encouragement.

"Because he's shutting down. Besides, drinks are the waitresses' job."

"Yeah but . . ." I narrowed my eyes at her. "Okay, okay. I'll

43

get it. It's not like I don't have anything else to do. Change the tablecloths, Tammy. Roll the silverware, Tammy . . ." she grumbled.

"Side work's part of the job," I reminded her as she stomped off into the kitchen.

"What's going on?" Nick stood in the door.

"Just the usual. Tammy trying to get Spiros to do her job."

"No," he said. "I mean, those two guys out there. They're just sitting there staring at Davon, and he looks scared to death."

I peeked out the wait station door. Nick was right. They were both glaring at Davon, wiping noses, knuckling their lips as though they were trying to send him silent messages. Tantalus wore a sardonic grin—a *just you wait, boy* grin.

Davon stared longingly at his battered blue pickup in the parking lot. Across the lot from Davon's truck was a black Dodge Ram with Big Foot tires that raised its stature to an automotive monolith. It was parked facing the street, ready to zoom out of the lot at a moment's notice. On the back window there was an iridescent sticker of an unrealistically equipped male horse followed by the slogan: REBEL STALLION AT STUD. Oh really!

"I don't know," I said. "Have you ever seen them before?"

"I don't think so."

"I think they must be after him for some reason. I wonder if they followed him here."

"Maybe. Look, go out there and talk to Davon. Try to calm him down. I'll keep an eye on them."

When I returned to the table with the coffeepot, Davon had torn his napkin to shreds. I poured him another cup, thinking that decaf might have been the better choice.

"Just stay here until they leave," I said.

"What? I'm sorry, I don't know what you're talking about, Miz Julia." But I knew he did.

"Okay," I said, playing along with him. "So, about you and April . . ."

Davon pushed his cup away and leaned forward. "What do you want to know?"

"April and I, we've been going together for three years. Her daddy didn't like me at all—but you probably know that already. Anyway, we've been fooling around for a while, and April—well, she got pregnant. So we got married."

"Did her father marry you?"

He laughed, his slightly uneven teeth sparkling, accenting the rich brown skin on his lips. But his eyes weren't laughing. "Got married in front of the judge soon as April turned eighteen. My mama and daddy, they stood with us."

"How did Reverend McNabb take it?"

Davon's glance strayed back up to the men on A deck. Their beer had come, two cold longnecks served with frosted glasses. Neither of them bothered to pour it out, just slugged it straight from the bottle. Tantalus held his thumb over the mouth of the bottle and gave it a good shake before pointing it at me. Beefy had quite a laugh over that one. Nick, back at the register, had drawn Tammy aside. She was arguing with him. I turned back to our customers.

They were watching us very closely. There was nothing casual in their interest. The beefy one picked his teeth and eyed Davon from under the bill of his baseball cap. He mumbled something to his companion—something that made the other one laugh. Tantalus caught my eyes and raked me up and down, coming back to meet my gaze with an amused glitter in his starlit eyes. He slowly slid his thumb off of the top of the bottle, letting the pressure release gradually. Then he wrapped his hand lovingly around the bottle neck and slid it up and down obscenely, eyeing me all the while. My stomach fluttered uneasily. This guy was definitely dangerous, at least to women. My face burned as I hastily turned back to Davon.

"Uh . . . you were telling me about Reverend McNabb?"

Davon's hand shook as he tried to lift his cup casually to his lips. He gave up making contact and set it back on the table with a thunk. "About like you'd expect. Wouldn't have anything to do with us—her mother, either."

"But they were at the funeral."

"Yeah, well . . . when the baby started coming, I naturally called them. They didn't say much. But then Miz McNabb, she showed up at the hospital."

"And her husband?"

"He came after Miz McNabb called him. After we found out . . . well, Damien, he was—"

Dead. I finished the sentence for myself, since Davon was unable to go on. He wiped his eyes with the back of his hand, grabbed a napkin, and blew his nose.

I could imagine the scene. Reverend McNabb holding forth about the sins of the father, urging April to divorce her husband now that there was to be no baby. And April, sinking deeper into the depression that was now driving her.

"What did he do, Davon? What did Reverend McNabb say?"

"Not much. He just sat there and held her hand. I couldn't believe it myself. He didn't speak to me, of course. But I didn't care. I just didn't want him to hurt April. And he didn't. When he left, he said he'd make the funeral arrangements. So I let him. I thought maybe it would help April—you know, to let him help her."

"So when did Fry come into the picture?"

"Right away." Davon's eyes went back to A deck. Now Tantalus was cleaning his nails at the table—with a very large knife. Davon picked up a steak knife from the now-scattered place setting and thumbed the blade, staring intently at the shiny steel.

"Davon, what is going on? Who are those guys?"

He didn't look at me. "Don't know. Just customers."

Tough customers, I thought. I glanced over at the register. Nick was gone. I could hear him in the wait station, his speech softly slurring in his native language. He returned just as Tammy appeared with a tray and two more beers. Nick grabbed her arm and pulled her aside. He shook his head over the two refills and an argument ensued.

"McNabb and Fry," Davon continued. "They've always been friends. So he called his buddy," he said with caustic emphasis. "And he told him about Damien and the funeral. That's when Fry called a meeting at the church. You probably know the rest."

I nodded. "I read about it in the paper. Did you try to see to Mr. Fry? Maybe try to talk him out of protesting the funeral?"

Davon didn't answer right away. He studied the table, carefully drew the knife blade across another napkin, watching as it rent the paper. He glanced back up at the deck to find Tantalus openly grinning and gesturing with his own knife as though they were engaged in some kind of swordplay. Davon turned quickly back to me, avoiding my eyes.

"Davon, tell me what's—"

"No," he said, shaking his head emphatically. He went on as if he hadn't heard me. "I never talked to him."

I didn't suppose talking to Fry would have done any good anyway. He hadn't struck me as a man who valued compromise. "All right. Then tell me this—where did April get the gun?"

Davon carefully set the knife on the table and rearranged the silverware. He crumpled up the torn napkins and stuffed them into his pocket before folding his hands in front of him.

"I don't know," he said. "And she won't tell me."

Tammy was at the table on A deck, gesturing to Beefy with empty hands. She pointed at Nick and shrugged as Beefy followed her finger, meeting Nick's gaze with an angry scowl. But Tantalus was considerably smoother. He held his empty bottle pointed indelicately at her slender body and curled his lips in a lazy grin. She giggled and ran her hands over her thighs. I winced.

Davon was standing, keys in hand. "I gotta go now, Miz Julia." He didn't wait for a response, but bolted through the door and out to his truck.

The two on A deck were on their feet, shoving Tammy aside, heading for the door. Meanwhile Spiros, with a plastic bucket and mop in hand, materialized between the register and the door. Water slopped onto the quarry tile. Soap slithered under the counter and oozed toward my feet. The pungent smell of ammonia burned in my nostrils.

"Hi. Fine." Spiros grinned and bobbed as the beefy one tried to elbow past him while Tantalus paid the check.

"No, no!" Spiros lurched in front of Beefy, pulled his sailor's cap off, and wiped his brow. *"Poli glistero!"* Beefy seemed to shrink a little next to the formidable Spiros.

"It's slippery," Nick translated. "He wants you to be careful."

"Like thees," Spiros said, rising up on his toes and gingerly tiptoeing through the water. He held up a finger. "You wait. I feex."

He grabbed the string mop and yanked it out of the bucket. Almost. The bucket rocked perilously and, aided by the toe of Spiros's shoe, thumped over, splattering water all over the customers' shoes and legs.

"Aw, shit," cried Beefy, as Davon's truck tore out of the lot.

But Tantalus said nothing—only glared at Spiros, then at Nick. He stood very still—anger coiled, ready to spring. A knotted vein popped out in his neck. I could almost see it pulsing.

Nick hurried around the side of the counter to survey the damage while Spiros pulled a bar mop out of his apron and mopped at Tantalus's legs. *"Signome, signome,"* he said. "Ver-ry sorr-ry."

Tantalus threw up his palms and silently backed away. Message clear. *Get the hell away from me.* Nick returned to the register, snagged a business card off the counter, and handed it to him.

"Here's the address. Get those cleaned and send me the bill." He grabbed another one and thrust it at Beefy. "You, too."

Nick's gaze locked with Tantalus's. There would be no apology. In fact, Nick's eyes twinkled, telegraphing a message: *I know your game, and I beat you.*

Tantalus turned to me, swept me with an appraising glance that lingered a second too long. He tucked the business card in his back pocket and pointed Beefy toward the door, turned abruptly, and sauntered over to me. He took my hand, kissed it lightly, and whispered in my ear.

"You'll be seeing us again," he said.

Nick was over the counter in a heartbeat, but not before Spiros had grabbed them by the collars and shoved them through the door. He spun around and barred Nick's way.

"*Asome!*" Nick growled. "I'm going after them."

"*Ohee!*"

They grappled at the door for a moment, Spiros letting go of Nick only after their tires had squealed out of the driveway. By then I had recovered my composure enough to speak.

"I'm okay, Nick. He didn't hurt me. He was just drunk. Spiros didn't want you to get hurt, that's all."

"He needs to mind his own business."

"Nick, don't be so hard on him. He was just—"

"*Signome, agori mou,*" Spiros said, his mustache quivering sorrowfully. He dropped a heavy hand on Nick's shoulder, but Nick shook him off and stalked away, ignoring the apology. In a second, we heard the office door slam.

"It's okay," I said. "He'll get over it."

Spiros shook his head sadly and picked up the mop and bucket. He stopped, glared out the window, and raised his fist at the Big Foot truck as it topped the hill on Broadway and roared out of sight.

"Caitiff!" he spat. I had to look that one up.

I had promised Davon to do all I could, which, I thought, would not be much. I could probably talk to Sam, although I didn't expect that he'd give me much information. But April hadn't been formally charged yet. Maybe she wouldn't be. Maybe some other lead would present itself, and Sam would see the folly of the whole thing.

April couldn't have killed Walter Fry. Could she? But we had been there, had seen her threaten him with the gun that killed him. We had seen in person what Sam had seen on tape. And I could understand why he would conclude, as he had, that April had carried out her threat. The truth was, I wasn't convinced that she hadn't. She was emotionally unstable—not at all the serenely confident young woman I had met in the jail cell. She could be focusing all of her blame for Damien's death on Fry—using him for a convenient scapegoat. From what I had seen of the deacon, I could hardly blame her.

"So what do you know about it?" I had called Rhonda in the hope of getting some inside information. She hesitated with an audible gasp.

"Okay," I said. "Let me just tell you what I know. I know April didn't kill that man. I wouldn't blame her if she had, but I'm pretty sure she didn't."

"Why? How can you be sure?" She had a point there. Why was I so sure? Because the girl I'd met in jail was a fighter. Murder, it seemed to me, was a form of capitulation. It was like an angry child striking out at an older, more powerful sibling because he knew he couldn't win any other way. But April had won. Damien was buried in the cemetery, just as she had wanted. She might have wanted to belittle and humiliate Fry, but I didn't believe she would want him dead. April was smart, and she was stubborn. Her opposition to her father amply demonstrated that. If anything, I thought, she would want Fry to live, just so she could take him on again, as she had her father. I tried to explain all this to Rhonda.

"Mmm. Maybe. But I don't know much to tell you anyway, Julia," she said. "Just that they're still detaining her for questioning. If she's charged, and I think she will be, it will be a couple of days before it goes to the grand jury. But unless there's new evidence, it's just about a sure thing that they're going to indict."

"What about the victim?"

"Sam didn't tell me much. He was a businessman. Owned Magnolia Mobile Home Park, I think. Maybe one or two other irons in the fire."

"What about his wife?"

"Her name's Elizabeth—think they call her Bitsy, though."

"Does she work?"

"No. Full-time housewife. Big in the church. Ladies' Circle, that kind of thing. Listen, Sam'd kill me if he knew I was talking about his case, but I'll tell you one other thing. They found a knife on the floor near the body."

"What kind of knife?"

"I don't know for sure—a kitchen knife, I think. Anyway, Fry's fingerprints and his wife's were the only ones on it. But you can't tell Sam I told you."

"He'll never know. I promise. Besides, I'm going to talk to him myself. But first I'm going to find out more about Walter Fry."

As soon as Rhonda and I hung up, I dialed the phone again. Miss Alma picked it up on the second ring. "Oh, Julia, have you heard?"

"About April? I'm afraid so."

"I was just listening to the radio—the Parnassus station. The newscaster said they have her in custody for Walter Fry's murder."

"Yes, and her husband's been here to see me. She has some crazy idea that I can help find the real murderer. I promised Davon I'd try," I said. "So I was wondering if you were game for a little subterfuge."

She most certainly was. Miss Alma, despite her eighty some-odd years, still embraces life enthusiastically. Although she's a native Texan, she has lived in Delphi for most of her adult life, and taught history in the public schools until her retirement. She taught most of the townies at one time or another. And she has a long memory.

"I just want to do a little harmless digging around. Are you willing to help me?"

"I don't hold with flouting the law, Julia. But yes, I think it's up to us to do everything we can to help that poor girl."

"Great! Now," I said, "today's Wednesday, so . . ."

Chapter Six

soph-ist \ˈsäf-əst\ *n* [L *sophista,* fr. Gk *sophistēs,* lit., expert, wise man, fr. *sophizesthai* to become wise, deceive, fr. *sophos* clever, wise] (ca 1542) . . . **3:** a captious or fallacious reasoner.

—*Merriam Webster's Ninth New Collegiate Dictionary*

The interior of Mount Sinai Tabernacle Church was as stark as its clapboard exterior. It was full to overflowing when Miss Alma and I arrived. We finally found standing room in the creaking balcony, along with the teenagers who had managed to escape their parents to join their peers. It was clear they were expecting a show.

"Do you suppose it's always like this on Wednesday night?" I whispered. Miss Alma shook her head and pointed to the front pew. A large woman, in a tight black sheath and a wide-brimmed black hat, sat with her head bowed. She clutched a wrinkled handkerchief in her hand, dabbing at her eyes now and then. Every eye in the church was trained on her grieving posture.

"Bitsy. Mrs. Fry," Miss Alma whispered to me. "Bitsy Hagan when I knew her." In front of Bitsy Fry the pulpit stood empty—waiting.

"Visitor, ma'am?" I nodded at the young usher who proffered a white card and a small red pencil. I took them automatically before realizing what they were for.

"I'll wait while you fill it out," he said, passing another one to Miss Alma.

It was a visitor's card. Name. Address. Spouse's name. I filled

them out and was pondering how to answer the next question—
"Would you like to be visited by our pastor?"—when the choir
filed in to take their seats in the loft. I thrust the card back at the
usher and turned my attention to the front of the church.

The organist tucked her pastel flowered skirt under her and
turned her gaze to the choir director. The organist was Joy Mc-
Nabb. Mount Sinai must be a family enterprise, I reflected. The
choir director raised his arms, and Joy's fingers plodded over the
keys, thundering the opening chords of "Cast Thy Burden on
the Lord." Allen McNabb entered the sanctuary from a door to
the right of the pulpit.

Bitsy tried to stand, but sank back to her bench as two of the
ushers came forward to assist her. Reverend McNabb watched
without a flicker of expression. The choir's collective glance
darted back and forth between their director and the mini drama
taking place in the first pew. The ushers hovered around Bitsy, taking her hand, whispering in her ear. The hat moved back and
forth as she responded to their condolences. The tenor faltered on
his solo as Bitsy once more rose to stand for the opening hymn.
One usher moved into the pew beside Mrs. Fry as the second retreated down the aisle. A collective sigh rose above the choir.

Joy McNabb ended the hymn with a heavy chord, dropped her
hands into her lap, and stared, expressionless, at her husband.
Allen McNabb walked to the pulpit, opened his Bible, and
thumped it down. He gazed out at the congregation for a moment, shook his head, and slapped the Bible closed again. Then he
stepped around the pulpit and stood at the head of the center
aisle.

"I have decided," he said, "to change tonight's lesson. Our own
beloved deacon and brother in Christ, Walter Fry, was violently
taken from us last night, while his wife was here, at Mount Sinai,
in the service of the church. It's only fitting that we suspend
tonight's regular service to join our sister, Elizabeth Fry, in grieving the loss of her husband." He turned his gaze on Bitsy.

She raised her tear-streaked face bravely, even ventured a bit-
tersweet smile for the pastor and turned it on the congregation.

"Sister Elizabeth—Bitsy," McNabb continued softly. "You know that we share your loss. But even as we speak about Walter, he is enjoying the company of the Lord."

A chorus of amens sang out of the congregation. Bitsy nodded rapidly and blew her nose into the mourning handkerchief. A few others in the church dabbed at their eyes.

"There are few who serve this church as Walter served it. His family heritage here was everything to him. He often told me he loved Mount Sinai more than anything on earth." McNabb favored the widow with a mirthless smile. "Except, of course, his spouse of twenty-eight years. That is right, Bitsy? Twenty-eight?" The hat bobbed.

"I don't need to enumerate all his accomplishments, but I must mention a few of them." He waved his arm behind him. "Our fellowship hall"—by which I took him to mean the large, tin modular building to the right of the church. "Walter, as you know, donated that building to the church. And the new organ—you all recall how tirelessly he campaigned for the money for that. We owe the music in our church to Walter Fry."

McNabb turned to the choir. "I hope each and every one of you will remember that, each time you practice, every time you raise your voices to the glory of God." Not to mention the glory of Walter Fry, I thought.

McNabb went on at some length, while the teenagers in the balcony giggled and whispered. Church gossip, very probably— just the thing I had been hoping to hear. I edged closer to them, but the whispers were drowned out by the choir as they launched into "Lord, I'm Coming Home."

At the conclusion of the hymn, Allen McNabb stood in front of his congregation. He waited, through the rustling in the seats and the thumps of closing hymnals. When the church was as silent as Walter Fry's waiting grave, McNabb stepped a little closer to the pews.

"Now," he said. "I have something else to say."

No mausoleum was ever more quiet. Even the teens in the balcony were silent, stiff with anticipation as to what Allen McNabb would say. It was, after all, his own daughter accused of taking the life of the deacon. And it was probably the most exciting thing to happen at Mount Sinai Tabernacle Church in anyone's memory. So the congregation held its collective breath, and I with it, as the Reverend McNabb gathered his thoughts. Finally he spoke.

"We have no secrets here at Mount Sinai Tabernacle. We are like Paul's beloved Romans, Corinthians, and Ephesians—knit as one in Christ." He held up interlaced fingers to the congregation, demonstrating his point.

"And so," he continued, "I want to bring everything into the open. Including my disagreement with Brother Walter in regard to my . . . to the child." A shudder of expectation waved across the church. This was what they had come to hear. A rarified form of gossip. Or maybe it would be a confession.

"Brother Walter opposed burying the child in our church cemetery. He based his arguments upon Scripture. And some of you followed him." I stared down into the sanctuary, watching with some satisfaction as a few members of the congregation shifted uncomfortably in their seats. With their champion gone, they were left to take responsibility for their own actions. But Allen McNabb's words had been uttered without recrimination.

"You must follow your own conscience in some matters, and I trust that you did. I studied and prayed over the issue, too. And I reached a different decision.

"You see, Jesus was a Jew because his mother, Mary, was a Jewess. The lineage of his race was passed to him through his mother—not through his earthly father, Joseph, but in keeping with the law of the Jews, through his mother. That was part of the Father's plan.

"My grandson's lineage was also passed to him through his mother. Therefore, Damien's race was white, and so, by ancient biblical precedent, he was entitled to be buried among others of his race." McNabb rocked back on his heels and stared at his congregation, challenging them to disagree.

I glanced at Miss Alma and found her shaking her head sadly. Thank heaven Davon wasn't there to be subjected to public insult and humiliation, as a member of a race not worthy to be buried in Mount Sinai Cemetery.

It seemed to me that Damien's grandfather was engaging in a bit of sophistry, but what was more alarming was his need to rationalize his acceptance of his own grandchild. I had to admit that he had come upon a dazzling solution to his problem. He would not commit himself to racial equality and risk offending some of his congregation. If Walter Fry had given money to the church, so might his widow be in a position to do the same. Perhaps even more. Nor would he openly support the daughter whom he had openly repudiated in the past. It was a masterful exercise in saving face.

The congregation murmured among themselves, their presence in a church all but forgotten. But McNabb wasn't finished. He held up his hand and called for silence.

"Brothers and sisters, please. I have more to say. As most of you know, my daughter, April, is being held for Brother Fry's murder. I can't comment on the crime at this time except to say that if, in fact, April did commit this murder, I will, as your pastor, act accordingly."

If? Act accordingly? What, exactly, did that mean?

" 'If thy right eye offend thee,' " he continued, " 'pluck it out, and cast it from thee: for it is profitable for thee that one of thy members should perish, and not that thy whole body should be cast into hell.' Matthew five: twenty-nine."

Allen McNabb would reject his daughter again, and the congregation approved. Bitsy Fry snuffled into her handkerchief. Heads nodded and amens were shouted. Joy McNabb stood up, silently slipping away from her organ and out a side door of the sanctuary. Miss Alma noticed her first and elbowed me.

"Let's try to talk to her," she whispered. I nodded and followed her out of the balcony and down the winding staircase to the first floor. As I pulled the door of the church shut behind me, Allen McNabb was being given a vote of confidence by his congregation.

Joy McNabb was not in the parking lot. After a quick check,

we followed the path around the side of the church and found her. She was standing over Damien's grave. We waited until she turned back toward the church and met her on the path. I reminded her who I was.

"I saw you leave the church and thought maybe I could catch you."

Joy twisted her skirt nervously in her hands. "What do you want?"

"We just wanted to know about April," I said. "How is she doing? When will she be released?"

Joy glanced past us, toward the lighted windows of the church. Voices were raised in song, without benefit of accompaniment. But the undercurrent of fervor seemed to carry them along, as though they needed no instrument to buoy them up.

"I haven't seen her. Allen won't let me . . . Well, her husband seems to be taking care of the arrangements. I believe she'll be released on bond—if he can come up with the money, of course."

I did not tell Joy that I knew as much, apparently, as she did—that Davon had been to see me, that April had asked for my help. I didn't think I wanted the information getting back to Allen Mc-Nabb.

"What," Miss Alma said, "can we do to help?"

Joy patted her breast and glanced around, fumbling for an answer. "I don't know. Nothing. I can't even help her myself. My own daughter and I can't . . . I can't do anything for her."

I have a theory that people tend to live up to their names. Dull, interesting, arrogant, foolish, we tend to fulfill other people's expectations of the name. Joy McNabb took a mighty thwack at the knees of that theory. Colorless and lackluster as she was, I wondered how she had managed to produce the vivacious, sparkling April whom I had met in jail. Maybe, at one time, she had been the essence of her name. I could well imagine that years of marriage to Allen McNabb would take most of the joy out of life. And as to April, the girl at the funeral was not the girl I had met in a cold, depressing jail cell. I knew that if nothing changed, April would, in ten years, be exactly like her mother.

Back in the car, I turned to Miss Alma. "What do you remember about Walter Fry? What was he like in high school?"

Miss Alma sighed and fumbled with the clasp on her purse. "I'm afraid I remember more than I'd like," she said. "As I told Louis, the students that most stand out in a teacher's mind are the very good and the very bad. I'm afraid Walter was the latter."

"A bad student?"

"Not in the traditional sense, no. His grades were excellent, which is, probably, the only reason he got away with so much. Our principal was not disposed to suspending good students. He had that 'boys will be boys' attitude that suffers hatred and cruelty as though they were just pranks."

"So you're saying Walter was cruel."

"Very. The sixties were a hard time, Julia. So much social change—mandated by law, so there was nothing that students could do about it. For many of them, it was unsettling to say the least. They didn't know what they believed anymore. Their parents were telling them one thing, and the law was telling them something else. Right or wrong as their views might have been, it was a bewildering time."

"So he was just another confused adolescent. Typical preacher's kid rebelling against his father?"

"Hardly," she said dryly. "To begin with, his father could scarcely be characterized as the typical preacher. He did not believe in sparing the rod, even for the most minor offenses. Walter came to school with bruises more often than I care to remember."

"His father abused him?"

"Yes, I think Walter was a victim of abuse, but the counselors could never get him to admit to it. And to be perfectly candid, he was not a likable young man. He did not generate a great deal of sympathy."

"Did you know Reverend Fry?"

"I had the uncomfortable experience of meeting him on a few occasions—parent conferences and open houses."

"What was he like?"

Miss Alma closed her eyes and laid her head back on the head-rest. "How well do you remember your history, Julia?" she said. But before I could respond, she went on. "Do you remember studying about the Puritans?"

"Pretty rigid," I ventured.

She nodded her head. "Multiply them times four and you would have Walter's father, the esteemed Reverend Fry."

"No wonder Walter rebelled."

"Walter went way beyond your average rebellion. He tormented the black boys in every way he knew how. Walter graduated in 1962 or 'sixty-three. You must remember that black militants were just beginning to rise to prominence. Most of those boys weren't caught up in the black power movement. They were just trying desperately to fit in somewhere.

"What about L.T.? Was he in the black power movement?"

"Well, Louis came along a few years later—after Walter had graduated. I doubt if they knew each other. But yes, Louis got involved in the movement later. He wasn't a militant, though—more a disciple of Dr. King. Nonviolent protest. I'm sure that's why he went to law school.

"Louis was such a capable young man," Miss Alma mused. "He still is. I've followed his career—I always did that with the students I thought showed promise—and it's been quite remarkable."

"He's such an attractive man," I said. "Married?"

Miss Alma frowned. "No. Surprisingly, he's not. I know he's dated a lot of women over the years. And he dated a girl his senior year—I remember, because I chaperoned the prom. He was crazy about her."

"What happened?"

Miss Alma shrugged. "I lost track of her. I guess she moved away. But Louis has always been so focused on social reform. You know, Julia, some men really are married to their work. A man like Louis would have trouble dividing his time between his work and a wife."

"So Walter Fry wouldn't have known L.T.," I said.

"Not in high school, and I doubt that their spheres of work overlapped. But Walter certainly knew other black boys, and he made their lives a living hell every time he could."

"What did he do?"

Miss Alma pulled a handkerchief out of her bag and daintily dabbed at her nose before twisting it between her hands. "Everything he could. He sabotaged their lockers and stole their books and homework. He tripped them in the halls and picked fights on the bus. Boys like Walter, who come from very rigid homes, often harbor a lot of anger. They've got to take it out on someone. I'm afraid the black boys were Walter's first choice for scapegoat."

"Didn't anyone do anything about it?"

"We couldn't prove it. I overheard him bragging about it one time and I marched him straight to the principal's office. But when it came down to it, and I was facing Reverend Fry and our principal across the desk, with Walter denying everything, I didn't have any proof. And Reverend Fry would never hear a bad word about his son. Perhaps he really believed that all that corporal punishment was keeping Walter in line. Besides, he was not much in sympathy with the integration movement. Walter was just carrying on his father's views—although to the great extreme."

"Was Bitsy one of your students too?"

Miss Alma shook her head. "Elizabeth moved to Delphi in, I believe, her senior year. She was not in my class and I don't think they were dating then. Walter was a good-looking boy then—"

"You're kidding," I said, recalling his heavy features and oily manner.

"No. The years didn't wear well on him. But he was charismatic in his own way. And adolescent girls are often attracted to rebellious boys—James Dean types, you know. The girls stuck to him like hair spray on a bouffant hairdo."

"I don't suppose you know anything about his private life? Who his friends were, things like that."

Miss Alma shot me a wry look. "Students seem to think that teachers live in a vacuum. They forget that we live in their neighborhoods, go to their churches. And we hear all the same gossip that everyone else hears. More, probably. Walter was particularly blind about it. He always thought he was fooling me.

"The only one in town who didn't know what Walter was doing," she continued, "was his father. Walter ran around with a rowdy crowd. In fact, I'd venture to say he was their leader and they were usually up to no good. They smoked and they drank—we didn't have to worry about drugs much then. He wasn't allowed to dance, so he didn't take part in the usual school activities. But I happen to know that he had a pretty active social life, if that's what you want to call it, on his own."

"You mean he—"

Miss Alma nodded sagely. "Any girl he could."

Which raised some interesting questions. Had Walter continued his amorous activities after marriage? Or had he resumed them during some sort of midlife crisis? And if so, did the grieving widow know anything about it?

Nick was whistling softly and packing the cafe records away when I got home. He was happier than he had been since the appearance of Richard Fortunata in our lives.

"I made copies of all of it," he said. "Canceled checks, forms, everything."

"And?"

"Tomorrow I'll drop them off at George Wolenski's office. He'll get it straightened out." I wished I could be as sure. But I told myself that it was just my mood—the depressing events of the evening—that cast a pall over his optimism. I heaped it all on his shoulders.

"I've got to do something for her, Nick. I can't just sit by and watch them convict her of murder. Even if she did do it, and I can't believe she did, heaven knows she had ample reason. And there's postpartum depression to be considered . . . But I have an idea."

61

Nick shoved a handful of files in the filing cabinet, slammed the drawer closed, and turned to me. "Stay out of it, Julia."

"Nick, you don't understand! She's a nice kid. And she was there, in jail . . . and her father—he's an SOB if ever I've seen one. And her mother's a dishrag . . . Nobody's going to help her. Davon's scared and—"

"There's nothing you can do for her."

"Nick, I just want to go see her in jail. Talk to her, that's all. If she's . . . well, I hate to say this, even to myself, but if she's lost it, I can get her some help. I know a couple of good psychiatrists, and I'm sure one of them would take her on pro bono." I think I even believed this myself, but Nick looked doubtful. He stroked his chin thoughtfully.

"That's all?" he said. "Just find her a psychiatrist and then stay out of it, right?"

"Right," I lied.

I was waiting for Sam when he dropped Rhonda off for work the next morning. I'd taken the deposit bag to the bank early and was casually alighting from the Honda when Sam and Rhonda pulled into the lot. I waved and ambled over to the driver's side of his unmarked cruiser.

"Hey, Sam, haven't seen you in a while. Been busy, huh?"

Sam shrugged his big shoulders. "Same ol', same ol', I guess. Hear you've been doing funerals lately. You know this girl—April?"

I smiled. "I met her when I was a guest of the county. You remember . . ."

It was one of Sam's sensitive spots, and I had no compunction about taking full advantage of it. A scarlet wave swept up his neck to the roots of his strawberry blond hair. "Yeah." He threw the cruiser in gear. "Well, gotta hit the road," he said.

"Without breakfast?" The aroma of sizzling bacon obligingly drifted up the vent hood and out into the parking lot, underscoring my point. "You know it's not good to start the day on black coffee. You'll think more clearly after biscuits and gravy. And grits. Sausage. Or maybe you're in the mood for pancakes this morning. With real butter?"

Rhonda eyed me suspiciously. "No pancakes, Sam," she said. "And no butter! Your cholesterol is way up."

Sam stared at her a minute before switching off the ignition. "That did it! Pancakes sound mighty good to me, Julia."

Sam does not like to be pushed around, nor, apparently, does he like to be told what to eat. Still, he shot his wife a worried glance before shoving the door open and heaving his broad girth out of the car. Rhonda didn't notice, though. She was glaring at me.

I shrugged and grinned. "Or maybe just toast and a little bran cereal." Sam hesitated outside the car. "And a couple of fried eggs, over easy," I added. "With hash browns . . ."

"Let's go," he growled.

Rhonda refused to serve him, and Sam refused to be served by Tammy. Nick took the tax records and left for George Wolenski's office the minute I returned. I couldn't have planned it better. I wanted Sam to myself. I put in his order and got us a couple of cups of coffee.

The sound system was cranked up to full throttle and Trisha Yearwood was warbling. *She's in love with the boy.* April and Davon sprang quickly to mind. Was April in love with Davon? No question how he felt about her, I thought. The sooner April was released, the sooner they could start putting their lives back together. I hurried to Sam's table and dropped into the seat across from him.

"You asked me if I knew April. I know her well enough to know she didn't kill Walter Fry, Sam."

"You do, huh? Kept in touch, did you?"

"Well, no. Not exactly. I went to see her at the funeral home. You know about the baby?"

Sam winced and nodded. "Yeah, I know all about it. And about the gun. You should have called me sooner. I might have been able to prevent all this." An accusing stare.

"Well, we just didn't want to make things worse for April. That kudzu's thick out there. I thought it was lost for good." But I hadn't sat down with Sam to be put on the defensive. "Obviously someone went back for it," I said. "For that matter, it may not be the same gun. You just saw it on the videotape, after all. One pistol looks like another and—"

"Ballistics."

"What do you mean?"

"Crime lab ran ballistics tests on the bullet we dug out of the siding on the church. They match the gun and the bullet that killed Fry."

"Oh."

I was saved further embarrassment by the order bell. "Zulia, order up."

I excused myself to pick up Sam's order: two eggs soft-scrambled with bacon and a side of buttermilk pancakes.

"Give me a couple of biscuits and two link sausage with that, will you, Spiros?" I added. Might as well butter him up good, so to speak.

"But about April," I said, setting the plates in front of him. "You don't honestly think she was involved in this murder. All right, she threatened him. But she was really stressed out, Sam. That doesn't mean she killed him. I'll bet half of Delphi would have liked to take out Walter Fry. He wasn't a very nice man."

Sam slathered butter over the top of his pancakes and flooded them with syrup. "Knew him well, huh?"

"Well, no." I hated to admit it, but I knew absolutely nothing about the man, except that he'd been an errant youth and that he didn't want Damien buried in the cemetery. But that alone said a lot.

"Besides," I added, "April's fingerprints *would* be on the gun. I'm not denying that she had it. Whoever retrieved it obviously wore gloves or something, and that could be anyone. And her husband told me April was at home all night. She wasn't even near Fry's house. So you don't have a bit of proof, Sam. Not one bit," I said firmly.

Sam listened to all this impassively. He deliberately worked his way through the mounds of food in front of him while I pointed out the myriad flaws in his investigation, the improbable leaps to erroneous conclusions, the impossibility of April being the culprit. I hit hard on her mental state at the funeral, and the likelihood of postpartum depression. I detailed the numbers of people in the vicinity at the time the gun was thrown into the thicket. I gave him a thumbnail sketch of the faces, postures, and attitudes of those in attendance. But the final coup, of course, was that April had been at home, alone, on the night of the murder.

"And you have proof of that?" he drawled, swiping his plate with a last chunk of biscuit.

"Well, no. But neither do you have proof she was there."

Finished, he sat back and dabbed at his mouth with a napkin. He refolded it, ran his thumbnails over the crease, and swallowed his last sip of coffee. "As a matter of fact, Julia," he answered quietly, "I do."

Chapter Seven

qualm \ˈkwäm *also* ˈkwom or kwälm\ *n* [origin un-known] (1530) **1:** a sudden attack of illness, faintness, or nausea **2:** a sudden access of usu. disturbing emotion (as of doubt, fear, or tenderness) **3:** a feeling of uneasiness about a point of conscience, honor, or propriety . . .
—*Merriam Webster's Ninth New Collegiate Dictionary*

Click. Click. Nick tossed his worry beads abstractedly as he turned the pages of the morning *Sun*. I pulled up a chair at the family table and eased into it, but I couldn't think of any way to ease into the conversation.

"I'm going to see April this afternoon," I said. *Click click click click click.*

"Sam said he'd let me in. I bought his breakfast, by the way."

Nick gaped at me over the top of the paper. His eyes, usually as deep brown and warm as a cup of morning coffee, were scalding.

"I knew I shouldn't have left you alone with him. I should have waited to leave until Sam finished his breakfast."

"Oh, what did George Wolenski have to say?"

Nick scowled at the diversionary tactic. "It's okay," he said. "He'll take care of it. He'll have to go over Fortunata's head, but he's pretty sure he can straighten it out. Don't try to change the subject."

"I'm just going to see if I can do anything for her, Nick. She's all alone. And I remember, all too well, what that's like . . ." I backed off and waited, feeling a bit manipulative. Nick has his soft spots, too. But I did remember the terrible loneliness and humiliation. And I wanted April to know that I was with her a hundred percent. Or maybe ninety-five. Sam's unexpected disclosure was nagging at me like a persistent itch.

Nick carefully folded the paper—into halves, quarters, eighths. He smoothed the folds and set it aside, crossing his arms over his chest. The picture of nonchalance. A veritable study in calm. But his right hand was tucked under his left arm, and beneath his calm his fingers were feverishly scurrying over his worry beads.

"Besides, Davon may have gotten her out by then. I thought I'd call before I go—just to see, you know, if she's still there. And I thought maybe I could bring Ted Cowan . . ." I snapped my fingers. "Which reminds me, I'd better give his office a call. If he's booked up this afternoon, we'll have to go at lunchtime. You can handle things here by yourself, can't you?" I jumped up and headed for the phone.

"Of course," I continued, "Rhonda and Tammy are both on the schedule. And Otis is due in at ten thirty. Spiros could practically handle everything by himself . . ."

At that, Spiros stuck his head out the wait station door. "Zulia! Hi. Fine."

"Oh, Spiros. *Kalimera!* You know, I wanted to talk to you about, um, the . . ."

"*Argotera, Spiros,*" Nick growled. "Later. Julia, sit down please," he added in that elaborately patient tone of voice that I detest.

"But Ted . . . And Spiros—"

"*Ohee, Zulia. Argotera.*" Spiros's bristling eyebrows furrowed sternly at me before he loped back toward the grill. I dropped back into my chair, resigned to the lecture that was to follow. I leaned toward Nick and tickled the side of his ear with the tip of my finger.

He pushed my hand away. "It's not funny. This is serious."

I composed my face and gave him wide-eyed and innocent. He narrowed his gaze. "You're going to see April."

"Yes. Yes I am."

"And you won't listen to reason."

"Of course I will. Say something reasonable."

He didn't smile. "You're determined to get involved in the whole mess."

"No, I'm not getting involved. I'm just going to see her, and let her know I'm on her side."

"Nothing I can say will stop you."

"Probably not," I agreed.

He stared at me a long moment. I gave as good as I got. At length he sighed deeply, stood up, shoved his worry beads into his pocket, and reached for his sailor's cap.

"You're hopeless," he muttered. "Let's go."

"I knew you'd come. I told Davon you'd know what to do." April chewed on a hangnail and tossed her ponytail nervously. Nick raised a skeptical eyebrow at me.

I faced her across a battered oak table in a stark room on the second floor of a county facility I knew all too well. Just being there made my stomach churn. But Sam had put us in the room himself, rather than have me facing her through a wire window in the visitors' room, for reasons that, any other time, would have made me bristle.

I'd overheard most of the whispered exchange between the sheriff and my husband. Sam wanted Nick with me. He had repeated, rather too emphatically, I thought, that he did not want me involved in his case—that he expected Nick to take control of the situation and keep me in check. Sam does not understand the dynamics of our relationship.

"April, I don't know what I can do."

"You can find the killer." A simple statement, uttered with complete conviction and underscored by a light squeeze of my hand. Eighteen is such an uncomplicated age.

"You have an attorney, April."

April snipped at the hangnail with sharp, white teeth and nodded. "Davon's daddy, he's got me L.T. Humphries."

"And he's the one who needs to handle your case."

She shook her head vehemently. "L.T.—I'm not sure he believes me. He's talking about depression and pleading manslaughter. Besides, he wants to get a detective on the case. But we can't afford a detective, and Davon's daddy—well, this is gonna bleed him dry. But you're a detective, Julia, and—"

"I'm no detective. I wouldn't have any idea where to start."

She waved her hand dismissively. "That's okay. You don't have to be a card-carrying cop. You know what to do."

I knew I should cut and run, and Nick's expression only confirmed my feeling. But one glance at April—that open, vulnerable face and the light of hope, expectation, in her expression. I couldn't explain her absolute trust in me, but I couldn't ignore it either.

"I suppose we could just talk to L.T.," I said, more to Nick than April. "Just find out what he has in mind. If he'll talk to us."

Nick's black brows came together, forming a sharp V over his eyes. "*Ohee,* Julia," he said, continuing in Greek. April wouldn't understand, but he hoped I would. "We're not getting involved. Sam—"

I turned back to April, waiting confidently. "Nick agrees with me. He says it wouldn't hurt just to talk to your lawyer." *Click click click . . .* "But first you have to tell me everything, April. Davon says you weren't anywhere near Walter Fry's house the night he was killed." She nodded, her ponytail vigorously bouncing over her shoulder as she worried the hangnail.

"But Sam, that is, the sheriff, says he has proof you were."

I studied her closely, noting the way her glance nervously shifted to the wire grid on the window that overlooked the parking lot before coming back to me. And my heart sank. She had been there. Sam was right.

"Proof, April. Think about it for a minute. What kind of proof does he have?"

She had chewed on the nail until a bright red rivulet trickled over her finger. She sucked it off and wiped her hands on her legs. "He doesn't know. I didn't want to tell him."

"Davon?" She nodded. "Tell him what, April?"

"He was evicting us."

"Who was? I don't understand."

April sighed and went to work on another finger. I reached over and pulled her hand firmly down onto the table. She spread her fingers and stared at them.

"Mr. Fry owned Magnolia Mobile Home Park. That's where we live, Davon and me. He used to not let blacks in there, but somebody sued him—like the NAACP or the ACLU or somebody like that. I don't know. Anyway, so he had to let us in. We paid everything—like the deposit and . . . you know, all that stuff."

"Then how could he evict you?"

"We were behind on the rent. Damien—we didn't have much insurance, 'cause Davon works for his daddy, and he's in business for himself. The hospital wanted a big deposit and we didn't want to go to Davon's daddy for more money, so . . . well, we had to let the rent slide. And then Mr. Fry, he got mad 'cause at the funeral I . . ." April hesitated. "See, it's all my fault, and I thought maybe I could do something—apologize and make him see that it wasn't Davon. But . . ."

"So you went to see him that night, while Davon was out." April nodded and angrily brushed away a tear that had insidiously trickled out of the corner of her eye. "What happened when you went to see him, April?"

Her eyes flashed, and for a moment I glimpsed the old April. The fighter. "He laughed," she said. "He told me he was just waiting for an excuse to throw me and my 'nigger boyfriend' out. We were behind on the rent, and he wasn't changing his mind, and that was that."

"Did he know you were married?"

"Yeah, he knew. But he said 'not in the eyes of God.' "

I glanced over at Nick. He was sitting forward now, brows still drawn, but a kind of cold fury had brightened his eyes.

April shrugged calmly. "So you see why I couldn't tell Davon. Besides, he was already threatening a lawsuit for . . . he called it my 'unprovoked attack in front of the media.' Unprovoked— can you believe that? After what he did? I mean, I just couldn't tell Davon what that man called him. Davon's a good man, Julia."

"Yes, he is. And he loves you very much."

"I know," she said, her hand going back to her mouth. "I know he does."

"This lawsuit—was it against you?"

April shrugged. "Me. Davon. Even Davon's daddy, although I don't know exactly how he came up with that one. Anyway, I didn't think he could win it. I thought a jury'd see what kind of man he was . . . and how he'd pushed me."

April was no fool. She had a pretty good idea how the whole thing would play out in a courtroom.

"So what happened then?"

"Nothing. I mean I apologized, and I cried and I begged him, but he wouldn't change his mind. I hated begging him. But we don't have any money—like for a deposit on a new place. And he wasn't giving us our deposit back. He said so. And he meant it."

"Okay. But what did you do then? What proof does Sam have? Did you touch anything?"

"Well, yeah, probably. The doorknob. The kitchen counter, stuff like that. But I don't think that's it. See, I ran away. I drove around for a while, and then I went home. And when I got home, I remembered."

"Remembered what?"

"The letter. I left the eviction notice on the table. I'd gotten it that day, before Davon got home. I hid it from Davon, and when he left I went right over to Mr. Fry's and then I got so upset I just left it there."

"In the envelope?" Nick said. April nodded. Nick pushed his hat back and stared out the window, slowly fingering his worry beads. I turned back to April, and she continued.

"I didn't go back for it. I decided I'd go talk to Miz Fry. She's my mama's friend and she doesn't have a mean bone in her body. I never understood how she could marry that man. But I thought if I could talk to her, well, maybe she could make him change his mind. But then they arrested me and . . . I don't know where Davon's gonna live while I'm in here."

"You have to tell Davon the truth, April. It's going to come out anyway. It's better if he hears it from you."

"I know. Unless you'd . . ."

"No," I said firmly. "That's up to you. Your attorney knows?"

"Yeah, but he promised not to say anything until I had a chance to tell Davon. He's coming this afternoon, I think. I'll tell him then."

I patted her hand. "Couples shouldn't have secrets from each other. I tell Nick everything." Nick gazed at me in astonishment, but he refrained from commenting.

"Did you see anyone else while you were there that night, April? Or did anyone see you?"

April thought about this for a moment. She tugged at a loose wisp of her hair and, frowning, tucked it back into the ponytail. "I don't think so. I didn't see anybody around. They got a couple of acres out there, back off the Industry Road right near the church. Can't see it from the street. So if anybody'd been around, I would've seen a car."

There was, of course, the possibility that she had seen a car—that she had recognized someone near the murder scene. That she was protecting someone. Someone like Davon.

"April, where was Davon that night?"

Her expression grew closed and remote. "I don't want to talk about that. Besides, Davon didn't have anything to do with any of this."

"Then why are you protecting him? Is something wrong with your marriage?"

April rocked jerkily back and forth in her chair, rubbing the palms of her hands on her thighs. "If there is, it's not his fault," she said.

"I didn't ask that. Why are you avoiding the question, April? Where was Davon?"

She wrapped her arms across her chest, hugging herself, and continued rocking. "He was out!" she cried, her voice shrill—fraught with fear. Or maybe it was something else.

"Something to do with . . . with Damien." Her voice dropped

off. "That's all," she added wearily. "That's all I can say about it. But he didn't murder Walter Fry."

"Well, somebody killed him that night. With the same gun you had at the church. Which brings me to the next question. Where did you get that gun, April? Did you buy it?"

"No."

"Then where did it come from?"

"It doesn't matter."

"Of course it matters!"

"Why?"

"Because, well . . ." I really didn't know why it mattered. Some detective I'd make. I glanced over at Nick, but I didn't get anything from him either. Lucy and Ricky go a-sleuthing. The gun mattered, I reasoned, because whoever had procured it for her knew she'd had it and that she'd be implicated in the murder. On the other hand, everyone at the cemetery also knew that.

"Trust me, Julia," she said firmly. "It doesn't matter." But I thought it probably did.

"The postmark," Nick said. "The letter was probably sent the day before Fry died. So they know she received it the day of the murder, and they've fingerprinted it and the house, and that's enough proof that she was there. She had motive and opportunity. And she had means. She was the last one seen with the murder weapon. You should have pushed her harder about the gun."

"Easy for you to say," I snapped. "You didn't open your mouth the whole time."

"She doesn't know me, and she doesn't have any reason to trust me. You're the one she thinks is V. I. Warsh—you know."

"Okay, okay. But you saw how upset she was. I didn't want her going ballistic on us." He chewed on that for a while as we trudged through the June heat to the car. I was biting my petulant tongue, wishing I hadn't been so quick to snap at him. I needed Nick's support now more than ever.

"All right," he said reluctantly. "I suppose there are other things we need to know first."

"I'm just not sure what to do next," I said carefully, mindful that his commitment to help April was halfhearted. "Any ideas?"

"Humphries," Nick said, pulling the car door open for me. "I think his office is in the Professional Building on Martin Luther King Avenue."

"Right," I said, suppressing a triumphant smile. "Do you think he'll talk to us? You know, client-attorney privilege and all that."

"Only one way to find out. Let's go."

The reception area of Humphries's office was deserted when we arrived. While not shabby, it was hardly the lavish office I'd expected for an attorney of Humphries's stature. A buxom, brown Naugahyde sofa nestled against one wall, flanked by a pair of mahogany veneer end tables arrayed with copies of *Ebony* and *Entrepreneur* magazines and several old copies of *ABA Journal.* On the other side of the room, a grouping of two gold velvet tub chairs and a third, identical table offered additional seating.

Photographs of L.T. Humphries lined the baseboards. I picked them up and studied them with considerable respect: A very young L.T. pictured with Coretta and Martin Luther King, Jr., L.T. on the steps of the Supreme Court building in Washington, L.T. marching at the head of an interracial group of women. The white woman next to him carried a sign that said MY BODY, MY CHOICE. A large framed reproduction of the Bill of Rights waited to be rehung in the vacant space over the couch. It would be flanked by additional photographs of Delphi landmarks: the original Delphi Ebenezer Baptist Church, which had been burned to the ground in 1969, and the Calloway County courthouse.

The receptionist's desk held the usual array of computer, telephone, and typewriter, as well as photographs of three black children ranging in age from toddler to teen. Nick leaned over it to glance at her appointment book. "There's nothing on it," he whispered.

I shrugged. "Let's sit down and wait. She's probably gone to the rest room or something." From behind her desk, down a narrow hallway, I could hear the whir of an office machine—a fax or copier. "Maybe she's back there," I said.

After ten minutes of perusing magazines and examining the photographs in greater detail, Nick stood up. "Let's go look for someone," he said. "I don't think she's here. Or at least she's not expecting anyone." I agreed and followed him behind the desk and down the hallway.

File boxes and cartons lined the walls. Nick rapped lightly on the door. "Hello? Anyone here?" he called as we made our way past the cartons. The buzzing grew louder, coming from a door that led off the hall to our right.

Louis Humphries stood with his back to us, perusing a file. He removed a handful of papers and fed them into the machine in front of him. Nick knocked on the wall again. This time Humphries spun around, startled, but relaxed when he saw us.

"Just a minute," he mouthed, and turned back to switch off the equipment. "Sorry," he said. "Makes quite a racket. They all do." He waved his arm over the machines around him—fax, copier, postage machine. We were in the mail room, apparently, and someone in Humphries's employ had a literary bent. Of sorts.

Between the copy machine and the paper shredder stood two gray garbage cans afixed with signs. The first said "You **CAN** help America preserve its resources. Recycle your aluminum here." The second stretched the theme a bit too far. "We'll be **SYC-A-MORE** trees are destroyed. Don't leave America **PINING** for our loss. Make recycling **POPLAR**. Take a **STAND** and recycle your paper here." As if in response to the recycling pixie's demands, Humphries pulled out the drawer to the paper shredder and dumped its contents into the can.

"Were you looking for me?"

He looked nothing like the man I had met at the funeral home, or later at the church, turned out in a well-cut sport coat and conservative tie. Instead, he was casually dressed in a red Sierra Club T-shirt and denim shorts, and had a remarkably trim physique for a man his age. He noticed my surprised expression and glanced ruefully down at his tennis shoes.

"We're getting ready to redecorate the office," he said. "I was just finishing packing up, culling out old files and getting rid of notes and things. Were you looking for me?" he repeated.

"Yes. We met at the Folsom funeral." I glanced out to the reception area. "Your secretary . . . There's no one—"

"Gave her a couple of days off. They'll be painting and moving in the new furniture over the weekend, and I need her help getting the office set up before we reopen on Monday. I was just finishing up odds and ends. I remember you. Mrs. Lamb, is it?"

"Lambros," I corrected him, and introduced him to Nick.

"Come on back to my office."

We followed him past a rest room, complete with shower and closet, and into an office in upheaval. His desk and the matching shelves had been pulled out into the center of the room away from the walls. The shelves were empty, their contents neatly stacked in boxes next to a broad mahogany desk. Soft apricot walls were freckled with paler squares of color, and beneath them more photographs and documents lined the baseboards. Only his law degree remained on the wall behind his desk chair. Lampshades had been removed and stacked like to-go cups, cords wrapped around lamp bases. Humphries unwrapped one and plugged it in, plunking a mismatched shade over the bulb.

"You've caught me at a busy time, I'm afraid." He dropped into a high-backed leather chair and waved us into a pair of matching armchairs in front of the desk. "Opened my practice here over twenty years ago, and I've resisted changing anything since. Sarah—she's my secretary—says it's typical of my gender. But I'm thinking about taking in a partner soon and . . ." He smiled. "I thought I ought to make the proposition a little more attractive."

I'd heard rumors that Louis Humphries had political ambitions, and the photographs underscored the probability. He'd need a partner to keep the practice going while he was on the campaign trail. Although he was still in the "No comment" stage, the move toward a partner suggested the rumors were true. I hoped they were. He was a man who exuded confidence and capability—undeniably attractive, too.

Humphries shook his head and grinned ruefully. "You can accumulate a lot of stuff in twenty years. Seemed like a good time to clean it out."

"We should have called for an appointment," I said. "But we won't take up a lot of your time." Humphries nodded at me and waited.

"We've come about April Folsom, Mr. Humphries."

"L.T.," he interrupted smoothly. "My friends call me L.T."

"All right. I'm Julia and my husband is Nick. But back to April—she's asked us to help, and we wondered what we could do." Humphries continued his steady gaze, but his brows glided together, creasing his smooth forehead.

"She has some crazy idea that we can help with the investigation," I explained.

"Investigation?"

"Of the murder. Walter Fry."

"Yes. I see. Or rather, frankly, I don't see. Are you private investigators?"

"Oh, no! We're just . . . interested friends. You see, I met April . . ." So I went into the whole story of how we'd been in jail at the same time. And how Nick and I had been forced to track down a murderer.

Humphries nodded. "I remember the case very well. A serious thing—human exploitation. I knew your name rang a bell." He steepled his fingers. "Actually," he continued, "both April and Davon mentioned you to me, although April wasn't making very much sense at the time and Davon didn't seem to understand why she was so hell-bent on getting you involved himself. Just what is it you think you can do to help?"

Chapter Eight

prag-mat-ic \prag-`mat-ik*also* **prag-mat-i-cal** \i-kəl*adj* [L *pragmaticus* skilled in law or business, fr. Gk *pragmatikos,* fr. *pragmat-, pragma* deed fr. *prassein* to do—more at PRACTICAL] (1616) . . . **2:** relating to matters of fact or practical affairs often to the exclusion of intellectual or artistic matters: practical as opposed to idealistic . . .

—*Merriam Webster's Ninth New Collegiate Dictionary*

I stared at L.T. Humphries, utterly at a loss. I had no idea what we could do to help, only that April expected us to do *something.* I decided to backtrack.

"Let me ask you something first. According to April, you wanted to hire a private investigator, right?" He nodded. "Okay, just what would you expect him to do?"

"Or her," he corrected me. L.T. Humphries was politically correct.

"Or her," I agreed, smiling.

Humphries folded his hands together and leaned forward, elbowing his desk. "Well, for one thing, he'd find out everything he could about the victim. Who else might stand to gain from his death, who might want him dead, who were his enemies—that kind of thing. He'd go out to the scene of the crime and look for evidence the police might have missed. He'd look for vulnerable spots in the DA's case."

"Vulnerable spots? Like what?"

"Did they handle the crime scene right? Did they preserve its integrity, or were sheriff's deputies stomping in and out and destroying potential evidence? He'd look into the background of the people on the scene, make sure no one had a grudge against Davon or April and tried to set them up." Humphries stopped, whistled through his teeth, and sat back in his deep leather chair. He shook his head.

"Look, I'm going to be honest with you. The only reason I suggested a PI in the first place is because Davon is determined to plead her not guilty, and he's sure we can find the killer. The truth is, Davon's been watching too much television."

"I'm sorry," I said. "I don't understand."

"Let me try to explain. I don't know whether April's guilty or not. All the evidence certainly points in that direction, but she's denying it. Even so, we have a better chance of pleading her guilty to manslaughter and trying to make the most of the extenuating circumstances—the loss of the baby, postpartum depression—than we have of winning a not-guilty plea to first-degree murder."

"But she didn't do it!"

"Frankly, Mrs. Lambros, I wish I felt as sure. You've seen her yourself. You were at the funeral when she threatened him."

"But no one in his right mind would follow through on an open, public threat knowing they'd be the primary suspect."

"Who's to say April's in her right mind? Have you ever seen her behave that way before?"

"Well—"

"There's even the possibility, although I think it's remote, that she doesn't remember doing it at all. More likely, she's in deep denial."

I wanted to protest, but I couldn't. It made a lot of sense. And Nick was just sitting there, listening. I felt he must agree with L.T. or he would speak up.

"Look," L.T. continued. "I'm being practical. A plea of guilty to manslaughter will not require a jury, which, under the circumstances, might be the best thing."

"Why?"

"Because April is involved in an interracial marriage. I might have a hard time finding a jury that will acquit her." To my puzzled expression he added, "Black people do not universally approve of racially mixed marriages any more than whites do, Mrs. Lambros. Either group might view her as rebelling against society's conventions and, by extension, very likely to follow through on the threats she made openly against the victim."

"But aren't we jumping the gun a little? She hasn't been indicted yet."

"No, but she will be. I'd stake my law practice on that."

"You mean because of her marriage," Nick said. "Isn't that point of view a little cynical?"

L.T. shook his head. "No, not because of her marriage. Although it could be a factor, depending on who's sitting on the grand jury," he added. "She's going to be indicted because of the weight of the evidence against her. Then we'll have to enter a plea. Murder is a whole lot worse than manslaughter, Mr. Lambros. A judge might be sympathetic to the death of her child and April's desire to see Damien buried in her own cemetery. He would understand the pressure she's been under. He'd make allowances for an unexpected act of violence precipitated by emotional crisis, and I think we could expect sentencing to be fairly light—minimal security and early parole. But I can guarantee you that in this instance, a jury will not be sympathetic to premeditated murder."

Nick and I exchanged glances. His said that L.T.'s arguments were sound. And much as I hated to admit it, they were.

"The best help you can be to Davon and April," L.T. continued, "is to convince them I'm right. I don't like it any better than you do, but what matters most here is saving that girl from life imprisonment or worse." He stood up and removed his law degree from the wall, pulled a crisp, white handkerchief from his back pocket, and swiped at the dusty frame.

"But it isn't fair," I countered.

He stopped wiping the frame and stared at the degree a long moment before fixing me with a rueful smile. "The law, Mrs. Lambros, is often not fair. But it is the law."

"You know," I said to Nick later, "even if I wanted to, I doubt that I could convince either one of them to accept a guilty plea, manslaughter or not."

Nick turned in to our parking lot and cut the ignition before he answered. He put his hand against my cheek and looked into my eyes. "How convinced are you, really, that she's innocent?" Truth can taste unpleasantly bitter. I swallowed hard.

"Not very," I answered. "But, like I told L.T., I don't see what difference it makes. What harm can it do to go ahead and dig? We may not find any evidence to exonerate her, but we're not likely to make her case any worse, either."

L.T. had agreed with this reasoning. In fact, he had agreed to help us as much as he could on the theory that if we could prove that other people had motives to kill Fry, he might be able to establish reasonable doubt. But he also added a warning.

"I wonder if you've thought about the potential consequences of this. If you're right and April didn't kill Fry, someone else did. If you're not careful, you could end up as his next victims. Besides, you don't have investigators' licenses and, I gather, you don't know much about the law. You could end up on its wrong side very easily—charged with impeding an investigation, for example. You'd better tread carefully. Now, having said that, what can I do to help you?"

The first thing we had asked of him was to find out the terms of Walter Fry's will, but L.T.'s part in the search would have to wait. His painters were coming that night and would work all through Friday. He had to be completely settled in his newly redecorated office before opening his doors Monday morning, which would mean a very busy weekend.

Our conversation was interrupted by a burly black man pushing a hand truck. Another man trailed behind him with blankets and drop cloths slung over his arms. L.T. jumped up to greet them affectionately. He introduced them to us as deacons of the Ebenezer Baptist Church of Delphi, explaining that they were there to pick up the office furniture, which he was donating to his congregation. He asked us to wait while he conferred briefly with them.

The couch and chairs in the reception room were to be used in the fellowship hall, while his desk and bookshelves and all the filing cabinets would go to the pastor's office. Although the men assured him that they could handle the job, L.T. insisted upon helping them move the couch, which was apparently quite heavy, out to the truck. They declined Nick's offer to assist.

"I'm glad you thought about the will," I said to Nick while we waited for L.T. to return. "It seems pretty obvious, doesn't it?" I paced L.T.'s office, picking up the pictures stacked against the walls and studying them abstractedly.

There was a photograph of an elderly woman—the type usually taken for church directories. She had grizzled hair, worn very short, and silver-rimmed glasses that enlarged her eyes to quarter size. Probably L.T.'s mother, I thought. And beside it another picture, this one clearly a high school yearbook photo, of a young woman wrapped in the time-honored black taffeta shawl. A strand of white pearls stood out in relief against the smooth black of her youthful skin. She was a pretty girl, with sparkling eyes looking out at a world waiting to be conquered. His sister, maybe, or his wife. But Miss Alma had said he never married. Some girl must still be regretting her loss, I reflected, glancing back at the photograph. A bold signature was scrawled across the bottom of the photograph—All my love always! Vanessa—more evidence of the spirited outlook of the eighteen-year-old. Which brought me back to April, who'd had the spirit crushed in her as surely as if she'd been mowed down by a semi. And she'd made it very clear. She was depending on us. But I hadn't even thought about the will, the most obvious place to begin.

"I wonder," I said, dropping back into my chair, "if we're really going to be any help at all. I feel like such an amateur."

"We are amateurs, Julia. All we can do is our best."

"Sarah's desk is staying. It was new last year. But I'm thinking about a new copy machine," L.T. said to one of the deacons as they rejoined us. "If I decide to go ahead with it, that one will go to the church."

The deacons worked around us, moving out the lamps, shelves, and empty file cabinets. Some of the legal files would be warehoused and subsequently microfilmed. L.T.'s secretary was making arrangements for that. And down the hall was a library and conference room, which we had not seen. L.T. excused himself again to help the men manipulate an enormous oak table through the narrow door.

"We need to get out of the way," Nick said, taking my hand and pulling me up. I had questions I was itching to ask L.T., but it was apparent we weren't going to get any more help from him then. He shook our hands warmly.

"Get back to me if you have any information. I'll follow up on the matter we discussed," he said. "And please—be careful."

It was after two o'clock by the time we got back to the cafe, and only a few lingering lunch customers dotted A and B decks. Rhonda was vacuuming C, while Tammy rolled silverware at the family table. I slapped two sandwiches together and joined Nick, who was sitting with Charley Albright on B deck.

"He did a lot for the church, that's for sure. You know, Allen McNabb was only a part-time preacher when we joined. Walter built up the church a lot. Donated that metal building, and that gave the youth a place to meet. Brought in new families—having a new youth program. Board voted to take Brother Allen on full-time last November." Charley stood up and grinned at me.

"Hello, Julia. Have a seat." Charley is a gentleman, a kind man with a ready smile and an open expression, which may well be exaggerated by a head as slick and bald as a cultured pearl. He waited until I had arranged our plates and taken the seat next to Nick before dropping back into his chair.

"So you belong to Mount Sinai?" I said. Charley didn't strike me as the type to enjoy the stern theology of Allen McNabb. But he nodded.

"Yeah. The wife got involved in their Ladies' Circle through a friend of hers and she wanted to join. It might not have been my first choice for a church, but I don't mind. I can stand anything for an hour a week if it keeps Cordelia happy."

"Did you know Fry well, Charley?"

"Nah. Not really. I don't do much socializing with the church. I leave that to Cordelia. Oh, I talked to him now and then, I suppose."

"And what did you think of him?"

Charley stirred in his chair, lifted his empty glass to his lips, scowled at the remaining ice, and set it back on the table. Nick went for more iced tea.

"I hate to say this, seeing he's dead now, but I didn't much like him. He did a lot of, well, posturing, I suppose you'd call it. Talking religion in one breath, and in the next complaining about—" Charley blushed and dropped his voice.

"He called them 'niggers.' Now, I've heard that word all my life, but I never got to where I liked it. Not, I'd say, a real Christian man. Seemed like he was always keeping the church divided, too. In factions. He liked to kind of scrutinize new members— ask around about them, look into their backgrounds. If he didn't like what he heard, he could make it mighty uncomfortable for them." Nick rejoined us with Charley's refill.

"But I thought you said he built up the church."

"Oh, he did. But he sort of handpicked the families that joined, you know? Didn't want anybody in the church whose background was—I think the word he liked was 'questionable.' "

"Like?"

"Drinkers. Divorcées. Mixed marriages. Ethnics." His glance went to Nick and darted away, embarrassed.

"Tell me something, Charley," Nick said. "Where did his money come from? He donated a building and he lived on a big piece of acreage. He must have had money."

"You know, I used to wonder that myself. He's got—had that trailer park, but I think it's only about eight units, if that. But

Bitsy drives an Acura, and Walter, believe it or not, drove a Jag. Didn't seem the type, did he?"

Nick fingered his worry beads and stared speculatively at his lunch. "I suppose a trailer park could bring in a lot of money, but . . ."

"I think he must have had other business interests in town." Charley swallowed the last of his tea and stood up. "Got to be on my way—empty vending machines await." He handed Nick his ticket and a couple of bills, dropping another one on the table for Tammy.

"I wonder," Nick said, after Charley had gone, "if L.T. can find out about Fry's businesses when he finds out the terms of the will. I'd like to know where his money came from and who's going to get it now. Think I'll try to catch him before he leaves."

When Nick had finished, I made a call of my own. Miss Alma was more than willing to help me out. Charley had made it clear that Nick might not be a welcome visitor at Mount Sinai, but that didn't mean that Miss Alma and I couldn't explore the possibility of joining a new church.

L.T. Humphries was better than his word. He had the information we wanted by late afternoon on Friday and delivered it to me over the telephone. He also had other news to impart.

"They formally charged April this afternoon," he said. I swallowed the news and let it flutter around in my stomach a minute.

"Will you be able to get her out on bail?"

"I hope so, but probably not until Monday, after she's arraigned. I'm afraid April's going to have to spend the weekend in jail."

Poor kid, I thought. But there was nothing I could do about it, being a person of absolutely no influence in the Delphi legal community. At least, though, I could get busy trying to help her from the outside. Which brought us back to the will.

"I think you'll find this very interesting. His wife, Elizabeth

Fry, is the primary heir. He had a half a mil in life insurance that will go to her, as well as most of his business interests, with one notable exception. Hey! Watch out with that desk, you're skinning up the woodwork! They just finished painting it. Sorry, Mrs. Lambros."

"How on earth did you find time to get the information for me?"

L.T. laughed. "Just a phone call. I knew who handled his legal work—an old law school buddy of mine. I had to put on a little pressure, though. Will's not public record yet, so don't let on how you found out, okay?"

"Sure. So she's the primary heir. That must mean someone else inherits, too."

"Several, actually. First there's a bequest to the church—three hundred and fifty thousand and one of his cars. The wife can decide which car goes. Then there are several smaller bequests— college tuition money for . . . uh . . . nieces, I guess. Hold on."

"No, the file cabinets go in that empty office on the right. Sarah, show these guys where that conference table goes, will you? Sorry, Mrs. Lambros, where were we?"

"Do you have their names? The nieces."

He did, and gave them to me. "Apparently one of them is at Emory. She's in her junior year and he's paid her tuition all the way. The other one started at Parnassus last September. Fry was paying for her, too. He just wanted to be sure that they were able to finish up if anything happened to him. There are several stipulations to the will, though. They have to pursue 'suitable' studies—"

"What does that mean?"

L.T. Humphries chuckled. "You probably won't like this. I don't think much of it either, but here it is. They have to pursue majors which Fry considered acceptable for a woman. Education was at the top of the list, but he also accepts nursing and the fine arts."

"What a—" I checked my impulse to render an opinion on Mr. Fry's parentage. It was not, after all, any of my business if his nieces wanted to accept his conditions. But it did help to fill in my picture of Walter Fry.

"The will also stipulates that if they quit school, the money goes to the church."

"Okay, you said the wife inherits most of his business interests. I guess that means the trailer park wasn't his only source of income?"

L.T. whistled. "Not by a long shot. He's got interests in businesses all over town. Holds stock in Delphi Tool and Die—his late brother's company, I think. Also got a wedge of computer pie— some other nephew's company. He owned a half interest in the Crosscreek shopping center property and . . . I saved the most interesting for last, he owned a half interest in the Vagabond."

"Excuse me, did you say the Vagabond?"

"I did, Mrs. Lambros. I did indeed. And even more interesting, Walter Fry changed his will three or four months ago. His half interest in the Vagabond doesn't go to the wife." L.T. paused a beat, the lawyer in him wringing every bit of drama he could out of the situation.

"The Vagabond," he continued, "goes to someone named Justine Leroy."

"The what?"

"The Vagabond! Can you believe that?"

Nick pushed his cap back on his brow and stared down at my list. "A beer joint."

"I think the correct euphemism is a 'country-western dance hall.' "

"And probably the most profitable place he's got. How about that? Didn't Charley say Fry was against drinking?"

"More or less. He said Fry didn't like drinkers."

"Unless, of course, he's serving them himself and raking in the money."

"But wait, you haven't heard the best part. L.T. said that Fry's attorney didn't know anything about this Justine Leroy, and he didn't probe. Just wrote the will the way Fry told him to. And there was a second life insurance policy, too, only it didn't go to his wife."

"Let me guess—Justine Leroy?"

"In a manner of speaking, yes. Actually, it was part of his original partnership agreement, that both partners hold life insurance in the amount of fifty thousand."

"That's really not all that much money," Nick said.

"No, but it probably was when they drew the agreement up. That was nineteen years ago, after all. Anyway, his partner is the beneficiary."

"Really? How very interesting," Nick said with emphasis.

I glanced at my watch—8:45 and getting dusky. We were on the Industry Road and heading toward the Vagabond with a vague plan of scoping out the place. Neither of us had ever been there, but we'd certainly heard the stories. Rumor had it that they checked you at the door for a gun, and according to local humorists, if you were clean, they gave you one. Obviously an urban legend. At least I hoped it was. The Vagabond certainly had a rough reputation.

We'd timed our arrival just as the crowds would be picking up and the parking lot would start getting crowded. Then we'd just sit there, unobtrusively, and see. Or we'd go in, maybe grab a beer and get a feeling for the joint. I didn't much care for that idea, though. I had a feeling the Vagabond wasn't going to be our kind of place.

The nieces, we thought, were the least likely candidates as murderers, since Fry was already paying for their schooling. Unless they'd had a rift, the chances were he'd keep on paying. And Bitsy Fry supposedly had an alibi for the time of the murder. The church as a whole would benefit, but churches don't commit murder. That left us with only one other person who would gain financially by Walter Fry's death—the mysterious Justine Leroy.

"But I thought that guy—you know, the big mouth that comes on the radio every morning—what's his name?" Nick said.

"Dudley, no Dub Something."

"Yeah. I thought he owned the Vagabond."

"Apparently he only owns half. Walter Fry was a silent partner."

The Vagabond was about a quarter mile to the Delphi side of Mount Sinai Tabernacle Church, and across the road—maybe a half mile from the Fry home. Magnolia Mobile Home Park was about two miles farther out, almost to the county line. Walter's main interests were neatly situated for him, I thought. We pulled into the lot and found a space about twenty feet from the door. A nice, steady flow of traffic followed us in—a fleet of muscular pickup trucks and four-by-fours, with the odd Mustang or Escort to break the monotony. Reputation notwithstanding, the Vagabond had a good business, especially on a Friday night.

It was a building constructed of afterthoughts. The entrance was centered in front of what appeared to be a small, red barn. I'd heard it had been a barbecue restaurant at one time, but that had been many years ago. Low, flat-roofed wings jutted out from either side of the barn—wings made up of sections marked by a gradual progression in siding from asbestos to clapboard to cedar shakes. They were all painted a deep barn red and looked as if they could use a new coat or two. A pair of John Wayne types stood on either side of the door checking IDs, affably clapping backs and waving people in. Twangy guitars whined in the background.

Most of the patrons were decked out like dancers on Nashville cable television—nubile girls in denim miniskirts and high-heeled boots that left superhighways of leg in between. Snug knit crop tops and pastel Stetsons added insult to injury. A survey of my own outfit was disconcerting. If I had a black pocketbook, they might mistake me for the Queen Mum.

And then there were the roosters—most of them young, with long, narrow necks, protruding Adam's apples, and western hats with shoulder-width brims. They were strutting the barnyard flashing mother-of-pearl buttons on their western shirts, and pegged jeans so tight they had to walk with a rolling gait to avoid some serious chafing. Nick doesn't own a tooled belt, and the closest thing he's got to a western shirt is a cotton knit that sports a polo player on the left breast.

"I don't think we'd better go in there, Nick. We don't look the part."

"How are we going to find out anything if we don't go in?"

"I don't know. But something will come to me."

Chapter Nine

an-guish \ˈaŋ-gwish\ *n* [ME *angwisshe,* fr. OF *angoisse,* fr.
L *angustiae,* pl., straits, distress fr. *angustus* narrow; akin
to OE *enge* narrow—more at ANGER] : extreme pain, distress, or anxiety **syn** see SORROW *vi:* to suffer anguish *vt:*
to cause to suffer anguish.

—*Merriam Webster's Ninth New Collegiate Dictionary*

We sat there awhile longer, watching the customers flash
their IDs and file in. I didn't see a single soul I knew. The bass
picked up—a two-step beat that rattled the dashboard in
the Honda. I had to admit it was catchy. Nick's feet beat out
the rhythm on the floorboard. I could imagine him, his
arm around my back, lightly moving me across the floor. It
was tempting.

"Let's come back another night, Nick. When we're dressed
for it. I haven't seen a single person yet who wasn't duded up like
they were looking for a rodeo. We'll look like a pair of greenhorns
in there."

"Green horns?"

"One word. Greenhorn. It means someone who's . . . Never
mind. Let's come back."

He agreed and pulled out, leaving our space to a boss pickup
with a serious gun rack in the window and a spotlight on the
hood. Customers were still pulling in, although the lot in front of
the place was full, speeding right around to another lot at the
back. We sat at the entrance, waiting for a break in the line of traffic, or at least for someone to signal a turn. Finally an old pickup
flicked his lights at us, signaling us out.

"Davon! Nick, wasn't that Davon's truck? What's he doing at the Vagabond?"

Nick glanced in the rearview mirror. "He's not. He passed it. Looks like maybe he's turning in at the church—"

"Nick, look out!"

A vehicle was barreling toward us and swerved into our lane, screeching around the line waiting to get into the Vagabond. Nick threw the wheel hard to the right as the truck came on, bearing down on us like a charging beast. The lights were high, throwing maximum beams into our eyes like the raging, fiery eyes of a wild animal. The horn bellowed as we hit the shoulder. Nick braked, throwing me against the door as the right front wheel hurtled into the ditch beside the road. I pushed myself away and turned in time to catch a glimpse of the back window before the taillights receded into the darkness.

"*Karioli!* Stupid son of a—are you all right?"

I was, although I expected to be bruised in the morning. "What's the matter with that guy? Didn't he see those cars? He had enough wattage to see all the way to Cincinnati."

"Probably a drunk. It's Friday night." Nick shoved the gearshift into park, pulled off his cap, and wiped his brow. "Are you sure you're okay?"

My knees felt a little funny, and I'd skinned my right elbow on the door, but most of the damage was fear—a queasy nausea that rose from a near miss. And from something else.

"That truck. I think it was up on those great big tires. I've seen it before. There was a sticker—I just saw some of it. Rebel something."

Nick jerked up and slapped his hat back on his head. "Are you sure?"

"Yeah. I just glimpsed it, but—"

"That's them, Julia."

"Them who?"

"The guys. The ones at the Oracle who were after Davon."

I was sitting up straight now, too, and checking my seat belt. "Nick, you don't think—"

"That's why they were in such a hurry. They're after him. Let's get up to the church. Maybe they didn't see where he turned."

But we couldn't move all that quickly. The right front tire spun, shooting a spray of gritty mud back under the car. Nick slammed his fist on the wheel, threw the car door open, and strode around to the front of the car. I clambered over the gearshift and was ready when he started to push. It took a handful of loose tree limbs behind the tire and a considerable amount of mud and sweat before we were out.

I spun the wheel and we flew onto the pavement, hanging a screaming U-turn in the middle of the Industry Road. My queasy stomach was busy tying itself in knots as I made a wide left and bounced onto the wooded driveway to the church.

"What are we going to do?"

"You're going to stay in the car while I look around. Maybe I'm wrong. Maybe he didn't turn in here. Besides, they probably missed it."

But they hadn't missed it. Davon's truck was parked in the far left corner of the lot, close to the walkway behind the church. The Big Foot Ram was pulled crossways behind his bumper—barring any quick exit.

The Honda lights swept the parking lot just in time to catch two figures racing toward the Big Foot. One of them hurled something into the truck bed. It landed with a heavy clank, followed shortly by the slamming of doors and squeal of tires as the gravel flew behind the retreating truck. Nick reached across me, grabbed the steering wheel, and gave it a hard twist, spinning the Honda as though it were on an invisible axis. I aimed the car toward the driveway and stood on the gas pedal.

"Should I follow them?" I shouted, as the lights retreated out of sight.

He shook his head. "No. I was trying to get some light on that license plate, but we were too far away."

I turned back before I reached the drive and headed for the space next to Davon's pickup. "It was them, though, wasn't it? Those horrible guys who followed him to the Oracle."

"Yeah, I'm pretty sure. It's not the only truck like that around town, but it's too coincidental. Just wish I'd gotten that plate." Nick jerked off his seat belt the minute I stopped the Honda, was out of the car and down the path to the back of the church. I stumbled behind him, groping in the darkness and trying to follow his shadowy figure in front of me.

The moon was a silvery hairline in the night sky, and the vapor lights in the parking lot did not turn the required curves to illuminate the cemetery. As my eyes got accustomed to the darkness, I began to make out the square shoulders of grave markers to my left and felt my way to the gate. Nick had left it open.

"Nick?" I half whispered. "Where are you?"

"Over here. To the right."

I found him on his knees next to Davon. The boy lay on his back, his head butted up against a granite marker. I dropped down beside him and laid my hand on his chest. It fluttered under my hand, a wretched, ragged, shuddering kind of breath, as though he were smothering.

"I don't think he can breathe! There's something caught in his—"

Before I could finish, Nick had heaved him onto his side. Davon's jaw dropped open, and the tip of his tongue darkened his lips. His chest rose and fell again, this time in deeper gasps. I sat back, able for the first time to breathe myself. But it was far from over.

"*Panaghia mou.* Julia, run back to the car. Bring some of those rags in the trunk. Hurry!"

I followed Nick's instructions, tripping over loose bricks in the path I hadn't even noticed in the light of day. My heart lunged up into my throat, where it beat wildly, and my mind raced ahead. Davon was hurt—badly. Where was the closest phone? Could I get into the church to call for help?

I grabbed the rags and detoured long enough to yank on the church doors, but they were locked, as I had expected. And what about those guys? I thought, as I staggered back to the cemetery.

We couldn't follow them and get help, too. If only we'd gotten that plate number.

But there was no more time to worry about it once I reached Nick. He was still bent over Davon, holding his head and trying to stanch the gushing streams of blood that I could feel, smell, almost taste, if not see. Nick grabbed the rags and started winding them around Davon's head. They turned dark as quickly as he got them wrapped.

"Here," he said. "Kneel down here and get your knees under his head." The blood continued to flow through the rags and onto my skirt as Nick pulled off his shirt.

"The church is locked. I couldn't get to a phone."

"Okay." He tossed me his shirt. "I'm going down to the Vagabond to call an ambulance. Wrap that around his head and try to stop that blood."

Then he was gone, and I was frantically lifting the dark, silent head, holding the shirt, pulling, turning, wrapping—blood, thick and sticky, oozing between my fingers and under my nails. Trying to remember any first aid—*don't push on the bones. Is that blood or fluid?* And praying. I never stopped praying.

"They're on their way." Nick stood over me with an old blanket from the trunk of the car. The blood flow was slowing down, the stains on the rags darkening. But Davon had not opened his eyes. We draped the blanket over his limp body and I carefully cradled his head on my lap. Nick stood up and glanced around.

"Oh my God," he moaned. "Look at that." I followed his pointing finger. Several pots of shrubs lay on their sides by the marker. Loose dirt was scattered to the left of the grave, but the holes had not been meant for planting. My stomach churned in horror. Damien's grave. Six inches of dirt spaded and tossed aside as his poor father lay bleeding beside it.

"How could anyone—oh God, Nick. They were going to . . ." Was there a word for this unspeakable act? Exhume the body? Too civilized. Too kind. Left to their own devices, they would have gouged the earth, torn the body from the grave, and . . . done what? I couldn't even think about that.

The sirens screamed, washing back over us, penetrating the windows of the Honda and reverberating against the walls. Nick slammed the accelerator to the floor in a struggle to keep up with the ambulance. Neither of us had said a word since leaving the cemetery. We both knew we would follow the ambulance to the hospital, and as to Damien's grave, words would define the unspeakable, giving it form and a sharp reality. Neither of us wanted to believe that such atrocities really could happen.

We passed the Vagabond, the speedometer needle sneaking past eighty. Nick never turned, concentrating on the ambulance lights ahead. But I did, got a hasty glimpse of a big truck on Big Foot tires, secreted behind the building. I didn't mention it to him. These guys were no normal bullies or roughnecks, and I didn't want to be following another ambulance—one with my husband strapped to a gurney, tubes snaking from his arms and a mask covering that straight, classic nose. Sam would take care of finding them, I hoped. And there would be time to tell Nick about it later. Maybe.

"Did you see anyone at the Vagabond?" I ventured carefully.

"No. I didn't go in. There's a phone booth outside." I breathed a little easier, knowing the nose would stay classic another day or two.

"We'll have to let April know about Davon."

"I'm sure Sam'll take care of that, Julia. The EMTs were going to radio ahead for a deputy to meet us at the hospital."

He was there when we arrived. The ambulance had gotten ahead of us in downtown traffic. We turned in to the hospital lot as they were pulling the gurney out the back doors. A nurse met them in the ER lobby. She got one look at Davon and spun around to the woman at the check-in desk.

"This is Folsom's son. Has anyone called her?" Our negative answers brought quick action on her part.

"Get on the phone to her right now. Tell her to get down here.

Davon's been hurt." She spun back around, directing her question to me. "Car accident?"

"No. He——" But the deputy intervened before I could finish.

"Just ask her to come on down. We'll straighten it out when she gets here." The EMTs had not waited, had wheeled Davon on back to an examining room. The nurse followed on their heels. The deputy turned to Nick. "You the people that found him?"

"At Mount Sinai Church, Deputy. He's been badly beaten." The deputy shook his head slightly, rolled his eyes toward the listening ears in the waiting room, and gestured for us to follow him down the hall. He pointed us to a couch in the waiting area outside of Radiography, dropped into a chair himself, opened a small folder, and pulled out a pen.

"Let's start with the victim's name."

"Davon Folsom."

The deputy scowled as he wrote the last name. "Folsom? Related to . . . No, he couldn't be. She's white."

"She's his wife," I said.

He stared at me blankly for a moment, allowing the truth to warm, simmer, come to a boil. "Aw shit." He pushed the pen back in the folder, snapped it closed, and stood up. "Stay here and wait for me. I gotta make a phone call."

I have seen Sam Lawless look pleased. He has three fundamental happy faces. Buy him lunch and he smiles like a jack-o'-lantern, all the while doing an aw-shucks shuffle. Put a big plate of crisp hash browns in front of him and he beams from the roots of his golden hair to the smooth, freckled tip of his chin. And when Rhonda enters a room, he puts on a 150-watt glow. He wasn't wearing any of those faces when he collapsed into the chair across from us in Radiography.

"All right, how did the two of you happen to find him?" He looked at me first, going for the weaker link, I suppose.

"Well, we . . . uh, we were out at——"

"We were driving up to Industry to check out a new supplier—" Nick interrupted me.

"At nine o'clock at night?"

Nick spread his hands out. Sam didn't notice the rigid, splayed fingers—a tip-off that something was amiss. "I couldn't go during the day, Sam. I was busy all day. Spiros's day off, you know. So I called the guy and he said he'd meet us tonight. Anyway," he continued, "Davon passed us on the road, and right after that a big truck passed us too. We saw him turn in to the church lot, and the truck followed him."

"So? They coulda been having a meeting at the church."

Nick glanced at me and took a deep breath. "Yeah, but I'd seen these guys before." He gave Sam the details of our encounter with them, and the way they were threatening Davon in the restaurant. Sam listened without expression until he'd finished. He shook his head and made little disgusted noises.

"You shoulda called me, Nick. Fact is, you shoulda told me all this when you came down to the office yesterday. You knew about it then."

"And what would you have done, Sam? Put him under police protection?"

Sam didn't have an answer for that. Calloway County is one of the smallest counties in the state. Delphi is an unincorporated town. The university has its own police force, but the rest of us have to rely on a small, overworked sheriff's force for our protection.

"All right. I suppose you got a point. So can you give me a description of these guys?"

Nick looked to me for that. I complied as best I could, giving him as accurate a physical description as I could recall. "Really evil-looking," I added, a description that Sam did not think would be too useful to his deputies.

"How is Davon?" Nick said.

Sam flipped his pad closed and stuffed it into his back pocket. "Still unconscious. I called the jail and told them to bring Miz Folsom right on over. His mama and daddy are already here."

As if to prove it, a clatter of wheels preceded an orderly pushing a gurney up the hall. Candice hurried alongside, fussing with the IV fluids and checking the insertion in her son's hand. Chester Folsom stumbled along beside her, his empty hands occasionally reaching out and drawing back—wanting to help, wanting to stay out of the way.

They were met at the door by a technician who ran from the other direction. She unlocked the door and the orderly and Candice followed her inside. Chester stood helplessly in the waiting area, staring after them. Sam stood up, put a big hand on Chester's shoulder, and turned him toward the chair.

"Sit down, Mr. Folsom. They've got to get a CAT scan. They'll be out when they're done."

Chester nodded and fell heavily onto the green plastic seat. His glance went from Sam to Nick to me. "We've met, Mr. Folsom," I reminded him. "At the funeral home."

He didn't say anything, just nodded slowly. His eyes went back to the ominously closed door to Radiography. He pounded a fist into his hand as he stared at it. Sam glanced our way, pursed his lips, and took a deep breath.

"I need to ask you some questions, Mr. Folsom. Are you up to answering a few questions while we wait?"

Chester turned away from the door, focusing his attention on Sam. "I guess so. But I wasn't there—at the church. It was Davon's night."

"Davon's night?" Sam looked back at us. Nick sat forward expectantly. "Davon's night for what, Mr. Folsom?" Sam repeated.

"To guard, of course. To guard the cemetery. We were taking turns, my son and me, watching over little Damien's grave."

"Why?"

Chester Folsom sighed deeply and turned deliberately away, avoiding all our eyes. "We've been gettin' threatenin' calls. Since before we buried him, we've been gettin' these calls tellin' us not to put the baby in the white cemetery or they'd . . ." His voice dropped to a whisper. "They'd dig him up. I guess they tried to do it and my boy got in the way."

Sam's quizzical expression strayed to us. Nick, his mouth etched in a bitter line, nodded in the affirmative. "Sweet Jesus," Sam whispered under his breath.

April arrived, under armed guard, soon after Sam finished taking Chester's statement. D'Anita appeared shortly thereafter, followed closely by L.T. Humphries. Davon had already been taken to surgery, where they would bore a hole in his skull and attempt to alleviate the pressure on his brain caused by multiple head injuries. April, Candice, and Chester had gone up to the Surgical Waiting Area. D'Anita and L.T. were still in Emergency, giving information to the young woman at the admissions desk.

"I'll want you to come into the station first thing in the morning," Sam said to us after the family left. "I'm gonna be tied up here most of the rest of the night."

"You already have our statements, Sam," Nick said. "There's nothing more we can tell you."

"I know, but I've got to have them in writing and signed. Besides, I want you to have a look at our mug shots and see if you can identify those guys. They sound like the kind of fellas who mighta made one or two overnight stops at the county in the past. If not, I'll start you working with a police artist—see if we can come up with a likeness for my boys to go on."

We agreed to be there as soon as we'd gotten the Oracle open and the breakfast rush under control. L.T. Humphries stopped us as we headed out the door. He was still dressed in a suit and tie.

"Got a minute? I've sent D'Anita on up to surgery, but I was hoping we could talk."

We agreed to have a quick cup of coffee with him in the hospital coffee shop, but finding it closed, the best we could do was a lukewarm version of same from one of Charley's vending machines. I made a mental note to mention it to Charley next time I saw him.

We took our places at a white Formica-topped table in the canteen area. L.T. loosened his tie and collar and sat back in his chair.

"First minute I've had to relax all day," he said. "Now, just what happened out there?" Nick gave him a complete rundown of the evening, beginning with our arrival at the cemetery.

"I wish I'd known about those calls. The church people would have helped them out. He should never have gone out there alone."

I watched as L.T. crushed the coffee cup under his large hands, thinking about the controlled anger reflected in them. Here was a black man of considerable stature in the community. I wondered if he still felt the sting of prejudice.

"It must be frightening," I ventured. "Knowing that there are people out there who hate you just because of the color of your skin or the shape of your eyes."

L.T. tossed the cup in the general direction of the trash. It hit the wall and bounced in. "One of my people's gifts," he said, grinning. "Yes, it's hard. But you can't let people like Walter Fry scare you into hiding. The law exists to protect us all, and I'd say the majority of the time it does.

"No," he continued. "Dogs like Fry can be made to heel. The guys we've all got to watch out for are the ones he influences—the ones who make the laws, both state and federal. They're the ones who can take away your fundamental rights, and when they do, the Walter Frys of the world will have dominion over us all. And the issue won't just be skin color—it'll be gender, nationality, even religion. I like to think of myself as one of the gatekeepers."

Once we were in the car, I turned to Nick. "Why didn't you tell Sam the truth?"

"I did. You heard me, I told him all about those guys following Davon."

"I meant about where we were. You know, the Vagabond."

Nick sighed patiently. "Because Sam would want to know why

we were there. And then we'd have to tell him what we knew about Fry's will, which, if you remember, L.T. Humphries specifically asked us not to do."

And why, I silently asked myself, had I not mentioned seeing a truck in the Vagabond parking lot? Because Nick would be angry when he found out I was trying to protect his nose. He'd think I doubted his ability to protect himself. And me. It wasn't the first imprudent decision I'd ever made.

Jack was sulking when we got home. After the initial *I was worried about you* wag, he took himself off to the den, slunk behind my favorite rocking chair, and poked his nose into the corner.

"What have we got to eat, Julia?" The answer was, of course, nothing.

"I don't know. Look in the fridge." This was followed by the usual muttering and grumbling that always accompany assaults on the Lambros refrigerator. The pickings are always slim, and more often than not, they're also blue.

"Come on, Jack. We couldn't help it. We had a little trouble."

"Julia, how old is this milk?"

"I don't know. Look at the expiration date on the carton. Want to go for a walk, Jack?"

"Yuk! It expired two weeks ago."

"Sorry. Where's your ball, Jack? Get your ball."

"Any fruit in here?"

"I think those strawberries Marjorie Vandeveer brought over are still good. Look in that pink plastic container. You are the only dog I've ever met who sulks. We couldn't help it, Jack. Now, come on out of there. Get your ball."

No amount of pleading, begging, or cajoling would bring him out. But there was always bribery. He's particularly partial to feta cheese. Before I had the container completely open, he was dancing at my feet. All was forgiven.

"Look at that," Nick said. "He smelled the cheese before you even got it open!"

"He heard it, Nick. He recognized the pop of the Tupperware lid." Nick would like to believe that Jack's a wonder dog. When I first brought him home, Nick accepted his presence only grudgingly, and with the proviso that it was a temporary visit. But Jack had proven his mettle as a protector, and Nick had reversed his stance. What followed was a period of male bonding during which Nick determined that Jack was the smartest canine ever to walk the earth.

"Oh yeah? Then why didn't he come running when I got these out?" He held up a container of strawberries. Jack yipped. "See? He agrees with me."

"Okay, fine. He's actually a bloodhound. He just thinks he's a Scottie. If we could just convince him otherwise, he'd grow flop ears and learn to wrinkle his brow." I tossed Jack the cheese and stuck the container back in the fridge. When I turned back around, he'd retreated to his sulking spot.

"Jack! Come out here. Oh, I give up," I said, turning to Nick. "You deal with him. I'm going to bed."

I guess I'd never really thought about how many faces there are in the world before—high foreheads, low foreheads; broad, stubby noses and long, patrician noses; square jaws on burly necks and soft chins receding into ostrich necks; thick lips, thin lips, no lips at all. And the many, many combinations and convolutions of the above. But after perusing three thick books of mug shots, I thought I must have seen them all. All, that is, except Davon's attackers.

Sam had left us closed up in his office with a stack of them, and gone downstairs to talk with April. They had just brought her back from the hospital. I suppose he wanted to find out how much she knew about the threatening phone calls and the guys who'd beaten up her husband.

Nick and I divided the stack of books and sat quietly concentrating on the faces—faces of every color, every age, every ethnic background. But none I recognized.

"Nick," I said, staring at a familiar scar. "I know this guy. I mean, I've met him."

Nick put down his book and came to look over my shoulder. "He's black, Julia. Those guys were white."

"I know. I didn't mean he was one of them. I just said I know him. He was at the funeral home with D'Anita. Somehow I didn't picture her hanging out with known felons, though."

Nick scratched his jaw and sat back down in his chair. "He may not be a known felon. I don't know where they get the pictures for these books. I suppose it's probably anybody who's been arrested." He picked up the last book in his stack and started thumbing the pages.

But he also set my mind whirling. I couldn't think about the pictures anymore. Something far more urgent was gnawing at me. I was still staring blindly at the mug shots when Sam returned from seeing April.

"How is she?" Nick said.

Sam shook his head. "Pretty shaken. She knew about the calls, and she knew where her husband and father-in-law were going night after night. Why the hell didn't they contact me?"

Neither of us had an answer for him. At length he shook his head sadly and went back to the business at hand. "Any luck?"

"None," Nick answered dismally.

"What about you, Julia?"

"No. But I'm not finished with this one yet. Sam, I want to ask you something." He raised an inquisitive eyebrow and nodded for me to go ahead.

"Am I in one of these books?"

Chapter Ten

pre·car·i·ous \pri-ˈkar-ē-əs, -ker-\ *adj* [L *precarius*
obtained by entreaty, uncertain—more at PRAYER]
(1646) . . . **3a:** dependent on chance circumstances, unknown conditions, or uncertain developments **b:** characterized by a lack of security or stability that threatens
with danger **syn** see DANGEROUS.

—*Merriam Webster's Ninth New Collegiate Dictionary*

I was not, apparently, featured among the rogues' gallery because I had not been convicted of a crime. Still, a disquieting chill
ran over my shoulders and tingled the back of my neck. My fingerprints were somewhere—in a computer, maybe, or just in the
files of the local Sheriff's Department. Although I have nothing to
hide, I didn't especially like it.

"So all these guys are known criminals?" I said, pointing to the
array of faces.

Sam shrugged. "More or less. Why?"

I hesitated, but only briefly. I had no reason to protect the
guy. In fact, if he was an escaped convict, known to be dangerous,
our killer might be easier to find than I'd thought. "Because I've
seen this guy before," I said, pointing to the face with the scarred
upper lip.

Sam peered over my shoulder a moment, muttered a number
under his breath, then lumbered to his computer and punched on
the keys. In a second a computer graphic of the same face appeared on the screen.

"Rodney Earl Carroll. Born in Delphi. Completed nine years
of school before he got himself tossed permanently. String of ju-
venile offenses. Picked up at age eighteen as an accessory in an

armed robbery. Served his time in a state facility and seems to have stayed clean. Been out a year and a half. Sees his parole officer regularly."

I felt ashamed. The past should be allowed to remain the past. But I was sure it was the same guy. The lip scar was so distinct, lifting the tissue on the left side. I stared at the picture. The name Rodney was ringing a bell.

Sam exited his program and spun around in his chair. "So where'd you see him?" he said, with, I thought, more than casual interest.

I shrugged. "I don't remember. Probably at the Oracle. So many people come and go, you know." He eyed me skeptically but didn't pursue it.

I went through the rest of the book with no results. Nick hadn't come up with anything either. Sam ushered us out of his office and on to the artist waiting to render a likeness from our memories. I didn't have much confidence in that process. My intuition, a faculty Nick seriously questions, was telling me that we'd be seeing them again. But it wouldn't be behind bars.

"Has there been any change?" I whispered, standing close to Davon's bedside. He was streaming with tubes and flanked by monitors. An EKG beeped regularly, like a stopwatch ticking off the seconds in a race. A tube inserted in the radial artery monitored his blood pressure, sending periodic blips across a miniature screen. An endotracheal tube kept his airway open while he was being mechanically ventilated. His head was heavily bandaged. I glanced involuntarily at my own hands, conscious of how much of his blood had seeped into my skin and under my fingernails.

Candice shook her head. "Skull fracture and subdural hematoma. Either he fell and hit his head on the markers, or they hit him with something." My mind went back to the clang of a shovel hitting the bed of the truck, and I winced. It was probably both.

"You needn't whisper," she continued. "I want him to hear

us—to know we're here pulling for him. Talk to him if you want."
She shrugged. "Who knows? It might help."

But I had no faith that our presence would bring Davon
around. In fact, I wondered what could possibly interest him in returning to the real world. His son was dead. His wife was in jail
for murder. His parents and sister loved him, but I wasn't sure that
would be enough. I patted his limp, outstretched hand, feeling
awkwardly unable to find any words of encouragement for him or
his family, either. I turned helplessly to Nick and saw, in his stoic
features, that he was feeling much the same way.

"Well, how are you doing with all this?" I said, turning my attention to Candice. She was still wearing the clothes she'd had on
the night before—a black knit pants outfit with bright appliquéd
flowers across the neckline and shoulders. It was rumpled, as
though she'd slept in it, which she probably had. Except that the
deep pouches under her eyes betrayed that although she may have
tried to sleep in the functional green plastic recliner next to the
bed, she had not had much success. She sighed so deeply her chest
rattled.

"As well as I can. I'm a nurse. I see a lot of this kind of thing.
Some patients make it, some don't." At this her voice broke and
tears bubbled and trickled over the bags under her eyes. "It's just
not the same when it's your own son."

I did not know Candice well enough to put my arm around
her, to comfort her. I didn't know her well enough to so much as
pat her hand. Instead, I reached for the tissues, awkwardly ten-
dering the box. She jerked one out and dabbed at her eyes and
nose.

"You're tired," I said. "If you get some rest, it won't seem so
hopeless." She nodded and dropped into the recliner.

"They wanted to keep him in ICU, but I called in all my favors.
I'm going to stay with him round the clock and that's all there is
to it. They can let me do it or they can try to keep me out of ICU,
but let me tell you, it won't be easy." Her jaw set stubbornly. I
knew from my own association with the hospital that Candice
Folsom had a reputation for being tough. Some of the doctors re-

ferred to her as an equal-opportunity bully, as quick to pick on the chief of surgery as the meekest nurse's aide. I could well believe that this was a battle Candice Folsom was going to win.

"I got them to agree to it, so long as we've got another nurse on the case at all times. I've picked them myself."

"Then at least you'll have some relief. How about the rest of the family?"

"I sent D'Anita and Chester home to get some rest early this morning. April, they let her stay here until this morning. She sat right there on the bed next to him, talkin' softly to him all night long." Candice shook her head. "I didn't know she had it in her. She's a strong little girl, that one."

I studied her as she said all this, unable to get any feeling for how Candice Folsom had accepted her white daughter-in-law. But whatever had gone before, I felt that from this time forward Candice would respect April, whether she grew to love her or not. Somehow it made me feel better about the whole family.

"You know," she said, "I've been a part of this hospital for a long time, but I've never been, well, on this side of the door, if you know what I mean. Oh, I had both my babies here, but that was different. That was a happy time. I've just never been the one sitting a vigil by the bedside of someone I love."

"How long is 'a long time,' Ms. Folsom?" I asked, hoping to get her mind on something besides her pain.

She counted backward under her breath. "Almost thirty years, I suppose. I did my training here. Started off in the ER on the eleven-to-seven shift. Now, there was a baptism of fire, let me tell you."

"I'm sure you saw a lot," I added ineffectually.

She agreed. "Car accidents, shootings in the projects, overdoses. And you know, back then, abortions weren't legal, either. We had our share of infections from dirty abortionists, and girls trying to get rid of those babies themselves . . ." She nibbled on her lower lip and shook her head.

"Have you always worked the ER?"

"Lord, no! I got out of there as soon as I could. Moved up to postpartum care as quick as I could get out."

"That must have been a relief. At least it's a happy place."

"In general," she agreed. "Of course, we still saw plenty of problems. In those days postpartum got the miscarriages and abortions too. I always felt so sorry for those little girls."

This was not a topic I particularly wanted to dwell on, especially since I had lost a baby myself. Being essentially a feminist, I understand the desperation that might drive a woman to abort a pregnancy—the tragic consequences of rape, incest, even one-night stands. I'm not eager to return to the days of self-mutilation and back-alley butchers. And I hate being characterized as unsympathetic and disloyal to my fellow women. I've tried to adopt the liberal point of view, even repeated the slogans to myself: *It's my body.* But my conscience always has a rejoinder: *No, not yours. This is another human being, another body attached to yours.* My mind is willing, but my heart is stronger.

I snapped back from my reverie to find that the conversation had proceeded without me and, thankfully, the subject had changed.

"And no one ever found out who the guy was?" Nick said.

Candice shrugged and looked at me. "She called out for him several times, but no one knew him. L.T. was pretty devastated by it. He was so young. You know, I think women are stronger than men in a crisis."

I'd missed her story, but I had to agree with her on her conclusion. April Folsom was Exhibit A—husband seriously injured and she accused of murder—still as placid as a frozen lake. But that metaphor was wrong somehow, implying that April was cold. She was just absolutely confident that things would work out all right. It said a lot to me about her faith. I just hoped she wasn't putting all of that faith in Nick and me.

"I've seen a lot of suffering women in my time. Battered wives—L.T. and I got to be friends serving on the Women's Shelter Board together. I've seen child abuse and postpartum psychosis."

Was there a message in all these memories? Did Candice think that her daughter-in-law might be suffering from postpartum depression? Depression, more than faith, might account for April's unruffled calm. She could be emotionally shut down. I voiced the question to Candice.

"I don't know," she murmured thoughtfully. "April has every reason to be depressed—carrying a baby to term and delivering a stillborn. And that family of hers—"

A nurse appeared at Davon's door, cutting off all conversation while she studied the monitors, changed his IV solution, and made notes in his chart. She seemed nervous, the natural consequence, I suppose, of having to perform even routine duties in front of the director of nursing. Especially when said director's son was the patient.

Chester Folsom arrived on the heels of the nurse's hasty departure. His arms were loaded—an overnight bag for Candice, a huge schefflera with an enormous purple bow, a pile of magazines, and a deck of cards. An optimistic armload for a patient who was still unconscious. Candice smiled gently at her husband and wordlessly offered him her chair, which started us all shuffling and offering to move to make room for Chester. He finally agreed to take Nick's place, but pulled the chair up close to the side of the bed.

"Did you close the shop today?"

He shot his wife a surprised glance. "Today and every day until my boy doesn't need me anymore. Until he's ready to get back on the job. Hasn't woken up yet?"

"No," Candice said softly. "Not yet."

We were in the way here. We could do nothing for Davon, and Candice and her husband needed time together—time to cry and time to pray. Nick was already motioning me toward the door. I stood up and Candice joined me.

"If you need anything . . . if there's anything either of us can do, you just call, all right?" To my surprise, Candice Folsom hugged me.

"I will. I know Davon thinks a lot of you two."

We were at the elevator before Chester Folsom caught up with us. "I wanted a private word with you," he said. "Candice—well, she doesn't know everything yet and I don't think she should until Davon comes around. It might be too much for her." He glanced around, down at his shoes, and up at the lighted numbers above the elevator.

"I know what you've done for my boy. And for my grandbaby. That sheriff, he told me. If you hadn't followed Davon, he would have died out there in the cemetery. I just wanted to say thanks." He offered Nick his hand tentatively.

"I'm glad we were there to help. I just wish we'd gotten there sooner," Nick said, returning the handshake. "We might have been able to prevent it."

Chester Folsom looked distressed. "You saved my boy's life and that's enough." We all stared at the elevator awkwardly for a long moment before Nick decided it was time to press Chester Folsom for more information.

"Tell me something, Mr. Folsom. Do you know who those men are? The sheriff asked us to look through pictures—"

"Mug shots," I explained.

"—but we didn't find them. Do you have any idea who they are? Why would they attack Davon like that?"

And why, I thought, would they vandalize Damien's grave? But I didn't say it. I didn't have to. It hung over us like a summer thunderstorm.

Chester Folsom shook his head slowly. "Got no idea. Could be any one of dozens of 'em that don't want to see a black baby in the white man's cemetery."

"When did the threats start?"

Chester closed his eyes, thinking back. "Soon's word got out we would be burying Damien at Mount Sinai. That Fry fella, he held a meetin' at the church. Started that very night. I took the call and then I called my son. He'd gotten one, too. Got worse the next day—callin' day and night at all hours, even the day of the funeral. That night I stayed out there at the cemetery, then Davon the next night. We were alternating, watching over the grave."

"But why didn't you tell the sheriff about it then?"

Chester Folsom looked away and sighed patiently. "There's no reason for you to understand this, Mr. Lambros. But the sheriff, well, he's never been a friend of the black man in Delphi."

I glanced over at Nick, at the lingering sadness in his eyes and the weary droop of his mouth. He knew as well as I that what Chester said was true. The previous sheriff, Cal Taylor, had been no friend to minorities.

"We're trying to help them, Mr. Folsom," Nick said. "We believe April is innocent of Fry's murder and we're trying to find a way to help them. If you think of anything—anything at all—that could be important, you call us."

Chester agreed, shaking Nick's hand before turning away to return to his wife and son. The elevator arrived and the doors whooshed open to reveal D'Anita waiting to alight. She cast a wary glance at us and caught sight of her father.

"Daddy!" she called, and pushed past us without a word of recognition.

"There," I said, "is the one member of the Folsom family who doesn't seem to like us very much."

"Mmm," Nick said, as he punched the elevator button and the doors closed. "I wonder why."

"There is a place of quiet rest, near to the heart of God . . ." Miss Alma's sweet soprano rang out confidently. I, however, was not quite as confident, and not particularly adept at faking it.

It was a pretty hymn, and Joy, who had returned to her organ, played it competently. But I didn't know it. I grew up with guitars and folk masses on Sunday mornings. And Nick, with his background of ancient mysteries, Byzantine chants, and incense, would have felt as if he'd landed on another planet.

Arriving early for the service, we'd taken a seat toward the back of the church where we could observe the worshipers as they came in. In the back of my mind I suppose I thought that Davon's attackers would appear at some point. But of course, they didn't. They were not churchgoing men. My one concern was running into Charley Albright, who knew far too much about us to believe that I was just visiting around, trying to find a church. But Charley had apparently slept in, and since I didn't know Cordelia, the Albrights presented no problem.

The service left me feeling confused. I'd had the impression that fundamentalist churches preached fire and damnation, slathering on guilt as thick as molasses on a short stack. It hadn't turned out quite that way. Allen McNabb, dour though he was, had preached a heartening sermon on the parable of the Prodigal Son. Its focus had been repentance and forgiveness—an interesting theme from a man who had repudiated his own child. I had to wonder whether he was not the least introspective or if he was trying to send a message to his congregation about his daughter. Either way, I'd gone to the church that morning prepared to beat my breast and acknowledge my base humanity, only to learn that my expectations were all wrong. Mount Sinai was nothing like I'd expected.

As we exited the church, I wondered how I was going to manage to penetrate this congregation deeply enough to find out anything significant about their deceased deacon. As it happened, Miss Alma provided the answer. She grabbed my arm, steering me to a group of older women clustered in the parking lot.

"Vivian?" A heavyset woman with fuzzy gray-blue hair like dryer lint turned and scanned the lot. When her gaze caught up with Miss Alma, her chins quivered with delight.

"Why, Alma Rayburn, what in the world? I haven't seen you in a dog's age." She hugged Miss Alma warmly. Miss Alma introduced her as Vivian Spaulding, a former math teacher at the high school. Apparently Ms. Spaulding, who was several decades Miss Alma's junior, had retired a few years previously. They had not seen one another since the retirement party.

"Julia and I have been visiting, trying to find a new church," Miss Alma explained. "I haven't been real happy at Second Baptist since Brother Kendall left," she said. "But that's all water under the bridge, anyway. Now I'm looking for a church with a solid Sunday school program and a strong women's group—you know what I mean, Vivian."

Vivian did. In fact, she assured us, Mount Sinai had exactly that kind of fellowship—an active women's group made up of women of all ages. She felt that encouraging young people to join gave the group a little more spice. Miss Alma and I heartily agreed.

"Of course," Vivian continued, "with so many women working these days, it's hard to get them to come out at night. Brother Walter didn't really approve of women working for just that reason. But I worked myself, so I'm more sympathetic. It's hard to stir up interest in rummage sales when your feet hurt and you've got seventy-five papers to grade.

"Anyway," she said, eventually coming back to the point, "we meet on Monday nights in the fellowship hall. If you'll come tomorrow night, I'll introduce you to the rest of the ladies and you can see for yourself."

Miss Alma and I quickly accepted her invitation, delighted in the smooth dovetailing of her offer and our plans. We agreed to meet her at seven o'clock. In the history of the Mount Sinai Tabernacle Ladies' Circle, no one had ever looked forward to a meeting more.

"You see?" Nick said, uncovering the basket. "Chicken, ice-cold sliced tomatoes and feta with basil, French bread, and—" he pulled out the bottle with a flourish "—*Roditis*—very cold. Get into your suit and let's get out of here."

Nick has a wide romantic streak in him. His skill at planning sentimental journeys on the spur of the moment is one of the things I love about him. It was a perfect day for a picnic—a warm summer Sunday wearing a clear, blue sky.

"Okay," I said. "Where to?"

Jack cavorted at our feet as Nick snapped on his leash and grabbed his ball. "I was thinking about Laurel Park."

It's a charming place, ten miles or so outside of Delphi and straight up. The view from the summit of Braeburn Mountain looks out upon miles of virginal pine forest and, in season, acres of blooming mountain laurel. Braes Falls starts somewhere near the middle of the mountain, tumbles over granite outcroppings and remarkably tenacious thickets, and forms a pool of crisp, clear water at the foot of the mountain. It's cold, hard swimming—the kind that reminds you you're alive. I couldn't wait.

I told Nick about my Monday night plans on the drive up to the park. "I'd rather you didn't go," he said.

"Why?"

"Because someone there is going to connect you with April. It could stir up trouble, and I won't be there with you."

"Nick," I answered patiently, "I'm just going to be gathering information. I'll be—"

"Discreet. Don't bother to say it. I've heard that before."

"I was going to say 'circumspect.' "

"Circum . . ."

"Spect. It means, literally, 'to look around,' to be prudent. Cautious. To be—"

"Discreet?"

"Besides, Miss Alma will be with me," I added hastily.

"Right," he said. "And who'll be with her?"

Nick pulled into a parking space at the base of the falls and cut the ignition. The park was surprisingly quiet for a summer Sunday, with several couples and young families dotted around the picnic area. But the spring semester at Parnassus was over and summer vacations had kicked in, taking faculty families off to Myrtle Beach, Hilton Head, and Savannah.

I gazed out at the pool and picnic area, nestled into a hollow at the base of the falls. To the right, steep, rocky cliffs led up to a horizon of thick pines, oaks, and hickory trees. On the left, the wooded embankment sloped more gradually and offered a walking trail for anyone hearty enough to try a hike to the top of the falls. The water roared as it cascaded over the cliffs and crashed on the rocks below. There it diverted into two streams—a large one that veered left and coursed under the base of the embankment, and a smaller one that filled the pool in front of us. A footbridge arched over both streams, spanning from one bank to the other.

"Look, all I'm saying is——"

Jack bounded from one side of the car to the other, his neon green tennis ball clamped firmly in his jaws. When the engine died, he threw his paws onto Nick's shoulders, dropped the ball in his lap, and let out a staccato string of "Growfs" in Nick's ear.

"Okay, Jack. Just a minute. Let me get your leash. Miss Alma is eighty—All right! You're all tangled up on the hand brake. Jack, stop! All right, come on."

They were out the door and bounding across the picnic area before I could pull the basket out of the hatchback. I made a mental note to save a piece of chicken for Jack. I owed him one.

Jack has many talents, most of which are useless, but he is not a swimmer. Unlike his fellow country dog Lassie, he would not even consider pulling either of us from a drowning pool if it meant getting his paws wet. Nor, I imagine, would he go for help. Fortunately, Nick swims very well, and I'm no slouch either. We hit the pool for a quick dip, clutching each other and shivering in the cold, while Jack yelped and danced on the sidelines.

"I'm hungry," Nick said, hoisting himself onto the granite ledge around the pool. "Let's have lunch." He stretched out a hand to pull me out.

We toweled off as quickly as we could, pulling sun-warmed T-shirts and shorts over our swimsuits, snagged our basket, and returned to the pool where we could grab a piece of sunlight while we ate. I peeled a lump of meat off a chicken breast and tore it to pieces for Jack, mindful to keep his square little snout away from the bones. The bread was crusty, the *Roditis* cold, and the sky clear. How much more perfect could it get?

"Now, about this meeting," Nick reminded me.

"Oh, Nick, let's not spoil the day. We're going to argue about this. I can feel it coming." I glanced up at the top of the falls. "Let's finish eating and hike up to the top. It's a much better way to spend our time. We can always argue when we get home."

Nick acquiesced and we packed away the basket and headed for the walking trail. Although it began as a fairly gradual climb, the way grew much steeper about a quarter of a mile up the path. Fortunately, it was broken up by frequent viewing points, complete with benches where out-of-shape climbers like me could catch their breath.

Jack, of course, was mainly concerned with territorial marking. Facing all those trees, he must have felt like Charlemagne on the brink of his campaign to conquer Europe. He so slowed our progress that it was a relief when he spied a chipmunk zipping along the path and took up his hunting posture—leaning forward, back legs splayed and rigid, tail and ears decidedly up. He watched the little animal a moment before emitting a low growl. The chipmunk darted into the brush as Jack strained at the leash. Nick unclipped it and let him go.

"What are you doing?"

"I want to see if he can track it," Nick said. "Look at him!" Jack was long gone, off the path and following his blunt little nose.

"You'd better go after him, Nick. He'll get lost."

He grabbed my hand and pulled me farther up the path. "He'll be okay. He'll find us when he's ready. I keep telling you he's smart. He'll follow our scent."

"Want to bet on that?"

"Sure. How much?"

"Oh, nothing so crass as money."

"Okay, what?"

"A massage. Every single night for a week." Nick gives a great massage.

He didn't even blink. "Okay, but if I win, I sleep late and you open every day next week." Yuk. I hate to open. It means I have to spend more time with the Buffaloes. On the other hand, it would give me more time to question Charley Albright.

The negotiations completed, I followed him reluctantly, checking back over my shoulder every few steps. Jack was nowhere in sight. We rounded the first turn in the path, Nick forging onward while I dragged my heels. There we stopped. I squeezed his hand tightly.

"Isn't that—"

"D'Anita Folsom," he said.

Chapter Eleven

ret-i-cent \-sənt\ *adj* [L *reticent-, reticens,* prp. of *reticere*
to keep silent, fr. *re- + tacere* to be silent—more at TACIT]
(1834) **1:** inclined to be silent or uncommunicative in
speech: RESERVED . . .
—*MerriamWebster's Ninth New Collegiate Dictionary*

The first observation point was beyond the footbridge and
about twenty feet above the pool. D'Anita Folsom sat on the
bench, concentrating so intently on the sketchpad in her lap that
she didn't notice us at all. She picked up a pair of binoculars and
gazed down at the pool a moment, set them down, and went
back to her sketch.

"D'Anita?" She glanced up sharply, her expression instantly
guarded. Nick and I walked casually toward her, giving her a few
seconds to collect herself.

"Are you an artist?" I said, looking at the pad in her lap. There
were four drawings on the paper, all swimmers in various stages
of activity.

"I'm an art student at Parnassus," she said, her chin tilting up
toward us. I'd seen this same tilt in Davon's chin—a proud, challenging angle of the head—but on D'Anita it seemed more ag-
gressive. I glanced back down at her work.

I didn't have to look twice to know that D'Anita Folsom was
very good. The sketches were simple line drawings that not only
captured the human figure, but gained its motion, with all the
power of arms thrusting through water and legs jackknifed to
dive. I recognized Nick's physique instantly.

"They're so good," I cried, pulling the pad off her lap. "And you can do it from this distance?"

"Apparently," she said dryly, reaching for her pad. But I had handed it over to Nick, who was thumbing back through her previous drawings.

"Well," I said, plumping myself down next to her on the stone bench. "I'm very impressed. What year are you in at Parnassus?"

"I'm a senior."

"Oh, I didn't realize . . . You must be older than Davon."

"Three years," she said. "Why?"

"No reason in particular." I picked up the binoculars and stared down at the pool. "I don't see how you do it. Those people down there are all moving."

"You have to know a lot about the human body," she said. "I'm studying their motion." It showed in her work. The swimmers looked as if they would soon lap the page and disappear.

"But why don't you go down to the pool, where you can see them better?"

"Because people are embarrassed if they think I'm sketching them. They leave."

That made sense. I was glad I was not one of her subjects, to be caught for all time in a swimsuit. I studied my thighs and vowed to retrieve my exercise video from the dusty corner of the shelf where it was moldering. My thirtyish thighs were not as firm as they had been in high school. There it was again—the magical age of eighteen. Which brought my thoughts around to April.

"I'm glad we ran into you," I said. "You know we're trying to help April?" She confirmed that Davon had said something about it before he was attacked.

"I'd like to ask you a couple of questions." I thought I felt her stiffen beside me, and glanced up at Nick, but he was still studying the pad.

"I don't know what I can tell you," she said. "I didn't know that deacon. I'd never seen him before, till he came to the funeral home the night before we buried Damien."

"Well, okay," I said. "I really wanted to ask you about April, anyway. Are you two close?"

D'Anita studied the toes of her tennis shoes. "Sure. We're pretty close. She's my sister-in-law." But despite this affirmation, there was no warmth in her voice. Was that pure D'Anita, or was it something else?

"You're closer to Davon?"

"He's my brother. I would be, don't you think?" she said wryly.

"Of course. So you'd probably know—has April been edgy or anything lately? Has he mentioned anything to you?"

"We don't talk about his marriage. That's their business, and I really don't see what any of it has to do with you trying to help April."

"I just wanted to know if she seemed different lately. If it's possible that she's so . . . unstable that she could really have tried to kill him."

D'Anita stood up and walked to the edge of the path to stare at the pool below. "I thought you said you were trying to help her. This doesn't sound much like help to me."

Okay, I thought. These verbal games were leading nowhere. I needed to get her cooperation, not antagonize her. But I wondered if there was anything I could do or say that wouldn't offend her. There she stood, her back to us sending the very clear message that she was not interested in helping us to help April.

"We're just trying to get to the bottom of it," I said wearily. Nick sidled up next to me, passing me the pad. I glanced up to find his finger to his lips. He flipped over a handful of pages and pointed. Before me was a beautifully rendered pencil drawing of Rodney Earl Whatever. I nodded quickly at Nick and turned the pages back over to the swimmers.

"Look," I added hastily. "I really believe she's innocent, but unless we find someone else who wanted to kill him, April's going down for the count."

D'Anita swung around on her heel, noticed the pad in my lap, and snatched it up. Her glance went to the page of swimmers before coming back to me. "I just don't know anything to help you, okay?"

"What about the gun? Do you have any idea where she got the gun?"

But she didn't get a chance to answer. A scuffling in the leaves behind me sent me leaping off the bench. Jack followed me, vaulting right over the bench to deposit a quivering little heap at my feet. He woofed happily and wagged his tail.

"Oh, Jack, no! Nick, he got it!" The little chipmunk's eyes were open and glazed over, but his body was still trembling.

Nick grinned broadly, the human version of our roguish canine. "I told you he was good."

D'Anita had not missed her opportunity. She grabbed the binoculars and dropped the cord around her neck, snagged her purse, and tucked her pencils away. She was leaving before we'd had time to get any information out of her.

"Wait, D'Anita. What about the gun? Do you know anything about the gun?"

"No, I have no idea. And now I've got to go. See ya," she said, stalking down the path.

"Great," I said, glaring at my two men. "We've lost her. Let's go."

I followed D'Anita's example and stomped away, glancing back only once. The boys were listlessly following me, tails tucked between their legs, but the chipmunk had disappeared.

"A little to the right," I said. "Mmm. Right there." Nick, feeling guilty about the near death of the chipmunk, had decided to forgo the bet. In fact, he'd even agreed to make good on one massage. I'm not above taking advantage of guilt.

"It says here that their jaws are very powerful and the feet are splayed so that when they dig, they throw the dirt outward. That way they can get in the hole easily." I shivered, wondering what Jack had been after in the kudzu, and turned the page of the book.

"But I don't see anything about them having unusual tracking abilities."

Nick kneaded my shoulders thoughtfully. "Well, we know Glenn took him to obedience school."

"Not that it helped," I interjected.

We had acquired Jack after his owner, Glenn Bohannon, died at the breakfast table in our restaurant. It was an incident I did not like to think about, especially the part where I was incarcerated for murder. But Glenn was, as Nick said, in law enforcement. Maybe Jack did have some sort of special training, as Nick seemed to think—like those dogs that are trained to sniff out drugs.

"I don't know," I said drowsily, not really caring either. Nick's hands had moved down to my lower back. "But I'd like to know more about why D'Anita's so hostile. She doesn't seem to want to help April at all, even though she said they're pretty close. I wish we could have kept her there talking longer."

"She did seem anxious to get away from us," Nick agreed. He rolled me over on the bed, took the book out of my hands, and set it on the nightstand. "Feel better?"

"Well . . ." I hesitated. "You know what would really be nice?" I waggled my eyebrows at him.

"Sorry," he said. "That wasn't part of the bet." I gave him a good shot with my elbow. "But," he continued, "I might be persuaded to oblige."

Vivian Spaulding rapped her gavel on the podium. "Ladies, please take your seats! Our program is about to begin."

Miss Alma steered me to a brown metal folding chair at the rear of the room where we waited expectantly for the others to get seated. The women ranged in age from the occasional mid-twenty-year-old to the far more common fifties and sixties. Miss Alma was probably the oldest woman in attendance, and I was among the younger ones.

Behind us the refreshment table held a variety of brownies and cookies. An ancient coffee urn was sluggishly perking in the corner. At the rate it was going, we'd be lucky to get coffee before Sunday morning. I hoped we'd get through the meeting quickly and move on to the eats. That was where we might have a real shot at learning something from these women.

".... so in spite of her recent loss, Bitsy has stalwartly insisted upon continuing her duties and she will present the devotional tonight."

The Ladies' Circle broke into soft applause as Bitsy Fry took her place at the podium. She wore a full skirt patterned with purple and fuchsia flowers and a matching purple crepe blouse. Even her flat pumps were purple. It was, in all, a rather garish outfit for a woman who was supposed to be in mourning. Her hair, minus the black hat she'd worn at church, was blond—cut short in layers that reminded me of chrysanthemum petals. She carried a large black leather-bound Bible which she thumped heavily onto the stand before gazing out at the audience.

"Before I begin, I'd like to take a moment to thank you all for your expressions of condolence. The spray y'all sent was gorgeous. Walter loved red carnations, as you all know. And the many cards and letters . . . the food . . ." Bitsy's hand fluttered over her breast, as though she could not go on.

Vivian stepped in quickly. "Bitsy, we all know how hard this is for you. Wouldn't you like Cordelia to give the devotional? Just tonight," she added.

Bitsy shook her head. "Walter would expect me to go on. I've brought his Bible and I'm going to read one of his favorite passages. Perhaps I'd best go to that."

Her fingers quivered as she leafed through the Bible, stopping now and again to study a passage before moving on. "I didn't really have time to prepare." She smiled apologetically at her audience. "What with preparations for the— Now, where is it?" She frowned as she turned the thin, gold-edged pages. "That's odd. What could have— Oh, here it is. All right. Now I'm ready."

She lifted the book and read steadily. " 'Remember how short my time is: wherefore has thou made all men in vain? What man is he that liveth, and shall not see death? Shall he deliver his soul from the hand to the grave? Selah.' " Her head came up and her eyes moved over the Ladies' Circle. "Psalm Eighty-nine: verses forty-seven and forty-eight."

Bitsy delivered quite a thoughtful and inspiring devotional on death of the body and life of the soul, calling up the memory of her departed spouse as an example. She remained calm throughout. Had I not known, I would never have guessed that she had lost her husband only a few short days before. By the end of her presentation, I had to admit that I was intrigued. Either she was a woman of great faith and self-control, or she really didn't much care about losing Walter. Personally, I was betting on the latter.

Following the devotional, Vivian presented her with a plaque donated by the Ladies' Circle in memory of Walter Fry. Said plaque would be installed in the fellowship hall, along with a set of volumes on Christian Family Living.

"Walter," Bitsy said, "cared so much about the family. Although we were never blessed with children of our own, he came to look upon every young member of the church as his own son or daughter. This would have meant so much to him." At this she choked up briefly. Vivian patted her shoulder and guided her back to her seat.

"Now, ladies," Vivian continued. "Before we go to the refreshment table, we have some business to finish. Let's begin with a report on this year's Fall Bake Sale," the plans for which were apparently going quite well.

Following the report, Bitsy Fry once again took the floor to remind the members of the circle that she was collecting clothing for the homeless coalition. "Now is the perfect time, ladies, to clear out your closets and get rid of those things you didn't wear all winter. I'll be collecting the clothing at my house all day tomorrow. On Thursday we'll be getting together to sort through and organize the clothing, so if y'all can come to help, you can bring your things then. There's a sign-up sheet for helpers on the refreshment table."

Now, really, this was a bit much. Here she was newly widowed and supposedly devastated by her husband's sudden death, organizing a clothing drive. I glanced around at the women in the room. Didn't anyone else think that Bitsy Fry was just a little too calm? But not a single face in the room registered surprise. Most of them were listening to the business reports. I tried to turn my attention back to Vivian Spaulding.

I'm not much of a joiner. A reluctant member of the Musewood Garden Club, I try very hard to confine my duties to attending an occasional meeting, casting my vote for further neighborhood beautification, and enjoying the fruits of the potluck luncheons. I did one term as treasurer, which was just enough to acquit me in the eyes of my fellow members and convince me that civic activities were not going to be my forte. I try to keep a low profile at meetings.

My gaze wandered around the room, noting the occasional familiar faces and tentative smiles of women who were probably customers at the Oracle. It is a hazard of the food service business that customers more often recognize me than I do them. Now and then I could attach certain features with their preferences—a woman who always asks for a seat next to the window, another who invariably asks about low-fat and vegetarian entrées, then orders a cheeseburger. I was in the middle of these musings when Miss Alma nudged me, pointing her chin to a woman several rows ahead of us and directly to my left. I swallowed hard, resisting the urge to hurdle over the seats and deliver a spontaneous sermon on courtesy and the offensive nature of public spitting. Miss Alma's elbow caught me just in time.

". . . so we'd like to welcome our newcomers and invite them to stay and join us for refreshments and a little time to visit. Alma, please stand up and let everyone know who you are, and introduce your young companion there."

Miss Alma hauled me to my feet, murmuring about her friend Julia. Bitsy Fry's expression was warm and welcoming. I smiled in return and cast around for those other familiar faces. Only one of them was paying attention. She squinted, studying me as though she were trying to recall where she had seen me before. At the cemetery, I thought, bracing myself for recognition. You're one of the late Walter Fry's minions, and you have some very nasty ways of expressing your opinion. I gave her one of my brightest smiles.

But she didn't seem to remember, and after the introduction we broke up quickly, moving toward the refreshments. I followed her as she collected a brownie and moved off to chat quietly in a corner with Bitsy Fry. I snagged a cup of coffee and eased their way, pretending interest in the church bulletin board, which hung conveniently on a wall near their seated figures.

"You know how much he'll be missed," consoled the spitter. "Walter was the only real leader this church has had since his daddy died. I had hopes for Brother Allen, but . . ." Her disappointed voice trailed off, leaving an expressive silence in its wake.

"Now, Nelda," Bitsy said. "Brother Allen and Walter had their little disagreements, but he's a fine preacher." Little disagreements?

"Yes," Nelda agreed, "I suppose, but just look at that daughter of his! Carrying on with that nigger boy—"

"You know, it's the strangest thing . . ." Bitsy interrupted, neatly derailing Nelda's train of thought. She tapped the Bible in her lap. "This is my Walter's Bible, you know. The print's larger than mine. You know how it is as we get older, Nelda. I'm having more trouble reading fine print. But I noticed—" She scowled at the book and shrugged. "Oh well, I don't suppose there's anything I can do about it now."

She turned her attention back to Nelda. "Do you have that problem? Your eyesight?"

Nelda did not. But she was having the occasional twinge of arthritis. She flexed her hands and examined her knuckles. "You see how large the right hand is? My sister—she moved to Tucson six, eight months ago—she says she has the same problem, but she thinks the dry air and heat help. She sent me this copper bracelet from Mexico . . ." Enough of Nelda's afflictions, I thought, moving away. She really needs her head treated. I moved over to Miss Alma, who was standing with Vivian.

"Bitsy is a remarkable woman," Vivian said, gazing fondly at her friend. "She was devastated by Walter's death, but she has tremendous faith. She positively insisted on doing the devotional tonight, in spite of the circumstances."

"Remarkable," Miss Alma agreed. "Is there any news about the—"

Vivian guided her away from the rest of the group, while I trailed behind. Her voice dropped to a whisper. "I wouldn't want to be overheard discussing it," Vivian explained, looking back over her shoulder. "But far as I know, our April's been indicted. I hear she got out today. Rumor had it that the judge was going to deny bail, but then her husband was attacked—did you know? Anyway, I guess the judge decided she wasn't liable to run, with her husband laid up in the hospital and all."

This was news to me. I was surprised that April hadn't come by to see me, but supposed she was spending every minute at Davon's bedside. Vivian ticked her tongue. "I'm not saying that the races shouldn't mix. I mean, I don't see anything really wrong with it, if they love each other. But April, being Brother Allen's daughter and all, well, it hurt the church. Divided us up, you know."

"How do the other women feel about it?" I said.

Vivian glanced around the room, as though mentally casting them on one side or the other. "Most of us just don't know what to think. There are a few, like Nelda over there, whose minds were pretty well made up that Walter was right. But the rest of us, we just want peace in the family, so to speak."

"I suppose," I ventured, "that Mrs. Fry must have agreed with her husband on the issue?"

Vivian shook her head slowly. "Bitsy Fry is a good woman. She wouldn't wish harm on a common housefly. No. I don't think she agreed with Walter. She just didn't oppose him. Brother Walter could be very . . . firm in his views." Vivian Spaulding was given to understatement.

Chapter Twelve

bi-zarre \bə-`zär\ *adj* [R, fr. It *bizarro*] (ca. 1648): strik-
ingly out of the ordinary: as **a:** odd, extravagant, or
eccentric in style or mode . . . **b:** involving sensa-
tional contrasts or incongruities **syn** see FANTASTIC.
——*Merriam Webster's Ninth New Collegiate Dictionary*

"I'm new to the church," I explained. "So, of course, I never
met your husband, but I wanted to express my condolences. I
was touched by your description of him—how he considered all
the children in the church his own. My husband and I don't have
children, that is, not yet. We hope we will in time."

Bitsy and I sat at the front of the room, while Miss Alma helped
Vivian clear the refreshment table and clean up. It was an opportunity I couldn't let pass, and Bitsy seemed more than willing
to talk with me. I wondered guiltily how she would feel if she
knew my real reasons for joining the Mount Sinai Tabernacle
Ladies' Circle.

"I understand exactly, my dear. Walter and I tried for a number of years without success." She reached over to pat my knee
with a plump hand. "Of course, that doesn't mean that you won't
have children eventually. Most couples do. You'll just have to be
patient."

"I'm sure you're right," I agreed quickly, eager to get off
this subject and on to the real point of my visit. "Your husband
was certainly generous to the church, putting up this building
and all."

"Oh my, yes! Not only that, but he left the church a substantial sum of money, too." I responded with an interested look.

"I don't need it, you see," she went on hastily, blushing, as though I might think she resented Walter's generous bequest to the church. "He left me comfortable and secure. But I'm sure you're not interested in my private affairs, after all."

Oh, how wrong she was. I was dying to ask about the two nieces and the mysterious Justine Leroy, but how? Bitsy herself paved the way. She smoothed her skirt and patted her chrysanthemum hair thoughtfully.

"Walter was always generous with the people he cared for. His brother's children—Raymond was taken from us at a young age—Walter did so much for them all. Put his nephew through college and helped him start a business. Computers, of all things! Walter didn't know a thing about them, but he helped Chip get this business going. It's a confusing time for us baby boomers, having to learn about computers. But then, I suppose you have one?"

"No, I don't. Did, er, Raymond have just the one son?"

"Oh no. There are two other nieces. Walter is—was—putting them through college. And he provided for them to finish their educations, so they'll be secure." Secure, I thought, doing what he wanted them to do—the only jobs he considered acceptable for women.

"How thoughtful of him. Did he have any other family?"

Bitsy shook her head sadly. "No. Just Raymond's children." Which told me only that Justine Leroy was not a relative of the late deacon. It didn't tell me who she was.

My first reaction to Miss Alma's news was dismay. "You signed us up to work on the clothing drive?" I pulled into her driveway and cut the engine. "It's not that I mind, Miss Alma, but I don't think I want to get that involved with this church, and it seems kind of deceitful to pretend that we're really going to join," I said. Miss Alma regarded me in silent amusement. "Well, okay, I know I've already deceived them, but . . ."

"Julia, I saw you talking to Elizabeth. Did you learn much?"

I shook my head. "A little. I know this Justine person isn't a relative. But I just met her. I didn't think I could push it that far." I met her steady gaze. "Oh, I get it. You think if we work on the clothing drive, she might open up . . ."

Miss Alma patted my hand. "Good night, my dear. I'll see you on Thursday."

"So, from what I gathered, this Justine Leroy, whoever she is, isn't a member of the family." I pulled my gown over my head and squirted toothpaste onto my brush.

Nick was pulling back the bedcovers. He stopped thoughtfully. "But she didn't say who she is?"

"No, and I thought that might be going too far—to ask, I mean. She'd have clammed up on me and I wouldn't be able to get another word out of her. That's why Miss Alma and I are going over there on Thursday to help sort clothing."

"Hmm. Look, be careful, will you? If somebody thinks you're asking around . . ."

"Mmf." I rinsed my mouth and grabbed a glass of water. "I know. I will. Miss Alma will be with me. You know how she is— she could get the walls to talk."

"So you're just going to pick up her brain, right? No searching through closets, no reading the mail, right?"

Although I privately admitted that this was an interesting idea, and one I hadn't thought of, I responded with appropriate outrage. "Nick! I don't do things like that. Besides, it's just *pick*. Pick her brain."

Nick stood at the dresser, counting his change and depositing it in his little wooden tray. "You know," he said, "it might be easier if you went there with some information of your own. I think it's time for us to meet Justine Leroy."

"And how are we going to do that?"

"I imagine we'll find her at the Vagabond."

It was Nick's turn at the sink, which bought me a few minutes to think. I hadn't told him about seeing the Big Foot in the parking lot. I knew he'd want to go out there and look for Davon's attackers. Tantalus and his buddy. Two men who thought nothing of beating Davon unconscious and digging up graves. Evil, ruthless men. Two of them. And Nick was one man—quick and sure-footed, but fairly small. No way I was letting him face those two alone. But I was going to have to tell him something. And he was going to be mad.

I grabbed Jack off the middle of the bed and dropped him on the floor. He curled his upper lip at me as I climbed into it myself and plumped up the pillows, then leapt back up with a defiant snarl. Nick followed closely behind, taking a moment to remove Jack from his side. "Stubborn dog," he muttered.

"I think," I said, trying to sound casual, "we should take Spiros to the Vagabond with us."

"Spiros? Why? I thought we were trying to fit in."

"Oh, I just think he might enjoy it. It would be a different experience for him, you know?"

"Different for everyone at the Vagabond, too. No, I don't think so."

I twirled a lock of his hair around my fingertip and tickled the tip of his ear. "You know, he never gets out," I said. "Except to take Miss Alma to the grocery store. I think he should be getting out more, meeting new people. Maybe a nice girl . . ."

He pushed my hand away and sat up higher in the bed. "Since when have you been concerned about Spiros's social life?"

"I just think he must be lonely, that's all."

It wasn't working. He eyed me skeptically and sighed deeply. "Okay, what's the real reason you want him to go along?"

Nick tapped a tattoo on the steering wheel with his fingertips and whistled softly through his teeth, now and again looking past me at the house. "Are you going to keep this up all night?" I said.

"Probably."

"Look, I've explained it to you over and over. I didn't want you to get hurt, that's all." It hadn't been a good day. In fact, from the moment I'd told Nick about the Big Foot, he'd been cool and distant. He doesn't lose his temper often, but sometimes I'd rather he did. That freeze-dry treatment of his is far worse than an all-out screaming fight. At least then I know what he's thinking.

"Spiros's going to be miserable if you keep this up. He's going to know something's wrong."

"Oh yeah," he said bitterly. "I forgot. We're getting Spiros out for a little fun tonight."

I let that one go. "Nick, I'm sorry. I apologize. I should have told you, all right? Now, can we forget it?"

In answer, he sat on the horn. "Look," he said, turning on me suddenly. "What I don't understand is why you didn't at least tell Sam your suspicions. You didn't hurt me, but you've hurt Davon and April, and you blew Sam's chance at picking them up."

"I guess I didn't think about it. I was thinking about your nose."

"My nose? What does my nose have to do with it?"

But Spiros's appearance on his front porch so absorbed our attention that I was saved from having to explain further. He grinned and waved, turning back to lock the door, while we stared.

Spiros is a big man. A very big man. He stands a good four inches over six feet, has herculean biceps and thighs like Doric columns. Said thighs were swathed in stiff, new denim that barely skimmed the tops of a pair of needle-nosed cowboy boots. Above a tooled leather belt, a bright white Ponderosa shirt that might have fit Atlas was topped by a black, fringed suede vest. The hat must have come directly from Hoss Cartwright's dressing room. He lumbered down the steps and came toward us, his mustache wildly twitching above a barely visible grin. The remainder of his chin was wrapped in bandanna print.

"Those boots must hurt his feet," I commented. He was walking oddly—sort of knock-kneed and sideways, with his right shoulder rolled forward and his right arm dangling loose at his side.

"Not the boots," Nick said, grinning reluctantly.

"Well, why's he walking that way?"

"He thinks he's John Wayne."

"Kai ee botes, apo tin Argentina." The Duke finished his inventory with the boots, which, apparently, he had acquired in Argentina, just as we were pulling into the parking lot at the Vagabond. Jeans from K Mart, vest and shirt from Mexico, and the belt and hat from a stop in the port of Houston. As a merchant seaman, Spiros had really gotten around. From the look of him, none of his souvenirs had ever been worn. He would not be an inconspicuous companion.

For a Tuesday night, the Vagabond had a tidy little crowd. It made me wonder if we were in the wrong business. The bass was already thumping—that must be Ed Winder and the Sidewinders, according to the portable sign on the side of the road. The bouncers were firmly planted at the door. I smoothed my denim skirt and examined the toes of my suede boots thoughtfully. They weren't really western, but covered my calves to the hem of my skirt. As long as no one looked too closely, they'd probably do.

Nick had come a little closer, with the help of a western shirt from Wal-Mart and a cowboy hat snagged from the window of a resale shop. Nick's one of those men who can wear hats. Even a faux Stetson looked right on him. In fact, it was quite becoming— like a real, live Marlboro man. I was seriously considering the attractive elements of this new man in my life when he grabbed my elbow and steered me toward the door. A flutter of nervous excitement tingled in my stomach, and I wished we'd formulated a plan on the drive out, instead of discussing Spiros's wardrobe.

"Nick," I whispered. "I think we should talk about this."

"I need to see some ID, ma'am." Too late. Now we were going in without a strategy. I flashed the cowboy my driver's license and stumbled through the door.

"Think you can pull this off without talking?" I said, as we searched for the table. Nick's command of English is vastly improved over what it was when we met. His accent, however, is as

134

thick as ever. We were going to stand out in this crowd like a Greek olive in a bowl of grits.

"No, I dun't," he said, sounding for all the world like Ricky Ricardo. *"Pame."*

Nick chose a dark booth that hunkered down to the right of the dance floor. I slid in as quickly and unobtrusively as possible and settled down to study the place. Smoke coiled in tubes of colored spotlights that glided over the dance floor. At the end of the room, a four-piece combo sat on a portable stage—two electric guitars, drums, and a bass. The lead singer, Ed Winder, was alternately crooning into a mike and leaning over to blow on a stationary harmonica. Clever fellow, Ed. The Sidewinders were singing backup and looking bored.

Most of the crowd was on the dance floor performing some sort of a line dance that was far too complicated for me to master in a single evening. Beside me, Nick's feet were already picking out the steps. It is a rare and somewhat embarrassing phenomenon to have a husband who can dance better than his wife. I gently laid a hand on his knee and growled, "We're here to find out about Justine, remember?"

He was spared having to answer by the approach of the waitress in a tight tank top and too short cutoffs—haute couture of Dogpatch. Certain parts of her anatomy seemed to arrive well before the rest of her.

"Hey," she drawled, her eyes brightly flashing between the two men. "What'll y'all have?"

"Gin and tonic," I said. She didn't bother to write it down, but nodded, acknowledging that I had said something. "And you boys?"

Neither man answered. I elbowed Nick. "She asked what you want to drink!"

"Neh? Oh, mia birra."

"Nick!" The lapse into his native tongue was a bad sign—a kind of regression into a more primitive state. His eyes were fastened on the early arrivals, and the waitress was not unaware of it. She pulled a check pad out of her hip pocket and leaned coyly over the table to write. I gave Nick's instep a good shot with the heel of my boot.

"Beer. Uh, Bud, I guess."

"What about you, Spiros? *Ti thelis na pyis?*"

"Whee-skee. A doo-bell."

"He means a double," I explained. She favored him with a wink and flounced away.

"Niko," Spiros said, pulling his notebook out of his pocket. We watched as his finger trailed up and down the pages until he found the word he was looking for. He grinned at Nick. "Voh-lup-too-us, eh?"

"Wan-ton," I corrected.

The bar was located on the other side of the dance floor, but only mirrored tiles and an immense portrait of a Rubenesque reclining nude were visible through the crowd. Thankfully, there was no sign of Tantalus and his buddy.

"Now, how do we find out about Justine Leroy?" I said.

"I don't know. Give me some time to get the layout of the place. Come on, let's dance." Nick grabbed my hand and pulled me out of the booth before I had a chance to resist.

"Nick, I don't know . . ."

"Simple. Come on, I'll show you."

And there we were—out there with the rest of them, Nick's right arm wrapped around my neck, western style. I tried to rest my hand on his shoulder, but he grabbed it and placed it on his hip. "Like that," he said. "Just act like you know what you're doing."

Ed was in fine form, soloing on a Tracy Byrd song: "Keeper of the Stars." I nestled into Nick's arms more comfortably and relaxed, letting him lead me around the floor.

" 'I hold everything, when I hold you in my arms, and I've got all I'll ever need, thanks to the Keeper of the Stars.' "

"Mmm." I was doing a little crooning myself. "Maybe we should come here more often. You know, I like this new look of yours. I've always had a thing for cowboys. And desperadoes." I hugged him a little tighter. He waggled his eyebrows at me.

"Keep that thought for later," he said, and swinging me around, waltzed us farther across the dance floor toward the bar just as Ed Winder wound down.

"What now?" I whispered in Nick's ear. The band broke into a tinny rendition of the Watermelon Crawl.

"I'm outta here," I said, but he grabbed my hand and pulled me back.

"Let's go to the bar," he said, and under his breath, *"Siga, siga."* Slowly, slowly. His undertone was telling me to be casual, unobtrusive.

"Let's sit this one out," I said when we got to the bar. "I want to see how the dance is done before I get out there." Nick ordered a couple of drinks from the bartender, whose badge declared him to be John.

John was a small fellow with Miss Clairol blond hair and a heavy case of postacne scars. His eyes were a deep blue, the color set off by the suspiciously red rims around his lids. He jutted out a square jaw when he spoke, as though daring anyone to question his masculinity, but his gestures were slightly effeminate, and his voice very soft. Not a bartender anyone was likely to spill his guts to, he seemed completely out of place at the Vagabond. We took our drinks and sipped them quietly, watching the dancers.

"Now, folks," Ed Winder drawled into the microphone, "we got us a special treat for y'all tonight, straight from the Lone Star State of Texas. Bonnie, c'mon up here."

A tall, slender dishwater blonde leapt onto the stage. She wore layers of soft, pastel calico prints—skirt, vest, peasant blouse— the kind of thing that makes me look like an overturned basket of laundry, and complemented the outfit with a pair of supple suede boots in the softest shade of dusty blue. Her hair hung to her shoulders in irregular layered strands. On her, the effect was decidedly sexy. On me, it would have looked like one of the string mops from the kitchen.

"Hey, y'all," she cried in a husky voice. "You know what Texas means?" The crowd did not.

"Comes from the Mexican word *Tejas*, meaning friendly. Are y'all friendly tonight?"

They were.

"All right then. I'm here to bring y'all a little bit of Texas. Who's gonna help me down off this ol' stage?" A posse arrived, six sets of male hands holding elbows, shoulders, and other parts that didn't need holding. Bonnie played along, adding a high kick as they swung her off the stage. She reached back to take a hand mike from Ed.

"Now then," she said. "We got us a dance in Texas that y'all need to learn. Everybody heard of the Cotton-Eyed Joe?" Ed's guitar twanged in the background.

"It's in-di-genous," she said carefully, "to my home state. So come on, y'all, let's get friendly. Now, you just line up . . ."

Nick saw his opportunity. He turned back to John, who was wiping his nose on the back of his hand. I stared thoughtfully at my glass.

"Is that Justine?" Nick said.

A sly smile crept over the bartender's lips. "Not hardly. That's Bonnie Wagner. She's traveling with Ed's band right now." His smile implied more.

"Well . . ." Nick glanced around the room. "Is Justine here?"

"Yeah," he said. "She's back in the back, talking with the boss. Why?"

"A friend said to look her up. Do you think we could talk to her?"

John eyed our empty glasses, letting his gaze move from them to the martini pitcher that held his tips on the bar. Nick pulled a ten and a five out of his pocket, ordered us two more drinks, and dropped the five in the pitcher. The Cotton-Eyed Joe was in full swing when John set the drinks and Nick's change in front of us, picked up a bar mop, and swiped it across the rutted wood surface. Nick stared at him a moment, picked up his change, and dropped it into the pitcher, adding a couple of singles on top.

John's mouth twitched. "I almost forgot," he said. "You wanted to see Justine." He turned to his left, heading back toward a door clearly marked "Office."

"You know," I said loudly, "I think we could see better over there." We scooted several seats down, closer to the office door, but Bonnie's instructions were too loud for us to hope to hear anything in the office. We didn't have to. We still got the picture.

The office was poorly lighted, allowing us a dim view of her. Justine Leroy stood with her back to us, her shoulders rigid, her fists balled. She faced a man who stood next to a desk lamp. A cone of light played up onto his face, eerily enhancing the menace fixed in his expression. His feet were planted wide, a necessity to hold up his considerable weight. His complexion was ruddy, his hair sandy brown and turning gray. He reminded me of a bull, ready to charge, and she, with her slim figure and erect posture, the toreador who was enjoying taunting him. John tapped her on the shoulder. She bit out a few words before he pulled the door closed again. His chin jutted forward and his blue eyes snapped as he returned to the bar.

"She's busy with Dub. She'll be out when she can," he added sullenly. Nick murmured his thanks and twitched his eyebrow at me. We turned back to the dancers on the floor.

"Oh no," I groaned. "Look."

jeop-ar-dy \jep-ərd-ē*n* [ME *jeopardie,* fr. AF *juparti* fr. OF *jeu parti* alternative, lit., divided game] **1:** exposure to or imminence of death, loss, or injury: DANGER **2:** the danger that an accused person is subjected to when on trial for a criminal offense.

—*Merriam Webster's Ninth New Collegiate Dictionary*

Spiros is surprisingly light on his feet, but with his enormous height and that Hollywood outfit, he was anything but inconspicuous as he cavorted across the floor to the Cotton-Eyed Joe.

"It was your idea to bring him," Nick reminded me.

"I know. But didn't you tell him—Oh, good." The music had stopped, and Spiros was surrounded by a crowd of women who seemed to be taken in by his John Wayne act. They must have been drinking tequila shooters.

Bonnie was hoisted back onto the stage. She threw her hair back and leaned into the microphone. "Ooo-wee!" she cried. "Ya'll do know how to be friendly." The crowd liked it.

"So," she said, pausing theatrically. "Let's get a little friendlier." The crowd liked that, too, as Bonnie swung into her own version of "Unchained Melody." Spiros chose one of his admirers and pulled her into the center of the floor.

"Come on," I said, grabbing Nick's hand. "I think we'd better try to get close to him."

"You wanted to see me?"

I had almost forgotten why we'd come to the Vagabond in the first place, and turned to Justine Leroy in surprise. I was even more surprised when I got a good look at her. I had not expected her to be so elegant, so poised. I had not expected the intelligent, perceptive eyes that met mine. And I certainly hadn't expected her to be black. Her skin was the soft brown of coffee ice cream.

"Yes," Nick said. "If you're Justine Leroy."

She raised an eyebrow and her pointed chin, appraising us both in a sweeping glance. Her gaze moved on to John, standing in the background and entirely too interested in our conversation. "I was tied up with Dub," Justine said. "I'm sorry you had to wait. Why don't you sit over there." She pointed to a table near the office door. "I'll be with you in just a minute."

We followed her instructions, taking seats where we could see the bar, dance floor, and office door. Justine, meanwhile, remained where she was, checking through the tickets. She questioned John about two of them, eyeing him doubtfully as he offered a sharp retort. She didn't like what he had to say. She led him along the bar, pointing out the spills that needed wiping, the snacks that needed replenishing, the glasses that needed polishing. He wiped his nose on a bar mop, which she summarily snatched from his hands and tossed under the counter, all the while keeping up a running discourse. She watched as he filled an order of drinks, eyeing the exact amount of liquor that went into each glass. Justine knew her business, and as the office door crashed open and her partner charged out, I was reminded that it *was* half hers. Another brief face-off at the bar followed, during which her partner apparently took up for John.

"Who is that guy?" Nick said.

"Dub something—I know, Dub Cantrell. You know, Nick, he's the one who comes on the radio every morning. 'Hey, folks, this is Dub Cantrell out at the Vagabond, and have I got a treat in store for you,' " I said, mimicking Dub's nasal drawl. "He doesn't look like his voice."

Dub Cantrell bombarded the local radio stations every morning. While the ads appeared most often on country stations, he wasn't above attacking fans of the soft and hard rock stations, too, carefully tailoring the ad to appeal to the listener. His ad on the classical station had raised advertising to new levels of absurdity when he pitched the Vagabond to a background of *Ode to Joy*. "Joyful, joyful we wait on thee," he wailed, insulting the intelligence of the listening public of Delphi. He was right up there with the local mobile home moguls and a used-truck salesman named Pinky who ran Pinky's Prestigious Pre-owned Pick-ups, locally known as "Pinky's Rinky Dinkies."

Dub cultivated his good-ol'-boy persona with, apparently, good results. The Vagabond was full. But the man who argued with Justine Leroy at the bar had no straw stuck in his hair. He wore a well-cut, if slightly rumpled, suit, and even from a distance I could see on his right hand a gold ring the size of an oxbow and studded with a massive diamond. Ol' Dub was doing all right. So, apparently, had Walter Fry. Which took me right back to Justine Leroy, who was, at that moment, pulling out her chair at the table.

"Sorry about that. Some problems that needed straightening out." My gaze went back to the bar. John's face was frozen in an expression of cold fury as he glared at us. Standing beside John was Dub Cantrell; his gaze drilled the back of Justine's head. Two words sprang abruptly to mind—*murderous intent*.

"I know how it is," Nick said. "I'm in the restaurant business."

"Oh, then you do know. There's always a problem. You can't get good help or," she said, with a glance over her shoulder, "they're somebody's nephew so you can't fire them." Justine looked down into her glass—sparkling water with a lemon slice. "Well, nephew or not, he's not going to blow my one chance . . ." Her voice trailed off as she seemed to remember that she didn't know us.

"I had a partner once," Nick lied. "Same problem—always hiring family. And he boiled the books, too."

"Cooked, Nick," I said. "The expression is . . ." But Justine looked up with renewed interest.

Nick's no fool. He nodded sagely. "Stealing—cash, product. Lying to the IRS."

"Tax problems?" she said quickly.

Hmm, I thought.

"Matter of fact, Nick's been doing the Taxes Two Step lately himself," I said, laughing at my own pun. Neither of my companions found it very funny. But Justine was definitely interested.

Nick nodded. "The IRS is claiming I owe them money, but I paid it a long time ago." He shook his head. "I wish they'd get their act together."

"Well, the thing is," Justine said, leaning forward and lowering her voice, "it wouldn't surprise me if we do owe them money. I can't get to the books or the canceled checks either."

"What does your accountant say?"

"Don't have one. Dub keeps the books."

Nick shot me a significant glance. "And what does he say about it?"

Justine shrugged. "You know how the IRS is. Dub says it's just an audit, no big deal. If they find we do owe them money, he thinks he can work a deal with the agent."

"That wouldn't be Richard Fortunata, by any chance?" I said.

Justine's eyes widened. "Do you know him? What's he like?"

"*Kali tihee,*" Nick muttered.

"What?"

"Good luck," I translated. "Fortunata's Nick's dance partner."

"Oh," she said, nonplussed. "If we owe the IRS money, it's gonna wreak havoc on our profits. And just when I thought I'd finally made some . . ." Justine viciously stabbed at the lemon slice with her straw. *Finish the thought,* I silently willed her. *Just when you thought you'd finally made some . . .*

Ed Winder had broken into a watered-down George Strait act—"Amarillo By Morning"—but there was no weeping fiddle to back him up. Justine looked over at the stage and, casually turning sideways in her chair, let her glance sweep on to the bar. I followed her eyes.

Dub Cantrell was glaring at us. Our eyes met and he turned away, punched the register, and withdrew a wad of bills, folding them and shoving them into his pocket.

"Look," Justine said. "When your partner was cooking the books—what did you do?"

Think fast, Nick. He did, answering her without hesitation. "I went over everything thoroughly. Uh . . . Dimitri, he did our bookkeeping. But I knew what to look for."

"But I don't," she said morosely. "I only became a partner here a couple of weeks ago. I haven't had time to—"

"I'd be happy to help you any way I can," Nick interjected.

Justine had to give this some thought. The Sidewinders were taking a break. Ed had switched on the canned music and headed for the bar. Justine's glance went back to Dub, now casually mixing drinks and conferring with Ed Winder.

"Of course, you could call in a C.P.A.," I suggested helpfully. This time Nick got my instep.

Justine shook her head. "If I knew that he was up to something . . . but I don't. I mean, I may be wrong. And I've got to keep some sort of working relationship with him. I don't really want him to know that I'm suspicious." She turned back to Nick, as though she had made a decision. "Were you serious about offering to help?"

"Sure," Nick said.

"Dub's going out of town for the weekend. Of course, John will be around on Saturday, but we're closed Sunday. Could you meet me—"

"What time?" Nick said quickly.

" ' . . . like a rhinestone cowboy . . .' " Glen Campbell was almost drowned out by the cheers coming from the corner of the bandstand.

"Oh no!"

His glasses dangled off one ear. He waved Hoss's hat in the air and howled—the Cretan version of "Yee-hah," I suppose. Spiros had found the mechanical bull.

"Nick, he'll break his neck on that thing!"

"He's knows what he's doing, Julia." This I doubted very much.

"Excuse me, sir." One of the doorkeeper-cum-bouncers stood over us. "Didn't I see you drive up in a beige Honda? Well," he went on to Nick's affirmative nod, "I was just out in the parking lot—checking the cars, ya know? I'm afraid you've got a flat."

"Oh darn, Nick, you'd better go ahead and change it now," I said, checking my watch. "It's getting kind of late and we have to open in the morning. I'll see if I can get Spiros off the bull."

"I'll help you with it," the bouncer offered, lingering at the table.

"Right. Thanks," Nick said, stood up, and followed the bouncer across the dance floor.

I turned back to Justine. "You were going to tell us what time—"

"Justine." Dub Cantrell now stood over us. "I need a word with you, if you don't mind."

"Right now?" she said impatiently.

"Sorry, but yeah, right now. We've got a scheduling problem. You've got the Buffalo Girls scheduled in for next week, and Winder claims you had him down for a two-week gig."

"Well, he's wrong. Our agreement was a week now and another week in September, and Ed knows that as well as I do."

"Didn't you have a contract?"

"Since when have we used contracts? Walter was always trying to get you—"

Dub coughed loudly. "Okay, whatever you say. But you're gonna have to straighten him out. We're probably gonna have to buy out the extra week."

Justine rolled her eyes. "All right, I'm coming." But Dub, not to be put off, waited at the table until she stood up.

"Excuse me," she said, turning back to me. She glanced down at her hand, held close in front of her body, and wiggled two fingers at me.

Two o'clock Sunday, they said.

A few of the customers had drifted back onto the dance floor, two-stepping to the canned music of Garth Brooks, but someone had started the bull again and Spiros was giving them their money's worth. I tried waving at him, but with all the wild jostling, I'm sure he couldn't focus on it. I don't know how he was keeping his whiskey down.

"How about a dance, pretty lady?" I swung around, prepared to advise my suitor to get himself a new line, caught my breath, and glanced around the dance floor. Where was Nick? How long did it take to change a tire, anyway?

"I'm sorry," I said. "I'm not much of a dancer. Thanks any—" But he'd caught my hand and, holding it firmly, dragged me toward the dance floor.

"Let go of my hand, please," I said, trying to shake him off. "I said, let go!" But Tantalus, for that's who it was, would not be denied his dance. The bouncers were nowhere to be seen and the rest of the dancers were gazing in each other's eyes or focused incredulously on Spiros and the bull.

"I like to dance close," he said, pulling me against him. In one swift move he had my left arm pinned against my back, under his right, and was holding my right hand in a vise grip. I stared at him stupefied, enraged, and scared witless. He cocked his head and nuzzled his cheek into my hair, casting the shadow of his hat across both our faces. I tried to turn, to look over my shoulder and signal Spiros, but my partner was far taller than I and had wedged my face against his shoulder with his chin.

"You remember me?" he whispered.

"No."

He lifted his chin and stared into my eyes. I swore I would never think of blue eyes as sexy again. A sardonic grin creased his all-too-handsome face and he winked. "Sure ya do!"

"What do you want?" I said.

"Just a dance. Now, you and me, we're gonna two-step right on over to the back door and out to my truck. I like my privacy."

I squeezed my eyes closed, fighting back the hot tears that were threatening to make me more helpless. Instead, memories played across my mind's screen—the way he cleaned his nails with the knife, and the way his eyes obscenely raked over me. And poor Davon lying helpless in his hospital bed. Oh my God, what would he do to me?

The speakers rattled with deafening bass, yet I could hear the shrieks coming from the bull pen. Spiros was still going at it and the tire change was taking too long. I had to get away now, before he could get me out to his truck. I twisted a little and tried to stomp down on his instep, but he was too quick-footed, jerking me harder against him, jerking my left arm up. Pain shot up my arm and into my shoulder.

"Don't be stupid," he whispered, smothering me against his chest.

He smelled of musk and held me so close I could see an ingrown hair on the side of his neck. He wouldn't like that. It would spoil his Clint Eastwood image.

I took a deep breath, praying I'd be heard over all the other noise. "Let me—"

Tantalus squeezed my thumb below the knuckle until I yelped in pain. "Shut up," he snarled, and continued dancing me toward the bar and the back door. His chin dug into my temple and my left arm was pinned so tightly under his that if I wriggled, he could simply jerk it up and snap it in two. And there was my elbow—the thought of it unhinged and dangling. My hand limp. My knees buckled and I started to sag to the floor. He pulled me up with a vicious jerk.

"Please," I said. "Just tell me what you want."

"I wanna know what the hell you're doing here."

"Dancing," I said, trying to ease my head out from under his chin.

"What else?" he said, applying new pressure to my thumb.

"Nothing," I whimpered. "Just having a good time. It's a public place."

"But you've never been here before."

"Yes I have," I argued, until he softly clasped the edge of my ear with his teeth. "Well, not inside," I amended.

"What're you talking to Justine for?" Teeth on ear again.

"Look, my husband and I are in the restaurant business. We got to talking and . . . I guess she's new at this. Anyway, she wanted advice."

I could see, peripherally, that we were nearing the back door on the opposite side of the bar from the office. It was marked

Emergency Use Only, but its alarm, I was sure, had been disengaged. He spun us around abruptly, so that he was pushing me toward the door. I was now invisible to the rest of the dance floor.

"What kind of advice?" His nibbling was starting to hurt—really hurt. And this, I thought, was only the beginning of what he was prepared to do to me. Warm blood trickled down into my ear and over the side of my jaw. A wave of nausea and pain swept over me. This was the time to pray, and pray, I did. *Please, God, send Nick. Please, God, help me.*

"Just business kind of stuff. Please, I'm going to be sick—"

"*Karioli!*"

Tantalus's hat flew back off his head, uncovering his face—openmouthed and scarlet with rage as he was wrenched away from me. He spat and blood trickled over his lower lip. Nick's right arm was tightly clamped around his neck, knee squarely lodged in the small of his back. Tantalus towered over him by almost a foot, but Nick's a soccer player—wiry, with wrestler's legs. He hurled Tantalus away from me, sending him careening toward the bar. He hit it with a revolting thud and rose up, smashing his head on a glass shelf. Shattered glass flew everywhere as he crumpled to the floor on his face. Before he could pull himself up, Nick was straddling him and tickling his carotid artery with a shard of glass.

"Son of a—"

"No, Nick. Don't!" Nick shot me an angry glance and reluctantly dropped the glass.

It probably would have been all right then if Tantalus's buddy hadn't seen the whole thing. I screamed, but not quite in time to warn Nick. He rolled off Tantalus and scrambled to his feet, only to be bulldozed again by Beefy. He had Nick's throat in his massive paws and was pounding his head on the floor. I kicked at the big man's backside, vainly trying to make contact with a more vulnerable spot. When that didn't work, I grabbed a barstool.

It did not work like it does in the movies. It did not splinter and knock Beefy within spitting distance of the netherworld. Instead, a shock wave traveled up my arms and into my shoulders, something like the kick of a twelve-gauge shotgun. I stared down at Beefy and Nick, unable to comprehend my failure until a hand at my elbow pulled me away. Beefy was big. Spiros was bigger. They reeled across the dance floor like a pair of circus bears.

Tantalus was staggering to his feet by then and lunging for Nick. Nick came off the floor in a handspring and threw a neat right cross. Tantalus fell back with a scream. Who would have known he had a glass jaw? The last I saw of Beefy, he was riding the bull.

"I can't hold 'em for your friend's assault, Nick," Sam said.

"Why not?" Nick was in his face, his dark eyes gleaming with rage.

Sam stepped backward a pace. "Because Folsom's still in a coma. Nobody else saw the attack."

"But I know it was them!"

I tugged at Nick's arm gently. "I don't feel too well," I said, dabbing at my ear with a bloody bar mop. "Could we please sit down?" Nick led me to a table next to the dance floor. Sam pulled out my chair.

He had insisted on calling the paramedics, who arrived just in time to defuse the tension. They cleansed and bandaged my ear and admonished me to see a doctor immediately, before turning to Nick's sliced fingers. Nick agreed to take me by the emergency room on the way home. It would probably mean a tetanus shot. I wondered if a rabies shot might also be in order.

Dub Cantrell had apparently left by the back door just about the time Nick flattened his opponent. Justine had been on the phone dialing 911. John, it seemed, had been somewhere under the bar. He watched us now, with a sort of wary amusement glittering in his eyes. It would all be duly reported to Dub, if not by Justine, then by this prominently placed, slimy little weasel. Justine, after repeated and profound apologies, had busied herself with the closing and cleanup.

"Look, knowing and seeing ain't the same thing, Nick. Hell,

I *know* Sherman marched through Georgia, but I didn't *see* him do it."

"All right." Nick sighed wearily. "I get your point. So what can we do?"

"Well, for starters, Julia can swear out a complaint for assault and battery." I glanced over at Tantalus and Beefy, leaning over the bar while Sam's men clamped them into cuffs. Tantalus's eyes met mine in the mirror, and for a moment I was really afraid. Again. I turned to Sam before my resolve could crumble.

"You want a complaint? You got a complaint. No problem," I said, sounding somewhat more confident than I felt. "But I want you to go for a restraining order, too, Sam."

"You got that right," Sam agreed, nodding, and took us both in with a sweeping gaze. "Now, will y'all please stay the hell outta my case?"

Jack gently licked my earlobe before moving on to my chin and nose. "Okay," I said, pushing him off my lap. "That's about all the sympathy I can stand."

Nick put a mug of warm cocoa in my hands and tucked the covers around me. I kicked them off. "It's summer, Nick. It's too hot for a blanket." I took a sip of the cocoa. He'd spiked it with a little rum. Not bad, even on an eighty-seven-degree night.

"The doctor said to take it easy and watch for signs of infection."

"Well, he didn't say to roast me."

A flicker of hurt crossed Nick's features. He dropped onto the bed and stroked my hair back off my forehead. "I'm sorry," he said.

"It's not your fault."

"But I should have been there. That tire—somebody let the air out."

"That little viper—what's his name? John?"

"No," Nick said. "He never left the bar. Must have been one of the other two. The big one, probably."

"Besides," I continued, "you got there just in time. I don't know what I would have done if you hadn't . . . Nick, what was he going to do to me?"

Nick pulled me into his arms and held me carefully, trying not to put pressure on my ear. The bite was small—a puncture wound that required cleaning and a little bandage. It was the bruising that really hurt. I felt Nick's jaws grind against my head.

"I'm going to make sure they keep that guy locked up for a thousand years," he said.

I shuddered and nuzzled deeper into my husband's arms. "I'm not sure they're going to be able to hold him long, Nick. A bite's probably just a misdemeanor."

"Don't worry," he said, rubbing my back in gentle circles. "He'll never hurt you again."

We didn't go in to the Oracle the next morning. After the previous night's "fee-stee-cuffs," as Spiros gleefully termed it, we were too exhausted to answer the six-o'clock call of the clock radio.

Dub Cantrell was in high form as, over the airwaves, he guaranteed me a night at the Vagabond that I would not soon forget. "Too true," I muttered, and slapped at the alarm with enough force to send Jack leaping off his chair with a guttural snarl. I rolled over, considered getting up, and quickly abandoned the idea. Rhonda and Spiros could be relied upon to get the coffee perking and bacon sizzling without us—a rare and fortunate condition in this business, I thought, as I drifted away again.

I was, however, up before Nick. My ear had throbbed throughout the night as I had restlessly tossed through a series of vivid nightmares which always seemed to end on the bed of a pickup truck. I'd probably kept Nick awake through most of it. I had vague, warm memories of being held and comforted, alternating with terrifying visions of battery and rape. The midmorning light pouring through my own bedroom window was a welcome gift.

After a cursory investigation of his bruises, which were legion, I left Nick snoring softly and stumbled into the kitchen to microwave a cup of day old-coffee. I have no principles when it comes to caffeine. Jack, not being a morning dog, had to be bribed into a quick trip into the yard. He was back, and waiting for a treat, before the microwave buzzed.

I hadn't even brushed my hair, and was standing in the kitchen in an oversized T-shirt, guzzling a dark and murky brew, when the doorbell rang. Without regard to my appearance, which, being only half-awake, I had forgotten, I threw open the door to a tall, slender man with an austerely sculpted face.

"Mrs. Lambros?" His astonished gaze took me in from my bare toes to the cumbersome bandage which had come unstuck and was dangling from my right ear. Jack raised his lip in a sneer and gave his best impersonation of a guard dog.

It was no way to face Allen McNabb.

pa-ter-fa-mil-i-as \pat-ər-fə-ˈmil-ē-əs, pät-, pāt-\
n pl **patres familias** \pā- trēz, pä-trās-\[L, fr. *pater* fa-
ther + *familias,* archaic gen. of *familia* household—more
at FATHER, FAMILY] **1:** the male head of a household **2:** the
father of a family.
                    —*Merriam Webster's Ninth New Collegiate Dictionary*

"Oh!" I said. "Reverend McNabb, isn't it?"

A dour smile cracked his face. He glanced at his watch. "It
must be earlier than I realized," he said, pointedly puzzling over
his watch.

"No . . . that is, my husband and I were up very late last night."

His glance went to my bandage, and his lips pinched together
with stern disapproval. "Is your husband at home?"

"Yes, but he didn't . . ." I fingered the bandage nervously. I
was only making matters worse. "Yes, yes, he is," I said, opening
the door wider. "Won't you come in?"

He stepped into the foyer and glanced down at a card in his
hand. "You didn't say whether you wanted to be visited or not, but
I was in the neighborhood . . ." So that was it. The visitor's card I
had filled out at the church. Allen McNabb was on a recruiting
mission.

I was not interested in being drafted into the ranks of the
Mount Sinai Tabernacle Christian soldiers on a permanent basis,
but even in my stupor I realized that this was a chance too good
to pass up.

". . . should come back at a more convenient time."

"No!" I think I rather startled him. "Now is good," I continued smoothly. "My husband and I aren't home very much. You just happened to catch us on an unusual day." I showed him into the living room. "Just let me run and slip into something . . . uh, change my clothes. I'll be with you in a minute."

"Nick!" I said, pulling off my T-shirt. "Wake up. We've got company."

He threw his arm across the bed and groped for me. Coming up with only empty air, he jimmied an eye open.

"I said, we've got company."

"*Ti eine?*"

"You won't believe me," I whispered, slipping into a pair of sandals. "It's Allen McNabb—April's father. Get up. Hurry!"

I left him sitting on the side of the bed, scratching his head and staring vacantly at the wall. By the time he threw on a pair of sweats and was semifit to join us, I had put on a fresh pot of coffee and was stalling McNabb with small talk. Nick appeared in the doorway, and for the first time I realized how bad the bruising was. He was walking stiffly and his neck was a mass of purple mounds, the result of Beefy's big paws hammering his head against the floor. That Reverend McNabb was shocked was apparent; that he figured we'd been battering each other, painfully transparent, although why he would vault to such a conclusion was beyond me. He obviously considered us very much in need of evangelizing, as he launched right into his agenda before either of us had a chance to explain.

Had we accepted Christ as our personal savior? We had. Were we able to turn to Him in our moment of need? I thought of the previous night and the way I had prayed for help, answering with an emphatic affirmative. Well then, did we currently belong to a church? This one was a bit tougher.

We were not, strictly speaking, members of a church, although we attended St. Jude's Catholic Church with semiregularity. We were, I felt, in a holding pattern. Nick was Greek Orthodox, and although there had been a recent increase in the number of Greeks in Delphi, mainly among the Parnassus student population, it was still insufficient to warrant a church. Occasionally the itinerant priest passed through Delphi, stopping long enough to celebrate a Liturgy and visit at the Oracle, but we were a long way from establishing a church. St. Jude's offered the only viable alternative and was comfortable for me, a Catholic from the cradle.

But I knew in my heart that Nick would never become a Catholic. His heritage of Orthodoxy was too deep—not only a question of faith, but a matter of culture. For my part, not having an Orthodox community in Delphi allowed me to indefinitely postpone a decision. Would I become Orthodox at some point? I did not, at that time, have any idea.

But none of this was shared with Allen McNabb. I didn't think he would really understand it. Instead, we affirmed that we attended St. Jude's.

"Tell me," he said. "Do they have a marital counseling program?" Out of the corner of my eye, I saw Nick stiffen. He had not missed the implications of the question. Since domestic violence is a problem that Nick abhors, this couldn't be sitting too well with him.

"Oh yes, an excellent program," I quickly assured him. "And family counseling as well."

"I assume, then, that you weren't looking for a church when you visited with us at Mount Sinai," he said. Nick and I exchanged glances across the living room before I plunged in.

"Not exactly. No." McNabb waited for me to expand on my answer. Nick was not forthcoming with any help.

"Actually, Reverend McNabb, I came to see you. You've probably forgotten, but we met before." I reminded him of our meeting at the funeral home and my renewed friendship with April. Aloof as he was, his expression grew even colder and more remote as I spoke.

"I'm afraid I don't understand," he said. "What did you want from me?"

"Well, I thought maybe there was something I could do to help. I know April must need all the support she can get from her friends and family."

"I couldn't possibly say what April needs. I have not understood that child since she was thirteen years old, and I certainly don't understand her now." Rising from his chair, he shook his head emphatically. "And I didn't come here to talk about my daughter with perfect strangers. I'll be leaving you now."

"Look, Reverend McNabb," I said, blocking his exit. "You and I both know that April did not kill Walter Fry. My husband and I are doing everything we can to help her attorney find the real murderer."

"You might start by convincing her to get another attorney— one of her own kind," he said. "I have no influence with my daughter, Mrs. Lambros. She has turned her back on her family. Why should she expect help from us now?"

"Because," I answered evenly, "she is your daughter and despite what you may think, she still loves you very much. Have you no feeling for her?"

"Of course I have feeling for her," he shot back angrily. "Do you have children, Mrs. Lambros?"

"No," I said.

Nick wrapped his arm around my shoulder and pulled me close to him. "My wife miscarried not too long ago," he said. He was keeping his anger admirably in check, I thought. A flicker of sympathy softened Allen McNabb's hard features, but disappeared as quickly as it had surfaced.

"Then you can't possibly know what it's like to have a child humiliate and betray you." He turned away from us, as though he would take a seat again. But instead he remained standing, speaking in a voice so low I had to strain to hear him.

"When she's little, she wraps her hand around your little finger and follows you wherever you go. She comes to you with her problems because she knows you'll solve them. Everything in her world is 'Daddy,' " he whispered softly.

"And then one day, that love, that trust, isn't there anymore. She'd rather be with her friends, listening to their filthy music. She won't come to church with you. People see her around town and they tell you all about it—who she's with, what she's doing. Oh yes, everyone loves to find fault in a preacher and his family.

"Walter knew that. He was a preacher's son himself. We tried to control her."

"We?"

He turned around, regarding me with some surprise. "Walter and I. His father didn't tolerate riotous living either. But April was incorrigible and she left me no choice but to cut her out of my life for the good of the church."

"But when it came down to it, you stood up against Walter Fry."

"You asked me whether I care about my daughter, Mrs. Lambros. The answer is yes. I love my daughter. And despite what you might believe about me, I loved my grandson, too. Besides, I was obligated to comply with the law. Walter could take a stand against it, but the law compelled me to bury Damien in our cemetery, and there was nothing he could do about it."

So there it was. Walter Fry was the most powerful man in Mount Sinai Tabernacle Church. He owned it; it was bought and paid for with gifts of a fellowship hall and bequests in his will. The church, as he viewed it, was the legacy of his father—to be cared for in his father's tradition. *His father didn't tolerate riotous living,* McNabb had said. He certainly would not have approved of the material gains such living provided.

I was beginning to get a slightly different picture of Walter Fry. He was a psychoanalyst's dream—a manifestation of just about every personality theory in existence. Id, ego, and super-ego at war, Oedipal conflicts, the child within him battling the adult—not to mention more current psychojargon. But Walter Fry was definitely not okay by anyone's standards.

Fry had continued the raging battle with his father long after the esteemed Reverend Fry was in the grave. Walter was a viper's nest of slippery, slithering conflicts. He must have been bursting with self-hatred—able to function only by projecting his guilt on everyone else.

Then there was his hatred for minorities. Here he could channel all his sublimated rage—against blacks, ethnics, probably women—against anyone who was different, more liberated than he. In April he had found the ultimate burnt offering. She, a woman and a preacher's daughter, had chosen a black man for her mate. Fry could manipulate, punish, and control her. He could expiate all his guilt on her altar. Or so he had subconsciously thought. But he had underestimated the courage of April McNabb Folsom.

Fry would have the church run as he wanted, using bribery and intimidation without qualm because his own mental health depended upon it. I wondered whether he had threatened Allen McNabb with losing his pastorate if he didn't get control over his daughter or cut her out of his life. Nick's train of thought was traveling the same track as mine.

"Walter Fry is dead," Nick said softly. "Won't you help April now?"

Allen McNabb shrugged. "She doesn't want my help. I went to see her at the jail, but she wouldn't have any part of me. You saw her at the funeral, how she defied me and threatened him. Besides," he added, "I don't know where she was that night."

And where, I wondered, was he?

"So the good news is," I said, fingering the fresh bandage on my ear, "Sam's got them locked up. I pressed charges against them this afternoon. Even if they do get out, and Sam will delay that as long as possible, they'll probably lie low for a while. They won't want to risk another trip to jail." I turned to Chester Folsom. "I think you can stop going out to the cemetery at night. They'd be stupid to go out there and try anything else."

Chester glanced over at Davon, still unconscious and hooked to beeping, blipping monitors as though he were some sort of technological creature instead of warm, living flesh. "You don't know people like that, Miz Lambros. They never give up." He shrugged. "But I haven't been going anyway. D'Anita's friend Rodney, he goes out there and watches over things so I can relieve my wife and April at the hospital."

"Has there been any change in Davon's condition?"

"The doc says he might be starting to come out of it. Brain swelling's down and his eyes—the pupils are about the same size. Candice says it's a good sign. Me, I just don't know."

Chester got up and moved over to the bedside, rearranging the covers around Davon's neck. It was the helpless gesture of a man who wanted desperately to help and comfort his son. He spoke quietly in Davon's ear.

"Come on, son. You wake up now, you hear me? I need you to wake up." He waited for a minute at the bedside, studying Davon's still features before returning to his seat.

"It isn't right, you know," he said. "Ever since he was a little fella, Davon wasn't like other boys. He's always been kinda gentle. Didn't get in fights like the other kids, unless he was fighting for D'Anita. He never took anything when it came to his sister. Not that she needed him fighting her battles for her," he added. "D'Anita's always been tougher than her brother. Nobody but nobody's gonna walk on our D'Anita.

"No, Davon was never like the others. He came home in the afternoon, got straight on his homework, and when he was done, he came down to the shop to help me out." Chester Folsom smiled sadly. "He knew how to change oil and adjust a carburetor by the time he was nine years old."

"Smart," Nick said, with an approving nod.

"He's smart, all right," Chester agreed. "You know he was going to Parnassus? Already finished one semester. He was gonna study engineering. But—"

We waited while he decided whether to go on. At length he continued. "April, she came along and Davon couldn't see past getting married with her. His mama and I . . . well, we wanted them to wait, but then there was the baby, and we thought he should do the right thing by the girl."

"But it meant a pretty big change of plans, didn't it?"

"Yes, a big change in his plans. But you know, Davon wanted that baby more than anything in this world. He loves April."

"I know he does," I said. "But it must have been hard for you to sit by and watch him blow his plans over a girl."

159

Chester Folsom glanced warily from Nick to me. I would have given anything to know what he was really thinking. He shrugged philosophically. "We haven't given up on college. Davon can do anything he puts his mind to. I told you he was smart. There's always night school. He can help me in the shop and go at night. April, she thinks it's a good idea, too."

We all inadvertently glanced at the still form on the bed, knowing too well that he was begging the question. The possibility existed, however remotely, that Davon would never regain consciousness. And even if he did, he might never regain the use of all of his faculties. The prospects were daunting. I even wondered if, should the worst happen, April loved Davon enough to stick by him. And that, I decided, might be exactly what Chester Folsom was thinking. But then, I reminded myself, there were good signs as well. The swelling and intracranial pressure were down, and he was breathing on his own. The trach tube had been removed and the ventilator pushed into a corner of the room where it remained as a reminder that progress, however slow, was progress after all.

"I was hoping to see April," I said quickly. "Did she go home?"

Chester shook his head. "L.T. picked her and Candice up an hour or so ago. Some kind of hearing at the courthouse. L.T. says it's routine. Case probably won't go to trial for at least two to three more weeks. Maybe not then."

"Why not?"

Chester examined the back of his hands thoughtfully. "L.T.'s wanting to change the plea to manslaughter. If April agrees, she won't have to go to a trial."

Nick and I exchanged glances. Apparently L.T. didn't have much faith in our investigative skills. He was still pushing for a manslaughter plea.

"Tell me, Mr. Folsom," Nick said. "Do you agree with him?"

"I'm no lawyer, Mr. Lambros. I don't know the first thing about any of it, but I know L.T. He's a good lawyer, and he's been a friend of the family for years. I trust him, and if that's what he thinks, then I'd advise April to listen." His eyes strayed to the bed as he continued. "I don't know how Davon's gonna take it when he wakes up, though."

"Davon," I reminded him, "was against it. He wanted April to plead not guilty, and I don't think she's going to change her mind."

"You may be right, Miz Lambros. I just don't know."

We sat in silence then, each occupied with his own thoughts. For my part, I was worried that we weren't making enough progress on the case to satisfy L.T. If I forced myself to be completely honest, I wasn't sure we knew much more than we had before we started. L.T. was pressuring April because time was running out and he didn't think he had a case. We had to prove that there were legions of potential murderers out there, and all of them had a reason to want a crack at Walter Fry.

Justine Leroy benefited from Fry's death. And if what Nick thought was true, so did Allen McNabb, if only because it released him from Fry's domination of the church. And what about Joy? If Fry had been responsible for the breach with her daughter, wasn't that reason enough to want to kill him?

Then there were the Folsoms to consider. The incident over the burial must have been humiliating and dehumanizing for them. Any one of them might have wanted to kill over it. Of all of them, D'Anita was the most hostile, and we were fairly sure that she was hanging out with at least one known criminal.

Dub Cantrell benefited from Fry's death, and he might have thought he would gain more than a small insurance policy. Did he know the terms of Fry's will? If he'd thought that Bitsy would inherit Fry's half of the Vagabond, he might have been greasing the way to a quick buy-out. Justine could be an unexpected fly in the naval jelly.

And finally I came to Bitsy Fry. Was she all that she appeared? Frankly, she had my sympathy—not because she'd lost her husband, but because she'd had to live with him for so many years. Maybe finally she'd just gotten fed up with it.

Chapter Fifteen

in·sin·u·ate \in-ˈsin-yə-wāt\ *v* **-at·ed; -at·ing** [L *insinuatus,* pp. of *insinuare,* fr. *in-* + *sinuare* to bend, curve, fr. *sinus* curve] . . . **2:** to introduce (as oneself) by stealthy, smooth, or artful means . . . to ingratiate oneself syn see INTRODUCE, SUGGEST.

—*Merriam Webster's Ninth New Collegiate Dictionary*

"Well, I have to agree with Nick," Miss Alma said, after I had explained the bandage on my ear. "I'm not sure it's a good idea for you to be going either."

"Oh, I'm all right. The tricky part is explaining the bandage. I think we'll just say that Jack got a little carried away playing ball and nipped my ear, all right?"

Miss Alma agreed, and that was the story we told when we arrived at Bitsy Fry's house. We were met at the door by Vivian Spaulding, who helped us with the six garbage bags full of clothing we hauled out of the car. I'd finally convinced Nick to part with the last suit he'd brought from Greece, along with assorted sweaters and pants he'd long since outgrown. Nick's put on a little weight since he stopped playing soccer regularly.

On my part, the decision was harder. I was tempted to get rid of the few maternity clothes I'd accumulated on the premise that the old wives' tale was true—disposing of them is the quickest route to pregnancy. Personally, I thought the expressway to pregnancy involved two people and was considerably more diverting, so I opted to keep the clothes. I did, however, reluctantly tender an assortment of woolen garments that harked back to my New England undergrad days. I'd kept them for those infrequent times when our mountain weather kicked in with snow-storms and bitter wind chills, but as Nick pointedly reminded me, the homeless spent far more time out in the cold than I.

Although a number of women from the church circle had dropped off clothes, only Vivian had stayed to help sort them. Bitsy Fry's washing machine was merrily chugging in the laundry room. "She insists on washing everything," Vivian explained. "Bitsy treats these people like her own family."

"All right," said Bitsy, peering over a load of clothes fresh from the dryer. "I think we'll sort by size and gender. Oh, hello, Alma. Julia." I was amazed that she could call our names to mind so quickly. "How nice of you to come and help."

Bitsy dumped the clothes on her dining room table—a ma-hogany Chippendale with a mirror gleam. Her cheeks were rosy from the warmth of the dryer, and her hair was slightly tousled, hanging in soft wisps around her face. A pretty young face emerged from the slightly corpulent folds, allowing me a glimpse of what a lovely young woman she must have been. But maybe it was not so much her regular features as her animated expression and the bright glow in her china blue eyes that stuck in my mind. It made me wonder how a man such as Walter Fry had ever at-tracted her in the first place. Surely the man must have had some redeeming qualities.

"Let's make the den the ladies' area, and put the men's and boys' clothes in the living room. We're washing everything as we go, and let's set aside anything that needs mending. I'll take care of those later. Watch for holes in the socks. They'll have to be darned."

I didn't know anyone darned socks anymore and expressed the thought. "Oh," Bitsy said vaguely, "I don't suppose many peo-ple do. Walter never wore a pair of darned socks in his life, but I do know how to do it. In fact, I'm quite good. And I don't want any socks going to the shelters with holes in them. These people deserve as good as we can give them.

"Now," she continued, becoming quite businesslike, "Alma, you and Vivian start sorting and folding these." She pointed to the pile on the dining table. "When you get finished, we'll stack them in the respective rooms. Julia and I will open all the bags and sort them for washing.

"I do hope someone included some underthings," she went on as she led me into the attached garage. To my horror the bags were stacked shoulder high over half the garage, and the air in there was as hot and thick as cream gravy. It was going to be a long day.

"People rarely seem to remember them—they just cut them up for rags. But you know, I think nice underthings give us such a feeling of . . . of dignity." Although I had never connected bras, panties, and Jockeys with dignity, I could see what she meant.

By midmorning we had only sorted a quarter of the bags. Bitsy insisted on hand-washing anything that looked remotely delicate at a big utility sink in the corner of the garage. She had strung a line from the garage door to the window and carefully pegged the hand-washing there to dry.

"You're quite a pro at this," I said. "I guess you've done it before."

Bitsy raked her hand through her hair and fanned herself with a pink satin slipper. "Oh my, yes, I've been doing these drives for about four years now, and I've got it down to a science. I even convinced Walter to buy me a heavy-duty washer and dryer last year. I can do so much more laundry at one time in them." A little frown tugged at the corners of her mouth. "I wish he could be here to see how much they helped."

At last, an entrée, and I couldn't think of a thing to say. I was there as a spy, on false pretenses—not because I was interested in the plight of the homeless. I felt like a worm.

Fortunately, Bitsy didn't notice my silence. In fact, she didn't just open the conversational door—she grabbed my hand and yanked me through it. "You know, there's been so much brouhaha about April's baby and all, and since you didn't know him, well, I don't want you to hear people talking and get the wrong idea about my husband. My Walter was a very generous man."

"He must have been—giving that building to the church and all."

She batted her hand at me, as if to say that was a minor thing. "Let me get us a Coke," she said. "I think we deserve a little rest, don't you?" Without waiting for an answer, she left, returning shortly with two cans of Coke, ice-cold and already beading with perspiration—not unlike me. She dropped down on an unopened bag, waited while the air squished out, and patted another one for me. I willingly complied.

"Of course," she said, continuing as though there had been no time lapse, "he made sure Raymond's children would get their education, and he left me very secure. I'll never have to worry about the roof over my head or putting food on the table."

And? my inner voice screamed. *What else? What was Justine Leroy to Walter Fry?* But Bitsy would not talk without a little prodding. I picked up a cane someone had contributed with the clothes and poked at the unopened bags.

"You know, I met someone the other day who knew your husband," I said casually.

Bitsy's reaction to the name Justine Leroy simply was to nod her head, confirming that she knew of Justine's existence. "Yes," she said, "Justine worked for my husband and his partner in one of his businesses."

"The Vagabond," I prompted her.

She responded with a deep sigh and a shake of her head. "Yes. The Vagabond," she repeated sadly.

I waited. Surely more would be forthcoming. Walter Fry's partnership in a country western dance hall and bar was very much at odds with his public persona. Even Bitsy must have realized that. She didn't disappoint me.

"You must wonder . . . Walter being a preacher's son and all. You see, Walter and his partner, Dub Cantrell, went to school together. Dub had been down on his luck for some time when he had the opportunity to buy the Vagabond. It was a barbecue restaurant at the time. Walter was doing very well in business, so he agreed to help Dub buy it and become a silent partner. It was quite a shock to my husband when Dub turned it into a dance hall, I can tell you that."

"I'm surprised he didn't sell out right away. I mean, he must have disapproved of the business."

Bitsy picked up a sweater lying on top of the stack of clothing and absentmindedly began pulling off the little pills that betrayed its years of use. "He did, of course. But he thought that if he stayed in, he might be able to influence Dub to tone the place down—gradually turn it back into a restaurant. Besides, he thought it would put him in contact with people who needed his help—you know, people who weren't saved."

Was Bitsy Fry really dim-witted enough to buy in to this subterfuge? But, I reminded myself, we can all be blind to the faults of the people we love. Besides, Walter, having had a lifetime of practice, was a very adept liar.

"But Walter didn't really work in the business. In fact, Dub and I were the only ones who knew he owned half of it. And, of course, I made it clear to him that I would never want any part in it."

"Well," I said, "I think it was nice that he left it to one of his employees. I hear it's a very profitable business. Justine should be doing pretty well." Bitsy glanced up at me, startled.

"Being in the restaurant business," I explained, "we naturally hear about how the other restaurants and bars in the area are doing. Nick belongs to the chamber of commerce, of course, and . . ."

She nodded knowingly. Bitsy was very naive. "Walter always helped his employees. He was very concerned about them all. If I tell you something, will you promise to keep it to yourself?" I certainly did.

"Well," she went on, "Walter had little pet charities that no one knew about. Sometimes he'd meet a young person and he'd say to me, 'Sugah'—he always called me 'sugah'—'Sugah,' he'd say, 'I'd like to help this young person out. Give them a good start in life, you know? How do you feel about it?'

"Well, of course, how could I refuse? We didn't have children of our own." Bitsy's voice was now almost inaudible. "Justine's black, you know. Well, of course you do, if you've met her. Walter always believed that the blacks should have equal opportunity." Separate but equal, I silently amended.

"And Justine's not the first, you know. There have been several others—two or three at least. One of them went to cosmetology school and another one became a stewardess. Why, one even became a teacher! Yes, that's three, isn't it?" Bitsy beamed triumphantly.

"But I don't understand. Why don't you want people to know? It's nothing to be ashamed of, after all."

Bitsy's head bobbed up and down, a chrysanthemum blowing in the wind. "Oh no! Walter never wanted anyone to know, though. I suppose he thought, well, some people might take advantage of him. I'm just honoring his request."

"He sounds very generous," I lied.

Bitsy patted my knee and gushed effusively. "You know, I knew there was some reason I was telling you my whole life story. You're so easy to talk to! But . . ." Her expression darkened. "You see, there are some people around here," she said, glancing about the empty garage. "They think Walter was prejudiced. But you can see he wasn't. He used to say to me, 'Sugah, if God didn't intend for them to be different, He would have made them white. But He didn't make them white. He made them black, and He gave them a place all their own in this world.'"

"I'm sure they were very grateful," I said dryly. "It must have made you proud."

"Oh," she said, "I never met any of them, and I don't even remember their names now. But I like to think of those young people out there, making their way in the world, and all because my Walter gave them a leg up."

Having finished with the sweater, she folded it neatly and stood up, glancing around at the bags and piles. "We have a lot of women's and children's clothes here," she said absently. "But we need more for the men. A lot more. I've set aside Walter's clothes . . ." Bitsy turned to me. "I wonder if you'd do me a favor. Walter's clothes are all clean and pressed. I've stacked them on his bed. But I don't think I can——" She broke off suddenly and turned away. I could see her dabbing at her eyes and composing herself.

"You'd like me to get them?" She nodded, a quiet sob her only answer.

I didn't wait for her to direct me to the bedroom. She needed a few minutes alone with her grief, and although the house was large, I was confident that I could find my way. Besides, I was eager to get a look around.

I found the master bedroom behind the third door I tried. There was no doubt I was in the right place. One of the single beds was piled high with neatly laundered and folded shirts, suits, and sport jackets still in their dry-cleaner bags, and boxes of shoes, underwear, and sundries. I took a minute to glance around the room.

Everything was spotless. White Martha Washington bed-spreads covered single beds with heavy mahogany headboards, an anachronism in any master bedroom dating after the fifties. Matching dressers, nightstands, and a single Duncan Phyfe chair that looked as though it had belonged in Grandma Fry's dining room completed the suite. The walls were a noncommittal mint green, decorated with large reproduction watercolors of southern flowers—magnolia, dogwood, and azalea blossoms. It was a serene room, much like Bitsy herself, but I thought it lacked character and told me little or nothing about their relationship. Perhaps that in itself said a lot.

Walter's nightstand held only a white ginger-jar lamp and princess phone. Bitsy's displayed a matching lamp, a stack of books, and a collection of sundries. Anxious to appear busy, I scooped up a carton of neatly shined shoes and carried them to the living room.

This was my chance, I reminded myself along the way. Now was the time to explore, look for information. *Snoop!* my conscience accused me. *April,* I reminded it. If I didn't do all I could, April McNabb Folsom would be convicted of a murder I didn't believe she had committed. My conscience thus assuaged, I returned to the bedroom primed to pry. First stop, the dressers.

Bitsy's chest was a low double dresser displaying a small assortment of crystal and gold filigreed jewelry boxes and cut-glass perfume bottles. I didn't have to open the boxes to see that they contained little more than a vast collection of Monet and Trifari costume jewelry reproductions. Walter had not believed in showering his wife with gold and gems. I would not open the dresser drawers. I do have my limits, after all.

Walter's bureau was of little more interest. There were photographs—high school yearbook photos, I supposed—of Raymond's children. A wooden change tray held an assortment of foreign coins, his watch, and his wedding band. I stared at the latter and felt a lump grow in my throat. Someday I might be staring at Nick's dresser the same way. I couldn't bear to think of life without Nick, and for the first time, felt how deep Bitsy's grief must go. I hurried back to the bed and grabbed a handful of hangers, tossing the jackets over my shoulder as I went.

I admired her, I realized, as I made my way to the living room with my load. She had to be grieving, but she had not allowed herself any respite from her work. And Bitsy's work clearly was taking care of others. She was, I had learned, chairman of the Homeless Coalition board, and ran the local soup kitchen with all the skill of a Fortune 500 chairman. *But you have to think about April.* Funny how capricious my conscience can be—just about the time it convinces me of one argument, it changes sides. I returned to the bedroom resolved to do better.

The closet door was closed. My hand stopped short of the knob, gut instinct reminding me that it was too risky to be found plundering in there. I wished I'd told Miss Alma what I was doing so that she could run interference for me. I'd try to catch her on the next trip to the living room. Instead, I moved on to Bitsy's bedside table for a quick inventory.

A tube of lilac-scented hand cream, an empty glass, and a small brown prescription bottle. I scanned the label—sleeping pills—and examined the contents. Of the thirty prescribed, at least twenty-five were still in the bottle. So if Bitsy was having trouble sleeping, she wasn't relying on drugs to put her out. Next to the pills, a stack of books, none of which was light reading, may have provided the answer—*Daily Devotions for Women, The Agony and the Ecstasy,* and a large, heavy Bible with gold-leafed pages. I recognized it as the one she had said was Walter's and verified it quickly. On the inside cover were listed three names—the first, written in a Spencerian hand, said:

> "To Henry Fry, Given to him on the occasion of his ordination, June 23, 1915, by his mother."

Below the inscription was a second, written in a heavier hand:

> "To my son, Charles Fry, as the mantle of God is passed. Ordination, May 26, 1939."

And at the bottom, a final name had been added. It said, simply, Walter Fry. A family tree of sorts had been laid out inside the back cover. It showed that Henry Fry'd had three sons and a daughter, that Charles Fry had fathered two sons, but that only one of them, Raymond, had children. Walter Fry had no issue.

I flipped the book open to the red ribbon marker. Psalms 116. And lightly marked in pencil, verse 15: *Precious in the sight of the Lord is the death of His godly ones.* Here, of course, was Bitsy's other prescription for grief.

"Julia, I—" Bitsy Fry stopped in the door of her bedroom and stared at me. *Act natural,* I told myself. Sure, act natural while you're digging into her private life.

"I couldn't help noticing your Bible. It's quite old," I added lamely, knowing that among family Bibles, it was probably just an adolescent. "And so beautifully illustrated. It reminds me of my mother's Bible—"

"Oh yes, it is fairly old," she said, as she came to stand beside me. "Both Walter's father and grandfather were preachers. You see . . ." she said, taking it from me and turning to the front cover. She read the inscriptions for me.

"Walter was so proud of this Bible. You can see what good care he took of it," she continued, as she turned the pages. She opened it to a painting of the resurrected Christ. "He especially loved this picture." She smoothed her palm over the illustrated page, allowing it to rest there for a minute. Then she frowned. "He must have been crushed when it was damaged." I raised a silently inquiring eyebrow.

Bitsy answered me by flipping through the book. "Let's see . . . Second Kings, First Chronicles, Second Chronicles . . ." she mused. "Yes, here it is."

I glanced at the page numbers—from page 440 it skipped to the opening of Nehemiah, page 447. Judging by the ragged edges, several pages had been torn from the binding.

"What happened?"

Bitsy closed the book. "I don't know. I only just discovered it myself when I was preparing the devotional for our meeting. He never mentioned it to me." She shrugged sadly. "He probably didn't want me to know. Walter kept things like that from me. Things he thought would hurt me."

Yes, I thought, that was becoming apparent. He helped young black people get a start in life but opposed Damien's burial in a white cemetery. He preached against riotous living but owned a half interest in a dance hall and bar. His wife worked on behalf of the homeless while he actively tried to evict a troubled tenant—and a friend's daughter at that! Yes, there would be a lot that Walter Fry would have had to keep from his wife. And I thought it probably didn't end there.

We resumed our work after a light lunch of salads and iced tea. As the four of us ate companionably, I detailed Nick's adventures with the IRS, which brought no more reaction than a few sympathetic murmurs from Vivian and Bitsy. I described finding him in our home office, with files and bank statements everywhere, went on to gripe about how much I disliked having an office at home.

"You never leave work behind you when you keep your records at home," I complained.

"Walter would agree with you completely," Bitsy said, refreshing our iced tea. "He never brought work home. He felt his home should be a peaceful refuge. I tried to make it that way for him," she added quietly.

So Walter's records would not be found here. That was what I'd really wanted to know. I had found out everything I could, short of exploring closets and bathrooms. I'd even instructed Miss Alma to check the pockets of Fry's clothes as she packed them into cartons. A shake of her head told me it had been a fruitless search. But despite the fact that I felt our work there was finished, I could not bring myself to leave Vivian and Bitsy facing the mounds of sorting, washing, drying, and folding alone. Which was how I happened to be there when Joy McNabb arrived midafternoon.

At the sound of her voice in the front foyer, I retreated to my post in the garage in the hope of not being discovered. I hadn't anticipated Bitsy's eagerness to display our cache of clothing still to be sorted. "It will go a long way toward helping," she said, as she ushered Joy into the garage.

"Julia here has been a huge help. I'm sorry, I don't know if you've met Julia."

Joy turned to me with a penetrating gaze. "Oh yes," Joy said. "We've met."

"So nice to see you again," I murmured uneasily, but Joy was not listening. Fanning herself with her open hand, she had turned to Bitsy.

"What a terribly hot day! I am absolutely parched," she said, rather pointedly.

Bitsy immediately excused herself to brew some more iced tea, leaving me alone to face Joy McNabb. She was, I decided, even more inscrutable than her husband.

"I didn't realize you had joined our little church," she said. Apparently Allen had not reported his visit of the day before.

"Well, I haven't exactly joined. But you see, Nick is Greek Orthodox, and he doesn't have a church here. So we thought if we could find one that met both our needs—"

"Really? And I thought you might just be checking up on us." She was not the nervous woman I had seen at the funeral home. In fact, I thought there was a slightly malevolent, maybe even amused, glint in her eye. It was the first time I'd seen any resemblance to April. A hundred lies scurried through my mind, but in the end I decided to be candid.

"If I were checking up on the church, if I were trying to help April, would you blow my cover?"

Joy turned away from me, walked to the dryer, and pulled out a load of clothes. She had folded three shirts before she answered. "Just what is it that you're trying to find out?"

"Who hated Walter Fry enough to kill him."

"Everyone. Some of us hated him for his views. Some because of the way he ran the church—and our lives. Some of us didn't like the way he treated Bitsy." This one was new.

"Oh?"

She shrugged nonchalantly. "There were rumors. We're not all as naive as—"

"Here you are. Let me give you a refill, too, Julia." Bitsy plied us with tea and small talk as Joy McNabb and I exchanged wary looks. As soon as Bitsy had gone to check on Vivian and Miss Alma, I rushed to Joy's side.

"If you know anything," I whispered, "tell me now." Joy turned to me, eyes blazing.

"I know that my daughter didn't kill anyone. I know that, despite what my husband says, April is a good, kind girl. And I know that Walter Fry deserved to die."

Chapter Sixteen

cri-sis \ˈkrī-səs\ *n, pl* **cri-ses** \ˈkrī-sēz\[L, fr. Gk *krisis,* lit., decision, fr. *krinein* to decide—more at CERTAIN] **1a:** the turning point for better or worse in an acute disease or fever **b:** a paroxysmal attack of pain, distress, or disordered function **c:** an emotionally significant event or radical change of status in a person's life . . .
—*Merriam Webster's Ninth New Collegiate Dictionary*

I recounted my confrontation with Joy McNabb to Miss Alma as I drove her home. "So I suppose either April's father or mother could be the killer."

Miss Alma shook her head decisively. "Joy McNabb was at the Circle meeting that night."

"How do you know? Did she tell you?"

"No. Vivian had her notebooks with her. I guess she and Bitsy were planning to take care of correspondence and update membership while the others washed and folded the clothes—they were expecting a better turnout for the clothing drive. Anyway, while she was in the powder room, I just looked at the attendance records. Joy McNabb was signed in as present that evening."

So unless she had slipped out of the meeting at some point during the evening, Joy had an alibi. It didn't make too much difference. I couldn't imagine her pulling a trigger anyway—except for that one second in the garage when all of her rage toward Walter Fry was revealed. Still, I thought we could safely check her off the suspect list. But I still wondered about her husband. Would he, could he, possibly have murdered Fry knowing, as he must have, that he would be implicating his own daughter? And, too, we had to consider Joy's other disquieting disclosure. *There were rumors...* What had she meant? Had Fry abused his wife?

I repeated to Miss Alma what Bitsy had told me about Walter's philanthropy. "I just can't get a handle on it all. Either she's really gullible or she's a wonderful actress—better than Helen Hayes, or Vivian Leigh, or Meryl Streep—"

"I understand what you're trying to say, my dear," Miss Alma interrupted. "You think she's very trusting."

"Well, yes. After all, she seems to trust me. But how can anyone be that naive? Walter Fry was a vicious racist. Surely she must realize that."

Miss Alma sighed patiently. "Julia, the issue of racism is not as black or white as our skin."

"Of course it is," I argued. "Either you're a racist or you're not."

"That, my dear, is typical Yankee talk." I wheeled on Miss Alma, shocked at a remark that was so unlike and, I thought, unworthy of her. She smiled gently. "I'm just trying to make a point, Julia. Everyone has their prejudices. Even you."

"Maybe so, but I'm not a racist," I retorted angrily.

"No? Perhaps not knowingly, and maybe 'racist' is too strong a word. Let me ask you something—how many black children did you go to school with?"

"A couple in elementary school. A few more when I got to high school. It was a consolidated school district. There just weren't many black families in our town."

"And why was that?"

"I don't know. I guess they couldn't afford to live there or—" I stopped abruptly, the truth of the matter coming home with a terrible clarity. *Somehow they were being kept out,* I finished silently. Miss Alma did not press the point.

"Prejudice," she went on, "is often a matter of learning—or perhaps I should say *not* learning. Let me give you an example. You're driving through Markettown in broad daylight. Your passenger door is unlocked. You stop at a light where a young man is standing on a corner. The young man is white." She stopped.

"So?" I prompted her.

"Exactly. So what? You wait for the light to change and drive on. Now what do you do if that young man is black? Be honest with yourself, my dear."

Her scenario was strangely disquieting. "I don't know," I mumbled lamely. "I guess I might be a little nervous."

"You wouldn't reach over and lock the door?"

"Um—well, I might. It would depend on . . ."

"How he looked? But you didn't ask me how the white man looked. You didn't even think about that."

"No, I . . ."

"Learning. Exposure. You've been taught, and the statistics verify, that more violent crime is committed by black people than white. Add in fear of the unknown. You didn't grow up with black people. You're not really sure whether you should be afraid or not. You don't know how to gauge whether a black person might, or might not, be dangerous. Is he wearing dreadlocks because they're popular with his culture, or because he's a Rastafarian, or because he belongs to a street gang?

"Now, if the young man were white, you'd make certain assumptions. Again, they may not be correct, but they'd probably be closer to the mark. If his hair is tied in a neat ponytail and he's carrying a backpack, you'd assume that he's . . ."

"A student at Parnassus," I supplied.

Miss Alma nodded. "But he could be dangerous. He could have a weapon in that backpack. And his hair is very long—an earmark of the nonconformist, perhaps."

"Well, yes, he could," I answered dubiously. "But most students carry backpacks, and long hair is no big deal. Lots of guys wear long hair. It doesn't make him a criminal."

"Exactly. You know all that. It's part of your culture. You are conditioned to understand it. I have a private theory," she continued carefully. "I'll tell it to you if you promise me you won't get angry."

"Okay, I promise. I think."

"In the North whites claim to love blacks, a heritage of the North's political position during the Civil War. They love them as a group—a race, if you will—because they think they should. But they are indifferent to them as individuals. There is little personal interaction between whites and blacks, therefore whites know little about the culture and folkways of the black community."

I couldn't pretend to like what she was saying, but I had promised not to get mad. I just listened.

"It's different in the South. People my age were often raised by black nannies and played with their children. Their husbands cut our yards and did odd jobs around the house." I opened my mouth, but she threw up her hand to stave off interruption.

"I know what you're going to say, but that's a different issue. That's about education and job skills. My point is that we knew them as people, and we liked and cared about them. We understood that they came from a different culture, even if we couldn't put that into words. And yes, as a race we feared them, as most people fear any large group which threatens change. Many people still do. But if the South were not burdened by its history, tell me which would be the more sensitive attitude."

I had no answer for her. Either way, she had painted a pretty dark picture. I silently pulled into her driveway and cut the engine. She grasped her purse and laid her hand on the handle of the door.

"And having said all that," she finished, "I will agree with what you're already thinking. Neither alternative is very desirable. We just have to keep working at it." She smiled enigmatically.

"You must have been a helluva teacher," I said.

"Oh," she said, nodding brightly, "I was."

Restaurants do not run themselves, although with Rhonda and Spiros on staff, Nick and I were fortunate to be able to come and go easily during the quiet hours. Nevertheless, in our frantic pursuit of Fry's killer, we had both neglected our duties. George Wolenski had called to say his first meeting with the IRS had gone well. They were trying to trace the missing checks and would be back in touch shortly. Nick was greatly relieved and felt it was a sign that things were beginning to go our way. We spent the next day trying to catch up—he on inventory and bills, while I returned to the hospital for a meeting.

One of my colleagues was going to take maternity leave at the end of the month and had asked that I step in for her. She had pared her caseload down to her most profound cases, which would allow me to continue working on a part-time basis, but these were patients whose histories required thorough review before I assumed their treatment.

I spent most of my day poring over their files—a singer with vocal nodules whose career depended on treatment, two aphasics who were in a crucial period of spontaneous recovery, and the stuttering group. The latter, all of whom required encouragement to stay in therapy, occupied the majority of my attention. Finally, there was a housewife with psychogenic aphonia. This last case I welcomed, in part because I found such cases very interesting, and in part because I knew it would mean consultations with Ted Cowan—an extremely competent psychologist. While I believed April was innocent of the murder, I still thought she might need some counseling when her ordeal was over. Consultation with Ted might be an opportunity to segue into a discussion of April, and even of the victim himself.

I had intended to stop by Davon's room before I left the hospital, but it was nearly four o'clock by the time I finished with the files. Nick would probably be finished with the closing and ready to head home by the time I arrived.

"Bal-der-dash!" Spiros's voice rose above the roar of the wet vac. Nick had purchased this appliance in the hope of inducing Otis to do a better job of cleaning the kitchen floor. The idea was to actually remove the dirt instead of simply moving it around. So far Nick had fished out two wine corks, a chunk of raw carrot, and a crumpled napkin, all of which had clogged the hose during Otis's indifferent operation. Otis switched off the wet vac, stared at Spiros, and scratched his head.

"I don't know what he's talking about, Miz Julia," he whined.

"He keeps on talking 'bout being balder than something. He ain't making no sense."

"Bal-der-dash!" Spiros shouted again, loping toward the back door. There Otis had piled black plastic trash bags, waiting to go to the Dumpster behind the Oracle. Spiros snatched one up and shook it. "Bal-der-dash out," he roared, pointing toward the back door.

"He means the trash. Take out the trash. You see, 'balderdash' probably translates as—"

Otis dropped the vacuum nozzle and hurried toward Spiros, waiting at the door. "Why didn't you just say so, anyway?" Otis hefted a couple of bags over his shoulder while Spiros nodded approvingly, threw the bolt, and held the back door open. He turned back to me with a grin.

"New word. Teach O-tees, *neh?*"

"You bet," I said. *"Pou eine o Nikos?"*

Spiros pointed to the closed door to the office. *"Telefono."*

I waited until Spiros returned to the grill before interrupting Nick. He was still on the telephone. "I'll tell Julia," he said. "We'll come by tomorrow." He dropped the telephone in the cradle and turned to me with a broad smile.

"That was April. Davon's awake."

Davon had begun responding to stimulation the night before, and by midafternoon on Friday he was awake, though slightly disoriented. "April said he recognized everybody—her, his parents. D'Anita. Even L.T.," Nick said.

"Then he's talking?"

"Must be."

We had been reluctant to intrude on the family so soon after Davon's awakening, but Nick said that April was insistent. He would want to thank us, she said, for finding him the night of the attack. Nick managed to put the visit off until Saturday. They didn't seem to have many friends and I doubted that April's parents would darken the door. Which left us, outsiders really, to help celebrate the reawakening of Davon Folsom. We stepped off the elevator and turned the corner, heading for Davon's room. His door was open, the light and noise spilling out into the corridor a sure sign, I thought, that he was recovering. But when we reached the door, it wasn't quite as I had expected.

Candice stood nose to nose with Sam, her hands on her hips and her feet planted firmly apart. His face was flushed and his eyes averted. Nick grabbed my elbow and drew me back out of sight.

"I am telling you that pushing him won't do any good. I've told you, and the doctor's told you, he'll remember when he remembers."

"Yes, ma'am. It's just that they were released on bail yesterday morning. We need to get a positive ID on 'em right away. We don't want these guys on the loose, you know?"

"Look, Sheriff, I don't want them on the streets any more than you do, but I can't do anything about that. He can't help not remembering, and when it comes right down to it, I don't think you want your identification tainted because their lawyer's claiming you coerced the patient. Do you?" Smart lady, Candice.

Sam sighed deeply. "No, ma'am, you're right. But the minute he remembers anything, you've got to call me." I peeked around the door in time to see Sam pull a card from his pocket and write something on the back.

"I'm giving you my home phone number here, but I'd appreciate it if you wouldn't give it out. But you call me day or night, all right?" Candice nodded and stuck the card in her pocket. In the background, Chester looked on with an astonished expression. *The sheriff, he's never been a friend of the black man in Delphi,* he'd said. Maybe now he would see things differently.

We intercepted Sam as he trudged out the door. He stopped short when he saw us, wordlessly shook his head, and started off down the hall.

"Hey, Sam, wait!" Nick caught up with him in a few long strides while I hurried along behind him. "What's the matter?"

Sam jammed his hat on his head and viciously stabbed the elevator button. "He doesn't remember."

"Davon? But I thought he recognized everybody."

"He did. The doctor's calling it retro—something."

"Retrograde amnesia," I said. "It means that he can't remember what immediately preceded losing consciousness. There wasn't enough time for it to go into long-term memory." The men waited. I stalled, knowing that the news I had to impart was not good. "He may never remember anything about it."

"Aw shit." Sam jabbed the button again. "Ain't that just swell. Here we're waiting for him to wake up, and now he doesn't remember anything."

"Give him time," I said. "Maybe something will come back. You've got to tread carefully here, Sam. If you push him—"

"Yeah, yeah. They'll accuse me of coercion. I know. But we don't have a helluva lot of time. Those boys are out on bail."

I was suffering from a queasy stomach, and Nick's temper was as taut as a stretched rubber band. "Who raised it for them?"

Sam shook his head. "They called some friend. Cox was bragging that they'd be out before the end of the week, and damned if they weren't, too."

Tantalus, I had learned when I pressed charges against him, was a thirty-four-year-old man named Stephen Ellis Cox. His friend was one Robert Vernon Willard. Their occupations were listed as "construction," but they were currently unemployed, which left them far too much time to zoom around Delphi in the Big Foot Ram trying to start trouble. And now they were out there on the streets again. It was not a happy prospect, but at least Sam had secured a restraining order to keep them away from me.

The elevator ground to a stop in front of us. We stepped aside as an orderly angled a gurney out the door and around the corner, returning a patient from surgery. Sam stepped on the elevator and shoved a foot in front of the door.

"Now, you see any signs of him coming around—remembering anything—you call me first thing. Don't you two go playing detective on this, you hear?" We solemnly assured him that we wouldn't think of it, as the doors eased closed.

"Hey, Sam?" Nick grabbed the door just in time. "Do you know who they went to for the bail money?"

Sam pushed his hat back on his forehead. "Some guy named Carter—no, Cantor—something like that. Why do you want to know?"

Nick let the door go and we turned back toward Davon's room as Sam's voice faded away down the elevator shaft.

Davon's voice was hoarse, his vocal cords edematous from the endotracheal tube that had, for several days, kept his airway open and his breathing regular. Still, his spirits seemed good considering all that he was facing. After all, he had not forgotten that his wife had been indicted for murder.

April sat on the bed beside him, smoothing her palm over his chest and fiddling with his bedcovers. She was wearing a ponytail and a pink tie-dyed T-shirt that was vintage sixties, and looked not one day more than her eighteen years. She smiled happily but said nothing, letting him speak for himself.

"Thanks," he said. "For everything. I know we've all been depending on you a lot . . ." He broke off, waiting, I think, for some good news from us. He wanted us to say that while he'd been asleep, we'd dug up enough evidence to exonerate April. We couldn't tell him that we really hadn't learned much at all.

"We're working on it," Nick said, with a peripheral glance at me.

"Don't try to talk, Davon. Those vocal cords are pretty raw. You could end up with granuloma. You don't want to have to see me professionally."

"That's right, son," Candice added gently. "You've been through a pretty rough patch. You need to take it real easy."

I backed away and let Nick tell Davon about the night of the attack. He listened carefully, his eyes trained on the wall ahead, as though he were desperately trying to remember.

"Be careful," I warned Nick. "You can't tip him off about the guys. He's got to identify them without any help from us." Nick just nodded and shot a glance from April to me. I squeezed her arm and gestured for her to follow me.

"Are you okay?" I said, when I'd gotten her into the hall.

She brushed a stray lock of hair out of her eyes and tried to poke it into her ponytail. "Yeah, I'm fine. I didn't think he was going to make it, Julia. Now that I know he's okay, I'm just sure it will all work out."

"Look, April, I have to be honest with you. We haven't learned that much. Now that Davon is awake, we're going to have to sit down and talk. You and me, I mean. You're still holding out on us about that gun."

She tugged at her T-shirt and turned away evasively. "I told you, the gun doesn't matter." Enough already.

I grabbed her shoulders and turned her around. "Listen to me. It matters," I said, trying to convey it in capital letters. "It matters a lot!"

Her chin came up and her eyes blazed. "Why? What difference does it make?"

"Because whoever gave you that gun in the first place may have expected you to use it—think, April! Did they encourage you to shoot him? When you didn't, they saw their chance. Your prints would be on the gun. They could finish Fry off and implicate you, all in a neatly wrapped little bundle!"

She backed away, her hands coming up to cover her ears. "No! Why? Why would Mr. Fry have had anything to do with—" But there she stopped, glancing wildly down the hall and back into Davon's room. When she had composed herself, she turned back to me.

"You're wrong, Julia. I'm sorry, but you're just wrong. The person who gave me the gun had no idea I was going to use it."

I wasn't convinced.

Chapter Seventeen

ex-po-sure \ik-ˈspō—zhər\(1606) **1:** the fact or con-
dition of being exposed . . . **2:** the act or an instance of
exposing: as **a:** disclosure of something secret **b:** the
treating of sensitized material (as film) to controlled
amounts of radiant energy . . .
—*Merriam Webster's Ninth New Collegiate Dictionary*

"He was better off asleep."

"Nick, that's a terrible thing to say!"

"I just mean that things look pretty bad to him right now. He's
worried sick about April. I hated to have to tell him the truth—
that we're getting nowhere—but he kept pushing me. Now he's
talking about getting out of the hospital so he can take care of
things himself."

"That doesn't sound too good," I said.

We pulled into the parking lot to find it packed with a late Saturday morning breakfast rush. Nick hurried to the kitchen, while
I pitched in to help Rhonda and Tammy deliver orders and bus tables. Given that it was a Saturday morning, our busiest breakfast
of the week, Otis should have been there early. But he had called
to say he'd be late. His grandmother was in the hospital. Again.

I was eager to meet Otis's grandma—quite a remarkable
woman with amazing recuperative powers. She'd been hospital-
ized off and on for a variety of illnesses ranging from the flu to
leukemia. She'd been tested for chronic fatigue syndrome, manic-
depressive tendencies, multiple sclerosis, and Lyme disease. Iron-
ically, she always seemed to develop these afflictions on Friday
nights, and they usually coincided with the disease featured in

the latest *Reader's Digest.* By my reckoning, she was due for prostate problems any day.

I stacked a load of dishes on the skirt of the dish machine, grabbed another bus tub, and hurried back into the dining room. Billy English was waiting to be seated. I put him at a two-top on C deck, where a big table of Parnassus students were hovered over a calculator trying to split their ticket. Billy knew what he wanted—a Greek omelette. I put in his order and finished bussing the tables. Otis would have a mound of dishes waiting for him by the time he got there, I realized with malicious satisfaction.

"Billy, I need your help with something," I said, as I put his order in front of him. I'd added a side of hash browns to sweeten the deal.

"Sure. Whatcha need?"

"A copy of the tape of Walter Fry's funeral. Can you get it for me?"

Billy buttered his biscuit and inserted a glob of strawberry preserves. "Got a copy. I taped it off the news—you know, keeping track of the competition. You can borrow it." He broke the biscuit and stuffed half of it in his mouth.

Billy works for *The Delphi Sun*, our local answer to *The Washington Post.* He'd helped us before, and in return had gotten the biggest story of his career, propelling him from part-time photographer and ad salesman to full-fledged reporter. I knew he'd do what he could to help.

"Course, it's edited," he said, sending a spray of crumbs across the table.

"Well, could you get me the uncut film?"

"Maybe. I've got a friend at WPAR. I'll call him on Monday." I was disappointed, and I guess it showed. "He's not in on Saturdays," he explained. "But you can have my tape today, and I'll see what I can do for you next week."

I left him pouring Tabasco over his omelette, glad that Spiros hadn't seen the destruction of his delicate balance of spinach, feta cheese, and dill. It would have hurt his feelings.

Billy delivered the tape after the lunch rush and reiterated that he would do his best to get a copy of the uncut footage for me as soon as possible. I grabbed Nick and pulled him out of the wait station, explaining what I'd gotten.

"You think it's going to be any help?"

"You never know. Maybe something happened that we've forgotten about."

We stopped on the way home to pick up Chinese takeout and settled ourselves and our Mongolian beef in front of the television. I love Chinese food, but the film quickly eradicated my appetite for it.

The camera zoomed in on the picketers as, in a voice-over, the newscaster explained why they were demonstrating. "This is Barbara Marshall, reporting from Mount Sinai Tabernacle Cemetery where today the body of Damien Folsom . . ."

The film then cut to April as she laid a flower on the wicker casket. I felt as though someone had inserted cold hands into my chest and squeezed my heart. From there we made a quick leap back to Barbara Marshall as she stood in front of the canopy in the cemetery. Although she was some distance away, we were all clearly visible—Nick, me, Miss Alma, and the family. The camera moved closer, lingering on the black faces partially shaded by the canopy.

Fry's voice droned in the background—" '. . . therefore give not . . .' " but Marshall's words overpowered him.

"Louis Thatcher Humphries, attorney for the Folsom family—"

"No!" April's voice cried out, and the camera swung around to follow her across the cemetery.

"My God, she's got a gun!" from Marshall. The camera jostled, giving us fragments of earth, granite markers, and wrought-iron gates as WPAR aired their journalists in the heat of the action. April's threats, and her humiliation, were caught for posterity as the film rolled on. Davon was shown, held back by his father while Candice rushed April to the car. L.T. Humphries, with D'Anita in tow, followed close behind. The segment concluded with a slightly rumpled Barbara Marshall closing the story in front of the empty church.

Nick and I stared at the snow on the screen. "Did you get anything out of that?"

He shook his head and snapped open a fortune cookie, read the strip of paper, and tossed it down in disgust.

"What does it say?"

"It gives me my lucky numbers for the day."

"Oh, right. They sell lottery tickets. Let's watch it again."

I had been spellbound by the scene, remembering it as it had happened and feeling, again, a horror for Allen McNabb's treatment of his fragile daughter. But I had not looked for details. Nick rewound the tape while I dumped my Mongolian beef in Jack's dish.

We rolled the tape and paused it, studying the picketers. "Look, Nick. Look at that," I said, pointing at the screen. "Isn't that Dub Cantrell?"

Nick agreed that it was. He was standing in front of Fry, trying to hold his attention as Walter's glance swept over the picket line. At length Fry turned back to him, smiled slightly, and shook his head. Cantrell stormed away, but lingered off to the side to glare at Fry.

"Well, well. So Dub Cantrell was there, and could have seen where the gun was."

"Yes," Nick said. "That's interesting."

We watched as the tape rolled on. I studied the faces of the family—Chester stood with his head down, and Candice's chin proudly tilted upward, grief pulling down the corners of her eyes and mouth. There was Joy McNabb, staring vacantly at her husband, as Allen intoned his prayers with no display of emotion. D'Anita was dabbing at her eyes with a handkerchief, which surprised me afresh. She didn't seem like a girl who harbored much compassion for anyone.

The camera tightened in on April and the gun in her hand, panned to a shocked Walter Fry and back to April just as she shoved her hands over her ears and the gun went off. Screaming provided the background as the camera backed off and caught the full impact of the slap and the gun hurled away.

I had to hand it to the cameraman. He'd certainly stayed cool and steady. He even took a long shot of the kudzu and zoomed in on the gun. He also caught the crowd as they dropped their signs and rushed to their cars. The family followed—muttering from Davon, and shouts from D'Anita. I thought I caught L.T.'s voice. ". . . in the car, D'Anita. You're making things worse—get in the car."

And then we were back to Barbara Marshall. But something was bothering me. I replayed the scene in my mind as Nick re-wound the tape. We had seen where the gun had landed, and I was sure that was where Nick and I had looked.

"Nick, stop the tape!" We were back to the flickering film as the cameraman raced across the cemetery. "No, fast forward it—almost to the end. There."

L.T. was pushing D'Anita into the car and she was fighting him, shouting back over her shoulder at Fry.

"Pause it!" I jumped up and pulled him over to the screen. "There! Do you see that?" I pointed to the screen where a hand-kerchief was suspended in midair. "Do you remember when we took Jack back to the cemetery with us—how he sniffed that handkerchief and then—"

"Followed the scent into the kudzu. He was tracking the scent. I told you he was good."

"But that means he was tracking . . . D'Anita."

"Oh, come in," Candice said, stepping back from the door. We followed her through the foyer and up a short flight of stairs to a comfortable living area. The house was a modest split level, fur-nished in tasteful contemporary pieces that emphasized comfort and utility. We were seated on a soft, cushy sofa covered in a jun-gle pattern of blues and greens.

I had hoped that Candice would be at the hospital and D'Anita would be home alone. We had not called ahead, instead had trumped up a reason to stop at the house. I picked up a plastic grocery bag and passed it over to Candice.

"We were just heading home from the grocery store," I explained. "I picked up a few things for Davon and I thought if someone was going to the hospital . . ."

"I was planning to leave in a little while. D'Anita has a date. I like to be here when the boy arrives."

I nodded, understanding Candice's point of view, and relieved to learn that D'Anita was at home. I gestured at the bag. "They're just some books—crossword puzzles and a couple of paperbacks," I said. "But we have plans tomorrow and I don't think we'll make it by to see him."

Candice opened the bag and glanced in. "I'm sure he'll be pleased to know you thought about him." She studied us politely.

I shifted my gaze around the room, unsure how to approach what was going to be a difficult situation. "Did D'Anita paint that?" I said, pointing to a large canvas framed in a rough wood that resembled barn siding.

Candice nodded. "She did that in high school."

We stood up and walked over to examine it together. It was a painting of three black men in khaki suits and white shoes. All three were leaping—caught in action, crouched in midair with their feet together and arms spread out behind them. Although her colors were a bit muddy, D'Anita had, in high school, shown the promise that she was now fulfilling. Her ability to capture movement was astonishing. I could almost feel the ground quake as their feet hit the earth. Even their shadows seemed to be in motion.

"They visited our church," Candice said. "They're members of the Zion Christian Church of Botswana. This is a ritual dance that they performed. D'Anita did the painting from high-speed photographs."

Nick had joined us at the painting. We were still admiring it when the artist herself walked in.

"Mama, do you have—" D'Anita came in fastening a large

wooden hoop earring to the back of her ear. She was wearing a black and brown batik broomstick skirt and a brown halter top, reminding me of a photograph from *National Geographic*. I felt that D'Anita was trying to establish her ethnicity. The painting of the dancers of Botswana was another piece of the same puzzle. She broke off when she saw us.

"Hi, D'Anita. We were just looking at this beautiful painting," I said. "Nick and I would really love to see some more of your work."

"I'm leaving in a few minutes. I have a date." She turned to her mother. "I just wanted to find out if you've got an extra barrel back for an earring. I've lost the one to this earring and the regular kind won't work on it."

"I'm not sure. I'll have to look." Candice turned away, and it looked as though D'Anita would follow her.

"Let me ask you something about this painting," I said. D'Anita glanced at her mother, but reluctantly turned back to us. As soon as Candice had cleared the door, I grabbed her arm. "We need to talk to you," I said in a low voice.

"I don't have time. I've got a date," she said, pulling her arm out of my grasp.

Nick stepped in between the two of us. "I think you'd better make time," he said. "We know about the gun."

D'Anita stepped back away from us, a flicker of panic in her eyes. She reached up to toy with the remaining earring, and I noticed that her fingers trembled a bit.

Nick put on a little more pressure. "If you don't talk to us, you're leaving us no choice but to go to the sheriff with this. Julia and I thought you should have an opportunity to explain, but if you're not willing—"

"No! I mean, we can talk about it. But not here, in front of my mother," she whispered.

"Then—"

"Will this work?" Candice had returned to the living room, a small gold barrel cradled in her open palm.

D'Anita grabbed it hastily and fiddled with her earring. The jewelry in place, she turned to her mother. "Mama," she said reluctantly, "Nick and Julia want to see some of my paintings. I'm going to take them downstairs for a few minutes. Will you stay up here and watch for Rodney?"

Candice agreed to do so and we followed D'Anita back down the stairs, across the foyer, and down a second flight of steps. She opened the door to what had once been a basement rec room, showed us in, and closed it firmly behind her. It smelled of turpentine and linseed oil.

The room was a daylight basement, with a set of sliding glass doors flanked by double windows stretching across the wall. Out in the backyard, several weathered tree stumps held large pots of pansies. Chester must have taken down the trees when D'Anita claimed the room as her studio, allowing her the light she needed to paint.

Stacked against the walls were canvases in varying degrees of completion. Most of them were practice canvases on hard cardboard backings and were, apparently, used for studies of motion, human anatomy, and portraiture. One was a study of rough, scarred hands, which I thought might well be Chester's. Another, charcoaled onto the canvas, was obviously a much younger Candice wearing a winged nurse's cap. The study had been executed from an early photograph which was propped against it. Beside it was another charcoal study of an aging woman dozing in a wheelchair. In the background, other very senior adults were depicted in activities ranging from checker playing to quilting. Most of them, including the woman in the wheelchair, were black. I recognized the setting—the Senior Center run by the Council on Aging. Nick picked up the second canvas and carried it into better lighting to study it.

D'Anita's easel stood at a forty-five-degree angle to the window, and on it was another familiar face. The portrait was not quite completed but very recognizable. Especially the repaired lip scar. Rodney's eyes were as deep and black as oil wells. The pink insides of his lower lids drooped below the whites, betraying a profound sadness I had not noticed in any of D'Anita's other paintings. His black skin was luminous, shining with blue highlights. D'Anita tapped her foot impatiently.

"I don't have much time," she whispered.

Nick set down the study of the dozing woman and motioned me away from the easel. I joined him to face her. "We know about the gun," I said. "We're trying to give you a chance to explain it. Why, D'Anita?"

She crossed her arms over her breasts, clenching her fists under her arms, and glared at us. "You won't understand," she said.

"We'll try."

She turned away and drifted over to the easel. "Because of him," she said, gesturing at the portrait. "I didn't want him to go back." I glanced at Nick, but he shrugged, as much in the dark as I was.

"I found it in his apartment and I took it. Rodney's an ex-con." She swung around on her heel so that her skirt spun out gracefully around her slender legs. "Please don't tell Mama and Daddy," she said. "They won't let me see him if they find out."

"You're twenty years old, D'Anita. They can't really stop you."

"No, I suppose not." She fingered the drawstring on her skirt. "But I don't want to hurt them."

"You know," I said, feeling an unlikely maternalism toward her. "Maybe you shouldn't be involved with him. If he's an ex-convict . . ."

The drawstring grew taught between her hands. It was not the first misstep I'd made with D'Anita. "You don't get it, do you? Just 'cause he made a mistake. He's straight now and he's going to stay straight." She turned her back to me and gazed out the window. "Oh it's always so easy for people like you," she continued. "You didn't grow up in a project, did you?"

"No, I didn't," I said, tempted to point out that, in fact, neither had she.

"Well, he did. On the streets mostly. His mama didn't want

him because . . . because of that harelip." I winced at her tactless choice of words.

"He's doing community service as part of his parole. I met him at the Senior Center. He's a good man. I'm gonna tell Mama and Daddy the truth about him . . . eventually. He needs a chance to prove himself first."

Nick glanced down at his watch and over at me. This was taking too much time. We couldn't afford to have Candice and Rodney interrupt us before we'd gotten to the point of our visit. "About the gun?" Nick prompted her.

"He's not supposed to have a weapon. It's a parole violation and they got him on armed robbery. He'd be back in prison in a heartbeat if anyone found out."

"Why did he have it?"

D'Anita shrugged. "He says he was keeping it for some buddy who just got out. That's why I took it. He shouldn't be so dumb."

"Why didn't you just throw it in the river or something?"

D'Anita sighed, as though I'd tried her patience a bit too much. "Because that buddy might come looking for it and then Rodney would be in deep . . . in trouble. But I couldn't keep it here," she said, gesturing around her. "So I gave it to April to hold for me and I told her not to tell anyone, even Davon. He'd go right to Mama and Daddy with the whole story. But I didn't know she was going to use it," she added defiantly.

So this was why April had refused to talk about the gun. She was protecting D'Anita and Rodney. Loyal to a fault. I wasn't sure I was buying the story about the prison buddy, but at least it explained a lot of other things, like D'Anita's hostility toward us. She was terrified that we were going to unearth the whole story, including her boyfriend's past.

"You should have come forward when they arrested April," I said.

"Why? What difference would it have made?"

"Well, for one thing," Nick said, "the district attorney thinks she went out and bought the gun on the street."

"Premeditated murder," I added. "The truth might have kept her from being indicted—at least on murder charges."

"Oh well," she said, her hands up in a helpless gesture and an amused glint in her eye.

"You can't mean you don't care," I said, horrified at her indifference. "I thought you and April were close."

"Yeah," D'Anita said, punctuating it with a sharp laugh. "She thinks so too. We got closer after I gave her the gun. It was our little secret, just between us girls.

"Okay, so she's indicted for murder and she goes to trial," D'Anita continued. "You think any jury's gonna convict her? Not a minister's daughter. Not a mother with a dead baby. Not a white girl," she added bitterly. "Me? Yeah," she said, pinching her deep brown skin. "But not her."

There was no arguing with her—no penetrating her anger. And for that matter, who was I to argue? I'd never been black, never been discriminated against because of my color. She might have been right, except for the fact that April, of all people, deserved better. I channeled my anger into another sharp question.

"Then why did you go back for the gun?"

"Back for the gun?" Her brows scissored in a perplexed frown. "I didn't. I left it with her. I didn't see it again until Damien's funeral."

I glanced over at Nick. He was studying her carefully, and I decided that, like me, he thought she was telling the truth. He took my hand and squeezed it.

"But you went back for it after the funeral. You must have," I said in response to her emphatic headshake.

"No, I didn't."

"Well, we tried to find someone to go back and dig the gun out of the kudzu," Nick said. "But you didn't answer your phone. Neither did Davon and April."

"We were at the church."

"Mount Sinai?"

"No. Ebenezer Baptist. We had a memorial service at our

church. A lot of our friends didn't feel comfortable . . ." *Going to Mount Sinai,* I finished for her. Of course not. Why would they?

"And you were all there? The whole family?" I asked, my heart lifting. Maybe April had an alibi we'd all overlooked. If we could prove that she was at the church when Nick and I went looking for the gun . . .

"Well, not Davon and April. They were too upset after the funeral. But Mama and Daddy and Rodney and I went. Someone from the family had to be there." Nick squeezed my hand again.

"Yes, of course," I said. But not April.

Chapter Eighteen

pur-loin \ p ər-ˈloin, ˈpər-\ *vt* [ME *purloinen* to put
away, render ineffectual, fr. AF *purloigner*, fr. OF *porloigner*
to put off, delay, fr. *por-* forward + *loing* at a distance, fr.
L *longe*, fr. *longus* long] (1548): to appropriate wrongfully
and often by a breach of trust **syn** see STEAL.

— *Merriam Webster's Ninth New Collegiate Dictionary*

We met Justine in the Vagabond parking lot at two o'clock
on Sunday. She motioned us to follow her to the back, where our
cars would not be visible from the road, and took us in the back
door, leading us through what had once been an actively used
kitchen. Nick's glance flickered over the equipment and he licked
his lips.

Nick's an equipment freak—always looking for a spare slicer,
fryer, cooler. Equipment failure is the bane of the business, and
since we can never afford to purchase it new—complete with
warranty and regular service contract—we're always repairing
mechanical artifacts that would carbon-date from the first millennium.

"Ever thought about selling some of this stuff?" Nick said, gesturing around him.

Justine shook her head. "I don't know why they've kept it all
these years. Kitchen's hardly ever used except for storage. I asked
Dub about it recently myself. We could knock out the walls and
move the bar back. It would give us sixty more seats, easy, and
widen the dance floor too."

"And?"

"He didn't like it. Probably because it was my idea—he's not crazy about having a black woman as a partner. Anyway, I'm thinking about looking into it myself—you know, get construction bids, talk to some banks. Find out what it would actually cost."

"Well, let me know if you decide to sell some of the equipment. I could use another steel table, and a slicer, and one of those steam tables, and . . ." I grabbed Nick's elbow and pulled him out of the kitchen.

Justine popped open a breaker box at the kitchen door and switched on one circuit of lights. There is something forlorn about an empty dance hall—without the glitter of shiny belt buckles and the noise of stomping boots, it comes off as just slightly shabby. But the Vagabond was more than shabby. It was frightening.

I was back, helplessly two-stepping my way toward who knew what? He might have raped me, beaten me. He might have killed me. I shuddered. Nick took my hand and gave it a light squeeze. At that moment I loved him more than ever. He really was my hero.

We followed Justine back into the office. It was a long, narrow room, darkly paneled with a single high window covered in nicotine-streaked beige drapes. Justine pulled back the drapes and dust motes swirled into columns of sunlight. A tall filing cabinet stood in one corner with a television angled for easy viewing on top of it. A heavy green metal desk crouched under the window, while its mate stood out in the room perpendicular to the opposite wall. This second desk held a computer and monitor, and on the walls above it were framed pictures of jungle animals and tropical birds. A cracked leather-look vinyl couch hunkered against the end wall.

"Jeez, I hate this office," she said, glancing around the room with distaste. Her gaze seemed to linger on the couch, with its stuffing foaming up out of the cracks in the upholstery. I made a mental note to find a seat elsewhere, unwilling to disturb anything that might be living in it.

"All right," Nick said. "Tell me exactly what we're looking for."
Justine raked her hands through her hair. "Well, that's just it.

I'm not exactly sure. All I really know is that an IRS agent was in here a couple of weeks ago—that was before Wal—er, Mr. Fry died. And then I found this in his desk when I was cleaning it out." She handed Nick a couple of sheets of paper as I peered over his shoulder. It was notification of an audit, addressed to FC Enterprises d/b/a the Vagabond, by the Internal Revenue Service. It was accompanied by a letter indicating that they had reason to believe that an error, perhaps even fraud, had been committed in the computation of paycheck withholding. Nick let out a low whistle.

"Fraud!" Justine nodded solemnly.

"Have you discussed it with your partner?" I said.

Justine sat down on the corner of a desk. "I've tried. He claims that they're wrong—that he paid the correct taxes, but the IRS records are screwed up."

Nick voiced exactly what I was thinking. "It's certainly possible. I've been down that road myself. But these are withholding. Not something you want to mess around with. Did Fry know about this?"

"I think he must have. He was spending a lot of time in here before he died. Trouble is, Dub keeps all the books on computer, and Walter didn't know much about computers."

Nick and I exchanged uncomfortable glances. Computers were not our area of expertise either. "What about you?" Nick asked.

Justine shrugged. "I know a little. I'm not real sophisticated with them, but I doubt if Dub is either. Trouble is, Dub has the files password-protected, and I haven't figured out the password yet. But I haven't given up."

She turned around and flipped a couple of switches, and the computer booted up. Nick dragged a chair up next to Justine, and I, left with the couch as my only alternative, took up a perch on what appeared to be Justine's desk. The top was clear, with only a pencil cup, a small ceramic ashtray, and a couple of framed photographs pushed into a corner. On the other corner, a large carton was stacked with files, a coffee mug that said "I'm the boss," and sundry bits and pieces of a man's working life. Justine had cleaned out Walter's desk, but had not yet disposed of his things. It might make interesting reading, I thought.

"I've tried everything I can think of—his wife's name, his street address, his birth date. It could be anything." Justine sat back in her chair and stared at the screen with its cursor flashing next to the word *Password:*.

Nick looked equally exasperated as he stood up and paced the room. He stopped in front of the desk and glared at the computer. "How about kids? Does he have kids?"

Justine nodded. "Three. Tried their names, too."

"Okay," he said. "Try combinations of them—initials, things like that."

Justine went back to work as Nick absently played with the objects on Cantrell's desk. He fingered a gold cigarette lighter, nervously flicking it until I took it out of his hands. Dub Cantrell had an amazing collection of executive toys on his desk—things to squeeze, pop, roll, and put in motion. He even had a little basketball hoop over his wastebasket. Nick tried them all, and I, just as methodically, took them away from him. He ended with a small ebony box, opened it and pulled out a deck of cards, which he shuffled. And shuffled.

"Nick, please! You're driving me crazy!"

"I'm sorry." He stared ruefully down at the cards.

"No go." Justine sat back again and lightly drummed her fingers on the keyboard. Nick started shuffling again.

They were pretty cards, I noticed as I gently removed them from his hands. On one deck tropical birds nested on a crimson background, while on the other, zebras and antelopes cavorted against a background of emerald green. The edges had once been gold-leafed, but the gold had been worn away with heavy use.

"Pretty," I said, handing them back to Nick. "Put them away, please, before you drive us nuts."

Nick studied the backs. "Try animals," he said, glancing up at the pictures. "Wild ones—like panthers, tigers, zebras." Again

Justine went back to work and again it yielded nothing. Nick turned the deck over in his hands.

"Wait a minute," he said, studying the cards' worn edges. "Try 'straight.' " No results. "How about 'flush'?" Justine shook her head as Nick continued to toss poker hands at her.

"How about 'royal flush'?"

"Bingo! I'm in." Justine laughed as she watched a directory pop up onto the screen. "Figures. Dub thinks he's a prince among men. I'm surprised he didn't use 'stud.' " She rubbed her hands together. "Now let's see what we can find."

I left them to it, opting instead to study the contents of Walter's desk, but his files yielded very little of interest. A copy of his partnership agreement with Dub Cantrell, which looked to me to be pretty standard stuff. Nevertheless, I skimmed it, verifying that the agreement called for a small life insurance policy to be held on both parties, with the benefits going to the business. Never having been involved in a partnership, I wasn't sure whether this was a standard clause, but I thought it made sense. If both partners were active in a business, and one was to die, a policy of this type would at least give the remaining partner time to find a replacement or some money to buy out an heir. But that reasoning also implied that Walter Fry was active in the business, a point that was reinforced by my next find.

At the time the contract was drawn, Walter held the controlling interest—two percent more than his partner. Which meant, I thought, that Walter could have done anything he wanted with the place—could have turned it back into a restaurant, or made it a grocery store, or peddled used socks through a drive-through window. It only underscored, again, the differences between the publicly pious Walter and the privately corrupt one.

A thick file of profit-and-loss statements came next, obviously precomputer and dating back some ten years. The Vagabond, I noted, was a very profitable enterprise. There were vendor files and handfuls of loose correspondence about billing errors, point-of-sale displays, and freebies that had never made it to the files. And there were files for utilities and fixed expenses, along with thick stacks of paid, unfiled bills. It looked to me as though Walter had taken more of an interest in the business than his wife thought. It also looked as though he needed a secretary.

I laid the files aside, pushed the loose papers and envelopes to the back of the box, and dug deeper, coming up with a framed picture of Bitsy Fry. It had been taken at least ten years ago, judging by the style of her clothing. This was a younger Bitsy, but with the same clear blue eyes, the same soft expression that seemed too gentle a companion for the disagreeable Mr. Fry. I set the picture aside with a baffled shake of the head.

Beneath the photograph there was a stack of catalogues—mobile homes and barware. And beneath the catalogues, a tattered copy of *Winning Is Everything*, a management handbook written by one of the legion of businessmen who make their living, not in the trenches of business, but as motivational speakers. Clearly, however, this was a philosophy old Walter had made his own.

At the bottom of the box was one last file. It held invoices for college tuition with check numbers duly noted—Raymond's children, I thought. But there was one for cosmetology school, student's name: Evelyn H———. The remainder of the name had been obliterated by a coffee spill. I made a note of it, recalling what Bitsy had said about Walter's generosity, and sighed. What had I really learned from all this? I asked myself. *Nothing,* I answered.

"Your supply costs are way up." Nick was pointing to a column of figures on the computer screen. "What do you make of that? You're doing about the same business you were last year."

Justine pursed her lips. "I don't know. It might mean somebody's stealing, but I haven't noticed any more deliveries than usual. Inventory's about the same as always."

"Well, let's deal with that later. Let's try to find the tax files."

"He's got all the files under these crazy names. Oh darn, here's another password protection."

"Okay, let's think poker."

I left them to that and wandered around the office. The file cabinet was locked. Justine glanced up briefly. "I don't have a key and I can't find Walter's," she said, and went back to her task. "Try 'blackjack.' "

Maybe I should go back through Walter's things, I thought. The key might be there somewhere if I looked carefully. I started laying out the contents on the desk methodically. Might as well organize them while I was about it, filing away the loose correspondence and bills. It was one little favor I could do for Bitsy, though she'd never know it was me, and I thought she deserved all the help she could get. I made neat little stacks of the files by type and watched as they overwhelmed the top of the desk.

I'd been through them all before, but I gave them each another cursory check and found nothing until I came to his contract file. There, tucked in between the pages, was a loose sheet of paper from a steno pad. Notes in a spiky little hand—columns of numbers in sequential order that meant nothing to me. "Look," I said, passing them to Nick. "What do you suppose this is?"

"There it is," Justine said. "Employees, deductions, year-to-date totals. Jeez, I didn't know John made that much. The little worm. Well, I'm going to do something about that!"

Nick shrugged and passed the paper back to me, staring at the figures on the screen. I could practically hear the keys whirring as his mental adding machine spun through the figures. "Looks about right," he said.

"The hell it does! That's not my take-home. My deductions are twice what he's showing here. Dub gave us all raises last year and my deductions went sky-high. He said it put me in a new bracket. Same with most of the others."

Nick grabbed a piece of paper and made a note of the monthly total in deductions. "Where does he keep the canceled checks and deposit slips?"

Justine gestured toward the filing cabinet. "But it's locked," she reminded him. "And I can't find a key anywhere."

It's a fairly simple matter to break into a filing cabinet, although it left a few scars in the brown enamel paint. "I'll just tell him I didn't realize it was locked," Justine said with a shrug. "I thought something was stuck in the drawer, so I pried it open. I was cleaning out Walter's desk and thought I should check the filing cabinet?" She looked at me for a critique of her story.

"It works for me. After all, what's he going to do, fire you? You're his partner, remember?"

"How many accounts do you have?" Nick asked, laying envelopes in neat rows on the office floor.

"I'm not sure. A general account, a payroll account, and a tax account, I think. Dub's not telling me much. To tell you the truth, I think he's looking for money to buy me out. He hasn't said anything about it yet, but he's going to be disappointed. I'm not going anywhere."

Nick had by now formed three columns of envelopes—bank statements and canceled checks—and assigned us each a column. "Open them, sort them by type if you can, and look them over," he said.

"What are we looking for?"

"Anything funny."

I took the general account, knowing that Nick would do better with taxes than I, and started sorting checks. Vendors. Utilities. Petty cash. It was all more or less like the checks we wrote every month at the Oracle.

"Funny," Nick said. "Each payroll period has one check to cash. The memo says deposit to tax account. Why doesn't he just deposit a check?" No one had an answer for that. "Listen," he said to Justine. "I'll read the dates out and you check to see if the deposits were made. January sixteenth."

"Got it."

"January thirty-first."

"Okay." I went back to my task.

Dub had written all the checks, I noticed, which pretty well jibed with Walter being a silent partner. And Dub was not above taking a few perks here and there. Large checks to local restaurants—the power lunch, I suppose. Checks to hotels.

"Justine, do you pay the bands' expenses when they come into town?"

"Usually, yeah. Meals and hotel. They pay transportation."

"Darn. Thought I might have found ol' Dub in flagrante delicto." A fleeting expression of distaste flickered across Justine's features.

"September thirtieth. You know, we should be verifying the amounts," Nick continued. "This one's four hundred fifty-eight dollars."

"Hold it. How much?" Nick repeated the figure.

"No way. Try two hundred seventy-two." We all stared at each other for a moment.

"Let's go back to the beginning," Nick said. "This time I'll give you date and figure."

The picture was becoming clear. Dub was withdrawing cash from the payroll account and depositing it into the tax account semimonthly, as he should. But the figures didn't match. Justine pulled up the payroll file on the computer again, and this time Nick pulled out his calculator.

"Okay, the figures he's depositing in the tax account match the withholding he's showing here."

"But he's withholding more than he's showing, I'm telling you," Justine said. "My take-home since the raise has been eight hundred and sixty-five dollars twice a month. He's showing a hundred dollars more. What's the deal, anyway?"

Nick punched the calculator off and poked it back in his pocket. "He's withholding extra money, drawing it out of the payroll account in cash, and depositing the correct amount. He's pocketing the rest."

"So in other words, he's stealing from us."

"Didn't you notice anything strange about your W-2 this year?"

"Well, I didn't check it. I'm always late getting my taxes in—and I had to pay this year, dammit. What a sneak!"

"Well, I'll bet somebody noticed it and turned them in to the IRS. That's why they're auditing you."

It was the *you* that did it. "Am I liable for what he did?"

Nick stroked his chin thoughtfully. "I don't know. Probably not, since it happened before you took over. But I'm betting Fry would have some liability. Either way, I'd get a lawyer if I were you. George Wolenski's a good man. I'm using him."

"Wait till I get my hands on him." Justine hit a key and the printer whirred.

Nick and I exchanged worried glances. The last thing we wanted was Justine tipping off Dub Cantrell that we were looking into his business. After considerable talking, she agreed to hold off and let the IRS do what it does best—intimidate.

"Found anything, Julia?"

"Just the usual. Didn't you say costs were up? I've got a huge stack of checks to vendors here. Who on earth is Rooster's?"

"Rooster's?" Justine repeated. "We don't deal with any vendors by that name."

"Well, I've got the checks right here. Look, here's one." I passed her the canceled check. "Look at the memo. It says 'ten cases Jim Beam.' "

"We get our whiskey and bourbon from Consolidated. Let me see those." I passed her the stack of Rooster's checks and listened as she muttered under her breath. "Scotch. Gin. Ale. What the hell's going on? Rooster's is a little bar over on the edge of Markettown."

"I know the place," Nick said.

"Well, we sure don't buy our liquor from them!"

Nick took the checks and ran up a quick total for the month of April. "I think Mr. Cantrell has a problem," he said. "And this one's not with the IRS."

"They match," Nick said, tapping the Rooster's checks into a neat stack. He handed Walter's sheet of columned numbers back to me. I took it, giddy with elation.

"You know what that means, don't you?" I said, grinning at the two of them. "It means that Walter knew Dub was up to something. He was probably going to confront Dub with it, if he hadn't already. And that means that Dub Cantrell had a good reason to want Fry out of his way. A motive for murder!"

"Murder?" Justine repeated, glancing from Nick to me, and back to Nick. "Dub?"

Nick glared at me and ground his jaws. Woops.

"Well, if that girl—what's her name—May? You know, if she didn't do it."

"April," Justine said. "Her name's April Folsom."

"That's right. April, not May. I guess I got them mixed up because—" But Justine was ominously silent, and greeted my innocent gaze with suspicion.

"Look," Nick said hurriedly. "I have a pretty good idea what these Rooster's checks are all about. Let me do a little checking up on them and get back to you. Meanwhile, go to the employees you trust and ask to see their paycheck stubs. Tell them you're thinking about raises and you need to see what their take-home is. When you get the figures, compare them to that," he continued, nodding at the printed sheets lying on the desk. "Try to figure out exactly how much he's been pocketing every month. But make sure you keep it very quiet. Somebody tipped off the IRS. It may be someone who works here now, or a disgruntled ex-employee. Either way, it could mean real trouble with the feds."

We left Justine reorganizing the bank statements and checks, returning them to the file cabinet. Nick didn't say anything until we got to the car.

"Nice going," he said. "You may have blown it for us."

"Sorry."

"If you remember, we were trying to find out what Justine's relationship to Walter Fry was."

"I know. I just got distracted, you know? I mean, all this business about his partner stealing and everything. I don't like that guy. I'd much rather he were the murderer."

"No one gave you the choice," Nick observed dryly.

"I wish they had. I don't think Justine would murder him. Did you see how outraged she was about Cantrell stealing? She's an honest person."

"Not necessarily. She's just very interested in money."

I had to give him that point. Justine was certainly motivated by the dollar. Which brought us right back where we started. What was Justine's relationship to Walter Fry?

"Evelyn," I said.

"What?"

"My hair. I think I need to have my hair done."

<h1>Chapter Nineteen</h1>

sub-ter-fuge \\ˈsəb-tər-fyüj\n [LL *subterfugium,* fr. L *subterfugere* to escape, evade, fr. *subter-* secretly (fr. *subter* underneath; akin to L *sub* under) +*fugere* to flee—more at UP, FUGITIVE] (1573) **1:** deception by artifice or stratagem in order to conceal, escape, or evade **2:** a deceptive device or stratagem **syn** see DECEPTION.
—*Merriam Webster's Ninth New Collegiate Dictionary*

It took me an hour the next morning to make the phone calls. There were three hairdressers named Evelyn working in Delphi. I had appointments with all of them and had to hurry to make the first one.

It was an ordinary cut-and-blow shop on Broadway, and Evelyn was due in at eleven. I was her first appointment of the day. They had shampooed my hair and I was waiting in the chair when she walked in and my heart sank. Evelyn was white.

"What do you need?"

"Oh," I said, "just trim a little off the top."

The second Evelyn was the right color. She worked in a shop close to downtown on the edge of a housing project, and stared at me across the shop.

"I haven't cut a white lady's hair in fifteen years. You sure you're in the right place?"

"You're Evelyn, aren't you? My friend, um, Annie recommended you."

"Annie Morgan or Annie Jeeter?"

"Annie Jeeter," I shot back, holding my breath.

Evelyn nodded reluctantly. "All right, sit down. Be with you shortly."

But when I was finally in her chair and staring at her reflection in the mirror, I knew I had the wrong Evelyn. She looked a lot older up close, with flecks of gray across her browline and at the temples.

"Now, what'd you want done?" she said.

Gulp. "What do you think about straightening it?"

At two o'clock I pulled into the parking lot at the Shear Delight and fingered my hair. It felt brittle. Straightening it had added length, and it was sticking out in tufts like a punk rocker. I hadn't let Evelyn blow-dry or set it, since I was running late for my next appointment. And I had no idea how I was going to explain the broom straw that was now growing out of my head. My entrance was met with startled silence.

The receptionist checked her book and verified that I had a three-o'clock appointment, which, her expression suggested, was not a minute too soon. She hustled me to a chair, explained that Evelyn was brushing someone out on the other side of the mauve striped partition and would be with me in a minute. But this time I knew I was in the right place. Evelyn Hall's license was taped onto the mirror. I concentrated on it, unable to bear my own reflection.

She came around the partition and froze. "Oh my," was the best greeting she could muster. Her petite frame was poured into her Calvins, and under a red and black brocade vest she wore a low-cut T-shirt that rounded out the picture of a very shapely figure. Her nails were longer than I like on a hairdresser, and painted a deep scarlet. In the face, she was a ringer for Whitney Houston.

"I know," I said. "I got tired of curls, so I straightened it. Now what do I do?"

Evelyn suppressed a smile and ran her fingers through what remained of my hair. She studied the shape of my face in the mirror, pulled my hair back to expose my ears, studied the hairline on my neck.

"Perming's out. It's already too damaged. I'd say we start with deep conditioning and then go to a good, short cut." She held up a lock between her index and middle fingers. "A very short cut." I groaned inwardly. The Shear Delight was a very pricey shop.

Evelyn was a friendly girl. We shampooed and talked. We warmed oil and massaged and talked. We conditioned and talked. She kept up a running banter with Patty, the shampoo girl, Tanya, the manicurist, and the other stylists. And finally we were back in front of the mirror.

"So how'd you get into hairdressing?"

Evelyn pulled open a drawer and grabbed a tiny pair of scissors and a fresh comb. She shrugged. "I tried a lot of things after I got out of high school. Worked at the mall for a while. Tended bar."

"That must have been interesting. Where'd you work?"

"Coupla places downtown. How do you feel about having it feathered around your face?"

"Fine. Just make it look presentable. Downtown?"

"At first. Then I went out to a place on the Industry Road. The Vagabond."

Pay dirt! "I've heard of it," I said. "Country western dance hall, right?"

"Uh-huh. You going to be blowing dry?"

"Probably. I'm looking for the easiest thing to take care of. Meet any good-looking cowboys?"

"One or two."

"Don't let her fool you," Tanya called from her table. "She had Wal-ter," she sang out.

Evelyn responded with a half-smile and a rude gesture. "Tanya and I go back to cosmetology school together. It's not something I'm proud of. She's got a few secrets of her own," she said. Fortunately, they weren't especially concerned with keeping them.

"Walter, huh? Big, good-looking. Narrow hips and all?" Yes, I was embarrassing myself, but I was never setting foot in the Shear Delight again. Frankly, I couldn't afford it.

Tanya let out a hoot. "Walter? Good-looking? Maybe if you're into cattle. He looked like an old bull." I grimaced, mentally acknowledging that it was an apt simile.

"Hey, Tanya, let up, will you? We both got what we wanted, okay? You're gonna have to keep conditioning this. You shampoo every day?"

I admitted I did.

"We're going to have to get you on this special treatment, then. A good shampoo with extra nutrients, followed by deep conditioning daily. If you don't have one, we retail a couple of them." I couldn't very well admit that I used Suave and considered it just fine.

"Right," I said. "I'll pick up something when I leave." In the mirror I could see Tanya tiptoeing toward us, her finger to her lips. "So are you still seeing Walter?"

"Oh Lord, no. Actually, he's—"

Tanya darted around behind the chair and whispered in my ear. "Evelyn was an old man's darling," she said, before Evelyn swatted her with the comb.

"Look who's talking! Tanya's into bikers—and she isn't particular about little things like teeth, if you know the type."

So that was it. I guess I had known it all along. Walter had a string of women on the side—young, black women. And apparently it was a quid pro quo. Evelyn went to cosmetology school. Justine inherited a dance hall. Evelyn hadn't been the first, but Justine was the last. Where would she have been if Walter Fry were still living?

I left the Shear Delight ninety-five dollars in the hole and carrying a shopping bag full of hair and scalp treatments I was going to have to explain to Nick. But at least I had the information I was looking for.

"*Mana mou!*"

I fingered my hair defensively. It prickled my fingers like chin stubble.

"What have you done? Where's your hair?" He circled me, studying my head as though it were a bust on a pedestal in the National Museum in Athens.

Thanks to the straightening chemicals, my hair had climbed the spectrum from a medium ash blond to cornsilk platinum. Among the preparations in my bag were shampoo and conditioners made of papaya, aloe, and awapuhi—whatever that was—and a toner intended to subdue any latent tendency toward brassiness. Evelyn had given me a good cut, and the little hair remaining feathered softly around my face before slashing severely over my ears. It was, I thought, a haircut that made a bold statement: Look at me—independent, strong-minded, efficient. It reclaimed all the feminist assertions of my early youth. I could bring home the bacon, fry it up in the pan . . . *I am woman—hear me . . . yawn.*

Nick stood in front of me, his hand folded under his chin, his index finger tapping his lips. I thought he was trying to suppress a smile.

"Well, it's done now, so if you don't like it . . . it'll grow out. That's the nice thing about hair. And anyway, it was worth it," I said, tucking my shopping bag behind the register.

"Exactly how much?"

"How much what?" I said evasively. "Oh, a lot. I found out everything I wanted to know."

"And it cost . . ."

"Less than a new pair of shoes." Hand-made imported Italian leather, I silently added. "I'm starved. Have you eaten?"

Nick replied in the negative. "Well, there's nothing to fix at home but soup, so we'd better get something before Spiros closes the kitchen down, if he hasn't already." We settled on Greek side salads and *stifatho*, a kind of savory stew.

I tracked Spiros down in the walk-in. "Zulia?" he said, staring wide-eyed at my head.

I pivoted on my heel. "It's the new me, Spiros."

He reached out tentatively to touch the top of my head, nodded happily, and shook his open palm. "Ve-ry hot! Like She-ned O'Cohnor."

Well, not quite. But at least he appreciated the change. I gave him our orders and returned to the dining room.

Nick greeted me with a broad smile. "I just talked to George Wolenski. They've taken Fortunata off the case and agreed to credit our account for everything—the payment we don't owe, plus penalties and interest. We'll get some kind of a correction from them next week."

I sagged into the chair, my knees weak with relief. I hadn't realized how much it was worrying me—that six thousand seven hundred twenty-three dollars. And forty-six cents. "Oh, Nick, that's wonderful. It's like finding money, isn't it? Now we can afford to put a new roof on the house, maybe take a vacation—"

"Julia, we never had the money in the first place."

"Oh. Yeah. Well, at least it's one less thing to worry about. That's something, isn't it?"

"Something. And here's something else." He was holding a videotape cassette, turning it over in his hands, which he pushed toward me. It was marked WPAR-TV.

"Billy just dropped it off. Said he promised to get it for you."

"It's the full tape of the funeral," I explained as I tucked it into the bag of hair preparations. "We can watch it later. First I want to tell you about my day."

"By all means," Nick said, with a wry smile. But I didn't feel up to discussing my hair, instead launching into the information I'd gotten from Evelyn Hall.

"So you see, apparently Walter Fry had particular taste in women. He preferred them young and black. At least, I think we can deduce that from the indications. Three or four young black

213

women, all helped to get schooling or good jobs. Justine's just the last of a string of them. And," I reminded him, "they slept in separate beds. He and Bitsy, I mean." Although I didn't say it to Nick, I thought that Walter's cache of beautiful black women fit in very well with everything else we knew about him—exploiting their sexuality as women while keeping them servile because of their race. What a sleaze. Of course, I had to admit to myself that the women didn't have to go along with him. They had made their own choice on that one.

"And the point of this is . . ."

"That Justine had a lot to gain by—" But I liked Justine. I didn't really want to believe that she was a murderer. "But of course, she's not the only one. Dub Cantrell was ripping off his partner and his employees, and he had them in a mess with the IRS, and . . ." I raked my hands through my nonexistent hair.

"I don't know, Nick. I'm starting to feel really confused. Did you find out anything about Rooster's?" We had agreed that Nick would probe to find out what was growing on the Buffalo grapevine about Rooster's Tavern.

He sat back, pulled out his worry beads, and gently spun them between his fingers. "I already know about Rooster's. It's a bar, but the bar's mostly a front for a high-stakes game."

"Poker?"

Nick nodded absently. "I asked Sonny about it this morning. You know, it's the first time I've ever seen him so quiet. He really didn't want to talk, Julia."

"Sonny? Not talking?"

"I had to push him—promise him I wouldn't repeat it."

"And?"

"Sonny plays at Rooster's once or twice a week. Most of the guys in the poker group do. He knows Dub Cantrell. Cantrell's a lousy poker player—always looking for the big score, the perfect hand. He's a pretty steady loser, but he won't quit."

"A candidate for Gambler's Anonymous. So the checks aren't for liquor at all."

Nick pushed his hat back on his brow and frowned. "Gambling debts. A lot of them. And Fry knew about them."

"Okay, so we have a motive for murder, right?"

"Probably. But we have to find out where Cantrell was that night."

"Great. How are we going to do that? We can't just walk in there and ask him, especially after the fight the other night."

Spiros set our plates on the table, glancing nervously between us as we sat silently staring at nothing. *"Then tou arresoun tou Nikou ta malya sou?"* he said quietly in my ear, pointing at my head.

"Neh. Ohee. Then exero," I said, indicating that I really didn't know how Nick felt about my hair.

Spiros's gaze shifted to Nick. *"Niko mou,"* he said plaintively. "Is nice! Like wolf!"

"A fox, *agori mou.* She looks foxy."

"Neh, neh. Fox-ee lad-ee."

Nick reassured Spiros that everything was all right. We were not fighting over my hair. This must be what it's like to have children—insecure children.

Nick picked up his fork and toyed with a chunk of feta cheese on his salad. "You may not like this," he said at length. "But I know how to find out—or at least get close to him. I'm going to the game at Rooster's with Sonny tomorrow night."

"Oh, Nick . . ."

We did not, however, have the chance to pursue the subject at that moment. A party of late lunch customers arrived. I looked up with some surprise to find April, Candice, and D'Anita waiting to be seated. We insisted that they join us at the family table instead.

April's face was pale, her lipstick and blush too bright a contrast against the pallor of her skin. She looked like a little girl who had been playing in her mother's makeup and smudged dark eye shadow all around her eyes. A closer look told me that the violet crescents under her eyes were not makeup.

D'Anita studied her menu and pointedly ignored us. Candice smiled and patted April's hand maternally. "We thought she needed to get out of the hospital for a while. Chester is sitting with Davon."

D'Anita was all attention then. "Poor April's been with my brother night and day since they let her out of jail." Poorly worded concern, I thought. "She needed a break."

"How is he?"

Candice smiled. "Much better. He's sitting up and starting to eat. His reflexes are good. We're going to get him up and walk him around some this afternoon. If he does all right, he'll be released tomorrow."

"But he still hasn't remembered anything," April added. "The doctor says he won't either. There wasn't enough time between him spotting them and . . ." She trailed off weakly, her features drooping back into a worried frown. I could have finished the sentence myself: *the attack*. I had been there and I knew there wasn't enough time. The doctor was right. Davon would never be able to identify them, and that would leave us both very vulnerable. I put my fork down—my appetite for salad and *stifatho* definitely gone.

I glanced over at Nick to find that his appetite had gone the way of mine. He was fingering his worry beads and staring out at the parking lot.

We must have argued for an hour after they left. Nick stubbornly refused to see the wisdom of my idea, but had nothing to offer in its place.

"It's the only way," I said. "You'll be there, so I'll be perfectly safe. If we don't try it, they're going to be out there on the loose, and neither Davon nor I will be safe then."

Nick shook his head obdurately. "It's too dangerous."

"Look at it this way," I persisted. "At least we'll be in control. I don't want to have to live the rest of my life wondering if, and when, he's going to come after me again. Look at what they did to Davon. Heaven knows what he might have done to me. This way we'll get them, and it will all be over."

He was thinking about it—setting it up in his mind. I could see, in his eyes, the details being planned, the safeguards checked. At length he tossed his beads on the table.

"Okay," he said. "But only if Sam agrees to it."

"Oh, Nick, I don't think we need to bring Sam into it," I said. But his jaw was tight, teeth clenching, hands rigidly splayed.

"Okay," I said, grabbing my purse and bag of hair treatments. "Let's go talk to him."

ex-tort \ik-ˈsto(ə)rt\ *vt* [L *extortus*, pp. of *extorquēre* to wrench out, extort, fr. *ex-* + *torquēre* to twist—more at TORTURE] (1529): to obtain from a person by force, intimidation, or undue or illegal power: WRING; *also:* to gain esp. by ingenuity or compelling argument **syn** see EDUCE.

—*Merriam Webster's Ninth New Collegiate Dictionary*

"I thought I told you two to stay out of my case!" Sam pounded his fist on the scarred oak of his desk.

Nick glanced at me and shook his head slightly. I took that to mean that I should not, at that moment, mention my idea.

"We're not involved in your case—really. Look, Sam," I said. "April is a friend of mine and I don't believe she killed Walter Fry. Especially not when there are about a hundred other people who probably wanted him dead. What is it they say in police work? *Cui bono.* Who benefits?"

"They say that in detective novels," Sam commented dryly. "In police work they say, 'Let's wrap this case up.' And that's what we've done. The DA had probable cause to arrest your friend. He took it to the grand jury, and they looked at the evidence. She'd been seen threatening Fry, she'd had the gun, and she was on the premises the night of the murder. She had means, motive, and opportunity." Sam ticked these off his fingers, holding all three up for us to see.

"The grand jury did the only thing sane people can do—they indicted her. She's got a good lawyer and she'll get a good defense. That's how the process works, and it doesn't leave room for messing around by a pair of amateurs who think, because they solved a crime once, that they're Nick and Nora Charles." He sat back and took a deep breath before continuing.

"Now I want you, Frickus," he said pointing to Nick, "to go home and take Fracas here with you."

"Fracas!"

Nick reached over and not-so-gently squeezed my knee. "All right," he said. "But at least let us tell you what we know." I nodded emphatically, silently sending the message that we were going nowhere until he had heard us out. Red-faced, he yanked open his desk drawer and scrabbled around in it, at length surfacing with a slightly flattened pack of unfiltered Camels.

"You quit two years ago," I said as he snapped a lighter and took a deep drag. "Does Rhonda know you've started again?"

"I haven't started again," he growled. "I just keep 'em around for times like this—when words and patience fail me."

I just love it when someone hands me a weapon and begs me to use it. I shot Nick a quick glance and bit the inside of my mouth, turning back to Sam with a grieved expression. "Rhonda would be so upset if she found out. You know how it is—you smoke one. Then another. Pretty soon you're back in the habit. And you're scrambling around, trying to hide it from your wife. It's on your breath. Your clothes . . . She's going to find out sooner or later."

Sam eyed me warily. "It's your call," I continued. "Sooner? Or later?"

Sam ground out the butt and reached for the pack again. Nick coughed politely. I waved my hand in front of my face. "Sure hope Rhonda doesn't smell it on me," I said.

"I'd like to think of this as a *sharing* of information," I said. "We share. You share."

"Now, look—" Sam spat a piece of loose tobacco off his tongue.

"Here's what we know," Nick said, quickly intervening. "We know that Walter Fry was a silent partner in the Vagabond, and that his partner, Cantrell, was stealing money from the business and their employees. He's being audited and I think he's going to find himself into the IRS for a lot of money."

"How do you know that?"

"Let's just say his current partner and I figured it out."

Despite his resistance, Sam was getting interested. "Okay, so he's in debt and he's stealing . . ."

"Well, Fry knew about it." Nick went on to explain how he knew, carefully sidestepping Sam's questions. Of course, should it become necessary to prove it, the checks would become evidence, which would mean the game would be up at Rooster's, which would, in turn, mean some very disgruntled Buffaloes. Nick wanted to avoid that if he could. It's inexplicable to me, but for some reason he hates to offend them.

"Fry was probably pretty angry, and he may have threatened Cantrell. Now, I doubt if Cantrell would be dumb enough to do it himself. In fact, I have a pretty good idea where he was that night. But those goons you were holding . . ." Nick pointed to the floor, and the holding cells that I knew too well were beneath Sam's office.

"You think he hired a hit?"

"I don't know. I think he might have. He had a life insurance policy, and the benefits went to the business. In other words, to his partner."

"Yeah, I know about that. Wasn't a very big policy, though."

"Maybe not. But if it was big enough to cover his debts . . ." Nick let that hang in the air.

Sam stared at us. I coughed and let my eyes drift to the pack of Camels. After a moment he grabbed a pad and scrawled a note on it. "All right, what else?"

We told him about Justine and Evelyn Hall, and about Walter's apparent predilection for extramarital affairs. "Justine would benefit, I suppose," I acknowledged reluctantly. "Although I really can't see her pulling a trigger."

"Some people can't quite see Ted Bundy as a serial killer either," Sam shot back. Well, at least he was paying attention. He went to his filing cabinet, pulled out a folder, and brought it back to his desk. He clipped the note to the outside and tossed it down, spilling the contents on top of his old-fashioned blotter. Nick had the pictures before Sam could stop him.

"Crime scene?"

"Yeah. You ought not to have those. DA would have my hide."

Nick grinned. "He's tough, huh? Like Rhonda?" Sam ignored the remark, but let Nick study the pictures at some length while he gathered up the remaining documents, shoving them back in the folder out of my reach. I didn't look at the photographs. I didn't want to see them. It would make the murder too real. In spite of the fact that Walter Fry was dead, and April was accused of his death, murder was still only a word. Photographs would make it a reality.

Nick handed the photographs back to Sam. "Something else . . ." he said. "I think you have to consider the wife, too."

"Oh, no way, Nick. Not Bitsy! You haven't met her, but she's   " I stopped when Sam shook his head.

"Checked up on her first thing. Alibi's ironclad. And she was there when the body was found."

"Oh, poor Bitsy. How terrible for her."

"I don't think she ever actually saw him," Sam drawled. He glanced back in the folder and double-checked. "The nephew officially identified him."

"What do you mean? You just said she found the body."

"No, it was found by a friend who was with her. Spaulding's the name. Vivian Spaulding."

"Of course," Nick said, "Bitsy could have hired a hit." I almost laughed out loud, imagining Bitsy Fry, in the dark of night, handing over vast quantities of currency to two thugs with whispered instructions to take her husband out. Yeah, right.

Although I could scarcely imagine Bitsy Fry contracting her husband's murder, it was not too difficult to imagine Stephen Ellis Cox and Robert Vernon Willard carrying it out. These were very dangerous men—the kind who drift around looking for a quick buck and a ripe victim. My mind went back to the Oracle, to the way they had enjoyed tormenting Davon and me. I skipped over the incident at the Vagabond, knowing that to rekindle that terror might actually dissolve my resolution. And resolved I was, to catch them and force them to show themselves for who they were. If I didn't do it, I would never feel completely safe again.

"And my money's on those two guys who beat up Davon," Nick added.

"Yeah," Sam said, dropping back into his chair. "We're never gonna prove it, though. I talked with the doc this morning. He says there's no chance that Folsom's ever gonna be able to remember being attacked."

He sighed deeply and leaned back, crossing his arms over his chest. "Even if he remembered a little something, the defense would tear it apart on the stand. They'd bring in expert testimony—some doc who'd say there's no way he could possibly remember, so the evidence would be tainted. Then they'd accuse me of coercing him . . ."

"Sam," I said. "Nick and I have an idea." Sam reached out and snagged the pack of Camels.

Nick sat at the kitchen table, a yellow lined pad in front of him. I was stretched out on the den floor halfheartedly doing leg lifts to one of the exercise tapes where women wearing designer exercise togs look as if they're enjoying it and would never think of sweating. I've about concluded that the only time I'll ever have buns of steel is when rigor sets in. Still, I persisted in making myself miserable. To my astonishment, Jack had joined me on the floor, rolled on his side, and lifted one leg. All that was missing was an insipid smile.

"There are three things we have to find out," Nick said, holding his pad up for me to see. "First, why did Fry leave the Vagabond to Justine?"

"I think we know the answer to that, Nick."

"Second, where were the other suspects at the time of the murder?"

"And third?" I said.

He wandered into the den and joined me in the end of the aerobic routine. He had no trouble keeping up or making the rapid step changes, which by now I should have known but never could seem to remember. His natural grace irritated me even more than the smiling dancers on the screen.

"I think we should try to talk to the Spaulding woman," he said, effortlessly lunging right and left. "Maybe she saw something that she hasn't told the sheriff. And anyway, how did she happen to find Walter Fry instead of his wife?"

"Interesting question," I gasped, and began jogging in place. We were in the cool-down phase, which I find is just as taxing as the rest of it. Jack danced at my heels, yipping and nipping at the strings of my tennis shoes. "I'll . . . call . . . Miss . . . Alma . . . if . . . I . . . live . . . through . . . this."

As I explained to Nick when the routine was finished and I had caught my breath, if anyone could get Vivian to talk to us, it would be Miss Alma. I called her and she agreed to get in touch with her friend, provided we took her along when we questioned Vivian. She called us back in a few minutes.

"She'll see us at ten o'clock," I repeated to Nick, after I'd hung up with Miss Alma.

I pulled off my sweatshirt and headed for the shower, mindful that I would first have to deep-condition my hair, followed by papaya, aloe, and awa—whatever shampoo and rich creme conditioner and dressing. Blow-drying must be done on low using a diffuser. Oh bother, I thought, and left it wet.

Nick was already in bed when I emerged. Jack was snuffling around in Nick's clothes, dropped on his favorite chair. The men in my life wage an ongoing battle over that chair. Jack has claimed it as his own. Nick insists on using it as his valet. Nick often smells slightly doggy.

"You know, we need to take all this to L.T., Julia. He needs the information for April's defense."

"If we wait a day or two, April may not need a defense," I said, wishing I felt as confident as I was trying to sound. Sam had eventually, very reluctantly, agreed to our plan. Even he could see that it was the only way we'd get those two off the streets. But I didn't want to talk about it, didn't want to betray how frightened I really was.

And now," I said, wrapping my arms around him, "I don't want to talk anymore about murder."

"Me neither. Let's talk about your hair."

I knew it would come up eventually. I contemplated which stand I should take—the outraged who-are-you-to-tell-me-how-to-wear-my-hair position, or the I-care-how-you-feel-because-I-want-to-please-you tack. I opted for the latter.

"Oh, Nick, I know you hate it. But I ran out of things for them to do to it—and then after Evelyn the Second straightened it, well, then it really needed help! You can't say anything that I haven't already said to myself."

"Actually," he said, his fingertips toying with the down at my temples, "I was going to say that I think it's kind of sexy."

"Oh, well then—"

Breakfast was hectic the next morning. Spiros had introduced a new breakfast item to attract the Buffaloes who regularly patronized Dinah's Donuts. *Loukoumades*—hot honey puffs, lightly flavored with orange and deep fried to a golden brown. I ladled warm cinnamon and honey syrup over them and sent them out the order window as fast as Tammy and Rhonda could pick them up. By the time ten o'clock arrived, Spiros was warmed up and bounding around the kitchen like a retriever puppy.

"We van-kweesh Dinah," he declared, holding a honey puff between his fingers.

"Probably not, unless you can figure out how to fill them with jelly," I muttered as I headed for the dining room. "We're late," I said to Nick, glancing at my watch. "Miss Alma will be standing on the corner. You know how prompt she is."

She was, in fact, right where I'd predicted she'd be. Fortunately, Vivian Spaulding lived in the Crosscreek section of town, a quick trip down Columbus Avenue from Markettown. We were only ten minutes late in arriving, and Miss Alma made our apologies for us. Vivian waved them away and set a coffee service on the table in front of us. Nick and I took chairs in front of the living room window, leaving the couch to Vivian and Miss Alma.

"You wanted to talk to me about something?" she said, passing us demitasse cups that would in no way quench anyone's need for morning caffeine.

Miss Alma took the initiative. "I'll be candid with you, Vivian. We need to talk with you about the night of Walter's murder."

"Oh dear," Vivian said, setting down her cup with a clatter. She fingered her bluish curls and smoothed the front of her dress.

"I'm sorry," Miss Alma continued. "I know it must be hard for you to talk about."

Vivian calmly folded her hands in her lap. "Yes, it is. It was a terrible ordeal. But they're going to call on me to testify, I know that. I'm going to have to testify, and that poor, darling girl is going to be sent to jail."

"Maybe not," I said quickly. "You may have information that could help."

"I'm afraid I really don't know anything. I've told the police everything already."

"Would you mind just going over it again with us?"

Vivian hesitated. "I'm not sure I should be talking to—"

"Vivian," Miss Alma broke in. Her voice was stern, her expression reproving. Her erect posture betrayed the authoritative teacher she must once have been. "Sometimes we have to break the rules. I know you ran your classroom by the book, but don't tell me that once in a while you didn't stretch and bend the rules for a special student. I know better. Now April needs your help, and I expect that you're going to do everything you can for her."

Vivian gazed down at her folded hands, knobby and dotted with age spots. "All right," she said meekly. "What do you want to know?"

"We want you to tell us everything that you remember about that night."

"Well," she said, gazing off into the middle distance, "Bitsy and I drove to the Ladies' Circle together that night. I picked her up, because she was on my way. We had some things to discuss— mainly the clothing drive."

But they hadn't had time to finish their conversation before the meeting started. It was almost nine o'clock when the Ladies' Circle wrapped things up. When they returned to the Fry house, Bitsy suggested that Vivian come in for a few minutes so they could finalize their plans for the clothing drive. She had stopped at the chest freezer in the garage to get a carton of ice cream and, knowing that Walter was at home, had sent Vivian on in.

"Which is how I happened to find him. He was lying on the kitchen floor, and I didn't have to check his pulse to know he was dead. He'd been shot—" Vivian shuddered and her voice dropped off to a whisper. "In the head." Miss Alma placed a hand over Vivian's, still folded in her lap.

"I'd never seen anything like that. I've seen bodies in caskets, of course. But this—"

"We understand," Miss Alma said. "Take your time. It's all right."

Vivian nodded. "I met Bitsy at the door as she was coming in with the ice cream. I couldn't tell her the truth about him. Not right then."

"What did you do?"

"I just asked her to wait a minute. Then I pulled the door closed behind me so she wouldn't be able to see poor Walter, and got her one of those folding lawn chairs."

This was the crucial point. If Bitsy had been expecting trouble, if she'd hired his murder, her reaction could tell us everything. I felt myself lean forward, holding my breath and wishing she'd get on with the story. After a second, she did.

"I told her there had been an accident, and I wanted her to sit quietly while I took care of it. She didn't understand. 'What kind of accident?' she said, trying to get by me. But she still didn't understand. What had happened? Where was Walter? He was supposed to be at home."

Vivian tried to pick up her demitasse, frowned at it, and set it back on the table. "I told her that the accident had involved Walter, and that there was nothing she could do for him. I'd grabbed Walter's Bible off the kitchen counter, and I put it in her hands and sat her down with it."

"How did she seem to be?"

"Stunned," Vivian said firmly.

"Didn't she want to go into the house?"

"You don't know Bitsy very well." Vivian smiled gently. "She has a rather passive nature. I told her I would take care of it, and she just nodded. Then I went back into the house and called the police. I locked the door in case she tried to come in, but I don't think she did. We waited for them in the garage."

"Did Bitsy say anything? Anything at all?"

"Nothing." Vivian shook her head. "She sat there in that lawn chair in the garage and read out loud."

"What did she read?"

"The Twenty-third Psalm. She just read it over and over."

"Vivian is a very reliable witness," Miss Alma said, when we were back in the car.

"She certainly keeps her cool." How she could have remained that calm, and kept Bitsy from falling apart, was beyond my understanding.

"She was a very good teacher, and you're right, she stays very composed in a crisis. During the late sixties and early seventies we had any number of bomb scares at school. And later, after I retired, they started having problems with drugs and violence. Vivian kept right on going through it all. She had a student pull a gun in her classroom one time, and she handled it so well she was voted Teacher of the Year by the faculty. If she says that's how it happened, I believe her."

Amazing, I thought, that this little blue-haired woman had worked in the trenches of public high schools for years and still managed to keep her sanity. I was glad that Bitsy'd had her to depend on the night Walter was murdered. We hadn't really learned anything, except that Bitsy was truly shocked by the murder. Somehow I felt relieved at that, and chastised myself for it.

Why did I have to dislike the victim but like all the suspects? It wasn't natural. Murderers were not likable people, and victims were usually innocent. Except that in this case the victim had been a loathsome man and, I reminded myself, my favorite candidates for murderers were classic—right out of *Deliverance*—evil. And I was going to have to face them one more time.

in-cu-bate \ '·in-kyƏ-bāt*vb* -bat-ed; -bat-ing [L *in-cubatus,* pp. of *incubare,* fr. *in* + cubare—more at HIP] *vt* (ca. 1721) **1:** to sit on (eggs) so as to hatch by the warmth of the body . . . **2:** to cause (as an idea) to develop . . .
—*Merriam Webster's Ninth New Collegiate Dictionary*

"Please," I said, for the fifth time that night. "Be careful."

Nick stuck his hat on his head, twirled his keys, and planted a kiss on the end of my nose. "I'll be back around two," he said.

Jack and I watched him back the car out of the garage and pull out of the driveway. We watched the Honda until it crested the hill beyond the house and was gone. I filled Jack's water dish and poured myself a very large glass of white zin.

"Here's to poker," I toasted, staring out the window, and nervously gulped down half the glass.

With those first couple of swallows, a comfortable euphoria set in. I hadn't wanted Nick to play that night, but I knew that if he didn't, nothing else would fall into place. It was the only way that Nick could legitimately get near Dub Cantrell.

Nick had played poker with the Buffs once a week for the last five years—since soon after we'd opened the Oracle. It was logical that he might move on to a bigger game, and he was known among at least half of the men who would be at Rooster's that night. He would be perfectly safe. No one would even question it. Still, I turned away from the window with a queasy stomach and resolved to spend the evening with Jack, catching up on the laundry and trying to betroth the inevitable bachelor socks.

I waited, half dozing on the couch, until well past 2:00 A.M. At two-thirty I was feeling uneasy. At three I was seriously considering calling Sam. At three-thirty I was panicky enough to do it, and had my hand on the phone when I heard the low rumble of the Honda in the garage.

What happened that night, I can only repeat as it was told to me, much later, in the dark, in the comfort and security of my husband's arms. Nick met Sonny outside of Rooster's at about seven o'clock. Sonny had already cleared it with Rooster's owner, Al Bantam, who did not himself play in the game. Bantam personally escorted Nick to the back of the bar, into a room that was designated for private parties only. A bar was set up in one corner, with Bantam himself mixing the drinks. There were already three players leaning on the bar trading golf stories when Nick arrived. They were introduced as Frank and Jimmy—and the third, one Dub Cantrell.

"Did he recognize you?"

"Not at first," Nick said. "Remember, I was wearing a Stetson that night." He had gone to Rooster's dressed far more like himself—jeans and a pale blue oxford cloth shirt. And of course, the requisite Greek sailor's cap. Nick is a little more superstitious than he lets on.

When the other three players had arrived, they took their seats. Nick scrambled for the chair next to Cantrell, claiming that the one under the window was always his lucky chair—an assertion his fellow players could accept. Sonny gaped at him but said nothing. Jimmy took the seat on Nick's other side, with Frank directly across from him. The rest of the players filled in the gaps. The cards were dealt, and Sonny quickly immersed himself in the game.

Dub Cantrell was, indeed, a poor poker player. He talked too much, flaunted his winnings too heartily, and lamented his losses too loudly. By the third hand he was already down several hundred dollars. It was Nick's deal and time to take the initiative.

"Al," Nick called. "Fix Mr. Cantrell another drink, will you? I owe him one."

"You do?" Cantrell stared at Nick, his eyes narrowed. "We've met before, haven't we? But I can't remember—"

"At the Vagabond," Nick cut in quickly, shuffled the cards, and began to deal. "The other night. The fight. You left before I had time to apologize for the damage."

Cantrell nervously fingered his cards before downing half his drink in one swallow. "I don't know who those old boys were," he said. "But I told . . . my partner I don't want 'em let back in till they straighten up. Vagabond's always been a safe place, even for single women." Cantrell shook his head morosely.

"Two," Sonny said, sliding his two rejected cards across the table. Nick complied, and Frank tossed in three.

"Well, it wasn't safe for my wife," Nick said.

"Yeah, I'm really sorry about that."

Nick shrugged philosophically. "Well, it happens to all of us. I'm in the restaurant business myself, and I know. People are always looking for opportunities to sue you. I had a customer who was going to sue me because some guy dinged his car in my parking lot," Nick said, as he raked in the discards and signaled Al to bring Dub a refill.

"I wanted him to know," Nick said later, "that we could go after him if we wanted to. I thought it might make him more cooperative."

Dub lit into his second drink. He must have been looking for a big win—possibly to defray the cost of that potential lawsuit—because he raised the stakes in a triple-figure leap. The others tossed in their hands, leaving it to Nick to face him off. As it happened, Nick was holding a full house—aces and jacks. Dub's three kings just weren't enough.

"Those guys are trouble. That wasn't the first problem I've had with them," Nick commented when the cards had been dealt again.

This seemed to interest Dub. "No?"

Nick took three cards but quickly folded his hand. He sat back and watched the rest of the hand played while he told Dub about their appearance at the Oracle. "I think they were chasing my customer—you've probably heard of him—Davon Folsom."

Dub didn't seem to know the name. "Sure you do," Nick said. "He and his wife had that baby your partner didn't want buried in the cemetery at Mount Sinai."

"Oh. Right." Dub drained the remainder of his Scotch. "Whatever happened about that anyway?" he asked casually, not realizing that Nick knew he'd been at the cemetery that morning. Nick told him about April waving the gun around at the funeral. "So she's the girl they've got on ice for his murder, huh? She still in jail?"

"Out on bail."

"Bail? With all that evidence against her? That's exactly what's wrong with our justice system."

"He said that?" I could scarcely believe my ears, but Nick responded with a nod and a twinkle of the eye.

"It gets better. I pointed out that with her husband in the hospital, she wasn't likely to go anywhere. Dub said he didn't know about Davon, which was the perfect opportunity."

Nick then recounted the attack on Davon and his tragic memory loss. "It was those same guys, you know," he said. "The same ones who'd been following him. One of them was the guy who attacked my wife. But we're going to get them."

The hand ended with the pot going to Frank and the deal went back to Nick, whose game of preference was Mexican Sweat. He called it and dealt the hand. Dub was downing his drinks so fast that his glass didn't have time to sweat, but he more than made up for it.

"Thought you said the guy couldn't remember."

"Oh, I did," Nick said, turning his cards over methodically. "But my wife's a therapist—" he omitted the part about it being speech therapy "—and they're going out to the cemetery tomorrow night to re-create the scene. She's pretty sure it will bring his memory right back. So," he continued, "you don't need to worry about them coming back and tearing up your place. I don't think they'll be going anywhere."

Dub folded his hand and excused himself to use the bathroom.

He came back mopping his brow, eased back into his chair, and ordered another drink. It was his deal, but he couldn't seem to shuffle the cards. He finally gave up and passed the deck to Nick for a cut. Nick tapped the deck with his forefinger—a sign of implicit trust.

"I told your partner—Justine, is it? You don't want anyone getting the idea that the Vagabond's open for brawling. She's a smart girl."

"Yeah," Dub growled. "Real smart."

"Partnerships are tough," Nick added. "I've been in them myself. But yours seems to be working out all right. How do you do it?"

"Aw, she's nothing but a dressed-up waitress. She'll do whatever I tell her." Dub apparently did not know Justine very well.

Although he'd accomplished what he'd gone to do, Nick couldn't resist probing a little further as the deal moved to Jimmy. Frank took a big pot with an incredible four aces and a wild joker. It was a big loss for Dub, who was betting heavily on his full house—eights and threes.

"Man, somebody change chairs with me," he groaned. Dub lamented each loss with a belt of Scotch, celebrated each win likewise—a habit, Nick tells me, that can be fatal to a poker player.

How did it happen that Dub had taken her for a partner? It seemed that Justine had inherited her half of the business. It was supposed to be a silent partnership. Dub was planning to teach her what that meant.

"Hell of a thing, after all these years, him leaving his half to a cheap trick like her. And a *nigger* tart at that!" Cantrell slammed his cards down on the table and stared fuzzily at them when he realized he'd won the hand. He went to the bar, returning with a tumbler of Scotch for himself and an order for drinks all around. His speech was beginning to slur as all that alcohol finally started working its sorcery.

"Ol' Walt never cared much about the business. I ran it the way I wanted to, and I don't plan on changing that now."

"He must have trusted you a lot," Nick said, sipping his drink slowly. "Shame about his death."

Cantrell studied his cards and smiled slowly. His mood became expansive, his tone forgiving. "We went back a lotta years, Walt and me. High school. Football. Girls."

Frank laughed expectantly. "High school girls. That was, what, the sixties? Before the days of 'free love'?"

"Not for Walt. Love was always free. If you knew where to look," he added.

Sonny, our inveterate gossip, came through right on cue. "Where did he look?"

Cantrell grinned lasciviously. "Let's just say ol' Walt's tastes ran to the exotic, if you get my drift." Unfortunately, he decided to elaborate. Justine had not been the first black woman in Walter Fry's experience—a fact we had already established independently. His taste for interracial amour had developed at a young age.

"But my wife knows Mrs. Fry. She's white, isn't she?" Nick said.

"I didn't say he wanted to marry any of 'em." The picture Cantrell drew for the men at the table was appallingly vivid. Walter was the dean of the use-'em-and-lose-'em school of relationships. Bitsy had been chosen—or as Dub put it, "loved"—by Walter for her virginal naïveté. She had not been a demanding lover, being far more interested in good works by day than by night. And she was nothing if not respectable—exactly the kind of helpmeet Walter was looking for. They had married immediately after graduation from Parnassus, had stayed together for . . . Dub squinted into space as he tried to figure it out.

"Twenty-eight, twenty-nine years."

Nick whistled softly. "And then she comes home one night and finds him on the kitchen floor. Murdered. Must have been tough." Dub acknowledged that it was.

"Did you go right over there?"

"Nah," Dub said. "Had a message on my answering machine when I got home. From the nephew."

"I'm surprised they didn't call you at the Vagabond."

Dub swished his last swallow of Scotch, held his empty glass up to Bantam, and shook his head. "I was playing that night—"

"Here?" Nods from the table affirmed that he had been there well past the estimated time of death—right around nine o'clock.

"Darn!" I said to Nick. "I was so sure Cantrell did it."

"He's got a big mouth, Julia, but he's not stupid. He'd never do it himself with that insurance policy riding on Fry's death. He'd have it done, making sure he was somewhere else when it happened."

The game ended with Cantrell seventeen hundred dollars in the hole. By prearrangement, he wrote a check to Rooster's even as Nick and the others looked on. Nick said he seemed positively jubilant about his loss, which was probably because he knew he had the insurance money for backup.

"He bought rum and Scotch tonight," Nick added wryly.

"You know," I said, as I tucked myself in further under Nick's arm, "I don't get this. Why would Bantam have him make checks out to the bar? Gambling's illegal, isn't it? So the money could be traced. And for that matter, what does Bantam get out of it anyway? It doesn't seem like he'd make all that much on drinks."

"He doesn't. First of all, he has the checks made out to the bar so he can run the money through his register."

"But he has to pay sales and income tax on it then. It wouldn't seem like he'd want to do that."

"Oh, but he does. That's what makes it all look legitimate. Everything checks out that way. There are no big, unexplained deposits in Bantam's checking account. He's washing it."

"Laundering it, Nick. Okay, but what does he get out of it?"

Nick sighed deeply. He must have thought my naïveté rivaled Bitsy's. "Probably half of the winnings. He had a couple of ringers in the game, Julia."

I sat up abruptly. "Who?"

"Frank and Jimmy. It wasn't just coincidence that each time one dealt, the other one took the pot."

"Does Sonny know?"

235

Nick grinned. "I doubt it. I'm going to tell him, but not just yet."

"Why not?"

"Because there's an outside chance that Dub really didn't have anything to do with the murder. Or he may have been too drunk to get the facts about tomorrow night, in which case we'll be sitting out there by ourselves. We may need to pry more out of him later. Consider it the ace up my sleeve."

I called Davon first thing the next morning. He and April had returned to their mobile home per Bitsy's permission. Davon would have to take it easy for a few days before returning to work, and then only part-time at first.

"Are you up to a trip down memory lane tonight?"

Davon patiently explained to me what the doctor had said— that he could not expect to ever remember the details of the attack. They were simply not stored anywhere in his brain. I let him finish before I explained our plan.

"I can go without you," I said. "They're itching to get their hands on me, too."

"No. I'll be there. You couldn't keep me away."

"We'll have to go together," I said. "And it might be best if we used your truck. But I'll drive for you." We agreed on a time. Nick would drop me off at Magnolia Mobile Home Park so that if anyone was observing us, we would be seen leaving together. Without Nick.

I punched line two on the phone and dialed *The Delphi Sun*. Billy English, steadfast reporter and friend, was happy to help out. I explained what I needed him to do and suggested he meet Nick at the Oracle. My third call was to Sam Lawless, and I was put right through to his office.

"Okay," I said. "We're set."

The office of Magnolia Mobile Home Park was closed, blinds drawn tight over the darkened windows. On the door hung a wreath of fading lilies and black ribbons. I couldn't imagine Bitsy running the place and wondered what she would do about handling Walter's businesses. But the thought did not occupy my mind for long. There were bigger things to worry about. We stopped in front of a trailer two doors away from the office. Nick took my face in his hands and spoke softly.

"I wish there was some other way," he said. "I'm scared."

I was scared too, but wasn't eager to add to his worries. He needed his head clear for the night to come.

"I'll be fine," I said, hoping to reassure him. I reached for the handle of the door, but turned back before I got out. "I'll see you later."

"I love you," was the last thing he said to me.

Davon was waiting for me. Claiming he was going to help Chester catch up on his work at the garage, he had sent April off on a trumped-up shopping trip with his mother.

"I don't want her worrying about me," he said. "And I don't want to get her hopes up either. It may not work." I agreed. April was fragile enough without adding to her worries. We climbed into his truck and pulled out of Magnolia Mobile Home Park.

Davon and I rattled into Mount Sinai's parking lot at eight-thirty, just as the last fingers of sunlight gave up their grasp on the horizon. The church was deserted, the cemetery as bleakly empty as they always are. I felt in my purse for the can of pepper spray— a last-minute what-if-something-goes-wrong purchase—and tucked it into the deep pocket of my denim skirt. Davon went to the bed of the truck and pulled out a tire iron.

"Now, wait a minute," I said. "You shouldn't need that, and if they see it, it might tip them off that something's afoot."

"I'll put it behind the marker," he said. "Just in case." I could scarcely argue with him, considering the lump in my pocket.

We picked our way cautiously back along the brick path toward the cemetery gate. Davon might not remember what had happened that night, but my memories were pretty fresh and disturbingly vivid. When we reached Damien's marker, I saw, to my great relief, that the grave had been neatly covered and a few blades of grass had already sprouted across the surface. I laid a bundle of daisies on the mound and stepped away, casually reading the other names on the markers while giving Davon a little time alone with his son.

A tall, spired monument stood about fifteen feet away from Damien's grave. I was sure it was new and realized, with a sinking feeling, that it had been erected since the last time I'd been out here. Walter Fry would be memorialized here for many years to come. He didn't deserve it, I thought, but Bitsy did.

"Now what?" Davon said, appearing at my side.

"Now we wait."

We didn't have to wait long. In the still evening, the slow crunch of gravel traveled across the church parking lot and drifted into the cemetery. A motor throttled down and two doors were closed in rapid succession. I met Davon's deep brown eyes and was chilled by the coldness I found in them. I shrugged as casually as I could.

"Curtain's going up."

Chapter Twenty-Two

de-lude \di-ˈlüd\ *vt* **de-lud-ed; de-lud-ing** [ME *de-luden,* fr. L *deludere,* fr. *de + ludere* to play—more at LU-DICROUS] **1:** to mislead the mind or judgment of: impose on: DECEIVE, TRICK **2:** FRUSTRATE, DISAPPOINT.
—*Merriam Webster's Ninth New Collegiate Dictionary*

I took Davon's arm and led him around behind the gravestone, instinctively wanting to put something between us and the two men who were coming toward us. I couldn't see them, of course, since night had fallen and the cemetery was only dimly lighted. But in my mind's eye I watched them swagger down the path and, spying us, slip furtively through the gate. They would probably skirt the central walkway in the cemetery, approaching us from the darkly wooded area on our right. We had to stay alert. And we had to appear to be doing what Nick had claimed, that is, trying to rekindle Davon's memory.

"So you had come out to protect Damien's grave," I said, trying to lead Davon along.

He passed his hand briefly over the marker. "Yes, ma'am. Parked my truck out there where it is now and came right on back here."

"Tell me the last thing you remember," I said.

"Seeing as I was gonna be out here anyway, I brought some little shrubs," he said. "Two azaleas to plant on either side of the marker. I was gonna put some monkey grass across the front. You know, right here at the base," he said, pointing to the foot of the marker.

I stared at him, the significance of what he was saying gradually unfolding. "The shovel!" I whispered. "Did you bring the shovel?"

He nodded slowly. "Yes, ma'am. I was gonna have to dig and mulch before I could set in the azaleas, you see . . ."

"Did you get the shovel back?"

He scratched his head. "No, I don't think——"

A soft scuff sounded in the grass to our right. I eased around slowly, peering into the darkness, unable to see more than the square granite shoulders of lonely headstones. But I knew they were there. I squeezed Davon's arm and shot a quick glance toward the trees.

"Had you started digging yet?" I said in a voice meant to be overheard.

"No, ma'am. I got down on my knees to lay it out, you know, see how it was going to look," he said, "but then I heard a couple of doors close."

"Out in the parking lot."

"Yes, ma'am. Well, I waited, but nobody came out here to the cemetery, so I figured it was just April's daddy at the church. So then I set the plants aside and started digging."

"Digging up trouble," said a voice off to my right. I turned on my heel to find Stephen Cox sauntering toward us from the shadows. But where was Willard?

Cox moved toward us on the slow, creeping feet of a predator. I watched the fluid movement with my lungs caught somewhere in my throat——unable to exhale, unable to draw a breath. I wasn't supposed to freeze like this. I was supposed to stay calm and in control. But the way the follicles on my scalp were buzzing with alarm, I could have counted every hair on my head.

He was smiling. His teeth gleamed like new porcelain, and his eyes sparkled with the cold brilliance of stars on a clear winter night. "Yep. Just had to dig up trouble, didn't you, boy?"

I let my glance shift to Davon long enough to find his eyes glazed and staring at the man who moved ever closer. I could have reached out and touched Cox with my hand, shivered at the very thought. He smelled of beer—warm, sour breath that reached me where I stood.

Davon gaped at him too, but with an abstracted, remote sort of concentration. " 'Digging up trouble,' " he repeated. "I remember."

But he couldn't! There were no traces—no electrical signals, no synapses firing, none of the ethereal elements of which memories are made. It was a bluff. It must be a bluff.

"I remember now," he said again. He rubbed his forehead, as if he were trying to bring the memory into focus. "You," he mumbled, "and two other guys—"

Two?

"—and Mr. Fry."

I spun toward Davon, baffled by the memories that couldn't exist, but did. "Fry? Fry's dead!"

Davon shot me a surprised glance. "I know." He raised his hand, pointing at Cox. "But he wasn't dead that day. Not yet, anyway."

"You crazy, boy?" Cox threw back his head and howled. "Your nigger friend here's as crazy as a loon, pretty lady."

But Davon was not to be stopped now. Memories were seeping into his conscious mind—memories that had been dammed up behind walls of grief and pain. And that phrase—"digging up trouble"—was the first crack in the dam. It wouldn't hold long.

"That's what all this is about. Digging up trouble," Davon said.

I grabbed Davon's arm and shook it. "What are you talking about? What do you remember?"

"That's what he said. 'Don't go digging up trouble. If you do, the boys'll have to handle it.' " Davon turned his full gaze on me. His eyes were dark and clear with a memory he had all but disregarded as insignificant. "I went to see Fry that day. The day he called the meeting at the church," he said.

"But you told me—"

"They were there—these two and that other guy. Big dude with light hair—"

"Dub Cantrell," I added automatically.

Davon nodded. "I thought he was talking about me—about

April and the baby. 'Don't go digging up trouble,' he said. 'The boys'll have to take care of it and . . . and you don't want that, Walt. Believe me, you don't want that.' "He turned back to Cox. "But they weren't talking about me at all, were they? It was something else—something between them." Like embezzlement, I thought.

"You knew I overheard what he said. That's why you followed me. And the rest of this," he said, waving his arm over Damien's grave, "the rest was just smoke screen. You thought you could lay it all off on Fry and his crowd. Get rid of me and blame him."

Cox laughed. "Think you're pretty slick, don't you?" he said, casually reaching behind his back. He was still deep in shadow, but a glint of light beside him told me all I needed to know. He had a knife—a wicked, shiny blade that could have been made for nothing but gutting helpless quarries.

"Damn. This situation's getting messy," Cox continued. "First you go telling her—"

"But he didn't tell me any—"

"Shut up," he said, pointing the knife at me.

"Then you won't die," he went on, adding a singsong cadence to his speech. "Then you go remembering things you shouldn't." He shook his head. "Too messy," he said, almost sadly.

Behind Cox, a shadow loomed and stepped into the light as Robert Vernon Willard presented himself. He rocked back on his heels and grinned.

"Howdy," he said. "Good ta see you folks again."

So now we knew. Dub had threatened to sic his dogs on Walter Fry, and Davon had witnessed it. But it wasn't enough. Despite Davon's accusations, Cox had said nothing to convict himself. I had to keep him talking until he did.

"I guess we underestimated you," I said, backing up a little toward the edge of the marker. "How did you know where to find us?"

Cox smiled—the same vain, reckless grin he'd flaunted at the Oracle. "Word gets around. That husband of yours ain't very bright, is he?"

"Nick?" I said innocently. "He wouldn't say anything."

"Hell, give a man a few drinks and a friendly poker game and he'll spill his guts."

"I don't understand what you mean."

He turned to Willard. "I'm beginning to think she's more your type," he said, returning a scornful gaze to me. "Do I have to spell it out for you? D-u-b. He told Dub!"

"So you just thought you'd come out here and polish us off the way you did Walter Fry?"

Cox shook his head. "Nah. Mighta had to take care of him eventually," he said. "But the nigger boy's wife got there first. Now, that's enough talk. You and I have an engagement. You ran out on me last time—right in the middle of our dance."

He was within a foot of me, the knife point moving closer to my neck. I tried to step back, feeling the cold granite monument against my legs. He reached out and softly drew the dull side of the knife across my cheek. "I'm gonna teach you a new dance tonight. I call it the Cuttin'-Eyed Joe."

It had gone too far. Cox had kept the blade out of sight until it was too late. And now, with that icy blade teasing my neck . . . one quick slash was all it would take. I had to help myself now. Or never. I slipped my hand into the pocket of my skirt, positioning my thumb carefully.

"You're mine," he whispered, drawing the honed steel edge down my neck toward my breasts. He leered at me as he started to slice through the thin cotton of my T-shirt. "Hey, Willard, did I ever tell you why they call it 'cleavage'?" Willard answered with a snicker.

Cox spun around to his buddy. "You get the nigger boy. I'm gonna take her—"

I was ready for him when he turned back to me. My aim was off, the full stream of gas coming closer to his neck than face. But it threw him off, if only for a moment. Long enough for me to fall backward over the marker and roll onto my side, pulling my legs into the fetal position. Davon had inhaled some of the gas fumes and doubled over on the grass, but Stephen Cox was still on his feet and staggering blindly toward me. He still had the knife.

Behind me, feet scuffling across the grass. A mighty whoop thundered in the air as Spiros shoved past Davon and went for Willard's throat. Nick dove over me, tackling Cox at the waist and knocking him to the ground. I was around the marker and wildly kicking at Cox's clenched fingers, but the hand was coming up, the knife pointed at Nick's back. I aimed carefully, leveled my foot against his forearm and stomped down with all my weight. The arm broke with a nauseating crack. Cox screamed in pain.

"Nick, stop!"

But this time he didn't. He pummeled Cox with his fists— dealing blow after blow until Stephen Cox's face was a bloody mass. It took two of Sam's deputies to pull Nick off. Even then he managed to get in a kick to the ribs before they jerked him back, locking his arms behind him. One of the deputies snapped on a pair of handcuffs.

"Just to keep you in line," he growled.

Spiros had Willard pinned to the ground, the very picture of the Greco-Roman wrestler. Sam pulled his gun and motioned Spiros off. He lumbered up, casually stepping back on Willard's knee. "*Signome,*" he said, doffing his sailor's cap as Willard writhed on the ground. "So-rry."

"I got it!" Billy emerged from behind Walter's monument. He tapped the videocam in his hand. "Cutting edge," he said. "In-frared. It's all there." He pushed the viewer in front of my face. "Wanta see?"

"No, thanks," I said, my knees crumpling under me. "I'll pass." And I did. Right out.

I joined them on C deck just as Billy was explaining to Chester how he'd happened to shoot the film. "The sheriff borrowed it from the state guys. They use 'em in undercover. But he wasn't so sure he knew how to run it, and I'd taken a class in video, so he let me do the filming."

I glanced around the table to be sure everyone was taken care of—plenty of drinks and appetizers. Chester presided at the head, with Billy to his left and D'Anita on his right. Next to her sat Rodney, across from Davon and April. Candice sat at the other end, with empty chairs on both sides of her. I pulled out one of the empty chairs and smiled.

"Happy group," I said.

She agreed, grabbed a plate of *spanakopitakia* and *tyropitakia*, and passed them to me. "These little things are go-od," she said. "I like the cheesy ones."

Spiros had prepared them especially for the party. Nick was in the kitchen now, helping him turn out a Greek-style leg of lamb that would carry them straight to rocky islands and clear blue water. We wanted dinner to be special for Davon and April—perhaps the one happy memory they would bring away from the whole incident. Toward that end I'd invited the McNabbs, too. They hadn't yet put in an appearance. I doubted they would.

"Where's L.T.?" I asked. "I thought he was coming."

"Atlanta," Candice said, licking butter off her fingertips. "You heard about that bombing?"

"The abortion clinic?"

Candice nodded. "They're one of his clients. That girl—the receptionist—she died."

"Oh no," I said. "I hadn't heard. I just don't understand it."

"Doesn't make any sense to me either."

"It's one of those volatile issues, you know? Where there's right and wrong on both sides."

Candice toyed with the straw in her iced tea glass. "You might think differently if you'd ever seen someone who's tried to do it themselves. Or had it done in some dirty office up an alley." She met my gaze steadily. "You don't forget that. The hemorrhaging. The pain. Lotta times they wait till it's too late before they try to get help. By the time they get themselves to the hospital, well . . ." She shook her head. "See it once and you never forget. A useless waste, that kind of death. It's easy when the issue's academic, but one personal experience with it is enough to change your mind. Vanessa was my first."

"Oh, there's Sam." Rhonda was waving at me across the dining room. Sam stood next to her, head down as he fiddled with the keys in his hand. I excused myself and joined them at the register.

"Hi! I was hoping you'd come," I said to Sam. He didn't look at me. "Sam?" I touched his elbow. "Why don't you come join the party?"

He glanced up and away again, drew a deep breath, and turned back to me. "I'm afraid I've got some bad news for you, Julia."

"They're not out again, are they?" I said, feeling a too familiar weakness behind my knees.

"Nah, they're not going anywhere. We got the shovel. It was still in the truck. It's just exactly like Folsom described it—crack down the haft, red blade, initials burned in the wood above the blade. Those boys were none too bright. It puts them right at the scene."

"Then what is it?"

Sam led me over to the family table and pulled out a chair. I dropped into it, waiting, overcome with misgiving. He took his time getting seated himself, pulled in his chair and rested his elbows on the table. "They didn't do it," he said.

I laughed. "Of course they did. They practically admitted it on the tape."

He shook his head firmly. "No. What they said was, well, Miz Folsom got there first."

"Surely you don't believe that? In the face of everything else?"

"It's not what I believe that counts, Julia. It's the facts."

"And?"

"Fact is, they couldn't have done it. They've got alibis."

"Right," I said, a burn creeping up my neck. "Who alibied them, Dub Cantrell?"

Sam shook his head slowly. "They were in the drunk tank that night, Julia. One of my deputies picked them up for drunk driving at five-forty-seven P.M. Cantrell bailed 'em out at nine the next morning."

I stared at Sam, unable to take it in. It must be a mistake. I knew they were guilty—it only made sense. Dub Cantrell had been heard threatening Fry's life. His thugs had made good the threat. Sam reached into his pocket and tossed a folded sheet of paper across the table at me. "Copy of the report. I knew you wouldn't believe me."

I unfolded it and read it. Stephen Ellis Cox and Robert Vernon Willard—stopped on the Industry Road just outside of the Vagabond at five-twenty-three. Picked up for speeding, DUI, and resisting arrest at five-forty-seven and remanded to the custody of Calloway County.

"Maybe they did it before—"

Sam shook his head. "When Miz Fry left for the meeting he was still alive. That was at six-forty-five. I talked to the DA this morning," he continued. I glanced over at the party on C deck before turning my gaze back to him.

"I'm afraid the charge against Miz Folsom still stands."

I suggested to Sam that he let me break the news, an offer he accepted readily. I thought it would be easier to take coming from me than the sheriff. When he was gone I hurried to the kitchen looking for Nick.

"You mean . . ."

I nodded slowly. "We've come full circle and April's still going to have to face trial unless we can do something about it. And fast."

"Do they know?"

"No. How am I ever going to tell them, Nick?"

Chapter Twenty-Three

ob·sti·nate \ˈäb-stə-nət*adj* [L *obstinatus*, pp. of *obstinare* to be resolved, fr. *ob-* in the way + *stinare* (akin to *stare* to stand)] **1:** perversely adhering to an opinion, purpose, or course in spite of reason, arguments, or persuasion **2:** not easily subdued, remedied, or removed . . .
—*Merriam Webster's Ninth New Collegiate Dictionary*

We decided to wait until L.T. had returned before breaking the bad news to April and Davon. I suppose I secretly hoped we'd discover the real murderer before we had to face them with the truth. It didn't seem likely, though. From what I could see, we were back where we'd started with little or nothing more going for us than we'd had before.

We pursued any number of wild theories. Maybe Cantrell had hired someone else to kill Fry. Or maybe Justine really had pulled the trigger. Allen McNabb was still a possibility . . .

But we were tired—tired of feeling guilty because we couldn't help. Tired of chasing thugs and goons, being threatened and having to defend ourselves. Tired of posing, lying, trapping. Sam was right. We were not Nick and Nora Charles, solving murders between walking the dog and swilling martinis.

We discussed it that night over an omelette and salad, agreeing to take one more stab at it before handing it back to L.T. along with a small check to help cover the cost of a real detective.

"Chester, Candice, D'Anita, and Rodney were at the Ebenezer church until six o'clock, so they couldn't have gone back for the gun. That lets them out," I said, checking off their names on my list.

"Unless," Nick said, pushing his plate aside, "the gun was there and we just didn't see it."

"No. I'm sure it was already gone." I followed that emphatic declaration with a sigh. "At least I hope it was. Otherwise, we're sunk. Joy McNabb and Bitsy Fry were at the Ladies' Circle meeting," I continued. "So even if one of them had gotten the gun, they couldn't have used it."

"What about April's father?"

"Maybe. I have no idea where he was that night."

"Wait a minute," Nick said. "That doesn't work anyway. His prints were on the gun barrel where he grabbed it away from April. If he'd gone to all the trouble to look for it, he would have wiped them off."

I agreed. "He wouldn't have left April's either," I said. "In spite of the way he's behaved, I think he meant it when he said he loves his daughter."

"All right. What about Justine?"

I drew a wide circle around her name. She was, in effect, the only suspect left. "But how did she know where the gun was?"

Nick shrugged. "Maybe she was there and we just didn't notice her."

I thought back to the tape. "No. I'm sure she wasn't. I didn't see her anywhere on the film, did you?"

Nick retrieved a film cartridge and popped it into the VCR. "No. But this is the uncut version, remember? Maybe it's different."

It was, but not substantially. There was more footage. Nick and I sat, eyes riveted to the screen. The entire service had been caught on video, the most poignant moments to be clipped for broadcasting. The camera panned the mourners under the canopy. Justine Leroy was not among them.

" '. . . give not your daughters unto their sons, neither take . . .' "

"Louis Thatcher Humphries . . ." said Barbara Marshall.

I left Nick in front of the TV and went to the bedroom, returning to the den with my Bible. I curled up on the couch with Jack, half watching the film as I went through the concordance—

daughters, sons, marriage, intermarriage. The tape was long over and Nick had rewound it when I found what I was looking for.

"Here it is," I said. " '. . . neither take their daughters unto your sons . . .' "

Nick grabbed his Greek Bible and flipped it open. "Where is it?"

"It's in—" I looked up at him. Something had sparked, but as yet I wasn't sure what it meant. "Ezra. Chapter nine, verse twelve."

"Do you see that?" I said. "It's between Chronicles and Nehemiah. Nick, I'm just sure those are the pages that were missing from Walter's Bible. But what does it mean?"

"Well, Sam didn't know that Fry's Bible was part of the crime scene because Vivian gave it to Bitsy before he got there. Vivian probably never realized it was important."

"And Bitsy was surprised when she found the pages ripped out. Walter hadn't mentioned anything to her about them. But, of course, she said he probably wouldn't have," I added despondently. "It may not mean anything at all."

"But look at what it says. That's what Fry was reading the day of the funeral. It has to mean something."

We studied our separate versions intently, but after thirty minutes neither of us had any theories to offer. Nick set his Bible aside and turned the tape back on. Cantrell talking to Fry, his face so flushed he looked like an ad for sunscreen. Picketers flinging muscadines and jeering at us as we entered the cemetery. Candice fanning herself with an open palm and L.T. wiping the back of his neck. What a hot day it had been—the kind of weather when tempers climb with the temperatures. No wonder April had lost it in the cemetery.

The camera focused on Allen McNabb, then cut away to the little white casket and April with the flower in her hand. The family followed her example. Fry's voice intruded on it all, and Barbara Marshall resumed her commentary. The camera zoomed in on the mourners and we got quick glances at Candice, D'Anita, and L.T. before catching April as she stalked between the head-stones. Here came the chase across the cemetery. Nick stopped the tape and rewound it a few frames.

"What are you doing?"

"Listen."

I closed my eyes so as not to be distracted by the action. Fry's voice came across clearly. "It's right here in the Word. Ezra nine: twelve."

"Okay," I said, opening my eyes. "So we're right about the passage."

He rewound the tape again. "Now watch."

McNabb. The casket. Candice and D'Anita. L.T. Nick paused the tape. "Look."

L.T.'s head had come away from D'Anita's ear. He had whipped around to stare across the cemetery at Fry. "He recognized that passage."

"He's probably heard it before. I'll bet it's pretty standard fare among racists," I said.

"But look at him."

His lips were parted and his eyes so wide the whites showed fully around his dark irises. It had happened so quickly we might never have noticed it. The camera found April and the chase was on. Nick hit rewind again, taking us back to the service in progress. A close-up of Candice fanning herself. Nick paused the tape.

"Do you see?"

I did. And I began to see other things—things I didn't like at all.

I went to the phone, dialed, and asked for D'Anita. After questioning her, I had her pass me to her mother. I had only one question for Candice and I desperately hoped she would not give me the answer I expected. I was gravely disappointed.

Black turtleneck. Black slacks. Black socks and shoes. "It's just a precaution," Nick said. "There probably won't be anyone there at this time of night."

I checked my watch. Twenty minutes past eleven. I pulled on the neck of my shirt and stood under the ceiling fan. The last time I'd gone out in this outfit in the middle of the night it had almost cost us our lives. I hoped we weren't heading for a replay.

We'd agreed that we had to have some proof to take to Sam. He'd gone along with us once, but neither of us thought he would do it twice. Especially when the theory seemed so thin, even to us. Although we'd racked our minds, we couldn't think of anything that would put closure to the case except a piece of physical evidence. And there was only one piece to be had. Nick and I were going after it.

I switched on the air conditioner full blast in the car and let the cool air bathe my face. "We could be wrong, you know."

Nick pulled out of Musewood and turned the car toward downtown Delphi. "We could be, but we're not."

We traveled the rest of the way in silence. I was consumed with the same thoughts I'd had before. How could I despise a victim and like his murderer? It rejected one of the natural laws of society. But so many of those laws had been overturned since the day Damien Folsom was born. And died.

Deacons were supposed to be fine, upstanding community members. Walter Fry fell far short of the mark. Racism was supposed to be a thing of the past, but some people lived with it every day of their lives. At the turn of the millennium, women were supposed to be empowered, but the only power Evelyn Hall and Justine Leroy had was their sex appeal. And worst of all, in a world where medical miracles are so commonplace they scarcely excite comment, babies were not supposed to die.

Nick switched off his lights just before he entered the parking lot behind the professional building. A white metal sign at the entrance declared it to be private parking for employees only, but we didn't figure anyone would care after hours and pulled into the first vacant space. We sat in the car for a minute, accustoming our eyes to the darkness and gauging the level of activity on the street. Then Nick unloaded the shovel and the garbage can from the hatch of the Honda.

There were two Dumpsters. One was the regular nasty, smelly kind full of decomposing food scraps and coffee grounds. In the June heat its bouquet was especially pungent. The second was a long, low unit divided into three sections. Each section had a slot about two feet high and three feet wide, like an exaggerated mail slot, opening on both sides. The three sections were labeled: RE-CYCLABLE PLASTICS, ALUMINUM, RECYCLABLE PAPER PRODUCTS. We dragged the trash can around to the back of the third, out of sight of the parking lot and street.

"Who's going in," I said. "You or me?"

"I'll go," Nick said, and hoisted himself through the opening. I glanced at the big Dumpster and decided to go along. I was inside before my astonished husband could protest.

"What are you doing?"

"I don't want to be out there with . . . whatever's out there with me." I shuddered. "There's nothing a rat likes better than a good juicy Dumpster." Nick rolled his eyes.

"Now what?" I said. We were standing on top of a mound of paper with little room to maneuver. There were stacks of newspapers, assorted junk mail, newsletters, and magazines. And there were balled-up sheets of copy paper, lined yellow legal paper, and printed forms. Nick squatted down and dug under the newspapers, pulling one out of the bottom of a stack. He dug in his pocket, brought out a penlight, and swept it over the paper.

"We're okay," he said. "They haven't picked up in three weeks."

Or, I thought, whoever deposited the papers held on to them for a while. But the thought was too discouraging to mention. Besides, I gathered Nick had figured that out for himself.

"We could be chasing wild chickens."

"Geese. A wild-goose chase."

"Whatever. Step over here," he said, pointing to the only available space—about two feet square. He grabbed the newspapers and stacked them where I had been. "This would be a lot easier if you'd get out."

"I'm not leaving."

Nick sighed and pointed at the papers. "Okay. Now stand on top of them." I did as ordered.

We continued this process, me moving from flat piles of newspapers to more precarious heaps of excess wastepaper as Nick sorted through the Dumpster. There still was no sign of what we were looking for.

"There," I whispered, pointing at his feet. "Can you see it?"

He flashed the penlight across the bottom of the Dumpster, where minuscule scraps of paper littered the metal floor. Nick flashed me a look of dismay. "Better get the shovel," he said.

It was stuck down in the trash can within easy reach, but maneuvering it through the slot was something else entirely. It hit the side of the Dumpster and reverberated like a gong.

"Shh!" Nick jerked it out of my hands and pushed me down in the Dumpster, following close behind me. Somewhere in the parking lot, a car door closed. Nick put his finger over his lips and eased up to peer out the slot. I was right with him.

We could barely make out the car parked next to our Honda, since it was black and furtively faded into the shadows. But a man stood with his back to us, a black briefcase on the ground at his feet. He was writing something—taking down our license plate number, I realized with a start. I jabbed Nick with my elbow.

"What if he calls the cops?" I mouthed at Nick. He patted my arm gently and pointed back out to the lot. The man was gone. Nick leaned out of the Dumpster in time to see the door to a private entrance snap shut.

"Okay, we've got to hurry up," he said, and began shoveling up confetti. I dodged the handle as it swung around and out the slot. Nick dumped the load into the trash can and pulled the shovel back in, glaring at me. "One of us is going to have to get out."

"Okay," I said, taking the shovel out of his hands. He glowered at me before clambering through the slot in the Dumpster to land softly on his feet.

"Hurry up!" he whispered. "He's going to come back, and we're going to have a hard time explaining this."

Even with Nick gone, it was tough work maneuvering that long handle inside the cramped interior of the Dumpster. After several tries I pushed the shovel out to Nick, grabbed a newspaper, and started heaping the confetti on top by hand. It was a much more efficient operation. Leave it to a woman to find the quickest way, I thought smugly. I'd accumulated a foot-deep pile of shredded paper in short order.

"We'd better leave some of it here," I whispered. "They have to be able to prove it was in this Dumpster."

Nick agreed and took my hand to help me out of the Dumpster. We peered into the trash can. How many millions of tiny scraps of paper must there be in there? It was going to be a very long night.

"I wish we had Spiros's glasses," I said, lamenting the tedious work of poring over the confetti. We spilled it out on the kitchen table, a cupful at a time, and picked through it with tweezers. Nick separated the colored and blank pieces to one side, painstakingly picking them up on his damp fingertips, flicking them aside, and pressing his fingers on a wet sponge to begin again. I did an overview and search, weeding out the paper fragments that had large type, colored marks, or were of a heavy weight. Even after all that, we were faced with half a cup of fragments to be examined more carefully.

My glance went to the trash can sitting in the middle of the kitchen floor. We'd been at it an hour and hadn't begun to make a dent in the mound of confetti that awaited us. I tossed the tweezers on the table and went to the fridge, pouring us each a glass of wine. Nick swept the latest rejects and dumped another cup onto the table.

I sighed. "There must be an easier way," I said.

Nick took a sip of his wine and set it aside, reaching for my hand. "Maybe we ought to turn it all over to Sam, Julia. He's got the equipment and manpower to do this. We don't."

I stared into my wine reflectively. "No," I said. "We could be wrong, and then we will have opened a hornet's nest. We'd just get stung. Sam would be furious. There might be charges for harassment or false arrest or something. All we have to find is one piece—just one piece of very thin paper." I went to the kitchen cabinet and pulled out a green pottery soup bowl.

"We'll put any possibles in here, and then we'll go back through them when we've finished with—" I eyed the trash can bleakly "—that."

Nick grabbed the measuring cup and scooped up another mound of confetti, dumping it on the table in front of me. He pressed his fingers to the sponge and started picking out the colored fragments. This time he finished quickly, sat back, and reached for his wine.

"If you're finished, you could help me," I reminded him sourly, at which he hastily bent back over the table.

"I don't see how we're going to get this finished tonight," he said. "It's already one-thirty."

The work was too tedious for the wee hours of the morning. My eyes were tired and my spirits drooping. We'd come home from the Dumpster on a crazed high, sure we had it all over Nick and Nora Charles when it came to smarts and guts. The high wore off quickly, leaving us to wonder if we were just, maybe, dumber. After all, do wealthy, cocktail-partying Brahmins clamber around in Dumpsters scooping up confetti at midnight? I think not.

"Okay," I said, once more tossing in the tweezers. "You're probably right. Nick?"

He was gazing at the paper fragments through his wineglass. "What are you doing?"

"Do we have any old jars with lids, Julia?"

"I guess so, somewhere. Why?"

He didn't answer but went to the kitchen cabinets, slamming one door after the next. At length he climbed up on a chair and immersed himself in the cabinet over the refrigerator. *"Eureka!"* he cried. Maybe Nick really shouldn't drink wine. He scrambled down with two empty, dusty jars—Hellmann's mayonnaise and Skippy peanut butter.

"What are you doing?"

"Watch," he said, rinsing them at the sink. He proceeded then to fill them with water to the top of the rim, screw on the caps, and wipe them down until they were bone-dry. He returned to the table and handed me one.

"Now, tilt it like this—no, not on its side. The air bubble gets in the way. Like this." He tilted the mayo jar in his hands, cap pointing away from his body. "Look."

"It works!"

Before me, the letters on a scrap of paper stood out wide and black and very readable—*Dea*—the salutation of a letter. I scanned the pool of confetti in front of me. It wouldn't be quick, but it would be better than nothing.

"Refracted light," he said in a self-congratulatory tone.

I kissed him and said the appropriate thing. "That's why I love you. You're just so smart."

We worked until three-thirty without success, but at least the mound in the trash can had diminished by half. I set down my jar with a thump.

"That's it for me. I can't do any more tonight. My eyes are crossing."

Nick was quick to agree. We shoved the trash can into the corner of the kitchen and pushed Jack out the back door. I flipped on the patio light and turned to Nick.

"Go on. I'll let him in. You have to open in the morning." I waved my hand in the general direction of the confetti on the table. "I'll finish tomorrow and call you if I find anything."

Nick stumbled off to bed while I went through the house turning off lights and checking locks. By the time I finished, Jack was yipping at the back door. I hit the kitchen light and turned to let him in, turned back and stared at the table.

The patio spotlight filtered in through the kitchen window, casting an eerie glow over the kitchen. I could see the vague shapes of the countertop and stove, could still make out the pattern on the tile floor. But what really caught my attention was the sparkle from the table. I moved to the left and it disappeared, moved back and it burst back into view. Move right and it's gone, back and . . . there it is. Slightly to the right of the field of confetti. At about two o'clock. I left Jack yipping at the door and slowly made my way to the table in the dark.

The sparkle was gone, but, I reminded myself, it had been somewhere around two o'clock. I raked away the fragments of paper, leaving a pool about two inches square, and backed up to the door. Move left, move right. A little farther. There! Somewhere in that two-inch square was a fragment of paper with a gold leaf edge—the result of a trip through a paper shredder.

Chapter Twenty-Four

ex-pe-di-ent \ik-'spēd-ē-ənt\ *adj* [ME, fr. MF or L; fr.
L *expedient-, expediens*, prp. of *expedire* to extricate,
arrange, be advantageous, fr. *ex-* + *ped-, pes* foot—more
at FOOT] **1:** suitable for achieving a particular end in a
given circumstance . . .

—*Merriam Webster's Ninth New Collegiate Dictionary*

"I am warning you," Sam said, wagging his finger in our
faces. "If this is another one of your half baked ideas, I'm going
to charge you with impeding an investigation, withholding evidence, and every other violation I can think of, from storing
snowballs in your walk-in to failing to provide a spittoon in a
public facility."

"A spittoon? You're joking. There's no such law."

Sam's face was a vivid scarlet and his expression thunderous.
"Local ordinances," he snapped, "come in handy sometimes." He
gave the elevator button a vicious stab.

Nick, always the voice of reason, held the doors back as Sam
and I entered the elevator. "You have to admit," he said, "the evidence is pretty convincing."

"What evidence? Some little speck of paper? Try convincing
the DA. Besides, you've been handling it. Who's to say you didn't
plant it there yourselves?"

"You know us better than that, Sam."

The elevator doors opened, presenting a wide hallway at the
end of which loomed a heavy mahogany door. The brass name-
plate next to the door was a new addition. Sam reluctantly followed us into the office. Nick gave the secretary our names.

"We have an appointment," he said.

Oddly enough, it had been L.T. who had called me. "We're getting down to the wire on formulating a defense," he said. "How's that investigation coming?"

"Um . . . as a matter of fact, we do have some new information for you. I wonder if we could come by this afternoon and talk about it."

L.T. put me on hold to consult his appointment calendar and was back on the line shortly. "How about two-thirty?" he said. I agreed that it was excellent. It gave us just enough time to touch base with Sam and show him what we had. Allowing plenty of time for him to berate and threaten us, followed by argument and overcoming his objections, we could just about make it by early afternoon.

Sarah led us back to L.T.'s office, down the hall and past the mail room. I nudged Sam and silently pointed at the office machines. He growled.

L.T. was standing at the window, gazing down at the street below. He was wearing a charcoal three-piece suit, a pale blue shirt, and a power tie of a predominantly crimson pattern. His black leather wing tips glistened like onyx. I was struck again by his good looks and the sure grace he conveyed even when standing still. He had a framed photograph in his hands, which he set back on his desk when we entered the office.

"Sheriff Lawless," he said, showing no surprise at Sam's appearance. He shook each of our hands in turn and gestured to the new leather wing chairs positioned in front of his desk. I glanced around the room. The walls had been painted ecru, and the woodwork and doors a deep forest green that matched the lush new carpet under our feet. All the pictures had been returned to the walls, and the law degree, newly reframed, held its former position on the wall behind the desk.

"It looks great," I said. "Like a whole new place." Sam and Nick agreed politely.

"Well, I can't take any credit for it. Sarah and the decorator did it all. But," L.T. went on, his gaze moving placidly from one of us to the next, "you really didn't come here to talk about decorating, did you?"

"No," Nick said quietly. "I'm afraid not." He reached into his pocket and brought out an envelope, passing it across the desk to L.T. "We came to talk about this."

L.T. pulled back the flap and glanced inside. "An empty envelope?"

"It isn't empty. Look again." This time L.T. examined it more carefully, stuck in his finger, and brought out a tiny fragment of paper. He raised his eyebrow and waited for Nick to go on. Sam coughed uncomfortably.

"We have a new suspect, L.T.," Nick said quietly.

L.T. sat back and knuckled his lips. "Suppose you tell me about it."

Nick studied the attorney for a long moment before beginning. "It all started almost thirty years ago with the death of a girl. Our suspect was in love with the girl. But he came home from college one summer and discovered that the girl was pregnant by another man. The man was Walter Fry."

In the background the copier kicked in with a low hum. A phone line shrilled and the fax machine started cranking out paper. But in L.T.'s office there was only a terrible, thunderous silence. L.T. rubbed his forehead and eyes with a neatly manicured hand.

"And this," he said, pointing to the tiny piece of paper, "is the only proof you have? It will never hold up in court."

"Maybe not, but I think," I said slowly, "that it's all we're going to need. One young girl already lost her life because of Walter Fry. I don't think you'll let that happen again. Will you?"

L.T.'s eyes met mine, his lips twitching into an involuntary smile. At length he shook his head. "I could have won the case, you know. Even on a first-degree murder charge. If I hadn't thought I could win it, I would never have let it go this far. I knew Fry had a lot of enemies, and I could have shown reasonable doubt if you had stayed out of it. But you were determined to help me." He laughed bitterly at the irony of it.

"But you wanted to plead her guilty to manslaughter," I reminded him.

"At first. But when you two turned up and started turning over all those rocks—with all those nasty worms underneath—well, I changed my mind. I didn't expect you to solve it, just give me a good, healthy list of enemies.

"I'll give you this much—I underestimated you." He reached for the telephone and buzzed his secretary. "Hold my calls, Sarah. And cancel the rest of my appointments for today. Give Phil Harper a call and see if he can fill in for me in court tomorrow. It's just a discovery hearing. And I'm probably going to need to consult with him later this afternoon on another matter. Alert him, will you? Find out when he'll be free."

He set the telephone back in its cradle, elbowed the desk, and folded his hands. We waited in silence as L.T. Humphries came to a decision. At length he dropped his folded hands on the desk and faced Sam.

"I am going to put you in a very difficult position, Sheriff. I have a statement to make, a statement which will clear April Folsom of any wrongdoing in the case of Walter Fry. I will make this statement only if you agree not to read the Miranda warning first."

"Now, look, Mr. Humphries—" Sam began, but L.T. stopped him with an abrupt gesture.

"Hear me out," he said. He opened the palm of his left hand and held it up. "You may, by some stretch of the imagination, have probable cause to make an arrest. But once you read me the Miranda warning, I will make no incriminating statements, and without them, I believe the district attorney will have trouble making a prima facie case against me. Frankly, if I were in his shoes, I'm not sure I'd even believe you, and the chances that I'd be willing to drop the charges against April are slim to none."

L.T. then raised his right hand, as if to counterbalance what he had just said. "However, if I make a statement prior to Mirandizing, you will have enough information to convince the DA to drop the charges against her. Then it will be up to your crime-scene people to gather enough physical evidence to pursue the case. Bear in mind that without the Miranda warning, not only will you be unable to use any statements I make today in court, but you will not be able to use that information to gather evidence against me." L.T. shrugged.

"I can't promise you that Forensics will be successful," he continued. "I'm always amazed, however, by what they can do. So it's up to you. Is exonerating April Folsom worth jeopardizing your case against me?"

We all turned to Sam, who shifted uneasily in his chair. "I'll have to check with the DA on this—"

"No. Did I forget to mention that? If the DA is brought in now, all bets are off. It's a tough call, and you're the only one who can make it."

Sam's thoughts must have been racing—sifting through the probabilities and calculating the odds. Mine certainly were. The only physical evidence Sam would have was the shredded pages of the Bible, which L.T. would doubtless imply had been planted by someone else. But the forensics people might be able to prove that they had been put through his office paper shredder, which would be considerably harder for him to explain away. Then there was Vivian's testimony that the Bible was removed from the crime scene—a fact the DA didn't even have, since we'd just told Sam about it ourselves. And maybe, if he was very lucky, there would be the odd fiber or print that might be turned up at the scene. But it was a gamble, and one that could mean everything to April. The agony etched in Sam's face told me that he was as aware of that as I.

"This may cost me my job, Mr. Humphries," he said at length. "But for the sake of that little girl—well, I'm willing to take that chance."

"Vanessa and I went to high school together," L.T. said. He held the photograph between his hands and gazed at it with a half-smile. "She was one of those girls—all sparkle and wit and drive. I was a big, gangly kid who wasn't interested in basketball or cars." His smile broadened. "Today they'd call me a geek."

Vanessa had seen something in the young, insecure Louis that she liked. It was the first time any girl had even looked his way, and he fell for her madly, hopelessly, and forever. He went away to Duke soon after graduation and they exchanged letters—hers lengthy and filled with energy scrawled on every page. She'd gotten a secretarial job at Parnassus and an apartment of her own, and life was good and rich and full. But Vanessa's letters were erratic, unlike his faithful twice-a-week reports about life at Duke and the future he dreamed about. Over that year, hers dribbled away.

"I had no idea that she might be seeing other men. My feelings for her were so intense, you see." His fingers curled rigidly around the picture frame, holding it as he had tried to hold on to her. "I should have realized she wouldn't be happy waiting. She was the kind of girl who wanted . . . well, she just wanted."

He had come home that summer determined to extract a commitment from Vanessa. He had planned it all carefully. Hopefully. He was attending school on a scholarship which included a stipend for living expenses. He would get a part-time job and she could find a job at Duke. With their combined salaries and his stipend, they could marry and live decently, if not comfortably. Their love would carry them through. He called her immediately, but she refused to see him.

"I went to her apartment, but she wouldn't answer the door. I just sat out on the street waiting for her to change her mind. I was so sure she would."

He had tried every few hours, always with the same result. Until the last time. It was late, and dark, and a light was burning in her window. But he hadn't seen it come on, concluded it had been burning all day and through the night before. He went back to the door, knocked and called out to her. This time he could hear her inside. She was moaning. Whimpering like an injured animal. He broke the window and went in.

L.T. broke off, running a gentle hand over her photograph as though he might be touching real, living flesh. It was all he had of her. Probably all he'd ever really had of his sparkling, witty, driven girl.

"She was lying in all that blood, her knees drawn up to her chest, gasping as though she couldn't get enough air."

L.T. glanced up at us. His eyes were glistening with tears that wouldn't spill over. It had happened over thirty years ago. He probably had few tears left for Vanessa.

"The blood," he whispered. "Blood everywhere—the bed, the carpet, the bathroom floor. The tub was slick with it. She had done it herself. There was a hanger . . ." He passed his hand over his eyes and drew it slowly down his other features.

"I put her in my car and took her to the hospital. I asked her who had done this to her, over and over—who did it? 'Ezra,' she whispered. 'Ezra.' "

L.T. rose and carried the photograph to the window. "Candice was working the ER that night. They took Vanessa in and started working on her while I paced in the waiting room and thought about killing Ezra." L.T.'s rich, mellow voice grew sharp and so caustic I could taste his rage. "You understand that I thought Ezra was the man who had . . . who was the father of her child."

"You knew she'd aborted a pregnancy?" I said.

L.T. nodded. "I'd seen it before, growing up in the projects. The bleeding. Yeah, I knew what it was. I would have raised her child if she'd only given me a chance." A sob caught in his throat, but he swallowed it away.

"Vanessa died twenty minutes after I got her to the hospital."

I reached over for Nick's hand, found it warm and soft and comforting. L.T. had lived his life alone, clinging to the memory of a girl who had once cared for him. Most of us put tragedy behind us and move on in life. By all appearances, L.T. had too. He was successful and prominent, and had much to offer another woman. And yet, deliberately or not, he had never allowed anyone to fill the void left by a girl named Vanessa.

"Do you know how hard I tried to find him? I spent that summer tracing Vanessa's movements, talking to her friends, asking questions at her work. There was no Ezra. Nobody knew anything about him. No one had ever heard her talk about him.

"I went back to school in the fall determined to find him. I wrote letters to everyone she knew, but no one knew who he was. They'd kept the affair very secret," L.T. said bitterly.

"Eventually—" he shrugged and sat back down at his desk— "I just ran out of leads and had to give up. But I never forgot. I came back here, went to law school, and set up my practice." L.T. folded his hands on his desk. "That's it."

"Not quite, Mr. Humphries," Sam said. "We haven't talked about Walter Fry."

L.T. reached behind him and pulled a book off his shelf, turning to a page marked by a scarlet satin ribbon. "I recognized the passage," he said. "I've heard it quoted before to buttress arguments against intermarriage. You hear a lot of that kind of thing. Go to a pro-choice or civil rights rally and someone's going to be waving a Bible under your nose." He shrugged. "You just stop paying attention."

He looked down at the page in front of him, reading slowly, almost under his breath. " 'For they have taken some of their daughters as wives for themselves and for their sons, so that the holy race has intermingled with the peoples of the lands . . .' "

He shook his head and snapped the book closed. "If Fry hadn't cited his source, I would never have known. I was supposed to be at the church—my church, that is—with the Folsoms. My Bible was in the car. I took D'Anita with me, seated her, then told her my beeper had gone off. I went out to the car and looked it up. Finally it all made sense—why I couldn't find Ezra.

"He went to Parnassus. She must have met him there. When she found out she was pregnant, she must have gone to him expecting him to marry her. All she got from that self-righteous bastard was this." He shook his Bible at us, its soft cover curling in his angry grasp. "Ezra, chapter and verse."

L.T. threw the Bible onto his desk, as though he held nothing but contempt for it. "I went back to Mount Sinai and got the gun. You know the rest."

"But we don't, Mr. Humphries," Sam said softly.

L.T. Humphries had waited, considering a course of action while his pain and rage silently smoldered. He had planned it carefully, knowing that Bitsy would be gone from the house that night.

The Frys lived on a secluded stretch of the Industry Road. He had parked at the Vagabond and hiked through the woods to the house. There he had confronted Walter Fry.

"If I had realized that April had been there earlier, I would have planned it differently, you see. It didn't matter about her prints on the gun—everyone had seen her threaten him with it. And I didn't know that Davon was going out to the cemetery at night. I just figured she'd have an alibi. So I wrapped the gun in my handkerchief and took it with me. But in spite of all that, it was not premeditated murder."

Sam, Nick, and I exchanged dubious glances. It certainly sounded as though he'd planned it—and very thoroughly at that. But L.T. wanted us to understand that murder was not what he'd had in mind.

"I could have used him," he said. "Fry had money and influence, and I went there planning to bring him over to my side. I only took the gun for persuasion."

"Your side?" I said. "Persuasion about what?"

"With his reputation, Fry could easily infiltrate the local antiabortion movements. They're becoming more dangerous every day. He could keep me informed.

"Or he could speak out in his own church. He could be a force for moving us forward—women's rights, minorities, the homeless. He could use his money and influence with the legislators.

He could contribute to my own campaign. He was a tool, don't you see? I was giving him a chance to make reparation for what he'd done. But . . ."

Fry did not know about Vanessa's abortion and death. In fact, he didn't even remember her. "If he had," L.T. said bitterly, "I might not have killed him. But don't you see, he never cared enough about her to find out. He'd thrown her away as though she were some . . . some old tissue, to be used—soiled—and discarded. And he still didn't care, even that night. Even though he knew he'd murdered her.

"Walter Fry was a man of absolutely no moral courage. He hid behind his Bible, waving it in my face just as he'd done to Vanessa. She must have felt so helpless in the face of it. She would have cried and begged him—the bastard.

"I warned him to back off, but he just kept on reading and ranting until I couldn't stand it anymore. I grabbed the book away from him and tore out his precious pages," he said, spitting the last with sour distaste.

"And then, Mr. Humphries?" Sam prompted him.

L.T. turned to us, his expression confused, his voice betraying the shock he must have felt that night. "He went nuts—started raving at me about his father and grandfather—and threatening to kill me. He picked up a carving knife and came at me."

L.T. Humphries shrugged. "I had the gun and I used it."

"And let Miz Folsom take the rap for it," Sam added.

L.T. turned on him, surprised. "But I knew I could get her off. She had so much going for her—the baby. Depression. And Fry had a lot of enemies, more even than I knew."

"Which is why you supplied us with the information about his will. You figured we'd track down something, at least, that would help you," Nick said.

"Yes. I didn't know you'd be quite this good. Until last night," he added. "I heard noise around the Dumpster—"

"The shovel," I said. "I hit it against the Dumpster by mistake."

L.T. confirmed it. "And I saw your car. I figured then that you knew." He shrugged again. "So now I'll make it work for me."

Nick and I exchanged confused glances. "How?"

L.T. smoothed his vest down over his flat abdomen, pulled a pair of glasses out of his breast pocket, and polished them with another of his sparkling white handkerchiefs. "This case will draw a lot of publicity. I won't make it easy for the prosecution and I'll drag it out as long and as loudly as I can. We'll unearth everyone who ever knew Walter Fry—everyone who ever had a grudge against him. Eventually we'll expose him for the hypocritical bastard he really was. In the end they may convict me. But I'll still be the real winner in the case."

"How?"

He stuffed his handkerchief in his pocket and put his glasses on, looking very much the intelligent, successful attorney that he was. His glance moved to each of our faces, the lawyer in him wringing every ounce of drama from the situation.

"Backlash," he said simply.

After reading him his rights, Sam took Louis Thatcher Humphries away in handcuffs. "Regulation," he explained, as L.T. offered his wrists to be manacled.

We left Sarah frantically calling Phil Harper, who had been alerted to expect a call from L.T.'s office. He could not have expected this. We followed Sam and L.T. into the elevator, each of us locked in with our own thoughts.

I did not agree with all of L.T.'s causes, but I had admired him as a man with the courage of his convictions. I couldn't see how he expected to win his case, although I suspected that when he had finally achieved his goal—to destroy Fry's public persona and create a popular distaste for anything associated with Walter Fry—he would change his plea to self-defense. I wasn't sure it would work. He had hidden so much, had connived to defend April for a crime she hadn't committed and, in so doing, had incited misery and fear in the rest of us. And he had gone to the Fry home with a gun wrapped in his handkerchief, protecting it from his fingerprints. That in itself might suggest premeditation.

But L.T. Humphries had made a career of taking adversity and making it work for the causes he espoused. Vanessa's death had devastated him, but it had also galvanized him into a plan of action he had followed his life long. The murder of Walter Fry was only one more step in his plan.

re·flec·tion \ri-ˈflek-shən\ *n* [ME, alter. of *reflexion,*
fr. LL *reflexion-, reflexio* act of bending back, fr. L *reflexus,*
pp. of *reflectere*] . . . **6:** a thought, idea, or opinion formed
or a remark made as a result of meditation . . .
——*Merriam Webster's Ninth New Collegiate Dictionary*

The charges against April were dropped the next morning,
after the district attorney had time to sort everything out. The ini
tial story had broken in the morning *Sun,* but it was full of gaps
and speculation as to why the prominent attorney had been arrested for Fry's murder. L.T. had been released several hours
later. Charges had not yet been filed against him. The DA had
made a brief statement to the press, indicating that the investigation was being reopened but he could not disclose any further information at this time.

The lunch rush had dwindled by the time I showed Sam to a
seat on B deck and took his order. He didn't look as if he'd been
to bed yet and he did not seem to be in a congenial frame of
mind. I waited until I had his cheeseburger, fries, and onion rings
in hand before tackling him with my questions.

"Well? How'd it go with the DA?"

"I'm on his shit list," he growled, bit into his cheeseburger, and
followed it with a large onion ring.

"I'm sorry, Sam," I said. "I don't know what else you could
have done. You're sworn to uphold the law. Surely that includes
protecting the innocent from wrongful conviction."

Sam shrugged philosophically. There's nothing like one of

Spiros's cheeseburgers and a mound of fries and onion rings to restore good humor. "Well, there's still some hope that we'll get him. They've sent the Dumpster and the paper shredder off to the state crime lab. That gold leaf on the paper may show up somewhere. And they're going back over all the other fibers found at the scene. We've impounded the Bible. There's some hope, I suppose, that we can lift an incriminating fingerprint. I took a statement from Miz Spaulding early this morning." At that he glared at me over the top of his burger. "Y'all shoulda told me about the Bible as soon as you found out about it."

"It just didn't seem that important, Sam."

"You see? That's why amateurs shouldn't be messing around in police business. If you'd just—"

"Sam Lawless!" Rhonda stood over us, her hands on her hips, the fire in her eyes blistering us both. "Julia, how could you? You know he can't control himself. Do you want him to have a heart attack?"

She turned her wrath on him. "What are you doing with those fries and onion rings? You know very well the doctor told you . . ."

I excused myself and beat a hasty retreat to the register, uncomfortably aware that I had just taken over the number one spot on Rhonda's list. Sonny was waiting for me with his lunch ticket. He pushed a five toward me as I rounded the counter and punched the total into the register.

"Tell Nick thanks for the tip," he grumbled.

"The tip?"

He blushed and tugged on the bill of his Delphi Vending baseball cap. "About the game at Rooster's. I told the rest of the guys. Just wish I knew how to get even with that son of a—oh, excuse me, Julia—Bantam." He shook his head and wandered out the door, still muttering to himself.

I watched Sonny leave, plotting his revenge on Al Bantam for all the times he'd been taken in by Bantam's ringers. Across the dining room, Joy McNabb was seated with her daughter and son-in-law. Even at a distance, I could tell that they'd only picked at their food, being far more intent on their other agenda. Their faces were solemn, but I noted with pleasure that occasionally April smiled, and once Davon even laughed out loud. Although I did not approve of L.T.'s methods, I wondered if, after all, some good might have come from the murder of Walter Fry.

I guess I had learned a little about myself along the way. Miss Alma had shown me that I was not as color-blind as I thought, and in dealing with the members of Mount Sinai Tabernacle Church, I'd discovered I had a pretty cynical view of strict religious fundamentalism. I'd made some snap judgments about Bitsy Fry, too—judgments I'd later learned were unfounded. All very discomforting revelations. But in all, Fry's death still left me with more questions than answers.

I returned to the newspaper, turning over to the meager World News column. In a world where a few taps on a computer key would connect us to the most remote spot on earth, why could we not yet connect with each other? Trouble continued in the Balkans and Eastern Europe. There, too, ethnic groups were engaged in a struggle for rights, freedom, and respect. It was not a new story, I reflected, and not unique to the descendants of black slaves. Who, in all history, had suffered more than the Jewish people? And the Greeks, themselves founders of our modern government, had lived under Turkish domination for four hundred years, deprived of education, religion, and basic rights. It had been going on for centuries and I could foresee nothing in our future that suggested it would change. Nevertheless, I hoped we wouldn't stop trying.

The mailman interrupted my troubled musings with a thick stack of envelopes. I sifted through them quickly, sorting the bills from the junk mail until I came to a brown window envelope. My hands trembled as I opened it.

"Unbelievable!" I shouted, clutching the envelope in my fist and stalking through the wait station. "This is ludicrous," in the grill.

"Zulia?" Spiros's brows were twitching over the rims of his glasses like a pair of bushy caterpillars, and his lips, half-hidden by his steel-wool mustache, were pursed in concern.

"*Argotera*, Spiros," I snapped. "Stupid, stupid, stupid," I muttered, past the hand sink and steam table, the racks of pots and stacks of dishes. I found Nick in the office trying to balance the checking accounts and waved the envelope under his nose.

"What's that?"

"Have a look," I said, pulling the contents out of the envelope—two pieces of paper, each the size and shape of a computer card. The first one was a check, made out to NJL, Inc., d/b/a the Oracle Cafe in the amount of $6,874. The second was a disclaimer . . . *If you choose to cash this check and in the future we determine that the United States Internal Revenue Service does not owe* . . .

Nick reached for the phone and punched in a series of numbers, talking to me over the ringing in the receiver. "Well, at least now they're paying us interest," he said. "George Wolenski, please."

I left him on the phone trying to make sense of our latest correspondence with the IRS and returned to the dining room. Rhonda was bussing April's table. I glanced out at the parking lot. April and Davon walked toward his truck side by side, their hands lingering close but not touching. Joy, slowly crossing the parking lot, stopped to wave at her daughter before entering her car. Davon said something to April and she laughed, giving him a playful shove before he grabbed her around the waist. An old man stepping down from the running board of his truck stopped to give them a second glance before heading toward the cafe.

"Zulia?" Spiros frantically tugged at my sleeve and waved a calendar page in my face. "Thees word," he said. "I know thees!"

He slapped the page on the counter and pointed eagerly.

> **in-ter-mi-na-ble** \in-ˈtərm-(ə)-nə-bəl\ *adj* [ME, fr
> LL *interminabilis,* fr L *in* + *terminare* to terminate]: having
> or seeming to have no end; *esp* wearisomely protracted
> syn INCESSANT, UNENDING, PERPETUAL, SISYPHEAN.

Spiros underscored the last synonym with his finger. "Thees word I know," he pronounced triumphantly. "Is Greek, *neh?*"

"Well, yes, but not just Greek," I said.

I still had the IRS envelope crumpled in my hand. Out in the parking lot, Davon's truck had left a haze in its wake. I wondered when, or if, I would see them both again.

"I have another word for you, Spiros. A better word," I said, snagging a pencil. I tore a ticket off Rhonda's pad and began to print in block letters:

PERSEV . . .